Praise for Ms. M Civilizati

The first line of the book, "Ming Cheng was born in the cruelest place on earth," is like a starter pistol, setting this zany, beautiful book into motion. Jan Alexander is a deft storyteller, who manages to create a world that is both wild and breathtaking. She takes us across this alternate world, and we willingly go. I warn you though. If you pick up *Ms. Ming*, you won't be able to put her down.

- N. West Moss, author of *The Subway Stops at Bryant Park*

Ms. Ming's Guide to Civilization is a witty and sobering account of contemporary China, with a touch of the absurd. For anyone who has had enough of the white expat male China novel, this book comes as a welcomed relief as Jan Alexander seamlessly weaves in modern social issues. An excellent choice for China novices and aficionados alike.

- Susan Blumberg-Kason, author of *Good Chinese Wife*

Real estate in heaven? An ancient god returning to earth for another chance? A wholly contemporary setting with folkloric elements? This is a world we haven't seen before, and Jan Alexander is an excellent guide, with a confident, charismatic writing style and complex characters.

- Beth Neff, author of *Getting Somewhere*

Ms. Ming's Guide
to
Civilization

Jan Alexander

Regal House Publishing

Published by
Regal House Publishing, LLC
Raleigh, NC 27612
All rights reserved

ISBN -13 (paperback): 9781947548046
ISBN -13 (epub): 9781947548053
ISBN -13 (mobi): 9781947548855
Library of Congress Control Number: 2019931665

Interior and cover design by Lafayette & Greene
lafayetteandgreene.com
Cover images © by C. B. Royal
Author photograph by Fred Gurner

Regal House Publishing, LLC
https://regalhousepublishing.com

Printed in the United States of America

For Jean-Marc

A Note from the Author

In this novel I find myself breaking and entering into the head of a character named Xiao Ming Cheng, who comes from China, a culture not my own. How I became a cultural burglar has something to do with my formal education in Chinese studies and years spent there. More than that, though, the time I spent in Ming's head told me that both imagination and identity extend far beyond geographic boundaries.

Ming's plight is born of the international divide between those engaged in the pursuit of dollars/euros/yuan, and those who see life as a quest for fulfillment, yet find that wealth is necessary to meet "the requirements of the imagination," as Henry James put it long ago.

I could borrow from Flaubert and say Ming c'est moi, the only known excuse we have in a long tradition of male authors appropriating the female mind and possibly an apocryphal quote at that. But we do know that Flaubert said of Madame Bovary, in a letter to Louis Colet: "... the heart I was studying was mine. How often have I felt at my best moments the cold of the scalpel that entered me in the flesh! Bovary (to a certain extent, as far as I could, so far as it was more general and human) will be in this respect, the sum of my psychological science..."

Ming, too, entered my being like a scalpel, appointing herself my mouthpiece as we both imagined a world order that has a place for scribblers and dreamers like ourselves.

PART I

The Spy in the Pagoda

Chapter One

Ming Cheng was born in the cruelest place on earth—a village that sprawled through six green hills, so far out west in Sichuan province that the maps had no names for what was there. The village lay beneath a dome of clouds, with rain that could bite right through her clothes. Hardly anyone came through and no one left; a bus was supposed to pass through town once a week, but many days it couldn't get through the clouds and was forced to take another route.

Ming's town was called Yang Guang, or Sunshine Village, and everyone thought that was a mean joke. Mama and Papa said the sun used to shine there, though. They could tell, from the deep gorge where the Tuo River ran, that a million years ago the rains had made a mighty river. Then the sun had dried it out, then the rains had come, then the sun, then the rains had come again and carved a deeper riverbed, then the sun again, and then the rain.

Mama and Papa had named her Xiao Ming, which meant "Little Bright One." They told her she was their bright little pearl, but Ming had a shard of mirror, and the mirror told her that was a joke too; she was an ugly girl, with grownup teeth coming in rotten. At least she wasn't a monkey.

There was a monkey hiding in the village, Ming knew—a monkey that could talk. She was only eight when she first saw him, and she kept it secret. If she'd told anyone that she'd met a talking monkey, the people would have called a struggle meeting, dragged her up the fourth hill to the amphitheater, put her on the stage, and pitched stones at her. "Enemy of the revolution, you believe in the olds, the superstitions!" they would have jeered.

Things were supposed to be different now that Mao Zedong was dead. He'd died the same year Ming was born, 1976. Chairman Mao had sent Mama and Papa to Sunshine Village because they were scientists, and the revolution needed them to help make silicon products for the Chinese army. So in 1969, they'd boarded a train from Beijing with at least a thousand other people, carrying just one suitcase, Mama pregnant with Ming's big brother Han, not knowing where they were going until the train stopped in the Sichuan city of Chengdu and a local army sergeant stepped on and called out their names.

The revolution still needed Mama and Papa. But now the people of Sunshine Village would watch their new leader, Deng Xiao Ping, on television, urging them to get rich so that they'd help make China strong and glorious, and they knew that somehow the new ways just couldn't get through the clouds that surrounded them.

Ming saw the monkey twice—the first time, in the pagoda. Except for the Red Guards who'd destroyed the old idols, nobody had gone near the pagoda in over a hundred years. Villagers said pale-haired foreign devils lived at the top of the pagoda, nine stories up, waiting to swat you with X-rays that would make you shrivel down into a tiny pebble. Ming wondered, though, if she might be able to persuade the foreign spies to whisk her away, outside the wall of clouds to some faraway land with beautiful flowers and lots to eat. So one day after school, she crept up to the doorway, trembling all over, but she made herself peek inside. There was only a thick blackness and a strong animal scent. Then, suddenly, she saw two fiery golden circles staring right back at her. With the light from those golden eyes she could just make out a monkey form.

"Are you the Monkey King?" she asked. The golden eyes were just like the ones in her old picture book, the one about the myth of the immortal Monkey King. Even Mao Zedong had turned out to be mortal, but the Monkey King, born, or so the legend said, from a stone egg, had reached the highest form of enlightenment. He had trained his mind so that his spirit could come back from the heavens; on earth, he could transform himself into seventy-two different shapes, from monkey to man, or from butterfly to gnat. He could also somersault across oceans and fly like a bird.

Papa had read stories to Ming about the Monkey King and how

mischievous he could be. In one story, the Monkey King got drunk on peach wine and stomped all over a banquet table. But he also protected the powerless, and he could fell a greedy warlord with one forward kick. What Ming loved most of all, however, was the ancient myth that the stone egg from which he had hatched was located somewhere along the cliffs near Sunshine Village. Papa had told her another tale, about how the Monkey King had flirted with many ladies, but his true love was a poor peasant maiden named Zenia, who had lived in Sunshine Village. There was an old superstition—not that anyone believed in superstitious old stories now—that the chilly rain was a curse Zenia had put upon the village when she was deprived of her Monkey King's love.

With those golden eyes practically daring her to believe in some terrible feudalist myth, Ming glanced behind her, terrified someone might have seen her venturing toward the old pagoda. When she turned back, the eyes and the monkey form were gone. She shivered, the winter chill biting through the holes in her jacket, and her stomach let out a savage growl. Sometimes when she closed her eyes, she saw pigs, tigers, *and* monkeys flying—Mama and Papa said these were hunger visions. Of course, this monkey, these eyes, had to be one of those visions. It was the last week of January and the pound of pork that Sichuan State Sunshine Village Silicon Works Enterprises had provided on the first of the month was long gone. Mama's vegetable patch lay beneath the cold ground, and all they had to eat was the rice Mama boiled three times to make it puffy.

As she walked home, Ming composed a poem in her head. "The monkey's golden eyes of fire / A land beyond the clouds, much higher."

Ming spotted the monkey again just a few days later. She was walking the long route home from school—the one Mama and Papa said she must *never* take because she might get lost in the pine grove, or fall off the cliff. Ming took the forbidden route whenever no one was around to see her turn into the pine woods, because getting lost seemed like a good way to have something exciting happen. A massive stone Buddha sat on the cliff; some sculptor in the nineteenth

5

century had carved it from granite, smoothing the big round thighs and belly and the flowing robes. For some reason, the sculptor had left the face incomplete, leaving a pocked slab of stone instead of a mouth to chant and eyes to guard the river. Beside the Buddha was a dark black hole of a cave. The earth could swallow you up if you went in there, people said.

The clouds grew darker as she wandered through the pine forest, and rain began to fall. Ming sloshed through fresh puddles down toward the Buddha. She opened her mouth to swallow raindrops and felt them tickle her throat. But they dissolved into nothing long before they might have reached the empty space that was her stomach. Then suddenly the monkey appeared from nowhere, leaping up to sit on the Buddha's shoulder. Ming stared at him, transfixed, wondering if she really was crazy.

"Do you have any peaches?" the monkey asked. His voice was deep, sending out sound waves that she could almost feel like a palpable force against her skin. Tears filled his eyes as he said the word *peaches*.

"What do peaches look like?"

"Or a banana?"

Ming had seen a bunch of bananas once in a movie at the village cinema.

"Modern Chinese people don't get hungry." She knew she was being mean, but people in Sunshine Village were always saying mean things. Everyone knew that the old rule about filling your stomach with good socialist thoughts instead of food was just another joke. The monkey probably saw food in his dreams, just as Ming did. The monkey stared down at her from his perch, his fiery eyes taking in the holes in her cotton jacket, her chafed hollow cheeks, and the chill bumps on her hands. Then he peered into her eyes as if he were looking right through to her soul.

"Help me," he pleaded.

Ming started to ask, "Help you what?" but the damp air made her cough before she could get the first word out. As she was coughing, the monkey raised his haunches, turned a somersault, and rolled

6

right over the edge of the cliff. Ming, catching her breath, ran to the cliff edge and peered over. He was nowhere to be seen. She shivered, figuring the current had washed his corpse downriver.

A loud cackle sounded from above, and there he was, in mid-air, soaring up and down and up again as if he were on a roller coaster to the sun.

I know why the magic Monkey King was hiding in the village, hungry and forlorn.

I'm Ming. He asked me to help him, and when I grew up I did. Zenia, too. The three of us changed the world, in fact. Not that I can promise a happy ending, though the story isn't over yet. Life is a battle where you win, then lose, then win, then lose, then you just might start all over again, like the eternal battle between the sun and the rain in the village where I was born.

For years afterward, Ming dreamt of riding the monkey's roller coaster to the sun, and in some ways, she actually did. When Ming was eleven, the Sunshine Village Communist Party officials granted some of the other scientist neighbors who'd come there to work in the silicon factory permission to move back to the cities they'd come from. Mama and Papa discovered that if they saved some money and gave it in an envelope to the local Party, they, too, could get permission. When Ming was twelve, they moved to the bustling city of Beijing.

Ming didn't mind climbing the seven floors to their new big-city apartment or dodging the million bicycles and cars when crossing the streets; nor did she mind the chemicals in the air that felt like needles piercing her nostrils. She could look above the tall buildings and see a yellowish sphere of sun, even on days when pollution made the air a chalky gray-white color. Ming loved looking in the stores with their glass cases full of medicinal mushrooms and herbs, bins of wrapped white candy, and headless mannequins wearing dresses.

She loved Beijing even though she didn't have many friends at her new school. The girls laughed at her, and she had heard them sneer—in their haughty Mandarin—at her ragged country clothes.

7

In school, Ming had read a story translated from English, about a group of writers who lived in America, in a place called New York City. Someday, she decided, she was going to find a way to get on a plane and get beyond even Beijing, to the city in America where everyone wanted to be a writer.

Her brother wanted to go to America too. Han had done very well on his Chinese university entrance exams—astonishingly well, his teachers had said, despite his childhood in a dirtwater country village. Han was accepted into Beijing University, or Bei Da as everyone called it—the best school in all of China. A professor from a place called Harvard Business School came to speak to students at Bei Da, and Han introduced himself and, apparently, made a big impression. Big enough that he ended up getting a scholarship to attend Harvard. Mama and Papa called that kind of good fortune "double happiness."

But then, in Ming's last year of high school, Mama and Papa had some serious trouble. One night, they woke to a thunderous knock on the door. Three policemen took Papa away, stating that he had committed some terrible crime—though they didn't say what the crime was. Mama told Ming the arrest was probably a result of their refusal to hire the local deputy minister of industry's mistress; they'd protested that they didn't have the budget and the girl didn't have any skills.

Mama and Papa, it occurred to Ming, still imagined they were serving a revolution where everyone was honorable and trying to make a better world. Papa spent nearly two months in prison. By the time they let Papa out, the local Party officials had accused the deputy minister himself of corruption. One day in March, the prison guard opened the door to Papa's cell and simply told him he could go. Mama said she didn't want to work for the government anymore, but things were changing once again and Mama had a big idea; they were going to start their own private enterprise. Lots of people were doing that now that the laws allowed them to. Mama had rented an old warehouse northwest of the city, in Badaling. The Party was busy there, bulldozing through woods to build the Beijing Badaling

Economic Development Zone, complete with industrial parks and office buildings, vast apartment blocks, and a broad stretch of road that led to the Great Wall of China. There, in the warehouse, Mama and Papa started a company they called Rising Phoenix. They hired about a dozen people, including some from the village, and they all got to work making silicone products once again. Instead of military products, however, they made silicone rubber that could be turned into molds for tires or toys or—as Mama and Papa knew but didn't like to talk about—sex toys.

Mama and Papa worked hard and saved their money, and after three years of frugal living, they bought a big section of land beyond the green hills of the Huyu Natural Scenic Area, amidst farms that were slowly surrendering to cement. They converted their land into an industrial park that housed their production facilities and residential apartments—for themselves as well as their workers and customers from out of town. By then, people were coming by the thousands from all over the world to worship at the altar of China's double-digit economic growth.

Mama and Papa put all their earnings into their company; they wouldn't even buy new towels to replace the threadbare ones they had brought with them from Sunshine Village. They worked hard, determined that Ming and Han both could have the opportunity to go to business school and help make China rich and powerful.

By the time Ming's parents were urging her to go abroad and study business, Han was settled back in Beijing, running a private equity firm with an American classmate from Harvard Business School. Mama and Papa said it was time for Ming to stop writing poems and stories and get an MBA.

Han coached Ming on the right things to say in the all-important business school application. For the required essay, she wrote two versions. One, Han had approved; the other was the one she sent. Han said, "Inform Harvard Business School what you can do for them, not what they can do for you." So in the essay that the admissions officers received, she wrote: *With a degree from Harvard Business School, I can achieve my dream of living in New York City and having a big office.*

9

Han said, "Show them that you're passionate about wanting to make a monumental difference in the business world, and that your love of writing somehow has something to do with that." So Ming wrote: *I've always kept a notebook for writing poetry. Someday I hope business people quote me, like we quote Chairman Mao in China.*

Two months later, Ming received a one-page letter from Harvard Business School that stated: *We had many excellent applicants, but unfortunately you were not chosen....* Papa sat, head in his hands, wiping tears with his handkerchief. Ming willed herself not to jump up and down with excitement; she'd have to go to business school at New York University instead, the school Mama, Papa, and Han had identified as her second choice. New York City—she played the name over and over in her mind. Ming had seen a movie where a scruffy guy with the curious name of Woody Allen had kept books about the meaning of life strewn about his apartment and made glamorous women laugh. Even the soundtrack had made her think of walk-up lofts, poetry slams, and drinking fine wine into the night. Eight million people lived in New York City and all of them would understand her.

But three years later, the magic roller coaster came to a screeching halt. Ming returned to Beijing. New York had people with big dreams and even a scruffy man who'd made her laugh, but it also had a crime ring, and Ming was now a fugitive from the law. Han put her to work at his firm as a poorly paid private equity research intern analyzing business plans and housed her in a cheap firm-owned apartment near the Beijing central business district. Every Sunday, Han piled his wife, his son, and Ming into his Lexus and they drove to Mama and Papa's apartment in Badaling.

One Sunday, in early February, three months after Ming's return to China, a friend from New York named Zoe Austin arrived in Beijing. That evening the Chengs gathered in the tiny box of a living room to welcome their visitor. Mama and Papa teetered in folding chairs, while Han, the son and princeling, kept up a back-and-forth motion in the rocking chair.

"Sit next to me," Zoe whispered to Ming in English, gesturing to a spot on the narrow Naugahyde sofa. Ming knew Zoe always had an opinion on what other people should be doing, as if everyone's life were a Broadway show and Zoe the infallible director. Ming's friend had neon-blue eyes and wore a black sweater that clung to her wiry frame like a long-term lover. When she spoke, her voice started out throaty, then rose with excitement, like a clap of cymbals in the New York tune "Rhapsody in Blue."

Han's quiet wife, Wu Xia, perched on the sofa at Ming's left, while her fat little son, five-year-old Bo Fu, bounced a ball against the floor.

Zoe brought out five gift boxes from the tote bag at her feet. "For you," Zoe said, handing her gifts out.

Ming watched Han tear tissue paper into little strips, revealing a slender pen box. Han pulled out the cotton batting from beneath the pen and ran his fingers over the bottom—as if he expected to discover a wad of cash or the key to a new BMW—then proceeded to twirl the cotton between his thumb and forefinger. He had a habit of playing with objects; Ming figured it had come from growing up without toys. Papa opened his gift to find an identical silver pen. For Mama and Wu Xia, Zoe had brought classic Chanel No. 5 in shiny, white boxes. For Bo Fu, a Yankees cap and baseball. He put the cap on and grinned, then tossed the ball to his father, who juggled it until Bo Fu asked for it back.

"We are grateful for your presents, however humble," said Papa. Even Papa, the old revolutionary, was caught up in the era of *more, more, more*. Americans were supposed to bring you property deeds and shares of corporations instead of shiny trifles. Papa, a small man who looked like he could blow over in a gust of wind, laughed a little and slapped his own cheek. Ming had always assumed this was a habit born of the revolution, when Papa had to perpetually apologize for having too much. Ming's grandfather had owned land before Mao came to power, and Papa had had to constantly demonstrate his support for the downtrodden, despite coming from the oppressor class.

Ming watched Zoe absorb the insult, bowing her head for a moment. Zoe came from "genteel poverty"—a term Ming had learned in New York. Her mother was a struggling actress, and Zoe a struggling graduate student; silver pens and *eau de cologne* would have cost her a semester's worth of books, but Zoe knew that one never arrived at a Chinese home empty-handed. She hadn't brought a gift for Ming—except for saying, "Sit next to me," and that was enough.

The black-clad visitor from New York looked Papa directly in the eye. "I'm very grateful to you all," she said. Zoe spoke Mandarin with scholarly, scrupulous enunciation, but the Manhattan rhythm pounded through every tone. "Perhaps Ming told you that this trip will help me start my dissertation. And when I'm a famous China scholar…" Her voice hinted at bigger gifts in the future.

Zoe had a sienna glow to her complexion, implying a parentage from some far-off coast, though she herself had no idea where that coast might be. She was striking rather than beautiful; the regal bump on her nose and the lynx-like way she smiled were artful signatures. Ming knew that her friend's exuberance was something she had deliberately cultivated as a matter of survival, and tomorrow Ming would begin to test those survival skills. They had two tickets for a flight to Chengdu and, from there, a bus to Sunshine Village.

Ming could still smell the salty fog and taste the bitter raindrops of her childhood home. While the villagers no longer lived on raindrops and thrice-boiled rice, only for Zoe would Ming blaze through the wall of clouds and help dig out empirical evidence of the Cultural Revolution at its most vicious. Officially, Ming was traveling under the authority of her brother's private equity firm, New Icarus Capital, assessing whether the Sichuan State Sunshine Village Silicon Works Enterprises might represent a potential investment. Han and Tom Wendall, his nice though married partner, were always looking for moribund, state-owned companies that they could buy cheaply and turn around. *And if I take my American scholar friend, everyone will assume that we are there to do academic research,* she'd told Han. Her brother had leapt at the prospect, as Ming had been sure he would.

Getting Zoe out here was Ming's way of bringing a touch of New York back into her life; it was one of those little deceptions Ming had devised to keep from going mad, along with the afternoons when she slipped away with Tom, who'd said, "You seem like you need saving." Studying herself in mirrors, Ming thought she detected a harsh twist to her lips and a steel glint in her eyes. She and Zoe were both twenty-seven, but whereas Zoe was all anticipation and city lights, for Ming the future seemed to promise only greedy moments of transient pleasure.

After her return to China, Ming had hacked off her waist-length hair; it had smelled too much like the Brooklyn loft she'd left behind. Then she'd paid a stylist to give her a bob that looked intentional. Han said the hairdo gave her a professional bearing. That was all he cared about. Ming wondered if her brother would have hired her if she had still possessed her old gnarled teeth. She had a perfect set of alabaster crowns now, ill-gotten beauties, and sometimes she looked in the mirror just to be sure they were still there, the handiwork of Dr. Perlmutter of Park Avenue who had charged her forty-two thousand American dollars.

"What are you getting your PhD in?" Han asked Zoe. He wore his Harvard Business School sweatshirt, as he always did when he wanted to show off. Ever since Han had returned from America, his face had seemed at war with itself. His smooth skin could crinkle into genuine love for his son or obligatory compassion for the rest of the world, yet he was developing a self-satisfied pudginess that seemed as if it wanted to overtake him.

"Developmental economic history," Zoe replied. *Economic* netted a smile of approval from Mr. Harvard Business School.

Han even said, with a heavy dose of magnanimity, "When you finish, if you decide you'd like to go into finance in China, come and see me."

"Ming tells us that everyone in New York wants to be a writer," Papa interjected, with a laugh.

"Well, a lot of them want to write at least one book or poem that will save the world." Zoe looked at Ming as if they shared a secret, and Ming dared imagine what it might feel like to be happy again. In New York, Zoe had often used those words, *Save the world*, and Ming

13

knew it meant *Save the world from greedy landlords and lives mired in anxious poverty and anything else that beat them down.*

"We didn't read the American writers in my day," Papa was telling Zoe, as if it were too late for him to ever read something new. "Have you read Pushkin? Tolstoy? We got all the Russian writers in translation. When I was twenty the Party sent me to Russia for six months." He slapped himself again.

Zoe nodded. "I was learning Chinese and I read *The Legend of the Monkey King* when I was a kid. Not great literature, but I liked that he was supposed to embody the reckless instability of genius." She rolled her eyes in self-mockery.

"There was a myth that he was born near Sunshine Village," said Papa.

"Tell our guest about the Monkey King while I get dinner," Mama said, laughing as she moved toward the kitchen. She was twice Papa's size. In Mama's old photo albums there were pictures of her as a strapping revolutionary girl, leading a brigade of girls with shovels. Ming had too much of Mama's sturdy build—bad luck now that delicate limbs were back in fashion.

Wu Xia rose to help her mother-in-law. Bo Fu tugged on his father's arm, nagging him to play a game, so Han slipped away to the computer in the corner, where he proceeded to blast Martians with his son. Ming stayed planted next to Zoe. She'd heard the story of the Monkey King and Sunshine Village a million times, but Papa added new details with each telling.

"The Monkey King sprang from a big rock, like a stone egg, the myth claims, and he lived in Sunshine Village," Papa began. "Villagers used to call him Handsome Monkey King, although his full name, Sun Wu Kong, means *Monkey Awakened to the Emptiness that is Nirvana.* He liked to drink, loved the ladies, and fell in love with a beautiful young girl called Zenia who tended the rice paddies and sold noodles at the market. Zenia knew that she would be planting rice until she died of exhaustion unless some rich man wanted her as a concubine, but she was a feisty girl and she had other ideas for herself. When she spied the Monkey King—in the form of a handsome man, strutting

14

about the village market—she called out to him, 'Can you teach me your martial arts?' The Monkey King, taking one look at the pretty girl, said he would be delighted to teach her."

Zoe smiled. Ming recalled that her American friend had a black belt in *qi gong*.

"So," Papa continued, "they met in secret every morning before the sun came up, and Zenia became a martial arts master in her own right. They fell in love, too, but the Monkey King was a rascal—he drank too much and was a terrible flirt. Zenia was humiliated.

"Then the village mayor sent a messenger to Zenia's parents, telling them the mayor would give them a lot of money if he could have her as a concubine. The mayor was an old man with a long beard that was always full of noodles because he liked to eat so much. Zenia had no choice but to obey, and she was furious at the Handsome Monkey King anyway. So she became the mayor's sixth concubine. The Monkey King, distraught, came to her in secret just before the mayor's guards came to fetch her, apologizing for his womanizing ways and promising to change, but it was too late. Still, Zenia, in her little room in the concubine quarters, would practice her martial arts exercises and the deep breathing—the first step toward achieving full enlightenment. She hoped that if she worked hard enough, she could send her soul outside her own body and be with the man she loved. Except the old mayor caught her practicing the deep breathing exercises and sent a guard to keep her from doing it. Zenia was so miserable, she stabbed herself with the guard's scabbard, and vowed, 'My tears will fall on the village until I can come back and be with my darling.' And the myth is that the dark clouds will stay there, spilling their bitter rain upon Sunshine Village, until Zenia and the Monkey King's souls meet on earth again."

"Almost makes me want to do my dissertation on ancient lore instead of the Third Front," Zoe said and laughed.

"Nope, no time for legends, we have to go conquer Sunshine Village and make money off it." Ming tossed her words in Han's direction.

Her brother looked up from his Martian-blasting and glared at her. "If we're smart enough to turn it into a money maker, it'll be good for everyone." He turned to Zoe. "Ming thinks *she* should get to write stories while the rest of us work."

Ming clenched her Dr. Perlmutter teeth, then let out a despairing wail that would have evolved into words, except Wu Xia came out of the kitchen bearing two sizzling platters just in time to stop her.

The Chengs ate well now. The Formica table jiggled under the fragrant weight of sweet-and-sour spare ribs, dumplings with a garlic soy sauce, pickled jellyfish, stir-fried bok choy, and soup brimming with plump seaweed.

"This is Ming's favorite dish," Papa said. He passed around the ribs, sizzling beneath slices of ginger and carrot, and cast a purposeful look at Ming, as if to say time to unite.

The vapors tickled Ming's nostrils and calmed her for the moment. "Mama boils them first; that's how they get so tender," she told Zoe. "Then she roasts them with honey and vinegar."

Wu Xia, seated opposite Ming, took just one small rib, as if to be polite. Wu Xia had sensible short hair and a delicate face with a tightness about it. It occurred to Ming that she had never seen Han gaze at his wife with love. Her sister-in-law tossed back her orange-blossom wine before she took a bite of anything. They had little Bo Fu, but Ming suspected it was habit and inertia that kept them together even more than their son.

Han picked up his chopsticks and pointed them at Bo Fu, making them open and close like a duck trying to talk. The little boy giggled.

Zoe devoured one rib after another, complimenting Mama and looking as happy to be there as Ming was miserable.

"So," Papa said to their guest, "you get to travel to Sunshine Village by plane and bus. Did Ming tell you about how we got there? One day, when Mama and I were young and working in Beijing, a Party official told us we were being sent off on a classified assignment, and two days later, we got on a night train to Beijing with about a thousand other people. None of us knew where they were sending us."

"Three days past Beijing, we stopped at a station," Mama told Zoe

16

as she put a platter of honeyed gluten balls and oranges on the table. "An army sergeant called out names at each stop and those people got off the train. After four stops, when we arrived at Chengdu, they called our names. From there we traveled three days by oxcart, no buses back then."

"Then," Papa interrupted, "we came to a wall of clouds and stopped at a village that was just one dirt street. Sunshine Village. Han was born there, while we lived in a dormitory with many other working families. Then Ming."

"By the time Ming was born we had our own apartment, but it was just one room," Han said. "She cried all the time and nobody could sleep—not even the neighbors."

"Ming always wanted people to hear her," said Papa. Ming could see the worry in his eyes. Papa had always looked at her that way; he seemed to think anything she did was going to get her into trouble. So often he'd told her: *If you're a writer, you might tell the wrong story and get in trouble.*

The following morning, Ming and Zoe took their seats on an Air China flight to Chengdu. Ming pulled out her notebook. In the air, with Zoe sitting next to her, she didn't have to play at being a private equity researcher. Even so, she sensed Zoe examining her, with questions that hung between them.

"Your father," Zoe observed, "loves stories and then he wonders why you want to be a writer."

Zoe smelled like books and peaches, Ming thought, the scent of a stroll past the stores along upper Broadway.

Ming sighed. "Sometimes I look at my parents and my brother and I wonder if I'm even related to them. There's a big stone Buddha in the village. I used to think I was hatched from rock somehow, like the Monkey King."

"I was hatched from rock too, in a way."

Ming knew that while she meant stone, Zoe meant rock music.

Chapter Two

When poring through Chinese history texts made her restless, Zoe Austin's instinctive reflex was to practice her leaps and lunges. She would jab the air and fell a phantom opponent with the kick that had won her a black belt—a kick that masqueraded as a frontal attack but swept in from the side. Then, inhaling deeply, she'd close her eyes and imagine an unearthly emptiness that was both terrifying and rousing, as if she were falling from the sky. And the incessant question would come into her mind: *Who am I?*

Her birth certificate recorded the day of her birth, April 8, 1976, which by complete coincidence happened to be Ming's birthday too. The space on the birth certificate that designated *Father*, however, had been left blank.

All Zoe knew was that half of her DNA came from someone her mother, Billie Austin, had encountered in a haze of rock and roll, cannabis, and cocaine. "I was knocked up," Billie had told her countless times, "and a voice spoke to me in the night and said, 'This child is going to save the world!'"

Zoe's mother had a Southern pedigree she wore with equal parts pride and loathing. The middle daughter of Stork and Mary Austin of Jackson, Mississippi—and the prettiest of the three sisters—Billie was always happiest when she was singing. Since she had a resonant alto voice and her daddy was a deacon, she became the youngest soloist ever at the Methodist church (the white one, of course) at the tender age of eleven. The deep green robe went particularly well, people in the congregation told Billie, with her rich auburn hair.

In high school Billie became the kind of girl people talked about. Not that she was a slut like the girls from the shacks. Her daddy was Winston Tyler Austin, after all—best known as Stork since his high school basketball star days. Besides being a deacon, Stork

Austin owned the town's biggest real estate company. No, people talked about Billie because she was often seen headed toward the woodsy place where teenagers parked and made out. "True love," she told Zoe years later, "is a matter of letting everything go. Even your better judgment." And it seemed that Billie had always been in love with someone. In her senior year, it had been the football co-captain; she went off to Ole Miss with him, despite earlier plans to run away to New York City the day she graduated. The love affair soon disintegrated into nasty accusations and beer bottle throwing, prompting her to join the Campus Crusade for Christ circuit, which had a spirit-lifting rock band going northeast that summer.

"Don't worry. I'm going to be a missionary," Billie had informed her father. Billie had an ability, particular to feisty Southern belles, to be simultaneously outspoken and chameleon-like; which is to say, she understood the value to be gained from telling people what they wanted to hear, especially her adoring father. She knew that Stork would shake his head over her going so far away, say "You'll be the death of me, girl," then let her do what she wanted.

Besides Billie, the band consisted of six other backup singers— two girls and four guys. The lead singer said "Hecky becky!" instead of swearing when his mic went dead. He laughed a little at his own prudery, glancing at Billie as if he hoped she'd laugh too, which she didn't. One night after a performance at a church in New Paltz, New York, she sneaked out the back door, where two boys who wore tight jeans and said "fucking" as a modifier to pretty much everything were waiting for her in a dented VW van.

After that, Billie traveled with a very different kind of band to the same windswept summer places that people were always visiting in movies: Cape Cod, the Hamptons, Connecticut. Before the Northeast had turned to the red and gold hues that matched her hair, Billie had run off to live with another musician in New York City. She lived with him, then another boyfriend and another, along with a moving parade of visitors and crashers, in a walkup in the East Village—back when the East Village still had cheap rents and stores with piles of dusty bolts in the windows. She spent a fall, then

19

a winter, and all the way into the next summer in a velvet haze, and it often felt like God was unzipping her blue jeans.

Somewhere in that haze, a celestial love came along. He was a guitar player. They moved in together that summer—a summer of making love all day when they weren't fighting and screaming at each other to get out and never come back. They'd get stoned and live on heat and lust; then they'd fight and he'd take his guitar and stay with one of the girls downstairs, or down the street; then he'd come back, repentant and dying for her, and they'd make love until dawn. Sometimes Billie found someone else to keep her company, but a white-hot force always lured her back to the man with the guitar. He wrote a song for her that went: "I'm here for you baby, I like to fix things." He wrote the song after she'd missed two periods.

Her girlfriends said don't worry, we'll pool our money and we'll all ride the subway with you out to the women's clinic in Flushing. Of course, getting rid of the baby was the only thing that made sense. Until the voice of God thundered through her head one night.

"This child is going to save the world!" Billie told the guitar player and everyone else who had tried to persuade her to go to the clinic. She took to wearing long white dresses and told the guitar player she thought this might be an immaculate conception and sex would taint things. That might have been the reason he called her "fucking cunt Virgin Mary" one night that December. She didn't remember why they had fought, and she tried to forget the bruises on her legs and her pregnant belly—the only traces left of him. He'd walked out, backpack and guitar case swinging down the hallway. "Don't ask—he never existed," she'd told Zoe over and over, as her hands assumed the position of prayer.

Billie suffered from lost time after that; she slept for days or maybe weeks, but then one morning she bounded out of bed and tightened a belt about her expanding waistline. She got a job as a waitress in a coffee house and enrolled in an acting class at NYU, financed via a credit card. Her parents would have had her locked up if they'd known what was really going on, but they had a pretty good idea by April when the divine evidence finally appeared.

In fact, Stork and Mary Austin fought for custody of the new baby, and Zoe spent the first years of her life with her grandparents. Billie showed up on Zoe's fifth birthday, full of tears and tenderness, with a story her parents hadn't heard before of a secret marriage to a theology student tragically killed in a private plane crash. Billie had provided him with an exotic history—a mother from a family of Brazilian landowners—which was her way of explaining the taste of piquant shores that seasoned Zoe's complexion.

The child, in fact, looked nothing like her mother except for a hair color loosely conjoined in the family of red; Zoe's hair was the color of a new copper penny. Billie had a hair-trigger kind of beauty, all porcelain and glitter in public but subject to thunderous pallor and migraines on a bad day. She was several inches too voluptuous to be a screen siren in the modern era, while her daughter had a wiry body that took to *qi gong* as if she were born to leap and inhale the wisdom of infinity.

By the time she was six and in first grade, Zoe knew she had some grown-up jobs to do. She learned how to make her own breakfast, administer cold compresses to a mother in bed, tune out parental meltdowns and bury herself in homework, get herself to her own child-actor auditions, and cultivate friends with fathers whose names were mentioned frequently in the *New York Times* or the *Wall Street Journal* for their corporate deals and accomplishments. The matter of her missing father plagued Zoe every time she was invited for dinner with an intact family, but, like her mother, she became adept at improvising her own life script.

Zoe had accompanied her mother from one school headmistress to another, embellishing a story that sometimes began with, "We're from Mississippi, you know. Her father was part Cherokee," but had innumerable variations. Another one Billie had tried was, "He was Persian. Very sadly, he went back to take care of his family's business when his father died, but because I didn't think Iran was a good place for a girl to grow up, he left us, abandoned… Can you imagine my child growing up in a harem…?" Her eyes teared up and her hands shook in her lap.

One of those stories provided Zoe with a scholarship to Brearley. Her mother had given her a script for that, too. "We can't afford for you to be a fashion queen, so you must be a brain instead," she told Zoe as she smoothed out her lower school tunic that first day. Zoe had learned a few things about playing a role. She became an opinion leader among the girls who cared about participating in juried art shows or getting the part of Lady Macbeth in the school play. It didn't hurt that she got a TV commercial, thanks to her mother's agent talking her up, which ran for years; as a result, everyone, even the cool girls, knew of her as the kid who leaped around the TV screen because a certain breakfast cereal gave her the stamina of Supergirl.

For two splendid years, mother and daughter lived in a cavernous Upper East Side apartment with a theatre director named Nathan, and Billie got good reviews for a bubbly ingénue role on Broadway. A few weeks after they moved in, though, Zoe started hearing loud voices from her mother's bedroom. The first time, she told herself that her mother and Nathan were just rehearsing some play about a fighting couple. After that, when she saw how they sometimes walked right past each other without speaking and other times they'd be tangled up together in one chair kissing, she knew anything might happen. Then one morning Billie stormed out of the bedroom, her face almost orange with rage. "Pack everything!" she snapped. "We're moving out."

Billie went to lots of auditions after that. Critics praised her soulful sexiness as a country singer in an indie film. But Billie blamed the role, and the hot-air-balloon sized falsies the director had insisted upon, for typecasting her. "I can lose this damn southern accent any time, honey," she railed to her daughter. "That asshole director said I don't have much dramatic range…bullshit! I can come across as a New York intellectual…can even sound British."

When Zoe was eleven, they moved from a walk-up with peeling linoleum on the East Side to a place just off West End Avenue that they both adored. Some of Billie's friends had meandered into the bourgeoisie; one had moved to Connecticut with her new husband

and let Billie move into her rent-controlled apartment. There was no doorman, and the apartment was a tad shabby, but in a way that Billie said was just right. They had saggy bookcases everywhere, hardwood floors they sanded and varnished themselves, an ancient claw-foot bathtub, and even a small terrace where Billie planted flowerboxes.

"This place fairly screams we are civilizers, not robber barons," she told Zoe. "Always remember you're a civilizer. We entertain people, enriching them in ways that are a lot more important than money."

In fact, they had to put on an act just to live there. It was an illegal sublet, and they had to pretend they were the friend, Brennan Leichtling, and her daughter. Fortunately, the real Brennan had been spending most of her time at her fiancé's house for several years, and the landlord and many of the neighbors didn't know what she looked like. When Zoe talked to the neighbors she was careful to refer to herself as Zoe Leichtling, and, if anyone asked, to say that Billie Austin was her mother's stage name.

"If the landlord ever figures it out, we're out on the street," Billie warned her. But so long as the landlord remained oblivious, there they lived, amidst a glorious clutter of antiques that Billie had inherited from a great aunt's house in Mississippi.

Billie cobbled together a living from occasional commercials and royalties, from part-time hours at a pet grooming business, and from Grandpa Stork, whom she called when they needed a handout. The job she loved the most, however, was the one that paid the least. She'd found a community center in Harlem where the director employed her to teach drama to middle school kids two afternoons a week.

"These kids..." she told Zoe, "you think *we're* poor...they don't even know there's a world out there, but they want to do something with their brains and their energy. They see drug dealers and pimps on the street, and it's not like they aspire to that. Why does everything have to be all about money?"

Even so, Zoe knew that she and her mother were always teetering on the edge. Sometimes a boyfriend with money would take them out to a fine restaurant, but then the next few would be struggling actors for whom Billie would buy things on credit. Near the end of every month, when the bills came due, Billie would spend at least one day in bed with a migraine. No lights allowed. By the twenty-eighth or twenty-ninth of the month, she would emerge from her stupor—hair in tangles and face blue-white and not so pretty—and solemnly place her checkbook on the kitchen table. It would sit there like a spiteful god. On the thirtieth, Billie would lay out the various bills in a fan pattern around the checkbook. "Okay, hold my hand," she would order Zoe. "Say a prayer."

As Billie wrote out the checks for rent, phone, utilities, and half a dozen credit cards, she would take pains to impress upon Zoe what a heart attack might feel like. "Your heart practically leaps out of your chest, then you can feel it going fffttt ffffffftttttt glop glop like an engine dying, all because you don't have enough in the bank to pay the credit card minimum so you use another credit card to do it," Billie told her.

"*Méiyǒu xīnzàng bìng fāzuò!*" Zoe pleaded after she learned how to say, "Don't have a heart attack" in Mandarin.

"You're showing off."

"You can't be having a heart attack if you can talk."

After the checks had gone off, the rest of the month was better. Sometimes at night they'd curl up together and watch television in Billie's big bed with the silk comforter. Once Billie said, "You're better company than most of the men I know; and to think, soon you're going to grow up and move on. Promise you'll visit me—assuming I still have a home?"

When Zoe was thirteen, she had an audition of her own for a few lines in a movie, but when they called out a list of kids they wanted to come back the next day, they didn't call her name. "I don't care. I'm going to be a director anyway, not an actress," Zoe told her mother. She didn't know what made her say that, except she had a vision in her mind of peering down at the world and wishing she could tell people which way to move and how to feel.

Zoe and her mother were curled up on Billie's bed, looking for something to watch on television. Zoe kept scrolling with the remote, trying to avoid any show where Billie would see actors she recognized and say, "I don't look as old as he does, do I?" or "How the hell did she get the role?" She stopped on PBS, a channel that seemed safe. The face of a man with shaggy dark hair filled the screen. Wire-rimmed glasses rested on a sculpted nose, and he had a gap between his front teeth. He spoke earnestly about his recently released book about China, his speech punctuated by awkward pauses and innumerable *ums* and *uhs*. Definitely not an actor, Zoe thought.

She pushed the button to hold the channel. "I want to know about China," Zoe told her mother, assuming that Billie would have preferred a more entertaining show. But Billie was staring intently at the man. He was talking about capitalism and democracy.

A caption flashed, identifying him as Charles Engelhorn, a Columbia professor and author of *The Price of China's New Wealth*.

"In the past," the man on TV explained, his dark eyes intense behind his glasses, "uhm, well, individuals in China were supposed to sacrifice everything for the revolution. Now, the imperative is to sacrifice everything to obtain wealth and make the country economically prosperous. That, uh, could mean, conversely, that if you're poor, you're nothing but a burden. You're holding the whole country back. It's the religion of China now, but, uh, I think it's a faith that could pick up followers everywhere."

Billie grabbed the remote and lowered the volume. "You know," she said softly, "that man could be your father."

"What...?" Zoe felt a lightning bolt charge through her limbs.

"Oh, I knew him when I was living in the East Village..." Billie looked strangely sorrowful.

Charles Engelhorn had dark hair, not like Zoe's. Still, he gestured on TV with lanky arms, and Zoe had long, thin arms too.

"It's funny how these things work," said Billie, apparently reading her mind. "Maybe your ability to speak Chinese is in your genes."

"Mom, I speak Chinese because I'm studying it."

"Too bad I can't call Professor Charles and tell him I have a smart daughter who speaks Chinese. I'm guessing he's not rich, but...."

"He's wearing a wedding ring. I saw that when he moved his hands around," Zoe pointed out.

25

The next morning, Billie sprang out of bed, announcing that she was starting one of her periodic juice fasts. Zoe threw beets and carrots into the machine and watched its jaws grind everything into a magenta liquid. As she poured the juice into tall glasses, she eyed Billie—all made up and wearing one of the filmy blouses she saved for auditions.

"Why can't you call that man?" Zoe demanded.

"Who, that Charles guy? I was mean to him. I should have been more practical, for your sake."

At school, Zoe watched girls get out of cars, their fathers behind the wheels, and others whose dads walked them to school every morning. That night she asked Billie if Professor Engelhorn was really her father.

"Aren't I enough for you? Two parents make life doubly complicated." Billie grabbed Zoe's hands as if leading her to salvation. "You were born to save the world. God sent me a message and you came along."

Zoe's lips quivered.

"Don't cry, baby."

"You were mean to him? Was he in love with you?"

"Yes, and don't act like that's a good thing. I did it on purpose, so he'd stop bothering me."

Over the next few days it occurred to Zoe that Columbia wasn't so far away. They lived a couple of blocks from a station where you could catch the Number 1 subway and take it right to the campus, although it was slightly beyond the reaches of where Billie allowed her to go alone. She even found the name "Engelhorn, Charles" in the phone book. He lived on Morningside Drive. She found it on a map—it was near Columbia, and she imagined getting on the uptown subway and going there. But what would she do once she arrived? Stand outside his building to catch some glimpse of him coming or going? Creepy, pathetic people did things like that.

Instead, Zoe filed the address and phone number away in the back of her mind and returned to her Mandarin textbook.

In martial arts class, she thought of her possible father as she

26

aimed for the sun with a kick across the side that looked like a forward kick but wasn't. When she leaped and kicked, Zoe imagined her fists and feet were knocking against the heavens, reaching for a message that would tell her who she was. In high school, she dated boys who used words like *imperative* and *conversely* and liked to talk about all the things they knew, sometimes in foreign languages.

"They don't look like much fun," Billie said, "but they'll make good marriage material someday. Let them be more in love with you than you are with them, otherwise you lose your head."

"I should have married that Charles guy," Billie would say from time to time, mostly around the time the bills were due. His name became a code word that meant "a positive bank balance" and "an apartment that was ours for life."

When it came time to apply to colleges, Zoe sent off carefully penned applications to a multitude of schools. A few in New England and Pennsylvania sent acceptance letters. So did Barnard—her top choice as a school and just across the street from Columbia. Small-town campuses, however, also held an appeal for Zoe.

"Why would you want to go to some cloistered college town and leave me when you can go to Barnard?" Billie pleaded. "Besides, how would we pay your room and board?"

Zoe dutifully enrolled at Barnard.

Billie didn't mention Charles Engelhorn again until two weeks before Zoe's freshman classes began. She pondered aloud, with no warning, "I wonder if that Charles guy is still there. If you meet him, don't mention me."

His name was listed in the campus directory of course, and as it turned out her Asian Political Economics 101 class was held in the same building as his office. She went as far as the front door of the East Asian Institute, where his office was, but it was a vast suite of faculty offices, and a student at the front desk asked, "Can I help you?" so Zoe pretended she was looking for the Human Rights Institute. But every day, yellow, blue, and pink flyers announcing seminars decorated bulletin boards beside the building's elevators, and one day in early October, Zoe spotted a yellow one announcing an upcoming brownbag lunchtime seminar with Charles Engelhorn, professor of Chinese history and government.

Zoe groaned to her friends that she had to attend some tedious talk for extra credit and slipped off to the building by herself. She arrived ten minutes early, but the room was already half full. Professor Engelhorn was there, sitting at the head of a long table. Zoe made her way through a dozen rows of folding chairs to the back of the room.

Up close, Professor Engelhorn looked even more important than he had on television, surrounded as he was by men and women who were saying things to him in the low tones of people who knew their words carried weight. Zoe met the great Professor Engelhorn's eyes for a moment. He'd grown a beard. A wistful smile played across his face, as if he were perpetually searching for something he couldn't quite define. His legs seemed too long for the chair.

Then she felt a tap on her shoulder.

"Excuse me, young lady," said a man behind her. "We have a crowd today, so this table is just for faculty and graduate students."

Her face on fire, Zoe moved to a folding chair. People talked of summers in China. Delicatessen bags rustled, and smells of deli meat and yogurt pervaded the room. She'd forgotten that "brown bag seminar" meant you were supposed to bring your lunch, though her stomach was way too knotted up to eat.

Professor Engelhorn opened the session talking about his summer in Beijing and news he'd heard of several Chinese businessmen being held under house arrest after they'd displeased one Party official or another. "And, um, some have gone to prison," he said. "Just over the summer, there was an egregious case of a physicist who'd served the Party for years in a remote place called Sunshine Village."

The village had been home to a factory that manufactured goods for the military, the professor explained, one of the many that Mao and Lin Biao had set up as part of the Third Front. The man in question, Mr. Cheng, and his wife, who was also a physicist, had felt honored to serve the revolution in a hardship outpost. Later, the Party had moved them to Beijing to run a quasi-government owned company that manufactured latex. In Beijing, the local minister of industry, whose duty it was to oversee the Chengs' company, had a mistress who needed a job in order to acquire a residence permit in the city. Professor Engelhorn smiled here and made eye contact with the important people around the long table. The minister, he went on, asked the Chengs to hire his mistress; they replied, however, that they didn't have a budget and the girl had no specific skills. Shortly thereafter, the police arrested Mr. Cheng on charges that were never made clear. His wife sought the advice of lawyers and urged everyone who'd worked with them over the years to write letters attesting to her husband's sterling character. What ultimately got Mr. Cheng out of prison, however, was that the minister himself fell out of favor.

"Once again, we see that your track record in China doesn't matter as much as whether you please the right people at the right moment," Professor Engelhorn said. "The more economic growth we get, the more we should keep an eye out for human rights violations related to business dealings."

Zoe raced home from her classes that evening and found Billie in her grooming-gig yoga pants—the ones that had dog hairs embedded in the threads—watching television and smoking a cigarette. Billie smoked only when the last day of callbacks for an audition had passed and no one had called.

"I saw him," Zoe announced.

"Who, baby?"

"Professor Charles. He gave a talk about these physicists who came from a remote Sichuan village. When he talked about the village I could *see* it. Rice fields, and a deep river gorge. He didn't describe it in detail, but I could see it—as if I had been there before, as if I knew the place!"

"Maybe you lived there in a past life."

"Dumb joke." Zoe stared at her mother, with her tousled auburn curls, her smudged eye makeup, and ashtray full of twisted butts. People with a good education didn't say things about past lives and messages from God, even in jest.

"Excuse me, Little Miss Seven Sisters."

Zoe attended other brownbag seminars with China scholars

during her freshman year, and Professor Engelhorn was usually there. She always sat in the middle of the spectator row. Speakers left fifteen minutes at the end of the presentation for questions from the audience. Someday, Zoe decided, she would raise her hand and ask a question.

In the middle of her sophomore year, she gathered her courage at a seminar and raised her hand. A professor visiting from Stanford and seated to Professor Engelhorn's right had spoken at length about the Three Gorges Dam. The Stanford professor pointed towards Zoe; his mouth tilted suggestively in a way that indicated an appreciation not for her raised hand so much as for her being young and dewy. His eyes scoped out the little points that were her breasts.

"I read that...um...a good portion of the workers on the dam are political prisoners?" *Oh hell, that was all wrong.*

"Is that a question?" the professor asked with a smug half-smile. "Yes, it's plausible."

That was all he said. Zoe sat immobile, on fire with shame, and stayed that way as those around her got up to leave, timing her exit to blend in with the crowd.

"Miss...?"

Professor Engelhorn was calling to her. She twirled around, and they were face to face.

"You might want to come next month," he said, mentioning that a famous Chinese political prisoner would be speaking.

Zoe opened her mouth to reply, but all that came out was air. She tried again. "I'm going to Beijing next year," she blurted out. It was the first that she'd thought of a junior year abroad, which would require yet another credit card, but there were things, she felt, that just *should* be true. "I plan to get a PhD in modern Chinese economic history. I hope I can study with you."

The professor smiled in a way that looked both flattered and put-upon. Up close he had a face that seemed too tight to spring into action, Zoe thought, and when he smiled, sadness cast a gravitational pull. He looked directly in her eyes, and she had a sense that he was trying to atone for the Stanford professor's impertinence by focusing

30

solely upon her face. "And what year are you now?" he asked.

"Sophomore." She might as well have said kindergarten.

"Well, come by in your senior year if you're still interested then." Then, turning, he directed a question to someone else hovering beside him: "So how was your trip?"

The only friend Zoe confided in about the possibility of Professor Engelhorn being her father was Jeffrey Kirschenbaum, whom she'd met in freshman poli sci class. Jeff was, by anyone's standards, a scruffy guy. He cultivated a night-bird complexion, kept a cigarette stub between his lips, and made a show of punctuating his sentences with declarative phrases like, "It all means a great deal of nothing." He could ramble on about overrated contemporary art and the messy state of the nation all in one sentence, then, a moment later, complain about his own philistine parents.

"How come we've never gotten it on?" Jeff pondered aloud, not for the first time, in the middle of their sophomore year. It was late at night, and the two of them were sprawled on his bed smoking a joint. Zoe didn't smoke often, but she liked listening to Jeff's incongruous musings and laughing into the night with him.

"Sex would ruin our beautiful friendship," Zoe told him, also not for the first time. It was an excuse. They could have slept together and still been friends, she thought. His hair was always rumpled, and his T-shirts littered the floor, but that did not bother her so much as the feeling that sex with Jeff would feel like wandering through dark roads with dead ends. Jeff seemed to have slouched into a spot where he was willing to stay forever, someplace that would always look like a college dorm, with books and shirts scattered about. He lived amidst found scraps of metal and Styrofoam—the corpus of art in progress—and tables covered in debris of old computers that he had pulled apart "to find their soul." Everything seemed to have a tortured significance to him, whereas Zoe knew that her own life must be compartmentalized and ordered so that she wouldn't end up in an illegal sublet with a perpetually negative bank balance. She reserved sex and romance for boys whose kisses felt like a trip to an easier world than her own.

31

Idling on Jeff's dorm bed, though, felt like a scene from a childhood she'd never had, conspiring with a brother and imagining kingdoms of their own.

"I'm going to China. I'm going to get a PhD in modern Chinese economic history."

"Can I come to China with you? I'll look for a beautiful Chinese girl and you'll find yourself a handsome young capitalist."

"Would that be so awful?"

"What, going out with capitalists?"

"I can't live the way my mom does."

"Okay, how about we go to China and set ourselves up as gurus?"

"I like that. Let's start a cult where wealthy people think they're coming to empower themselves, to get even richer, but we'll brainwash them into supporting struggling artists." They both giggled.

"You're not cut out to spend your life going through old Chinese manuscripts in dusty libraries. Even if you don't have ADD like me." Jeff always made his attention deficit disorder sound like a badge of superior intelligence. He had changed majors four times, although it appeared that he was starting to settle on art. "My dad almost got a PhD. He loved military history, but he said nobody gets tenure anymore. You get contracts, two years at a time in Podunk, Mississippi, then next year Podunk, Wyoming. I could've been born in Podunk, Somewhere, instead of Podunk, New Jersey."

"Professor Engelhorn—the guy I want for my adviser—has tenure."

"Tenure schmenure. We could take a road trip across the US. I'll make a movie about it and we'll get rich."

It was a fantasy she let herself entertain through one more drag.

"You're really ambitious, aren't you? I don't mean in a money-making way. I was thinking I'd call the movie *On the Road with Zoe* and we'd go looking for your father."

"Funny thing…my real father could be right *here*."

That was when Zoe told Jeff how she'd seen Professor Charles Engelhorn on television, and how Billie had said he'd loved her once.

"Wow. I bet your mom was hot when she was young. I would've

been in love with her too. Hey, if you are his kid, you can go to Barnard or Columbia completely tuition free."

Zoe understood that tenured professors weren't rich, but Professor Engelhorn was enough of an academic star that they probably paid him well and he probably lived in a faculty apartment. She'd been in a couple of them; they were big, old-fashioned residences, full of polished parquet, and walls hung with art from India and Madagascar and ancient Persia. Faculty children rode tricycles in the hallways. No one ever worried about paying the rent or losing the apartment.

"Don't worry," Jeff said. "It'll all work out. For both of us."

A big toe poked through a hole in his sock. He wasn't quite clean, yet his sweat had a rather pleasant grassy smell, combined with a whiff of suburban New Jersey, popcorn, and green cannabis.

"Well, what am I going to do now?" Zoe insisted, poking Jeff's bare toe with her own foot.

"If I were a forty-year-old professor, I'd like to have you as my star protégée."

"You can't tell anybody that he might be my father. I mean, he might not be, right?" Zoe didn't want to ponder this possibility because Professor Engelhorn as a father figure had taken root and become entrenched in her psyche, much like the way her muscles obeyed her mind once she'd learned the sideways kick and it had become a reflexive action.

"Puleeeze. You think Uncle Jeffrey would spill your secret?"

⌘

With the help of her mother's credit cards, Zoe spent the spring semester of her junior year at Bei Da, and two years later she embarked upon the master's program in Chinese history. While she had not obtained a full fellowship—the one that took care of all tuition and living expenses—Zoe managed to get a small grant for the first year. The grant required work-study hours, so she worked part-time in the office of the department, answering the phone, Xeroxing papers, and writing up expense reports.

For the first few weeks, Professor Engelhorn kept calling her "Melanie," the name of the girl who'd had the job the year before.

"Actually, my name,"—it seemed a bold move to correct him—"is Zoe. Zoe Austin." Charles Engelhorn's face reddened for a moment, she was sure.

Zoe took Professor Engelhorn's seminar, "Origins of the Chinese Revolutionary Movement," in the second semester. She studied every night for a month before the first test and made an A. After that, she felt bold enough to say a few things when he passed her desk, like, "How are you today, Professor Engelhorn?"

Department gossip had already been a significant source of information. Professor Engelhorn was married with two young sons, but Sara—a friend working on her dissertation—told Zoe that the professor and his wife led separate lives. On his desk, Professor Engelhorn kept a family photo of his wife, an elegant Chinese woman with a meticulous hairdo and fabulous cheekbones, and his two dark-haired sons. Despite Mrs. Engelhorn's apparent composure, her face looked anxious, as if the photographer had set her in the pose and then told her the studio was on fire. The boys had somber Eurasian eyes. Sara said Professor Engelhorn's wife was "a piece of work."

"She's an investment banker and she travels a lot," Sara told Zoe. "And, apparently, she had an affair. They stay together because of the kids. Sad, I'd say he deserves better. He likes to intimidate his new students, but if you make it through, he's your friend for life."

In April, Zoe, her mouth so dry she wasn't sure if words would come out, approached Professor Engelhorn to ask if he would agree to be her primary thesis adviser the following year. "Um, well, I'd like to do something, you know…"

"Take a deep breath."

"I've read about villages that became industry towns under Mao for state-owned enterprises. So when those enterprises fizzled out, what happened to the people there?"

Momentum gathered in her mind. "Anyway, I was thinking of examining the towns that had no real reason to exist in the modern system, the towns that Lin Biao set up as his line of military contractors—"

"Do you mean the Third Front?" He was plunked in a chair in his big office, like some kind of wiseman with a novice standing at his feet. "Mao and the whole Party apparatus set up the villages. It was just later, after Lin Biao betrayed Mao, that they spread a story that Lin had sent all those scientists and workers to the boondocks as a ploy to run a secret network of military manufacturing facilities as one of his last gasps at power."

Zoe felt like an eight-year-old who'd failed to do her homework.

"Be careful about assumptions. What do you hope to contribute to the history of the Third Front?" He stretched upward, until he was standing over her, as if he were about to drill her head open and pour knowledge in.

"Um, I'd really like to find a specific village and, you know, study its last fifty years, one where there was plenty of drama...."

"Well, you can start your research with these." He pulled three books down from his shelves.

In May of that year, Zoe got up the nerve to tell him that, since his teaching assistant was going to spend the following year conducting research in China, she was interested in the job. "Assuming I survive, of course."

There were fifteen master's candidates in her class and Professor Engelhorn had said, on the first night of his seminar, "If three of you make it to the PhD program, and then through orals, and then finish your dissertation, that will be about the normal odds."

That afternoon he reacted with his familiar flattered-though-put-upon gaze. "Sit down."

"Are you absolutely sure you want to be a scholar?" he asked when she was seated.

"Of course. If I wanted an MBA, I'd be there."

"I think it's my duty to remind you, if you take fifty newly minted PhDs in the humanities, the likelihood of two of them ending up with tenured jobs at any school, let alone an Ivy League one, is slim. The odds are that you'll have to ply your trade in a series of contract jobs or adjunct jobs, roaming around as an academic nomad."

Nomad. When Professor Engelhorn said "two out of fifty," what Zoe heard was that at least one of those fifty would get tenure at a top school, and didn't she deserve to be that one? It might be tenure at Harvard or Yale or Princeton, in which case she and her New York-based financier husband—she had started dating Jeff's friend Danny Hirsch that year—and two precocious children would work out some kind of commuting compromise.

"It's brave of you," Professor Engelhorn continued. "I mean, going for something as difficult as China. I fell into this because my grandfather had been posted all over Asia with the State Department, and then my father was a professor of Russian literature at Harvard. I wanted to do something similar but different. I guess if my dad had worked for General Motors, I'd be making cars."

He made her feel like an impostor.

When she left his office, she considered locking herself in a toilet stall and crying all afternoon.

Yet the day he said, "The TA job is yours in September—if you want it." He sounded as if he really thought she might have better things to do.

Her second year in the master's program began like a reward; first, she became Professor Engelhorn's TA—obligated to attend his classes, grade all of his student papers, and sit in on the discussion every time a student came to complain about a grade. The job paid her tuition and provided a stipend—just enough that when three scholar friends pleaded with Zoe to be the fourth roommate in their student apartment so that they could all afford the rent, she said yes. "It's time I grew up," she admonished Billie, who had a boyfriend coming around from time to time that year and called Zoe asking her to come home only when she and the boyfriend fought. By then, it was March and the graduate students had received word that their building was scheduled for demolition at the end of the school year to make way for a luxury condo development. The graduate student residents began taking turns holding what they called Armageddon parties.

As Professor Engelhorn's teaching assistant, Zoe found that students frequently came into his office after hours, hanging around talking about anything—their dissertations, Chinese scandals, cranky lovers, certifiable parents, inorganic wheat allergies. She observed that while the students were unloading, Professor Engelhorn was just avoiding going home. Sometimes he would suggest going out for a beer.

They would crowd around a table at the Abbey Pub and an eager cluster of students would ask Professor Engelhorn what he thought of this or that news from China or this or that new book, while another core would talk about who they were dating or who they thought was hot. A few teased Zoe about how she was going to be looking at Shanghai someday from the perch of a penthouse built by the famous Hirsch Builders—Danny's father.

One such night in May, she invited two dozen students and the professor to a party she and her roommates were throwing that Friday night—their turn at hosting the end of the world. Professor Engelhorn said he was going to be addressing a group of Columbia and NYU students from China on Friday night. "They call themselves an assorted crew of malcontents who don't believe a free market will make everything all right."

"They can all come. Armageddon should be overpopulated," Zoe assured him.

It was at that party that a confluence of karmic influences caused Ming and Zoe to meet.

It was a cool night, but open windows were no match for the inferno of body heat. Zoe, standing against the kitchen counter between Danny and Jeff, watched friends of friends of friends jostle for air rights.

"Does a crowd make us feel more or less loved?" Danny wondered. He poured a frosty bottle of South Hampton barley ale for the three of them. Danny had a fresh-scrubbed face that could sometimes deflate with an incongruous inner gloom, and a body that was just a little too thin, as if he were still growing into his adult role. Zoe's mother had pronounced him "not shallow but callow, not repulsive but not hot." His shirt smelled as rarified as the men's department at Barney's.

Jeff raised his glass and said, "To the evolution of barley malt. Hey, there'll be strangers fornicating in your bed by the time you try to clean up."

Jeff wore a T-shirt with a faded picture of McDonald's arches above the words "Pave the rainforest." Zoe herself wore an I-have-no-time-for-fashion tank top from her martial arts academy.

"We might love the reinforcement of a crowd but hate the people in it," Danny went on.

Jeff had turned away, his gaze fixed upon a Chinese girl whose Rapunzel-of-the-Orient tresses grazed his elbow. "I didn't know my tasteless friend Zoe was going to use my art this way," he murmured to the girl, and pointed out the photographs of homeless people tacked on the walls and cabinets.

"Those pictures are, uh, I would say, deeply disturbing," the girl said, her voice fierce with approval. She wore a tee shirt and mini-skirt as black as her hair, her shirt short enough to reveal a sunburst tattoo easy enough to hide from straight-laced Chinese parents. She spoke English with a versatile vocabulary but with the accent of a recent arrival.

"I'm Ming," she said. She stopped suddenly and closed her mouth, but Zoe had already observed the gray third-world stumps that passed for teeth.

"Zoe spent a year at Bei Da," Jeff said. "Can you tell I visited her there? I learned how to say Bei Jing instead of Beizhing—"

"I speak Lhasa-Yipso dialect," Danny muttered, and squeezed Zoe's waist as if he were a space alien trying to pull her away.

Ming tossed a confused look at him, then turned to Zoe. "I am here to study an MBA at NYU. Surprise to my parents, in my heart I am a writer."

"Maybe the world isn't ready for your genius," Danny persisted. Zoe punched him lightly. That was the code word, between the three of them, for bad art. She saw that Ming got it; the girl lowered her head like a creature in retreat.

"Where are you from?" Zoe asked—dumb small talk to ease hard feelings. Danny turned to talk to a group in the corner.

"Beijing." Ming tossed her hair. "But I wasted my childhood in Sichuan, you know Sichuan? It was a Lin Biao classified project in an awful," she gave a shudder, "little village...."

"A Third Front village? Praise..."

Zoe caught the words on the way out. She had almost shouted, "Praise the Lord!"

Around them party guests were expounding on assassinating Republican politicians, the advantages of Zoloft over Paxil, how technology was going to create an empire of its own in the new millennium, and why theatre critics were all bombastic bootlickers. But absolutely no one in that crowd would have known quite how to react if they'd heard some alien in their midst howl the words, "Praise the Lord!" Especially if the words tumbled out in a Mississippi pulpit twang.

"I've been talking about the Third Front line of defense in the provinces with my adviser," she went on, grasping to recover her poise. "He said that the villages might be a good dissertation topic. If the committee decides I'm PhD material, that is."

Jeff patted her shoulder.

"Do you drive cars?" Ming asked the two of them.

"Sure, I grew up in New Joisey, suburbia, but I try not to go back," said Jeff.

"I would like to drop out from school and go across America all the way," said Ming.

"You wanna see billboards and Bible thumpers and amber waves of grain?" Jeff's pale cheeks lit up with sudden color. "I've always wanted to take a foreigner on the road."

"First, we all go see America, then Zoe comes with me to Sunshine Village," Ming half-promised.

When Jeff left the party, Ming left with him. A month later they were married.

Chapter Three

The bus ride to Chengdu took four and a half hours. Ming and Zoe shared a thermos of tea, some bean paste rolls, and one of the two magenta Day-Glo dragonfruits Zoe had bought at the market outside the Chengdu airport. Zoe pulled out her old Swiss Army knife with the blade that wouldn't quite retract and sliced the rubbery rind in perfect strips.

"I remember your mom had a summer dress this color," Ming mused, holding up a strip of dragonfruit rind, and she felt herself sigh with longing for the place she'd had to leave.

"One hill after another," Zoe snapped back. "Must have been a rough ride by oxcart." The way she glared told Ming that this was going to be the rule: no talk about New York.

Ming let her pink strips fall to the floor, along with the banana peels, peanut shells, and cigarette butts that other passengers dropped as the morning wore on.

Just after one o'clock, she sniffed a familiar salty smell, and the old bus wheezed its way through a wall of clouds.

"Next stop, Sunshine Village!" the bus conductor announced.

The two travelers stomped over the carpet of detritus to exit the bus. Outside, the white misty air swirled through the black grime of Market Street. A swarm of villagers, gathered to greet the incoming bus, stared the new arrivals up and down. Ming looked very official in black trousers, high heels, and a yellow wool coat; the townspeople doubtless would have suspected her of being the investment firm conscript she really was if not for the fact that she was with an American in hiking boots, dressed as if China were nothing more than a mountain to scale.

No one was expecting them. New Icarus Capital had a practice of sending researchers out to inspect old state-owned companies in surprise attacks. If they had forewarning, the villagers would erect a stage set to make the company look far more valuable than it was.

True, there was always the danger of some local authority detaining unexpected visitors just to let them know they weren't wanted. Han had a plan for that; Zoe was to flash her Columbia University ID card, which would convey vague suggestions of American ex-presidents and network reporters descending in her wake.

Market Street, the center of Sunshine Village, ran for two and a half blocks, and was lined with cement buildings of two and three stories high. At dirt floor storefronts, merchants sold cabbages and oranges and the occasional bar of soap. Sweaty cooks stirred vats of chicken broth, their customers slurping noodles at Formica tables, playing mahjong, minding babies, and watching soap operas on overhead television screens.

At the end of the two and a half blocks, where the storefronts gave way to a meadow, the visitors halted. Two dozen or so men swarmed about, muttering amongst themselves, smoking, spitting, and carrying signs that read *Unemployed Machinist Needs Work* and *Experienced Payroll Manager, Laid Off*.

Zoe stared. *You don't have the freedom to stare,* Ming thought, but all she said was, "C'mon." She pointed to an unpaved road that wound uphill. "There used to be a guesthouse this way."

They passed a few sparser storefronts that seemed to sell nothing but oranges. From the crest of the hill, they looked down upon an undulating valley, the grass brown and frosty between clumps of yellow rapeseed. In the distance was the spire of a pagoda. It was there that a big-boned young woman appeared, trudging up the hill and waving at them, with a face so sour she might have been about to handcuff them. But she didn't look like any kind of police officer, not in her purple parka and two pigtails tied up in a rainbow of plastic baubles.

Ming shuddered.

"Xiao Ming Cheng?" The woman's voice was a melodic alto.

"Lulu Pang?" Lulu had been a year behind Ming in school. Ming recalled a hideous day when she was taking a shower in the community bathhouse and Lulu, then a chubby eleven year old, had flung open the curtain, pointed at Ming's budding breasts and

41

pubic hair, giggled, and sang out, "Ming has hair!" After which, Ming had recurring nightmares about parading through Sunshine Village naked, while the townspeople pointed and laughed.

"We welcome you to Sunshine Village." Lulu seized their suitcases. "You will come and stay at my mother's guest house. Why didn't you telephone? We use email now, too. We would have made up special rooms for you."

"This is my friend Zuo Yi," Ming said. "She's a China scholar at Columbia University."

Lulu cast a disapproving sidelong glance at Zoe. "Welcome," she said in a rote tone that sounded like she was reading from an unfamiliar script. "We get many foreign guests now, from America, Taiwan, Japan, Switzerland..."

They had no choice but to follow Lulu down the other side of the hill, along a narrower dirt path to a cement courtyard and behind it, a forlorn slab of a building washed in peeling pink paint. An older woman with plump pouches for cheeks—as if she had gobbled up the previous visitors—appeared at the front door. She gave the girls a contorted smile that looked out of practice, but pumped Ming's hand and gushed, "Xiao Ming Cheng? All grown up. You came without letting me know?" She stared at Ming and her city clothes, then her gaze crossed over to Zoe and her utter American-ness. "You come from America? My cousin went there."

"Mrs. Pang," Ming whispered to Zoe as they followed the older woman up a narrow flight of stairs. "Lulu's mother. She used to work as an office manager for my parents."

Above, they traversed an unlit hallway, their footsteps echoing on the cement floor. Mrs. Pang reached into her pocket and pulled out a ring with a dozen keys and unlocked a door, which opened into a small suite. There was a front room with four stiff-backed chairs, and a thick brocade curtain that reeked of mildew. Mrs. Pang picked up a corner of the curtain and led them into a room with one double bed and one single bed. She turned on a switch and a blast of crematory heat filled the bedroom.

"You must be very tired," Mrs. Pang pronounced. Her cheeks

grew fatter. "Two beds, see? And you have a private bath, with hot water."

"How much?" asked Zoe.

"Don't worry, you are our guests, we settle when you go."

Price improvisation, Ming thought.

Another young woman entered, head bowed, carrying a tray laden with a tea thermos, four oranges, and two paper-thin towels.

"Let's go back out," Zoe said as soon as the two visitors were alone. It was ice-cold in the front room. Zoe tried to yank the curtain aside. "Shit. If this would move, we could distribute the heat…."

Ming turned the knob on the front door. It didn't budge. "We have a smiling jailor."

"Shit! Try again."

"I think they'll come let us out when the town is cleaned up."

"Cleaned up?"

"The men," Ming reminded her. "Those protesters will rot in prison so that we can see the town all spiffed up and presentable."

"When you take over the company, you can let the men out. Shit, shit, shit. I should get word about a human rights violation to Professor Engel—" Zoe stopped herself and turned her back to Ming.

"How is he?" Ming felt her voice coming out in little-girl falsetto. An involuntary reflex that happened when she had cause to be contrite. *Nothing happened with him*, she had to remind herself.

Instead of answering, Zoe picked up the teapot. "Think there's a microphone hidden somewhere in the room?" She poured the tea, and the small room was filled with the fragrance of a summer garden.

"Sichuan jasmine. Grows all around here," said Ming. "When I was little they used to ration two shreds of leaf to a cup for the grownups and one shred to the children. We might as well take showers. You want to go first? Not very nice towels. Maybe you like this one?"

Ming handed Zoe a faded blue-and-green-striped towel.

Zoe pulled out a bar of wrapped soap. "My mom put more money on her credit card to send me off with some nice peach-mango soap."

When Zoe came out of the shower, Ming was sprawled out on the small bed, tapping at her laptop. Zoe claimed a few square inches of floor to do modified *qi gong* stretches and kicks. Then she settled into a chair. Ming looked up from her writing occasionally and saw Zoe trying to bury herself in a scholarly book, except that she kept glancing up at the cracks in the ceiling as if the squiggles contained a message. The oxygen grew thin.

At last, somewhere in eternity, they heard the sound of metal scraping metal. Then a knock on the door.

Lulu stepped inside. "Did you have a nice rest? Are you hungry?" she asked. "I will show you the town now."

⌘

They were outdoors, finally, ambling down the hill and onto Market Street. The protesters were gone—nothing but a puddle of water on the ground where they'd been. Ming could almost smell blood spilt then hosed away.

"We have many restaurants now," said Lulu, their designated minder.

They wandered into a market stall where Ming and Zoe ordered bowls of steaming noodles. A critical customer from New York would have pronounced the broth lukewarm and the clots of fatty gray meat beyond disgusting, but New York was far away. Zoe poured jasmine tea into three cups.

"You have great hair," Zoe told Lulu. Lulu's hair was indeed glossy, the color of black jade and so thick that her pigtails nuzzled her shoulders like twin panther cubs. "You could be a hair model."

Basking in Zoe's effervescence, Lulu looked more wistful than sour. "I would like," she said, "to study the hospitality industry."

When they left the restaurant the clouds were the color of smoke. On the eastern side of town they could see the tiny figures of peasants trekking home from the fields. Ming turned up the hill toward the pagoda that loomed against the northern sky.

"It is not so nice there," Lulu protested. Ming ignored her and steered Zoe toward the poplar trees that formed a circle around the

44

ancient tower. While Lulu planted herself behind a tree, Ming showed Zoe the friezes carved in crumbling stone. Each wall depicted a scene from the Seven Sages of the Bamboo Grove. The sages lifted wine cups at a long table in one, stood debating the universe in another, wrote poetry in a third—their robes flowed gracefully, their long fingers, tapered and elegant, but there were only gouged holes where their heads had once been. *Red Guards came with stonecutters and broke their heads off before you were born,* Papa had told her.

"Let's sneak out tonight and climb up here," Ming pleaded as they approached the dark doorway to the pagoda. Within they could see the dim twist of a staircase that no one had climbed in a hundred years. "I know you're not afraid of anything."

"I'm afraid of plunging through a rotting stair and breaking both my legs and getting gnawed to death by rats."

Suddenly a thud sounded from inside. Ming and Zoe stopped. And then, from the blackness, a man emerged.

He was young, with emaciated limbs and feet black with coal dust. Pants hung in threads on his skeletal frame; his hair was long and wild. He froze, momentarily, at the sight of them, his eyes scoping them out like two golden torches. Then he sprinted past them and took off like a creature in flight, vanishing behind the pagoda. Yet a ray of light seemed to linger.

Chapter Four

One day when Ming was ten years old, she ventured down to the cave beside the big Buddha dragging runty little Wu Li Nan along behind her. It wasn't a deliberate plan, just an idea that came to her after the big boys punched him, stupid boy that he was. Li Nan's uncle in Hong Kong had sent him a shiny green parka, like nothing you could buy in China, and he had to show it off. Ming saw the bullies, Tang, Yeng, and Eng, punching Li Nan and ripping off his beautiful jacket and pulling it to shreds. Li Nan, Ming knew, would hide in the rice fields until he was sure they'd gone home.

It was strange that the two of them were friends: the girl whom teachers described as the best student in the class and the boy who seldom did his homework. Instead of studying, Li Nan was always betting on things—soccer games on television, ping pong at school—and he'd set up betting pools of stones since no one had money to play with. But in fact, he was Ming's only friend. There was a group of five girls who used to let her walk home with them sometimes, but ever since she got into trouble for doing their homework for them—the teacher had noticed the similarity of the characters, despite Ming's efforts to vary the writing—the girls wouldn't talk to her. They got smacked on their hands for the homework incident, while Ming got a lecture about how she shouldn't let lazy people take advantage of her. Now, when she passed the five girls they'd make fun of her ugly teeth.

That particular day, Ming found Li Nan crouched behind the stalks in the rice paddy with a telltale stain on his crotch.

"Pee-peed in your pants!" She couldn't resist taunting him; it made her forget, for just a moment, the hunger that was rattling through her brain. That was when she got a big idea. "You can come with me and I'll show you something scary," she told him. "But it'll eat you in one bite if you cry. Even the big boys are afraid to go there."

Ming led Li Nan past the pink, scum-covered pond where the bullfrogs were going *urp-urrrurrp*, then through the grove of pine trees. The clouds were the color of ashes by the time they arrived at the Buddha on the cliff. Drizzle bit through the holes in Ming's jacket.

"It's so foggy, if a wolf comes along and eats us no one will find our bones 'til spring," she told her snively little friend. Actually, he'd stopped sniffling and crying. He followed her to the mouth of the cave.

"We're monkeys. *Reeepp'eee eeee*. You have to talk like a monkey. There's monkeys inside and they'll kill you unless you make like you're one of them."

"I'm not a monkey!" he insisted. Still, he got down on all fours, the way she showed him, and they crawled inside the hole. "I can't see!"

It was pitch black, but as their eyes adjusted they could see crystals hanging from the ceiling like icicles and rising up from the earthen floor like toadstools. Li Nan made a funny sound, like "*Aaaarrrrraaaaarrrrr!*" that made Ming's feet tremble for a second.

"Eat the toadstools!" She shouted it out like an order, trying to be louder than his shriek. "They aren't poison. They're candy."

Li Nan pretended to pick one and give it to her. "This one's free," he said. "Now you have to buy more from me."

"I found the candy. You pay me!"

"I stole it. Put your money in my pocket."

The darkness was making him brave. He took her hand and put it in his pocket. She felt a big hole there, and he was pulling her hand through the hole and then she screamed. She was touching the thing between his legs. He giggled. Maybe it was funny—she wasn't sure, but since it made him laugh she giggled too, and squeezed the thing, which made him laugh more.

"You wanna know a secret? I'm going to get rich when I'm big," Li Nan said. Then, suddenly, he made the "*AAAARRRRaarrrr!*" noise again, even louder. "Look!"

Down on the ground was something white and round. Even in

the dark, Ming could see two holes and below them a hollow mouth with a dead grin.

Li Nan bent down and picked it up. It was a human head, with nothing left but the bones.

Ming knocked on Li Nan's head. "It has no brains," she declared. "Like you!"

This was the best day of her life, she decided. Then she heard a splashing sound, and smelled the sharp stink of urine. Li Nan was making *pee pee* in the bone head. They both laughed.

That was when the static of a loudspeaker sounded in the distance, and a voice issued the usual five o'clock greeting: "Good evening, comrades." Five o'clock! They were going to be late getting home.

"My mama's gonna box my ears!" said Li Nan. He looked almost proud of it.

"My papa's gonna yell 'til he turns purple," Ming said.

Li Nan hoisted his knees high in time to the music on the loudspeaker. Ming lifted her knees in unison, left, right, left, right, and they marched down the dirt road toward the village. Coal smoke curled out of the factory chimneys, black smudges against the graying sky. Scrambling down the hillside, Ming and Li Nan saw their mothers in a cluster of a dozen or so women heading home after the day's work.

Mama spotted Ming and raced over, her broad face hot with fury as she pulled Ming by the arm. "Where have you been?"

Mrs. Wu looked down at her son, then at Ming. "You whore!" Mrs. Wu shrieked. She was always saying that. Ming knew it meant something really wicked and it made her feel cold inside. She twisted her free hand, afraid to look at it. Maybe both hands had turned the color of blood from touching Li Nan where she wasn't supposed to.

"Ming's a whore!" Li Nan flashed a vicious grin at Ming, then looked up at his mother as if he thought she might reward him.

Mama pulled Ming along until they got to their compound. Outside, in the concrete square with neighbors gathering to watch, Mama scrubbed Ming's face raw with lye soap and dried it roughly with a torn towel.

"No!" Ming screamed and cried and sobbed loud enough so that the magic monkey would hear her cries, be filled with pity, and snatch her away, but of course there weren't really any magic monkeys.

"Hush!" screamed Mama. Up above, through the clouds that perpetually covered the village, lightning split the sky in half.

⌘

Li Nan grew up to be fearless, and he went to New York before Ming did. His parents, who had come to Beijing to work for Mama and Papa's company, were always bragging that their son was getting rich in America, although others whispered that he was involved in some kind of criminal scheme, or maybe more than one. Before Ming left for New York, Mama and Papa told Ming to stay away from Li Nan; Mrs. Wu, however, gave her his cell phone number.

"He'll always help his friends from home," Mrs. Wu had said, but something in her eyes made Ming feel like a wicked whore all over again.

Ming arrived in New York with two thousand dollars. A lot of money, her parents kept saying, though even in Beijing these days it would barely pay a month's rent in a city apartment. She had a partial scholarship, but all it covered was tuition, and she had to pay her living expenses. Her parents' customers were all in China and therefore had only domestic *renminbi* to pay them, and though everyone said China's national currency was going to be traded all over the world someday, for now it was worth nothing in other countries. Anyway, Mama and Papa thought everyone should work for their money. Her brother claimed he didn't have any cash to spare, and besides, he said, it was important that Ming learn how to make her own way. Two thousand dollars was just enough to buy books for business school and obtain a basement apartment that she shared with twelve other Chinese students and a colony of rats. Ming had nothing left for the second month's rent. So she visited Li Nan and he gave her a cash loan. "I can always lend money to friends from home," he said.

Then she had to start paying him back.

A few months into business school Ming started a blog that

consisted of a fictional series of sexual encounters by a black-haired temptress called Mimi. Mimi was working her way through all of the men in New York according to the letters of the alphabet. She jumped into bed with Andrew and licked dulce de leche ice cream off his dick. Ben tied her to a bedpost with silk cords; Cyril was a conductor who insisted she spank him on the bottom with his baton.

While the blog was entirely fictional, the author did draw inspiration from her own life. Li Nan had presented her with the cash, in an envelope. He watched while she riffled through the bills, caressing the numbers, scrutinizing the crisp shades of green.

"You don't have to worry about paying me back," he said, almost in a whisper. He sat behind a metal desk in a barren office, a single joss stick curling out smoke that, in Ming's mind, took a Bodhisattva shape. "You just work for me. I have a lot of friends. But they're lonely. For you, it's a perfect job. You can get your mind off business school and study human psychology—you'll find a million stories to write."

Then he called his colleague Brian in from the adjoining room. Brian had a mouth that turned downward on the left side, as if something tasted bad, and a snake tattoo on each hand. He gave Ming a piece of paper with the name of a man, the address of a hotel, and the number of a room. "You'll make plenty of money," Brian said in his gravelly voice. He looked her up and down and she had a sense he was looking for weak spots where he might plunge a knife if she didn't come through with a lot of money.

The hotel room reeked of infected semen, and Ming was convinced her insides were going to rot. But the man gave her three hundred dollars. "You should get your teeth fixed. You could make a lot more if you had better teeth," the customer told her.

She met men who wanted her to tie them up, and another who lay in the bathtub and asked her to douse him in a bath of piss. Li Nan always let her keep half of the earnings. Some of the men didn't even want her to stay long enough to wash up in their rooms, so she'd have to sit on the subway with their juices snaking along her thighs and stinging like acid.

Ming worked for Li Nan two to three nights a week. The rest of the time she tried to be someone else—a student, a writer, and an explorer. She wandered through the ecosystems of New York City: the shiny magic place called Park Avenue, where flowers bloomed on the oasis between the traffic lanes and doormen, dressed like royal admirals, stood outside the buildings, and the tenement streets where the people seemed to have nothing but defiance to keep them from cracking in half.

Unlike her roommates, Ming avoided political meetings. Groups scared her, gathering for the purpose of identifying an enemy who might end up being one of those present. But one Friday in May, her malcontent roommates told her about a party up near Columbia and she decided to go.

At that party, Ming couldn't help but observe a guy in a torn T-shirt gazing at her. She could practically smell his unwashed hair across the room, but appreciated the way his eyes followed her. A yellow fever type, for certain. The West was full of men who had fantasies of whores with virginal voices teaching them a hundred mysteries-of-the-Orient sex positions. But Ming liked his eyes, and she liked how the copper-haired woman standing next to him seemed imbued with light. She glided over to their warm circle.

"Williamsburg is the capital of hip. My squalor is cooler than your squalor," Jeff crooned over the subway screech the night they met, as they rode the L train to his place in Brooklyn. He lived in three hundred square feet of space, a one-third share of a loft, three floors up on an elevator that swayed.

Up close, Jeff felt just as she'd suspected; when he kissed her, sweat dripped from his face to hers and if she moved an inch away from him he'd move an inch closer.

"Let's just be friends," she said, and the condom she'd brought along stayed in the bottom of her purse.

He shrugged. "I'm always the guy who doesn't get laid."

Ming slept on a pile of quilts in the corner, and in the morning Jeff made exquisite coffee. He ground French roast beans, steeped them in a French filter, and made a great show of asking, "Café au

51

lait, mademoiselle?" He even used a little steaming device to make the milk bubbly.

Somehow Ming didn't leave. She didn't even go back to school when it came time to take her finals. She had studied a little bit, then kicked her books into Jeff's laundry pile. I'll die of asphyxiation in the exam room, she realized. This loft with the cracked skylights was a kingdom where she belonged, living where the gods of wit and talent reigned. Zoe and other friends were always passing through, drinking cheap wine and talking about exhibition spaces and rehearsals and dissertations, even while they worried aloud about how to pay their bills.

True, it was suicide to drop out of business school. Ming's student visa was due to expire at the end of the month. But Jeff said something about "damsel in distress," and Ming found herself uttering the words "green card marriage."

A dozen of Jeff's friends came with them to city hall on a Friday afternoon in June. Zoe came without Danny. "He's in the Hamptons," she said, and Ming thought her friend looked more relieved than disappointed. "He promised his old girlfriend, Liesel Morgan, he'd go to a charity gala out there." Zoe emphasized the name "Liesel Morgan" as though that were someone Ming should have heard of. "And you are both invited, as the bride and groom, to go tomorrow afternoon. His wedding present."

The Hirsch estate in East Hampton had a deceptively modest facade of weathered redwood, with a solarium on the ocean side. Danny and Zoe ushered the newlyweds through a room where museum-white walls burst with modern and contemporary art. On the west wall, Rauschenberg and Pollock abstracts and Warhol movie stars sized up the visitors. The east wall was decorated with a collage of cigarette packs and splashes of primary colors; a giant sculpture of Cheerios, Ritz crackers, Tampax, and Crayolas boxes; and a life-sized sculpture of a crashed car.

Danny left Ming and Jeff ensconced at an aluminum patio table shaped like an amoeba while he and Zoe prepared lunch.

"Is this a table or something from an auto body shop?" cracked

Jeff, rubbing his hand on the aluminum and leaving a dull smear.

When Zoe and Danny emerged from the house half an hour later, their faces were flushed. People in love went indoors and found secret spots to get it on; that much Ming knew. Such a sun-kissed mussiness about them.

Or maybe they'd been fighting.

"Danny thinks writing my dissertation about a Sichuan village is too subaltern," Zoe announced, as she passed around a huge bowl of salad.

The salad filled the air with the lush perfume of lime. Ming drew up a forkful of green papaya and tender beef shreds flavored with garlic and chili peppers.

"Riesling?" Danny asked. He poured wine. "Guess you're not a spice wimp, being from Sichuan. I just told Zoe—no offense, Ming—but I don't think there's anything commercially viable about the story of your childhood and how you were so hungry that you saw a talking monkey. Academia likes history that looks to the future. When I tell people that my girlfriend's getting a PhD in Chinese economic history, they ask me what's going to happen there. Like I'm supposed to know how long we have 'til China overtakes America as a superpower! I told Zoe she ought to study the big state-owned companies under Mao, and how they contributed to China becoming a force in the world today. Then she can write her ticket as a high-paid consultant on top of teaching."

Ming helped herself to more salad.

"I like a girl with a hearty appetite. So...where do you go in New York for real Sichuan cuisine?" Danny asked.

"Real Sichuan cuisine in Communist China was rice gruel," Jeff injected. "Ming's mother cooked the rice over and over because they had to make it last all month."

"It's still communist," Danny pointed out.

"And her father got rice gruel with roaches for protein when he was a political prisoner—"

"He wasn't quite a political prisoner," Zoe interjected.

"Li Nan, a friend from my village, took me to this place in

Chinatown when I first came to New York. I didn't have much money when I first arrived, and he…took me out to eat. You would never be able to find this restaurant; it's on the second floor and there's no sign, but the owners are from Sichuan and they cook very good Sichuan food. I think they made dog but they wouldn't admit it. Li Nan is not always, shall we say, on the right side of the law," Ming confided.

"Danny's grandpa was a crook. Every fine estate starts with one," Jeff observed.

"Put this in your mouth so we can start roasting you," said Zoe. She pretended to shove an apple at Jeff, but instead started slicing the apples into seedless quarters.

Danny passed the plate to Ming. She mumbled, "No, thank you."

"Ming doesn't eat apples," Jeff said.

⌘

"I like it here much better than the Hamptons," Ming told her new husband that night. Grimy Brooklyn heat sneered through the skylights. She was sitting atop her pile of quilts. "I am quite sure Danny doesn't like me."

Jeff was silent, which seemed to be his way of agreeing. That night Ming massaged his shoulders, then let him massage hers, and pulled him on the bed. He didn't even let her touch his hard-on; he kissed her, down to her toes. He asked, too often, too tentatively, "Do you like that?" A true love, she thought, would know what she liked just by the way their bodies melded. Still, it was nice to sit up in bed with Jeff after they made love, laughing as he read aloud from a paperback copy of *On the Road*. He spread a map of the United States on the floor and showed her a thin line called Route 66. It was an open road where dreamers drove and kept going until they ran out of luck or out of gas, he told her. Ming and Jeff decided they'd take the trip someday.

They let the rest of that long summer grow prickly with dreams; they went to art galleries and visited an agent who liked Jeff's portfolio; they ventured into Tiffany's and Bergdorf and Jimmy

Choo, and Jeff watched as Ming fondled silver high-heeled sandals that cost $725. It would take five slimy hotel encounters to buy shoes like that, she calculated in her mind, and going without food for two weeks.

Jeff was always finding things in the streets. He'd carry wicker chairs home on the subway, and broken plates and old computers, but only Macs. He kept his computers on a long table in his makeshift room. On one computer he composed his own weird poetry into voice-activated software; on another, he made digital pictures of pretty faces look like gorilla masks. A week into their marriage, he discovered a photo on the internet from the Hamptons party of Liesel Morgan, the vanilla-haired, financial analyst ex who was, Jeff said, after Danny. "Clichéd party shot...." Jeff railed. "Awful lighting." Ming laughed as she watched him photoshop Liesel Morgan into a cavewoman. At moments like that, they were vengeance warriors in an army of two.

⌘

Ming still worked some nights for Li Nan. She told Jeff she was helping her parents sell to the American market and sometimes had to go to dinner with prospective clients.

On other nights, to tease her, Jeff would read Ming's blog aloud. "He had a regatta tan on every part, and Mimi rubbed him below deck...are you kidding me? This is so bad it'll probably make you rich. Too bad you're not really a hooker. Sick twisted reality sells."

Ming told her family that she'd found a husband in New York. If she'd tried to tell them she needed money, they'd say come back here and work for us. It was a pyrrhic victory, to have officially become a poor artist. A victory that extended even beyond the Cheng household to her entire pragmatic homeland.

"I feel like the family I should have been born to is right here," she told Jeff and the roommates one night while they lounged on Salvation Army chairs and hashed out the world's problems.

"Yeah, we're a nuclear family. Looks like fusion, but it's really all fission," said Jeff.

The ideal kingdom, where Ming really longed to live, however, was the illegal sublet on the Upper West Side that Billie Austin inhabited with Zoe. The Austins' apartment had mismatched shelves that overflowed with books, antique furniture, and flowery porcelain that was chipped around the edges.

"We live on a theater set, don't you see?" Zoe mourned. "And someday the show is gonna close and it'll all come crashing down."

But you're the performers, the whole city is a stage set for you, Ming thought. New York. If she said it aloud Zoe would counter-attack; Ming knew better than to contradict her friend when she had that all-is-drama look about her.

One sultry evening in July, Billie invited Ming to stay for dinner. "We have our terrace garden," Billie said. "Screw the Hamptons, though to be in Manhattan in July is an admission of failure." Even so, Ming detected a thread of hope in her voice—it was only Tuesday and there was still plenty of time for a weekend invitation to materialize, for love to appear, or an agent to call.

Though it was evening, Billie wore a straw hat on the terrace, going on about how a few rays of sun could age her by ten years. She told Ming about an audition she'd had yesterday. She'd worn a pound of makeup to hide the circles under her eyes, she claimed, because it was nine in the morning. "Can you imagine, me, who just doesn't do mornings? Poor Zoe always had to make her own breakfast. So you're a writer, Ming?"

No one had ever called Ming a writer before.

"I'm writing erotic stories."

"Mmmmmm." Zoe's *mmmmming* was over an ear of corn. "Try some," she said, passing the platter to Ming.

Ming shook her head.

"In her country it's for hogs," Billie said.

"You've never even been to China," Zoe chastised.

"I saw something about farming in China on TV, and how many farms did my daughter see in Beijing? That CNN correspondent, what's her name, Rhonda Rogers, she did a special on the un-booming parts of China."

56

"Jeff says she looks like a mummy with her Botox," Ming parroted.

"I think she had a lip job, too," said Billie. "Crazy, you wouldn't catch me risking ruin with Botox even if I could afford it. But when you get rich—erotica sells, so I know you'll be a bestselling author someday—don't do that thing Asian actresses do, you know, getting eye jobs to look more Caucasian. Ming is lovely, don't you think, Zoe honey?"

"I need cosmetic surgery," Ming pointed out.

"Only on your teeth, otherwise you're perfect. Exotic and strong. You could be an actress but don't, it's a thankless life."

"I need a job. But I think people won't hire me because my teeth. And…" she hung her head with more humiliation than was strictly necessary. "I cannot eat hard things. Like corn. Or apples."

"Oh my god." Zoe shoved her plate aside as if she didn't deserve it.

"Good god, girl," Billie said. "You've got to get your teeth fixed. I wish I had all the bucks in the world to give you."

They sat waiting for a set of perfect teeth to drop from the sky.

Finally Billie spoke up, "We didn't have such great teeth in Mississippi either. Mine were dingy once upon a time. Zoe doesn't know how lucky she is; just look at those incisors that nature filed to perfection."

"People get their teeth done in Thailand cheaply," Zoe offered.

"Oh, please, this little mouth needs the best in the business, and she's going to have to go back so many times she'd have to spend the whole year in Asia. You can't do that when you're trying to get a green card, can you darling? When I needed help I went to this guy, Dr. Richard Perlmutter. He'll be expensive. But I say go into debt for it, then write your bestseller with your pretty teeth to help you sell it."

Dr. Perlmutter wasn't taking new patients before his August vacation, a self-important female voice informed her. "You sound like you wanna do it soon. I have something the first week in September." The woman on the phone pronounced it "Septembah." Jeff had told Ming about those old-style Brooklyn accents.

The initial consultation would cost two hundred dollars.

"Do you have pain?"

"Yes."

"It's considered cosmetic, but if you have pain your insurance might pay some. Bonding teeth, if the doctah says that's what you need, is about $1500," the woman on the phone said. "No, that's per tooth."

Afterward, Ming held up a hand mirror and counted her teeth. There were twenty-eight of them since a dentist in China had yanked out her wisdom teeth. Forty-two thousand dollars.

"Do you have health insurance?" she asked her spouse.

"Health insurance? Ha, ha. Health insurance, she asks. This is my health insurance." He held up two crossed fingers. "Do you know how much health insurance costs?"

Ming called Han. "Forty-two thousand dollars." She said it twice before he reacted.

Her brother told her that if she'd go back to business school she could get a job that would pay for all the perfect teeth she wanted. Besides, his money was tied up, he said. "When are we going to meet Jeff? You know there's plenty of opportunity for you both in China. And if he doesn't make enough money to help you, why did you marry him?"

The wonderful, wonderful Billie Austin came forward with the two hundred dollars for the first office visit. "I call my father and tell him I'm doing missionary work sometimes," she said. "If your mouth isn't a mission I don't know what is."

So the gods sent Ming to Dr. Richard Perlmutter.

The dentist to the stars was a man who exuded conscientious contentment. He had pictures of his wife and three children around the office, and one of himself running in a marathon. He gave Ming a brochure with pictures showing how, with his etching tools, he would scrape on a paste of acrylic resins combined with tiny crystals of quartz and silicon dioxide, all of which he'd measured and mixed to just the right shade of white. He had some sample colors, and he showed Ming a white of fine bone teacups that he said would go beautifully with her skin tone.

Dr. Perlmutter told her, that first week in September, that he could fit her with a temporary façade. "That won't cost much. But your teeth need permanent bonding. Probably will need root canal work. They'll be a lot healthier."

"I don't have much money." Ming let her voice rise several octaves and her eyes push out plump tears.

"Don't sweat the small stuff."

In the street outside of Dr. Perlmutter's office, Ming made a phone call, then wandered in the direction of Chinatown. She felt her teeth pinching. All her life they'd hurt.

Li Nan moved often and he'd given her a cryptic address. "Baxter below Grand, above fish. Four." That meant fourth floor.

"I need more money, but I can't keep doing, y'know. My husband would kill me if he found out I was entertaining your friends," she pleaded.

Li Nan's grownup body was like a balloon stuffed with dumplings. He wore a crisp polo shirt and Italian loafers without socks. His teeth were crooked and yellow, but not nearly as bad as Ming's. They'd all woken up on fire with stomach cramps as children, had all spat vile pus into their bedpans, yet Ming could trace the putrid colors of every childhood disease in her teeth while Li Nan had only a wispy ghost of jaundice.

"My husband lost his job."

Jeff had been on call with a magazine to shoot parties but they hadn't called lately, so it wasn't exactly a lie. Ming let tears flow down her cheeks. Li Nan had moved into a new office with a mahogany desk, but the walls were empty. An air conditioner whirred and dripped into a plastic bucket.

"Anyway," she said, "I could make more money with better teeth. I need to get my teeth done. It's my dream."

"It is true, you would be so pretty with new teeth." Li Nan held up his wrist to show her his watch, decorated with small diamonds around the bezel. "You see this? Here is a very beautiful face, I think. It tells me the time in Asia and Europe and the phase of the moon. This beautiful watch cost five thousand dollars. I understand now, having the best makes you a better person. You cannot, of course,

59

give people handouts. But you could come to work for me here in the office."

Li Nan picked up a wad of black velvet. Inside was a gemstone with myriad surfaces casting blue, green, and violet fire. It felt like getting close to a star.

"These come from a mine not too far from the old salt mines in our village," Li Nan said. "We call them Sichuan opals. Guess how much they cost?"

"A lot."

He looked pleased. "There is nothing else like these available in America, not yet...."

Ming went to work in a room where twenty or so young men and women sat at small metal desks and talked on phones. "This is so-and-so from Shearson Barnett...." they'd say in English, Mandarin, and a babel of other tongues. They used different names for themselves every day, and they varied the name of the company, too. Sometimes they'd say "Zurich Partners Exchange" or "Merrill Logan."

Li Nan trained the brokers to start from a script: "Do you like beautiful jewels? I have a great investment opportunity, but there's a very limited supply. No risk, it will never lose value. Before people used credit cards they kept valuable objects that could be liquidated in times of need. We are a cutting-edge investment house, and we got into partnerships with these mines before anyone else did. That's how we get to offer these to special clients at special prices."

They got names of people to call from lists that Li Nan had "obtained," as he put it, from various brokerage firms. His requirement was that each broker make a sale to at least one out of every seven prospects, and you got fired if you missed your quota of twenty sales a week.

Ming sold nothing her first two weeks. Li Nan stood behind her listening, and he yelled at her in front of everyone, saying she didn't sound confident. But he gave her a second chance. In the third week, she learned to sound like every prospect's best friend. "I wish you could see the beautiful colors in this stone," she would say.

Twenty sales a week, four a day, five percent commission, paid in cash. Ming made a little over five thousand dollars her fourth week, minus what she still owed Li Nan for his initial loan, and, as he told her when he gave her the money, he had to take out two percent of her first six months' earnings for the training. Few people lasted more than three months. Still, she kept twenty-five hundred dollars and got two teeth done.

After two months Li Nan promoted her, so that she made follow-up calls instead of cold calls. She called people who had already bought, saying, "The gems have appreciated, and we have a one-time opportunity for you to buy more." Three months into the new sales pitch, she choked.

"You know there's no such thing as a bad week here. You either sell or you're out the door," said Li Nan. "I'm sorry. But you are an old friend. Maybe you'd like to try something different for a while?" He brought in Brian, who gave Ming the social security number, address, and date of birth for someone named Wing Yu Guan. All Ming had to do was get a home equity line of credit in Wing Yu Guan's name, then transfer the money to another account.

Over the next six months, little white jewels sprouted in her mouth.

"Fourteen to go," Dr. Perlmutter told her, and held up a mirror so she could admire his work. That was on a Monday. That Wednesday she went to the newest office in Chinatown—they'd moved a couple of times by then, and this space was over a gift shop—and saw a security guard sitting outside the door that led upstairs. She kept walking.

"I got laid off," she told Jeff that night. Ming's husband of convenience knew only that she'd been working for some kind of brokerage firm in Chinatown.

"Aw….and with your nice teeth too. Don't worry, we'll find you something."

Jeff was experimenting with sculptures of found objects that he turned into extraterrestrial creatures, and they had half a dozen inanimate roommates. There was the dog he was still putting together that had a cracked hand mirror for a head. Ming picked up the dog and held it close, so that all she could see was Dr. Perlmutter's beautiful construction, the only part of her that could truly claim it knew nothing of what she'd done before. She let Jeff see that she was stifling tears.

Two days later he held his hand out and said, "Take this." In his hand was a credit card.

"Eight thousand dollar limit. Some bank that would like to fuck me over just sent it. You're in charge of paying it off. In return for this I'm calling Zoe's friend who has that catering gig. I think they pay about fifteen an hour. I'm not so good at math but if you stick with catering, I figure you can pay off your Doctor Pearly Teeth in approximately three hundred years."

Dear, sweet, foolish Jeff. His credit card wasn't quite enough to finish the job but Dr. Perlmutter's receptionist waved an arm, jingling her diamond bangles and said, "We'll bill you."

By mid-summer, a year after Billie first told her about Dr. Perlmutter, Ming was able to look in a mirror and see a young writer/caterer who could walk up to people with an appetizer tray and an appetizing smile. In her white shirt and black bow tie—she'd had to spend five hours' income after taxes on the uniform—she was just like the others, looking out for the party guest who might be a famous writer or a handsome man who really wasn't married, as opposed to those who'd slipped their rings off.

In November of that year, another man appeared on the Mimi blog. She called him The Professor. An older man. Married but not happy. With him, Mimi spent hours talking about literature and the state of the world and why nothing was ever enough for most people, and Mimi called it an intellectual infatuation. They weren't sleeping together. He was a professor of comparative literature at NYU. That part Ming completely invented.

In reality, she had met a certain older professor. In late October, Zoe had called Ming and said, "I got you a speaking gig. No money, but it's a worthy cause. I'll coach you if you'd like. You know how the rich always want to have edifying experiences? So, Danny's mom said to me a couple of nights ago, 'Darling, it would be a coup, an utter coup, to have your Chinese friend whose father was imprisoned talk about her life at a benefit I'm giving.'"

The benefit, Zoe said, was for a Chinese human rights group. Suzanne Hirsch, her potential mother-in-law, had asked her to line up a few experts who could tell horror stories between the main course and dessert. Professor Charles Engelhorn was going to be there, along with a young man who had recently been released from a *lao gai*.

"Just talk about how your parents got assigned to the village, and then they got out only to be the victims of a corrupt official." Zoe didn't leave room in the conversation for Ming to say no.

Ming's wardrobe didn't include speaking-at-a-charity-gala attire, but she combed through limp gowns at a thrift shop and found a dress made of ivory lace, with a high neck. Jeff snickered when she modeled it for him. "Makes you look like a poetess who writes things like, 'My Sunday morning carriage ride, through the lord's field of demurest daffodils….'"

"Zoe didn't give me a lot of time."

"I know. I'm not supposed to tell you…"

"What?"

"Nothing." He was obviously bursting to tell her. He mentioned the name of a famous Chinese writer now living in Princeton. "They had her lined up, but she canceled, said she was doing something in London. You're a substitute."

On the afternoon before the affair, a Thursday, she tried on the poetess lace dress once again. Jeff was Photoshopping something.

"Danny is away on business and might not get home in time tonight," she said, examining the battered red pumps that were her only option.

"Poor Zoe, just has to marry a power broker," Jeff said.

Ming nodded. The dress cut into her neck. "It must feel so strange to not even know who your father is."

"Well, of course…." Jeff seemed to be bursting again.

"Of course what?"

"Nothing for your big ears."

"Are my ears too big?" she checked in a mirror.

"Mirror, mirror, on the wall, Ming is not the fairest of all because she's so vain she doesn't even care about her friend."

"I'd do anything for Zoe."

"Well, I can't tell you anything."

"So don't."

"Why do you think she got into this China thing? She thinks Charles Engelhorn might be her father. I'm never supposed to tell anyone. You let it out, you die."

That night, Ming was to meet Zoe at a coffee shop on Madison Avenue near the Hirsches' penthouse so that they could arrive together. When Zoe entered the coffee shop, heads turned in her direction. She wore long earrings, probably borrowed from her mom, and lipstick.

"You should always dress like that," Ming said. She wondered if Zoe could see through to her brain and this strange secret that Jeff had etched upon it.

In the Hirsches' apartment, though, Ming observed that Zoe's earrings were just servile tinsel amidst all the diamonds and emeralds. Suzanne Hirsch was wearing a ruby necklace. The rich all looked as if they'd just swept in from somewhere else—the status was in their voices and the things they said, and the jewels were supposed to look like an afterthought, Ming saw. Suzanne had a wholesome face that looked as if it really belonged to the sea breezes off of East Hampton.

"I'm so happy you could come." With a start, Ming realized Suzanne was talking to her. "And have you met Charles Engelhorn?" A tall man with shaggy gray-flecked hair stood looking at her. "I had such a fascinating visit to Beijing a few years ago. I almost became a Chinese art scholar, many years ago, but I got married instead," Suzanne said, with a luxuriant smile of regret. It was hard to tell if she was really regretful, or just trying to make her guests feel like their lives were worth an ounce of envy.

"Suzanne!" Someone came in and wrapped her in a hug.

"So you're a writer, I hear," said Charles Engelhorn.

He had a tight beard and wore a not-quite-expensive-enough-for-this-crowd suit. She observed his gap-toothed smile and arms that stretched as if they didn't quite know where they would stop.

She nodded. "I blog erotic stories and poems."

She watched him squirm, then start stroking his beard as if that was what he'd meant to do. "Do you know, I've traveled all over China but never got to Sichuan?"

When they were at the table and it was Professor Engelhorn's turn to speak, he talked about Ming. "I'll be brief because we have two real-life stories from China tonight," he told the fifty or so guests. He said that nearly ten years ago he'd been in Beijing and heard about a local man, a physicist and manager of a state-owned division, who had been arrested on unstated charges but in reality had just fallen afoul of a corrupt local official. "I've just now, tonight, found myself sitting next to that man's daughter," he said.

Then he went on to talk about the just-released prisoner and how his crime had been to organize a protest against a group of corrupt officials in another town. Ming flashed a Dr. Perlmutter smile at the young hero just out of the *lao gai*. He nodded with an expression that said smiling was for pampered fools. When the former political prisoner stood, he spoke in Mandarin with Professor Engelhorn translating, telling of a guard who beat him if he didn't split rocks fast enough. The hero looked too broken. Ming saw Danny slip into the room and to a table where the guests whispered to him instead of listening to the speaker. When it was Ming's turn to address the crowd, she made a point of slowing down for effect in the places Zoe had told her to.

The next day an email from an unfamiliar address showed up, signed "Charles." The message was short, just, "It was good to meet you. I'm glad to hear that your parents are doing well now. Maybe someday I'll get to Sichuan."

Ming huddled in a corner even though Jeff wasn't home, waiting for her fingers to play out a response. What came out was, "I rarely wish to go back and explore my birthplace. But if you were to visit there, I think you might find it..." she sat for a while with her hands in limbo. The word she finally wrote was "salty."

65

Sunshine Village was, in fact, a salty place. Around 250 B.C., a provincial governor had discovered the salt mines, and for many centuries, the economy had revolved around that most valuable of commodities in the days before refrigeration, a commodity that emperors believed would arouse even the most homesick among their underage concubines. Illegitimate princelings throughout China were conceived in a salted frenzy.

"Come by and chat sometime if you're around the Columbia campus," the professor wrote back. Two days later, she sat across from him in a tiny coffee bar, fifteen blocks from campus. Ming kept glancing around, fearing Zoe or someone who knew her would wander in.

"I never want to go back to China," Ming told him. "I love New York."

"So you're living the life of a young writer in Brooklyn?" he asked. American men, she'd found, seemed to like it when she talked about living beneath skylights and dropping out of business school to write. Maybe someday she'd meet a man who would listen if she told him about Li Nan and the awful things. She toyed with the idea that the professor might be that man. For the moment, she told him about her artsy roommates and their day-to-day angst. She told him about her marriage but said she and Jeff were just good friends, doing it for the green card. She told him that Zoe was also her good friend.

"I love Zoe's mom, too. She's a beautiful actress." The background music stopped, the chatter around them grew silent. At least that was the way it seemed. And Charles—he had said to call him Charles—sat upright, suddenly stiff.

"Sounds like your father's pleasing the Party now," he said, as if suddenly remembering his authority. He said to watch for something more insidious as China grew richer and more aware that the eyes of the world were upon them. "We might call a lot of what the media and advertising do in this country brainwashing, but if there's a society that's going to turn up in the future with the most sophisticated form of brainwashing, I'd put my money on China."

He seemed to think he knew more about her homeland than she

did, but it was nice to listen to a man who actually had something to say. She thought she could see the traces of a shy and pimply youth, like a pentimento beneath his middle-aged face. Maybe he'd talked about books to the young Billie Austin, and maybe she'd liked it for a little while. But Jeff had told her Billie had been mean to Charles Engelhorn, and Ming had a sudden sense of wanting to protect that young boy and tell him things were going to work out very well for him.

The next day, Ming decided to be bold enough to email him. "I enjoyed talking with you." The next step was up to him.

He emailed back, "I enjoyed talking with you too."

After that, weeks passed without any messages from Charles. Then she got an idea. She wrote to him and said she had a book she thought he'd appreciate—by the eighth-century poet Du Fu, who wrote his most famous poems in Sichuan. She copied a line from the poem "My Thatched Hut."

"...my window contains peaks with a thousand years of ice my gate harbors boats from ten thousand miles downriver."

"I can bring it by sometime," she wrote.

Two days later he wrote back. "Sure, bring it by when you have a chance."

But it all came to an end before she even got to his office.

On her way home from a catering job that same night, in mid-December dampness, Ming spotted a figure huddled across the street from her building, a man with bear-like shoulders and a face wrapped in a muffler. It was impossible to tell if the man was one of Li Nan's henchmen or a plainclothes cop. If the law had found Li Nan they'd also come looking for his employees. She sauntered on, sat in a restaurant that was open until two a.m., but eventually she had to go home. The hulk was still waiting in the shadows.

She slept late the next morning. She turned over many times and felt the sunlight caress her face. Jeff had gone out somewhere.

Her cell phone rang and she saw that it was her parents' number in China.

Mama still had a voice as strong as a rock. "We went to see Li

67

Nan's family tonight…" It was, after all, nearly midnight in China. "They didn't want us to come in, they want to hide in shame."

"What?" Ming played innocent.

"Folks here are saying," Mama spoke slowly, with meaning, "he was running some kind of company that committed fraud and identity theft. The police raided his office a while ago, but, just this week, they found him. Come home for the holidays. We'll welcome your husband, too. You don't have to go back, either. Han has a job for you."

Mama, dear Mama, who always figured out everything, even how to save face.

Li Nan and his thugs would serve their sentences, then change their names if they had to, tap into offshore accounts and start over, because this was America. But there was that steel that would inhabit your soul. Could you ever shake it off if you'd been a criminal?

Ming had knelt and asked Buddha for favors before. Her whole family had, even though they knew it was superstitious nonsense that just made you feel better for the moment. She knelt then, for just a few minutes, before she started throwing things into two suitcases. She begged the gods for a dozen favors, including that no one would barge in, no roommates and especially not Jeff. She left her husband-of-convenience a note saying her father was sick and she had to be in China, just for a while. She left fifty dollars with the note. Not enough to cover anything, just a token of false promises. She stole a platinum wig and a pair of sunglasses that Jeff had picked up somewhere, and left through the backdoor in the basement.

Jeff would get by. He—and Zoe and her mom, and the roommates in the loft—could still trust in the gods that ruled their shabby but oh-so-civilized kingdom. Ming had nothing left, except maybe the god of private equity.

Chapter Five

"That guy was like an ancient Chinese hermit," Zoe contemplated the morning after their arrival in Sunshine Village, "with eyes like fire. I dreamt about those eyes."

The man in the pagoda. *I've seen a creature with fiery eyes before*, Ming thought.

The overheated bedroom seemed to swirl with rainbow lights flashing from the dingy walls. Then, before she had a chance to say something about the man, the phone rang.

"Did you have a good sleep?" asked the ubiquitous Lulu. The directors of Sunshine Industries invited Ming and her American guest to lunch that day, she said.

The grass and the rapeseed and even the clouds looked like a palette of vivid brown, yellow, and silver, Ming thought as she and Zoe made their way to the executive dining room at noon, with Lulu trailing them.

Three young men and one old man sat at a round table. They stood up in unison when Ming, Zoe, and Lulu entered the room. Ming recognized them all, weathered though they were. Guo Tang Fei, now the company director, and his old friends, Yeng and Eng. The three boys who'd bullied Li Nan. Tang still had his wavy hair. Yeng was almost bald. Eng was tall and reedy. The fourth man was Mr. Pang, Lulu's father, who introduced himself as the director who'd just retired. He was, Ming recalled, about twenty years older than Lulu's mother. He'd been a large man, but his back was stooped now and his pants draped around a belt.

"Please sit," said Mr. Pang. They encircled a Sichuan hot pot bubbling with the savory aroma of chicken broth and ginger. A waitress brought in platters of vegetables and raw chicken and beef, and they all picked up one morsel at a time with their chopsticks, steaming the ingredients in the hot pot and slowly filling their own individual bowls. Ming watched their hosts smack and slurp as if small bites would never be enough; it seemed they hadn't forgotten how it felt to have nothing to eat but thrice-boiled rice.

They stopped slurping only when the waitress brought in a plate piled high with slimy clumps. Everyone gazed at the platter.

"Ah, pig brains," Tang Fei exclaimed. He was looking at Zoe as if he wanted to smile but wasn't sure if that would impress her. "Eat plenty of these and you'll finish your PhD, no problem." He grabbed one of the slimy brains with his chopsticks; it had the circumference of a dinner plate, and Ming watched him wrestle it, then another and another, into the hot pot. When the brains were cooked he eased them onto a spare platter, cut them into large cubes with chopsticks, and passed the platter around.

Yeng gobbled down one clump of pig brain after another, then looked at Zoe as if he, too, wanted her to notice him. "Ming was the smartest kid in school," he pronounced. "There was a kid named Li Nan who was the dumbest. He went to New York too, and he got very rich."

"Until he got caught, that is," Lulu snickered.

Ming felt her little-girl falsetto take over, against her will. "I talked to him once or twice in New York. He said he makes dreams come true."

She reached for the pig brain platter, intending to stuff her mouth and say no more, but only a single clump was left, and it wasn't polite to take the last one. Odd, how fast the delicacy had disappeared.

Zoe had turned to examining her teacup. "Ming and I have been talking about how someone ought to start a business exporting this jasmine tea," she told their hosts.

Thank you for changing the subject, Ming uttered silently.

"Unfortunately, we don't have a lot of private businesses operating in Sunshine Village," Lulu said.

"We don't need private businesses. We're the only state-owned company in Sichuan that's doing very well," Tang Fei said. "We expect to see a profit of forty percent this year." Ming interpreted the giggle in his voice as a blip from some spot in the stratosphere

70

where numbers were free for the offing. "We found that we could cut our workforce by sixty percent and still get more accomplished by requiring that everyone work six days a week. We were spending so much money sending people off on vacations every summer, you see. We are much more like America now; two-week vacations and workers pay for their own vacations and housing."

"I'm writing about the history of Sunshine Village for my dissertation," said Zoe. "Did you all grow up here?"

Mr. Pang spoke up, his voice thin and gravelly. "I came here as part of a military unit when there was nothing here but a few peasants working the land," he said. He cleared his throat and spat on the floor. Old revolutionaries in China were always spitting, just to flaunt how lower-class they could be.

"We were going to build something big and beautiful," Mr. Pang went on. "China didn't need to grow rice everywhere, we needed a powerful country with a strong economy. So we built a factory with our own hands, then brought more people here and built a town."

"Did people think it was going to become a workers' paradise?" Zoe asked.

Mr. Pang laughed. "Yeah, the village cadres reminded us China was going to be a workers' paradise every time we went to get our food rations. The peasants petitioned us because we were taking land, land that belonged to the state, of course. We built a good school, a good hospital, for everyone. Some of the peasants even got new jobs in the factory." He stopped and coughed a wet, hacking cough before he resumed talking. "Some people think paradise is being part of a strong country. Somebody else won't agree." Then he lit a cigarette.

Old Mr. Pang was killing himself with cigarettes, Ming surmised. And, in fact, when everyone got up to leave, Lulu pulled Ming aside and said, "I have to take my father to the doctor this afternoon." They would be gone a couple of days, she said. Her father needed radiation, and for that they had to go to the town of Fushun. "My mother will look after you and the American, though," Lulu promised.

Ming wondered if Mrs. Pang was going to follow them or just hear reports from the villagers about every move they made.

"Also"— Lulu lowered her voice to a conspiratorial whisper—"Tang Fei invites you to visit the factory tomorrow morning. We're sorry, though, we can't get clearance for the foreigner to visit."

Ming interpreted that to mean that they were embarrassed to have foreigners see their sorry little factory. Zoe was going to be very disappointed.

She told Zoe they were on their own, but she left out the part about Tang Fei's invitation. The two of them tromped over the grasses outside, headed in the direction of the guest house, and Zoe was silent, gazing at the gray sky as if she were contemplating a storm.

A sparrow circled around them. Zoe glared at the bird, then spoke. "This place is full of ghosts and spirits. And no one's telling me the truth about anything. Forty percent profit? Puh-leaze." Her tone accused Ming of lying too. "Everyone except old Mr. Pang, and I'm guessing he's eaten up with lung cancer and who knows how long he has. I want to talk to the peasants. I don't expect them to be noble, pure, pastoral folks or anything, but what do you think they might have to say about the invasion of the military factory people? And the hermit in the pagoda?"

"No one's going to admit he exists. It's like my talking monkey— he's a superstition. Maybe he *is* my talking monkey. The Monkey King could affect—"

"Seventy-two transformations."

They stopped talking. Ming shivered, and she saw that Zoe was shaking, too. They had reached a hilltop, and they stood there in spite of the chilly mist. Zoe kickboxed against the wall of fog, and let out a defiant *aaarrgghh* sound. Then she looked at Ming and said, "Show me more of the village."

That was what they were here for, after all. Ming led Zoe to the west, along the dirt path to the riverbank where the big Buddha sat. The cliff was so high that clouds gathered around the Buddha's neck. "Like he's wearing a Shakespearean ruff!" Zoe exclaimed. She took out a spiral notebook from her jacket pocket and wrote some notes, looking very purposeful.

72

From there they made their way to the northeastern part of town, skipping through rice fields, past a trio of ducks swimming in a pink-scum pond. Plantain trees had shed their green bark in the rain the day before and left a slippery detritus in their path.

The rice stalks were short in winter, but the fields were flooded and peasants were at work, emptying wheelbarrows of mulch into the gullies. They still wore dark blue work suits, just as they had in Ming's childhood. Their backs were curved from stooping. Some walked barefoot, even though they could contract parasitic worms in the paddy water that way. When Ming was a child, the village council had provided them with galoshes, but the peasants had complained that the boots weren't comfortable. Three hogs wallowed beside a farmhouse, and geese honked in the distance. You could always tell you were getting close to the rice fields by the fat flies and the smell of manure; that hadn't changed either. Pig manure and human night soil—always a fresh supply, with a whiff of disease. The tillers of the soil had always scared Ming. They'd had black dirt embedded in their skin and their clothes, snot streaks and sores on their faces. In school, the children, when they came to school at all, would stare between her legs; they'd spit and curse, and the teachers barely bothered to call upon them in class.

"There, you can see your peasants at work," she told Zoe.

"You say it with disdain."

"It was one thing to build a socialist state for everyone and honor those who grew the rice," Ming admitted. "But there were the peasant kids and the factory kids, and we didn't talk to each other."

"What if you provided everyone with an equal education?" Zoe pondered. "Even if they work the farm or sweep the streets, they could go to night classes and learn just for the sake of, you know, filling their minds with possibilities? A revolution where everyone learns from the learned instead of the Maoist business of the learned learning from the peasants…"

The two of them clomped through the rice fields toward a cluster of buildings. The closest one, with its squat cinderblock walls overtaken with moss and mold, looked abandoned.

"That was my dentist's office," Ming said, and shuddered.

"I should see all the buildings I can." Zoe stopped outside the door. "Especially since this one might fall down before your capital gets here."

Ming felt a cold sweat break out on her forehead. Still, perhaps if Zoe saw the old dental clinic, she'd begin to understand. So Ming led her friend down the dank cavity of a hallway, made a right turn, and then pushed open the third door on the left. Inside, a vinyl chair was overturned on the floor, moldy-colored stuffing spilling out like internal organs. Dangling from the ceiling was a drill, half crumbled with rust, but the end was still pointed enough to stab a little girl.

"Can you imagine—my teeth were always decayed when I was a kid, so I'd come here and the dentist would drill out my cavities with this thing." She pointed an accusing finger at the rusty contraption. "I'd scream and try to punch at him, so he started tying my hands down. They didn't have Novocain and I was sure I was going to die from the pain."

Zoe stared at the drill, and at Ming's beautiful new mouth.

When they were back outside, Ming pointed out another crumbling brick building, just down the dirt road. A sign outside said, in faded characters, Sunshine Village Hospital.

"That's where I had to go when I got pneumonia. There were mosquitoes all over and I had to lie underneath netting."

They strode to the entryway and saw that no one was on duty at the front desk so they went in. The halls were dark except for a few twitching lights from the rooms, and the air reeked of urine. Through an open door they saw a man in a dingy doctor's smock trying to get a skeletal patient to make some motions with his two leg stumps. In another room a woman lay muttering as a nurse wadded up blood-soaked sheets.

On the second floor a man with gray-flecked hair and a look of sullen authority appeared. "Are you looking for something?" he asked.

Ming bowed her head.

"I'm the hospital director. Why are you here?" the man demanded.

74

"*Chiirrrpppp!*" The sound came from within Ming's pocket. "*Chiirrrppppp!*"

She started to speak, but, suddenly, a cricket leapt from her pocket to her arm. The green insect rubbed its legs together, hopped onto the hospital director's head, then bounded onto the grimy hospital wall.

Ming seized the moment to gain the upper hand. "What's this... bugs in the hospital?" she shouted. Without taking time to glance back, she seized Zoe's arm and they fled. She heard the hospital director, behind them, mutter something about "foreign human rights activists...."

"Well, since he brought it up, I'll just have to let Human Rights Watch know about the conditions in this hospital," Zoe exclaimed, almost giddy. "What kind of things do you think they do here? Organ transplants? Forced abortions?"

"They might just be embarrassed at how filthy it is. But did you see the cricket that jumped out of my pocket?"

Zoe nodded. "Some spirit's looking out for us."

They were a few feet from the hospital entrance when a peasant woman with a pale little boy in her arms edged up to them. "Miss, please...my little one's sick, and...we need money to go in there and get his medicine." She was a handsome woman of indeterminate age, with jet black hair and the complexion of a well-worn saddle. One eye was clouded blue; that was the river blindness peasants got from the parasites in the rice paddies.

"Don't," warned Ming, but Zoe fished in her bag and handed the woman twenty yuan.

The woman examined the bill and turned it over as if she thought there might be more on the other side. It was worth little more than two dollars in the U.S. She shook her head despairingly. "We need a thousand yuan just for his medicine."

"You see? C'mon," said Ming, and collared her friend away.

"If I marry Danny," Zoe pondered aloud as they walked on, "I'll come back here and give them money to start a free clinic."

Hunched in their coats beneath a chilly drizzle, the two trudged back toward the inn. A multitude of farmworkers were also making their way home, mothers carrying toddlers on their backs as they pulled wagons loaded with onions and cabbage. They walked in silence except for their footsteps sloshing through the mud and grass, the call of geese, the chortle of bullfrogs, and the ghostly whistling of wind.

⌘

In their room, a piece of paper was sitting on the table. Zoe dove for it, then looked befuddled as she scanned the message. "I don't understand this." She handed it to Ming.

The paper contained a short note, written in an ancient classical style. The anonymous writer had borrowed one of their ballpoint pens and torn a page from a ledger notebook—but despite the humble delivery, the characters resonated with the authority of an imperial scholar. It took Ming a few minutes to realize that the words ran right to left in the manner of a distant century.

Perhaps I can help you. I humbly request a small favor in return. A pleasant repast today, but I have many years of hunger to recover. Come to pagoda. You must not be seen.

For a long time, Ming and Zoe stared at each other.

"There are no classical scholars in Sunshine Village," Ming said finally. "Even if somebody left this as a joke, who could write like this?"

Zoe had a strange look about her, as if she were peering into space. "I swear...the writing here. It reminds me of something."

It reminds me of something too, Ming was thinking.

"I know. The jasmine tea is laced with hallucinogens." Zoe laughed with no conviction.

"I saw a talking monkey." Ming eyeballed the peanuts and oranges on their table. She detected an off-kilter smell in the dank room and could swear it had an animal undertone. Maybe she was hallucinating. She used to get strange sensations in her childhood. She'd see darkness even with her eyes open, then she'd hear that someone had

76

died. A chill would blast through her chest, and then she'd hear that the villagers had turned a comrade over to the community committee for counterrevolutionary activities. What she felt now was something entirely different, more like a chill through her bones and an absence of gravity, as if she could somersault across the river right behind the talking monkey.

"We're going there," Zoe commanded. If she was afraid, she didn't show it; instead she kicked the air and flexed her limbs.

That night, Ming set the alarm clock to wake them at eleven thirty. She lay in the bed without covers, knowing the cold would rouse her just in case she tried to snooze after the alarm went off. When the alarm rang, she saw Zoe bolt upright.

They had gathered two oranges, two handfuls of peanuts, and the second dragonfruit Zoe brought from Chengdu. To these meagre offerings, Zoe added her Swiss Army knife with the blade that didn't quite retract—because how else would a hermit slice into a dragonfruit rind that had the rubbery thickness of a tire? They wrapped their bundle in the blue-and-green-striped towel, still fragrant with Zoe's peach-mango soap.

With flashlights concealed in their bag, Ming and Zoe crept through the courtyard beneath a melon slice of moon. A line of geese stretched across the clouds like a guiding arrow.

They walked soundlessly on the grass, past dark houses and a cluster of trees, up a hill with rice paddies, and then below to where the pagoda stood silent. A distant *hoo hoo* from an owl seemed as brash as a drumroll.

At the doorway to the pagoda, Zoe turned on the flashlight. From inside a foul blackness and a muffled whoosh of flying mites accosted them.

Ming moved an inch forward and jumped, startled, when something touched her.

"Pssst!" It was Zoe, her voice gruff after their long silence. They moved through the doorway in miniscule steps, brushing through cobwebs, and trying to not think of scurrying creatures underfoot. Ming began to hum a soft Chinese folk song as she knelt down, spread out the towel, and arranged the offerings in a circle around the dragonfruit.

Then the darkness stirred.

"*RRREEEeeeeeep!*" The shriek was a few notches away from human.

The ragged hermit stood before them, his eyes bright as beacons. Zoe aimed the flashlight down at his threadbare pants and bare feet, then toward the towel.

He reached down and grabbed the peanuts, smacking his mouth as he devoured them, leaving a pile of cracked shells scattered across the dirt floor.

"Niiii....niiii..." The man seemed to be forming distinct Mandarin words. "Ni, huh ni," he repeated, glaring at them as his body trembled.

"You and you...have mere trifles for a starving man." His voice was almost operatic, full of sound waves. Just like—yes, a voice Ming remembered. "And this," the emaciated recluse said, holding the dragonfruit to his lips. "This is like a painted woman with a thick hide. How, I beg to inquire, do you get through to her?" In answer, Zoe beamed the flashlight down on the knife, which he picked up and examined, before pulling out the blade, the scissors, and the corkscrew, one by one.

He was a madman, Ming decided, as she carefully backed away. A madman who spoke beautifully.

"Do I know you?" she ventured.

His fiery eyes penetrated both of them. Then he turned to the dragonfruit, his gaze yearning as if there really were a lover trapped beneath its rind.

"This is all the food we could find," Zoe said.

"I would expect more from two such enterprising maidens."

"Maidens?" Zoe didn't suppress her snicker.

Ming, too, almost laughed. "How about showing some manners and saying, 'Kind thanks, gracious maidens, for the favor'?"

"Show me your light machine," the madman commanded, reaching out a filthy hand. Zoe passed him the flashlight. He slid his fingers along the slick surface, and jumped back with surprise when he hit upon the button that flicked the light on. He held it upward, exposing the rotted ceiling beams. Then he aimed the light at the two visitors, making them squint.

"In my travels, I once saw a beautiful, young maiden as graceful as the moon, so filled with virtue that she left her mother and father to give food to wayfarers," he began. "But she was an evil fiend in disguise. You give me a knife that is smaller than a tiger's claw. You propose, I presume, that I catch a sparrow on the blade, or stop a rabbit in his tracks? I will eat once again and grow fat. For would you have me believe that the populace eat daily in this prosperous twentieth century…?"

"The twenty-first," Ming interjected.

He rubbed his chin. "The twenty-first century? And still, men fight to be king of the beasts? They still gather their money and hoard it like food for the winter, and let others starve? No doubt it is your conclusion that I am mad. Isn't all of mankind mad? You go and ask after the men that they made disappear the day you came to town. Ah, but Sun Wu Kong, the once-great warrior, could save them, if they let me!"

He jumped up suddenly, kicking his heels like a newborn fawn as he lurched forward.

Zoe, in a flash, flew at him. Ming could make out the vision of her friend's knee thrusting out, her feet dancing then leaping, her body swooping behind the crazed man, sending him tumbling with a side kick.

The man leapt to his feet, an agile opponent, but suddenly withered, crouching with his head in his hands.

"Go…" he shouted, waving them away.

Ming seized the flashlight—leaving the knife behind—and they fled.

They stopped just beyond the trees. "I don't know what made me do that," Zoe whispered. "But it's not like I hurt him."

When they were back in their beds, Ming uttered what had been on her mind all the way back. "He called himself Sun Wu Kong."

"Napoleon. Shakespeare. Monkey King. Just a crazy man ranting."

79

Zoe sounded only partly convinced, though. When the sun rose, Ming turned on her computer and wrote: "Life is like climbing a mountain, but just when you can see a summit you tumble back into the valley and have to start all over again. I thought I saw a peak last night."

She thought of sending an email to Tom Wendall, but there was no time to delay. She showered, then dressed quickly. It was only eight, early to appear at Tang Fei's office, but she had a plan to slip out and leave a note for Zoe. It was the escape plan of a coward, running away before Zoe could stomp and kick and say, "Take me with you."

Ming was buttoning her blouse in the front room when Zoe peered around the door, her face a buoyant sunrise.

"I'm sorry, but Tang said I should come alone. He claims some of what they do is classified. I think he just doesn't trust foreigners, but I'll try to talk to him about that. Anyway, I'll tell you all about it."

"I can't use secondary research," Zoe protested.

"Stay here. I won't be long."

⌘

"Stay here" was a provocation. Zoe stretched her hamstrings and warmed up her glutes. In her tee shirt and panties, she sliced the air with her arms and lunged to each side over her knees. After thirty minutes, gleaming with sweat, she showered, devouring the scent of peach-mango soap as if it were breakfast. She sipped from the thermos of jasmine tea that the housekeeper had brought, but there would be no time for the dining room, and no time to dally if she was to go out on her own.

Zoe could still feel those golden eyes boring through her in the dank pagoda.

Perhaps I can help you, the note had read. Even though she couldn't read classical Chinese, there was something about the swirls of his handwriting that had felt like some kind of answer to questions she didn't even realize she had. Maybe she was going crazy in this ghost-rattled village. She drank a little more jasmine tea, half-wishing for a vision that would explain things. How had he managed to get the note into their room? Surely he wouldn't have given it to Mrs. Pang or the chambermaid.

The Monkey King, of course, could assume the transformation of a bug, or make himself invisible. Where had she read that story about the Monkey King lording it over someone? She could practically hear the words: "I'm an enlightened being. I will return to earth in my magic form and remember all. You'll return as a mortal, and all you'll know is your mortal incarnation."

The door wasn't locked—at least Ming wasn't holding her prisoner. Zoe walked outside and made her way to the northeast, where the rice fields were. Each step was like slicing through the opaque fog, but the smell of the stagnant pink pond reassured her that she was heading in the right direction. She had five hundred yuan in her pocket, money she was prepared to use to make friends in the most hardscrabble part of town and help them out in return for research. Danny would call it subaltern research, but surely the peasants had stories to tell.

Just beyond the rice fields, Zoe came to a sod hut where an old man sat smoking. "Do you know the woman with the blue eye and a sick little boy?" she asked. The man's rheumy eyes opened wide at the sight of a foreign devil. He looked her up and down, but finally nodded, and pointed to the right.

"Third house down the hill," he said.

At the bottom of the hill, along a dirt path, she found two houses made of white stucco that had grown muddy with age, each with rice-paper guardian demons draped across the doorways. Geese and chickens pecked out front. A woman was cutting noodles at a table outside the first house. At the second, black smoke from the chimney curled through the fog.

She didn't see the third house until she reached the very end of the path—a sod shack, the color of the soil and barely visible even close up. At the doorway, with no actual door in sight, Zoe peered in and saw the sick boy, lying on a cot beneath a filthy pink quilt and staring

81

up at the straw roof. The interior was dimmer than the outside, but Zoe could make out a well-trodden dirt floor. A rough-hewn table stood against the rear wall next to a small iron stove.

Catching sight of her, the boy screamed.

"Don't be afraid," Zoe said in a soft voice, tentatively edging over the threshold. "I'm here to help you. How do you feel?"

The boy screamed again, his eyes streaming yellow mucus. "Where is your mama?" Zoe asked.

"My mama dead. Auntie there," he whimpered, pointing toward the rice fields.

Zoe thanked him and went off to the paddies, where she spotted the blue-eyed woman who had approached her at the hospital. The woman was sorting bales of straw from a wheelbarrow and throwing them onto the fields. A girl of about twelve or thirteen trudged a row behind, kicking up soil with her bare feet. She wondered if the village had stopped giving out boots and now the peasants couldn't afford them.

"Hello," Zoe called out, trying to assume an I-just-happened-to-be-in-the-neighborhood sort of cadence. "I met you yesterday…"

The woman threw down an armful of straw, then stopped to inspect the intruder, her good eye lingering on Zoe's copper hair. "They say you're a human rights activist," she said.

"Well… not really."

"A reporter?"

"I'm here to write about the village."

"*The Wall Street Journal*? BBC?"

Who said the peasants weren't aware of the world? "You know Columbia University? In America. I am writing…a book. My dissertation."

The woman considered that, her mouth dropping in disappointment. "Why don't you go into business and make money?" She coughed out a bitter laugh.

"Can I talk to you?"

"Not now. We have to work," the woman said, and reached back into her wheelbarrow.

Zoe turned away, thinking that maybe if she returned tomorrow, they'd know she was determined.

"Miss!" a reedy voice called out.

The young girl had caught up with her.

"My mother told me not to bother you. But I want to ask you something. I think you must be a nice lady."

"Thank you. What's your name?"

"Kwan Jing Yin." The girl looked down. "My mother is Yu Li. She's embarrassed, that's all. Maybe she blames you, but it isn't your fault. My father worked in the factory and he lost his job. The people who run the factory made everyone work even though they couldn't pay any salaries. They kept promising that they would pay next month, then the month after that. Then, they said go, you're fired. And now my father, he has gone..."

"Where?"

"He was demonstrating in the village, but they, y'know, the village committee, locked the workers up in the jail because they don't want you to see him. What is your name, miss?"

"Zuo Yi Au Tin."

"That is a pretty name. Are you a teacher, Miss Zuo Yi?"

"Well...yes."

"Would you help me learn, maybe? I had to stop going to school when we didn't have money to pay the fees. I used to make pretty good grades and I miss it *so* much. They took most of my books but..."

"Who took them?"

"Come now, please? I told my mother I won't help cover up the soil. It's the part I hate the most. It hurts my back to bend down with that heavy straw. I'm thirteen and I don't care if my father beats me when he comes home. They know I won't do a good job anyway."

And so it was that Zoe found herself spending the morning in the peasant hut, and promising to come back the next day.

Ming frowned when Zoe told her about it. "It's not safe there."

"But I have to..."

"Be careful. Don't take money with you," Ming relented, finally.

On her way out the next morning, Zoe bought soap and towels and matches at one storefront on Market Street. At another, she purchased a big aluminum pot, and at another a plucked chicken, a cabbage, fruit, and some bean paste buns. The shopping left her with twenty yuan and some coins in her pocket.

At the shack, the boy was coughing up phlegm, and Jing Yin sat on the cot beside him with a bucket. The little room reeked of sickness.

"Oh, Miss Zuo Yi!" Jing Yin jumped up, smoothed her hair, and frowned at the spittle tracks on her shirt. "I'm so sorry…it was bad all night."

Zoe filled the new pot she'd brought with water from the pump outside, turned several knobs on the stovetop until she got a burner to light, and deposited the chicken in the pot to stew. Jing Yin ate some of the oranges, bananas, and buns. Even Jing Yin's sick little cousin gobbled down a bean paste bun. When he finished eating, spots of color had blossomed on his pallid cheeks.

"I wanted to do the homework but I was up with him." Jing Yin looked longingly at her neglected books—three of them, stashed in a corner. "Can you sit a little while? Do you know the story of the Garden of Eden? Some people from a church came to my school once. I like that story."

As it happened, Zoe had often watched her grandfather, the deacon, conduct services for the children's congregation and tell them about Adam and Eve. Stork Austin used to hiss like the serpent as he pulled an apple from his pocket. Zoe told Jing Yin and her cousin that a big bang in the cosmos created earth; she told them of the evolution of one-celled creatures in the ocean and the arrival of dinosaurs, followed by the apes.

"Two apes woke up one morning and found that they'd evolved into a man and a woman," she told the kids. She leapt like a creature reborn. "They realized they could speak, and they spoke to God, who told them their names were Adam and Eve, then plucked them up and sent them to live in a paradise with green trees and lots of flowers and fresh streams. But then one day Eve saw a serpent." Zoe hissed the way her grandfather used to. "The serpent told her she should eat an apple from the Tree of Knowledge, and then she'd see all kinds of amazing things that God didn't want her to know about."

Jing Yin clapped at the end. "They say Sunshine Village was paradise once too," she said. "I know a sad but beautiful story about the Handsome Monkey King."

Zoe listened, for the second time, to the tale of the Monkey King and his sweetheart. Except in Jing Yin's version, Zenia died of grief.

"She cried herself to death," Jing Yin declared. "And they say her tears still fall over the village, which accounts for the constant rain and fog."

The girl had undeniable talent, Zoe was thinking, the makings of an actress or performance artist if she just had someone to train her properly. These days a peasant with ambition might be able to find her way out of Sunshine Village. Watching Jing Yin and mulling over what it would take to get her to a good school somewhere else in China, Zoe didn't notice two figures at the doorway until the boy emitted a croupy shriek from his sickbed.

Two young men stomped over the threshold. Both were slight of build but seemed to be forged entirely of iron. They wore only tee shirts against the cold, their arms warpainted with tattoos, their two faces like a double-barreled shotgun.

Before Zoe had fully risen to her feet, one of the intruders came from behind and seized her breast with a tattooed hand. She jumped up and gave a backward kick to push him away, but he came at her from the front, with a switchblade pointed at her chest. He grinned and made a pantomime of slicing off one breast at a time. Zoe tried to sense a weakness in her opponent, but by then he had the knife pressed up against her chest. Her limbs and even her brain seemed paralyzed. She felt a rush of warm water, wetter than any celestial tears, and registered that she'd peed in her pants.

Somehow she felt a thought return—and with a swift kick to her opponent's groin, she sent the knife hurling to the ground. *Grab it, poke his eyes out.* But Zoe was shaking, and the other man seized it first, shoving her shoulder and forcing her to the ground.

"Ugly bitch." He ripped her pocket and the twenty yuan tumbled out. He seized the money, then sliced her blouse in one swift movement, the buttons bouncing onto the dirt floor.

The man spat in the dirt. He looked at the buttons on the floor, glared at Jing Yin, and snarled, "Pick up those and give them to me, girl." While she was on her knees, pulling tiny buttons from the dust, he said, "You tell your mama you're way short."

The other man surveyed the room, and Zoe watched him light upon the shiny pot on the stove. "Something brand new," he snarled, then walked over and seized the handles without paying attention to the flame below. "Fuck!" he screamed as he threw the chicken and water onto the dirt floor, muttering something about the Kwan family burning his hands, as if it were their fault.

They left with Zoe's cash, the new pot with shards of Zoe's blouse wrapped around it to keep from burning them more, and a can filled with rice.

Jing Yin and her cousin huddled against each other on the bed, the boy's face the color of ashes. Jing Yin's lips quivered and Zoe saw rage building to a simmer on her thirteen-year-old face. "Go, please, Miss Zuo Yi. You can't come back here. They'll come after you again. You must be careful everywhere. They know you now."

"I'll tell the police."

"They are police helpers. They buy houses here to make money from rent. They own our house and we can't pay the rent, so they take our TV and everything, even your buttons. They work for the police bureau part time. They know where my father is."

"Oh...god. What if I got you the money? A lot of money?"

Jing Yin shrugged. "They always want more. They'll be after you, too."

Chapter Six

The night after Ming vanished from New York, Danny invited Jeff over. Zoe plied the abandoned husband with single malt scotch. The three of them gathered around Danny's computer, and Jeff read aloud from a certain blog.

"Sheeeiiitttt. 'His cock had a curve like the crescent moon...'" Jeff's hair flailed out like wild grass, and cold gray sweat beads broke out on his forehead.

"You're making that up." Danny looked for himself. "Ha, my man Jeff doesn't lie."

Zoe read a few lines aloud from a more recent post, about Mimi meeting a professor at a park bench in Washington Square on a snowy night. Then, as they talked and the snow fell upon them, they both turned into fearless peregrine falcons and began to fly.

"I hate to say it, but there's a glimmer of talent," said Danny. He poured more whisky for Jeff. "Your loving wife ought to work on that. I know because I fantasized about dropping out of business school and writing magical realism prose a million times."

Zoe didn't point out that Danny could quit his job any time he wanted. Rich people were always self-conscious about being rich. Nor did she speculate aloud on something she was thinking, that maybe Danny had taken such a dislike to Ming because she had a kind of courage he didn't, letting the world see her literary experiments.

"She seemed like a disruptive force," Danny went on, as if he'd read Zoe's mind. "From the moment she parted bodies at your party and came tossing her hair at us. I felt like she wanted, I dunno, to take a piece of our souls."

Jeff got up and opened his backpack, strewing papers across a table. "You guys have gotta see this. Exhibit A. Invoices from Dr. Perlmutter. She paid most of them. She put eight thousand bucks on *my* credit card. She owes them five thousand, and they keep sending the bills. But she paid off another twenty-nine thousand. Where did she get the money, you might astutely and legitimately ask? Well here's a clue. I came home and all her stuff was gone; she left only this bullshit note, and then the doorbell rang and what the fuck, there's a police detective looking for guess who. She left her cell phone, by the way. The cop pointed out that it's a tracker."

Zoe sank into her chair and everything seemed to swirl. She heard Jeff say, "Your China fixer is a wanted criminal," and a voice in her own head thunder *this is the end of your dissertation*. She heard Danny say, "I knew she was bad news."

Sometime in the middle of the night, she woke up with a name rollicking through her mind. Ming had talked about her parents' company a lot. She'd said they called it Rising Phoenix because it was their own rebirth. It was awfully hard to disappear in the twenty-first century. She padded into Danny's study, took out her laptop, and Googled the name. She found a Chinese website for a silicon company in Beijing, and a phone number.

It was two a.m. in New York, three the following afternoon in Beijing. She dialed the number. A receptionist answered and connected her to Mr. Cheng.

"Zoe. We've heard so much about you." Ming's father's voice resounded with hospitality rather than surprise. "We hope we'll meet you. And you know her husband?" He grasped at the word as if Ming's having a husband made everything all right.

"How is your health?"

"Health ... oh, I have high blood pressure but I'm taking walks, I'm fine, feeling pretty good consider...." He stopped himself. "Oh. I had a scare...."

So Ming had lied about her father being sick. Zoe could hear the cover-up in his voice, as if he understood that Ming had come up with a face-saving excuse for leaving her beloved New York. Zoe understood, too, that Jeff was probably right about everything. She inhaled, gave herself the line, "How is Ming?"

Mr. Cheng seemed like a cordial man, eager to improvise his own script. He said Ming was working hard for her brother's business, making money for them, and there were plenty of opportunities for her husband in China too. Zoe could almost hear bells tinkling in his voice over the word "husband." Ming had told him about Zoe's dissertation, he said, and she should come soon too, so that she could see the village before it changed. Dead air, then Mr. Cheng said it was hard to reach Ming because she was always at meetings, "but I'll tell her you called."

"Fuck," Jeff spat out later that morning. "Now you've destroyed my fantasy that she's been bumped off and I'm rid of her." Jeff stayed. Zoe found him dozing on Danny's sofa that evening when she came in from her classes. He moved into the spare bedroom that night, and filled it with crumpled papers and the stink of stale scotch.

⌘

Over a month of Christmas festivities and wintry nights, Zoe waited. Ming didn't call back. Jeff, who eventually went back to his place in Brooklyn, called every day. "I can't pay my rent. My wife left me with a humongous debt and I'm too depressed to work."

She didn't tell Jeff, or Danny, that something in the name Sunshine Village felt like a lodestar calling. It made no sense even to her. She didn't tell them, either, that she'd found some maps in the China collection at the school library and had pored over the route because wasn't it better to go on her own than lose all the time she'd put into studying the Third Front?

In the second week of January, Ming left a message on Zoe's cell phone.

That night, Zoe crept out of the bedroom while Danny was sleeping and returned the call.

"Hello…Zoe?" Ming said her name as if it were the answer to a prayer. "I'm at lunch now with an American colleague." Ming sent giggle waves across two hemispheres. "We have an idea for Sunshine Village. Can you come?"

The way Ming had giggled—it was just like the way she'd giggled when she'd announced she was marrying Jeff, Zoe decided as she lay awake that night. More the vibrations of a lunchtime tryst than a work meeting.

She told Danny the next morning that she was going to Sunshine Village. "I know, I know," she acknowledged, "but I can handle Ming."

"Suit yourself. I hope you find plenty of cocks that curve like the new moon."

"You're going to lose Danny if you go to China," Billie warned.

"We don't have a game-playing relationship."

"That's a game itself, pretending there's no game. And how do you plan to pay for your ticket? I was counting on you to marry Danny and pay off my credit cards, you know."

How to pay for the trip was a problem, of course. Her only real hope was that Professor Engelhorn would know what to do; maybe he'd be able to dig up a grant. She called him and asked. Large insects fluttered in her head.

"Of course. We'll come up with something," he said on the phone, "when the department opens again in January."

But in January, he told her everyone was scrimping. There was one possible grant, but they wouldn't even start looking at applications until March.

"I have my orals this semester anyway," Zoe muttered, feeling tears threaten to pour out.

"Yeah…but it's an opportunity you should seize. Can you use the village in your orals?"

"I can't afford to go." The words burned her throat like smoke from a rancid cigarette.

"Let me see what else I can do."

A couple of days later, Professor Engelhorn called her into his office again. He said she absolutely must keep this a secret, but he would advance her the money. He wrote out a check for two thousand dollars. "I'm afraid this won't be five-star travel," he said with a rueful half-smile.

Zoe was spilling tears dangerously close to his signature.

Jeff yelled and banged his fists when she told him. "I'm finally over Ming and I'm boycotting all goods made in China to prove it, which means I'll have to stop buying clothes and go naked, and now you're going off to see the fucking, lying, cheating, evil seductress Dragon Lady?"

"You should come too." Zoe wasn't above imagining a showdown.

"You're the China hand. I don't even want to be a China ass. By the way, the detective came back and said if she ever tries to come back to the US they've got her in a database. But there's something else you should know."

He was just mad, Zoe figured. She told him to stop over-dramatizing, that she'd thought it over a million times and was prepared to travel to Sunshine Village on her own if Ming flaked out. Jeff insisted she sit down, though.

"Ming had some kind of thing for the man you think might be your father."

Zoe said, "bullshit," but it felt like a barren defense.

"There was one clue that slipped her devious little mind. She cancelled her cell phone subscription but the bill came. So I went through all the numbers. Lots of guys. Lots of calls to China and from China. And then there were some calls to this number with an 854 prefix, so I knew it was Columbia. So, I called it at three in the morning and the voicemail said, 'This is Charles Engelhorn at the East Asian Institute, please leave a message and I'll have my underling Zoe deal with your plebian business…'"

"They met. Doesn't mean they were having an affair."

"I didn't say they were having an affair. She called him; he didn't call her. My deduction, dear Zoe, is *she* was pursuing *him*."

Jeff's smile was like that of a child caught in the act.

Everything swirled around her once again. All those days and nights Jeff and his bride-of-convenience had spent together in their screened-off space; Jeff would have searched the world for stories that would entertain Ming, except he had something at the ready. Zoe had seen the way Ming inched away while Jeff kept inching toward her, the way he'd hung his arms around her, and she'd looked as if the man glomming on to her were a noose. He would have offered

91

Ming all that he had—credit cards, objects of art, and, especially, gossip that the two of them could ponder for infinity, like the tale of how Professor Engelhorn just might be Zoe's father.

Zoe opened her mouth to chastise him, but she knew it would do no good. Jeff loved to hear himself talk. You might as well punish a dog for barking, a sparrow for warbling.

Chapter Seven

The same morning that two thugs defeated Zoe, Ming met Tang Fei at the entrance to Sunshine Village Silicon Works Enterprises. He was ready to show her the silicon dioxide research lab—where her parents had once worked.

It was spotless, as a silicon research lab was supposed to be, but Ming spied a thick layer of dust on the windowsill and suspected that a cleanup crew had been brought in for her benefit.

Two men in white coats sat at computer consoles, while several others were bent over small sheets of silicon, busy with forceps. They'd had an entire day to prepare themselves for this brief performance, Ming realized. She imagined getting back to Beijing and laughing with Tom about how it should be called Potemkin Silicon Works Enterprises.

"We're working on the production of a silicon battery," said Tang Fei. "Silicon dioxide has thousands of uses. You probably used some in your toothpaste this morning."

Ming ran her tongue over Dr. Perlmutter's little sculptures. Tang Fei told her Sunshine Village Silicon Works Enterprises had evolved from the production of Plexiglas for military planes and jeeps, and they were now manufacturing optical fibers for export. "But like any good manufacturing facility, we pride ourselves on a diversified portfolio," Tang Fei said. He showed her a brochure that had pictures of dozens of silicon products—gloves, spatulas, lipstick, packets of silica gel, baby pacifiers, green rubber watchbands, a pair of breast implants, even a life-sized sex doll.

"You make all of these things?"

Tang Fei looked down at the brochure, then, as if realizing he could embellish only so much, admitted, "We just supply the raw material."

"The world runs on silicon," he added, sounding more salesmanly.

Ming had done a beastly thing, raising Tang Fei's hopes just by being there. The company had no blood left, and behind all of Tang's boasts was a plea for a cash transfusion. He'd told her yesterday that he knew all about New Icarus Capital. She realized the hot pot lunch had been the beginning of a courtship ritual. The directors would have preferred to meet with Han and Tom, but a low-level researcher was better than no one.

Han and Tom would see through Tang Fei's fictitious revenue and profit figures; Tang Fei had produced numbers but couldn't name any customers. Ming had escaped this cruel village only to return as a bearer of false hope, and somehow the sight of Tang Fei, former schoolyard bully, now prostrating himself before Ming with her gold-rimmed New Icarus Capital business cards left her feeling like a toxic ion in the air. Cruel people like Tang knew about begging for kindness and getting kicked instead.

Trudging back in the direction of the guest house, Ming knew she should find a cell phone friendly spot where she could call the office and admit that the deal she'd been so eager to chase was a bust.

Veering toward a circle of poplar trees, she fished into her handbag for her cell phone. Something she didn't recognize was in there. She pulled out a cylinder of paper, tightly coiled like an ancient scroll. On it was a note, in a delicate swirl of classical characters.

My deepest apologies for my lack of hospitality, she read. *I need your help and it appears that you need mine too. Come, by yourself I implore, to the place where we talked when you were small and hungry. If I may trouble you, I am more rational when I'm fed. Something fermented would be excellent as well.*

Ming's heart pounded. The handwriting was the same as that on the note that had materialized two days before. *The place where we talked.* She knew just where to go. *I'm not really a private equity intern, I'm an explorer of the unknown.* No time to call the office now. She sprinted off to Market Street and bought six pork buns, four oranges, and three bottles of beer, then climbed up the hill to the cliff where the big Buddha watched over the river and the mouth of the cave.

Creeping into the musty silence of the cave, she heard the sound of breathing, a breath that sighed with defeat and despair. As her eyes adjusted to the dark, she made out a man-creature sitting in lotus position, eyes closed. Before him, on a blue and green striped towel that she recognized, sat the dragonfruit and Zoe's Swiss Army knife.

Ming whistled the long lewd whistle of the magpies that came in summer.

The man, acting oblivious, recited silent words.

He might be a madman, Ming reminded herself. Perhaps she was crazy too.

Then his fiery eyes opened. He stared at Ming and she wondered if the whole afternoon might pass with his eyes burning into her.

"Your name is Cheng Xiao Ming," he proclaimed, finally, with the gravity of an imperial edict. "Is anyone with you?"

"I came by myself, as you implored. Now I implore you, come outside." The dankness was making her bones rattle.

She crept backward toward the exit and watched him rise and follow her, blinking in the foggy daylight. Ming perched herself on the big Buddha's left thigh and watched while the hermit stretched his arms to the sky, then began to leap up and bounce down upon his toes, as if he were testing a trampoline.

"I brought you something to make you more rational." Ming held out her offerings. The hermit devoured three of the pork buns without looking up. Then he bit the cap off a beer bottle and guzzled the entire contents. He tossed the bottle to the ground, where it rolled along the dirt, and emitted a thunderous belch.

"S'cuse me. I'm not usually so unrefined."

"Really?" Ming folded her arms across her chest and eyeballed him from his oil slick of hair to his soot-stained feet. "Actually, if you could just dive into a vat of disinfectant and win an Armani shopping spree, you wouldn't look half bad." The hermit, seemingly emboldened by the beer, sat down on the Buddha's knee and began to edge up the thigh closer to her. She could see the bugs crawling upon him.

"When I was small and hungry, twice I saw a monkey. Once the monkey talked to me, right here. I was afraid to tell anyone."

"I remember you. You thought you were too good for the other children." He dug into the grocery bag and bit the top off the second beer bottle. "And you have something else you're hiding, I know. I can read your true nature."

"I...I wanted so much...I'm a..." She shivered in the fog, felt a lump in her throat that contained the confession *criminal, though not by choice.* But the crazed hermit interrupted her.

"Let me tell you a story, Miss Ming." He edged his filthy head closer to hers, as if to conspire. "There once was a magic stone high on a mountain that developed a magic womb, which produced a magic egg. When the wind blew on the egg, it hatched, and out came a monkey. He would play with other monkeys born from flesh and blood mothers; they would climb trees, chase dragonflies, and bathe in a waterfall over a mountain stream. But the rock-womb monkey was the only one brave enough to chase the waterfall all the way to its source in the Kingdom of the Water Curtain. And for this, the other monkeys made him their king. The Monkey King, desiring answers to questions that plagued him, sought out the Patriarch of the Immortals, who taught him to cultivate conduct and thereby become, himself, an immortal. The Patriarch named him Sun Wu Kong, 'Monkey Awakened to the Emptiness that is Nirvana.'

"I had a blissful childhood." He cast a nostalgic gaze out at the river. "You, to your great misfortune, were born in awful times. Long ago there was a forest here, full of strange beasts—wolves, tigers, leopards, deer, wild cats, raccoons, horses, orangutans, bears, little dogs, big dogs, wild boar—and they all paid homage to me because I was the Monkey King. So long ago." For a moment he looked as if he might start sobbing. "But when I returned to earth, it was as if I had plunged into hell. You knew that hell. I landed there," he pointed to the cave, "at the passageway to the Kingdom of the Water Curtain."

"So you really are the Monkey King?" Ming let out a laugh of superiority, even though she wished she could believe him. "All the logic of the modern world says you're just a psychopath who happens to be a master of classical calligraphy and sleight of hand."

He seemed lost in his own cloud of memories, though, and paid no attention to her words. "And when I came back to earth, to the place from where I had come, it was much changed from how I had remembered. The trees no longer bore fruit; there were no wild silkworms, no tigers to skin. Instead there were people, everywhere, people in the same hideous blue clothes.

"One night, a peasant man spied me scooping some sorry little minnows out of the river. He had a big knife and he came at me with it pointed at my chest. Everyone was hungry then. He was trying to stab me so he could roast me on a fire in the cave and feed me to his family."

"Ha, I thought you were immortal!"

"I am immortal, but I have a heart just like you. A knife can destroy my flesh and then I have to go back up there"—he waved one dirt-stained hand up toward the sky—"and start all over. Anyway, listen to my story so you'll understand some things. I was dreadfully out of practice but I quickly inhaled enlightenment, just as he lunged at me, and I made my chest bend a knife. Fortunately for me, the peasant was so weak from hunger he collapsed on the spot."

"You killed him?"

"To be a primate is to be a warrior. You are a young maiden, but you ought to know that." He looked as if he were considering his own words for a moment or two, then continued. "If you have true perception you can dine on the wind and sleep in the dew. You can live with nothing, in the cold, buffeted by the wind and sleeping on rocks, and it's still better than existing as a savage who eats his fellow man. Or lays him off from his corp-or-ation so New Icarus Capital can get even fatter than it already is."

"How do you know about that?" Ming gasped.

"The walls have ears in modern China and so do sparrows and crickets."

Ming opened her mouth to tell him she was tired of delusions and everything else in Sunshine Village, but he interrupted. "To answer your question, I didn't kill the man who tried to kill me. I admit, I didn't try to revive him, and he wasn't breathing. I said a few blessings, wishing him a better incarnation. The poor fool, his eyes were wide open, staring, and looked as starved for enlightenment as anyone I'd ever seen. It was damn lonely in the cave, so I twisted the head off the corpse, and I sat by him, talking to him.

"I can, of course, perform seventy-two transformations, but decided that no animal form was safe, and turning myself into a man was little better than appearing as the Monkey King, but it felt like a natural state to me. I left the cave for the pagoda, because the villagers were all afraid to go there. And rightly so—it's full of felled spirits, but the ghosts and I made a pact."

"Oh my god, the skull...?" Ming shook her own head. The hermit put a filthy hand on her shoulder, and she tried not to cringe. Then he began to cry, and the tears left clean streaks upon his cheeks. "I think you really are the Monkey King. I grew up so hungry I swallowed raindrops, and that ought to give me a license to believe in miracles."

The hermit leapt up to the Buddha's shoulder, pounded his own sunken chest and called out, "You mortals can't touch me!" Then he soared in one arc over the riverbank.

"Yoo hoo..." echoed across the black water. He waved to her, a figure on the other bank. She could see him bend his knees and thrust upward, turning somersaults across the river again, and landing inches from her on his filthy feet.

After that they sat together for a while, silent and swinging their legs over those of the Buddha beneath them. The man who seemed to be the Monkey King slurped his warm beer while Ming turned her gaze to the thick veil of clouds that covered the village.

"I hate this damn place," Ming said, finally. "I hate Beijing. I hate my job. I have nowhere to go."

"The village is part of you. Mend Sunshine Village and you'll mend yourself." He guzzled down the final drop of beer. "The poor old wise man Confucius—and I did like to sit at his table up there in the heavens, although he had a falling out with every protégée who disagreed with him—he said the heavens were harmonious. But what did he know back then? He hated war profiteering on earth and imagined that there was a place on the other side of life where enlightenment dwelt. You know people like that, I'm sure. They live in China and think there's a paradise at Harvard Business School, they live in America and think everyone in Asia does nothing but chant mantras all day. Still, it was pretty blissful up there for me, and those of like mind, for several hundred years. I have a story to tell you. That's why I'm here instead of in the heavens. The earth is in dire need of enlightenment, not chanting but real enlightenment.

"It was in the heavenly kingdom of the Jade Emperor where I spent those halcyon centuries. You get there, as it happens, through that passage in the cave, and if you tunnel through it you reach the sea, and you soar past the birds, so giddy that you would swear you were completely drunk. Life on the clouds is blissful, the air fresh as a spring meadow, the wine exquisite. You wear silk robes, bask in the sunshine, never hungry or tired." He scratched his head, pulling out a crawling insect. "At least it used to be that way.

"Just before I left, Siddhartha made a bundle selling short at the celestial stock exchange. Plato did pretty well, too. He started an advertising agency with property developers; all he talked about was how much he'd paid for this condo and how much he got for that one. Poor Confucius—one of the few who didn't buy in—was homeless and ranting."

"Maybe they got bored? Eternity lounging around on clouds drinking wine—I'd get restless," Ming said.

"Oh, you humans kept us well entertained." He snickered. "We'd poke a little hole through the clouds and observe the insanity on earth. We'd watch the governments everywhere and the people they governed, and speculate on what each should do, and they always seemed to do just the opposite of what they ought to. Over the centuries I picked my favorite countries to watch, and I learned their languages. You see, I can speak perfect English," he said in a plummy Oxford accent.

"*Je parle francais*, too. And Italian. And Czech because I started watching Franz Kafka. And Pa-Russky. I knew Persian and Arabic in their glory days. And Yiddish. So evocative. We would laugh

99

uproariously and call people schmuck or mensch, and, excuse my vulgarity, schtup."

Ming felt a deep pang for New York.

"But your point has validity; bliss is by definition temporary, even for immortals. Sam Clemens—one of my drinking buddies—had said heaven lacked humor because the secret source of humor is not joy but sorrow. Once he arrived in heaven, he realized how wrong he'd been. The other thing about the heavens is that we were always falling in love. If you have love, you have sorrow. And I had a great love, my Zenia. Seduction is the key, and the only thing that can keep you enthralled for all eternity. You love as if nothing could ever stop you. Then you fight, then twenty years later you resolve the conflict, only to start fighting about it again ten minutes later—"

"So what did you do, have a fight with your girlfriend and run out?"

"I came back for something that's important to you," he said, his fierce golden eyes looking irritated. "Don't fidget. You don't know it but you have eternity to hear me out."

"No offense, but you don't look much like a wise sage in this form."

"I was on the Nirvana Selection Committee, and despite my best efforts, every now and then someone with inadequate credentials would talk their way in. We geniuses were unkind. We had our own pecking order. Soren Kierkegaard could make mincemeat of my words every time I tried to offer proof that there is no defining essence except what we believe it to be. Fyodor Dostoyevsky set Andrew Carnegie weeping with frustration when the rich man told the great author he related completely to Raskolnikov's view of himself as an ubermensch and thought it was a shortcoming of the law that he had to go to Siberia...."

"So you all waved your dicks around, like I'm so impressed. Where were the women?"

"Oh, did I not tell you about Virginia Woolf? Zenia and I spent many a happy hour in her company. We had a bit of a *ménage à trois*. Everyone was in love with Virginia. There were a number of gifted women. Li Qingzhao, the ancient poet with the melancholy lyrics, like 'Ten thousand songs of farewell failed to detain the loved one.' When Will Shakespeare read his sonnets, a lot of us jeered and said they were just a derivative of the love poems Li had been writing in the heavens. Will admitted that a Chinese woman had whispered sonnets to him in his dreams.

"We liked to be muses to mortals who had grand aspirations, you see, those who dreamt of literature, art, and music, and who would move civilization forward. What we didn't expect was an invasion of mortals who craved nothing except what money could buy them. They bought friends and favors on earth, and they found a similar route to paradise.

"It was those souls who paid their way to heaven and started telling the gods about privatization. The idea that everyone would respect the place more if they had to pay for it. Some of them began experimenting, with an eye to creating discrepancies. That was the beginning, you see. They made finer wines, fancier garments. We cared little for such things, but they invited us to their clouds and we became accustomed to drinking the true nectar of the gods. Another clever bastard manufactured a dirty, cold rain that poured relentlessly over our old clouds, while in their gardens the air was pure and fresh and precisely the right temperature. When Zenia and I ventured into one of their gardens, a guard stopped us and said we'd have to pay admission.

"Oh, they were shrewd. We had no currency, of course, so one of the market economy gurus started cranking out little plastic cards. The gardens became private property, and prices soared. The enlightened ones became obsessed with bargain-hunting; they'd fix up their clouds and sell them for profit. Confucius would have nothing of it. Then Zenia and I realized that our own dark, miserable cloud was shrinking. It was so small we kept bumping into each other, like caged animals, and we started fighting again. It was too late to buy a garden cloud. In fact, a slumlord had bought our cloud out from under us and he kept jacking up our rent. We worked at a number of jobs during the day, and spent many a sleepless night trying to figure out how we were ever going to pay our debts. We didn't have the energy to contemplate the universe.

"And then, just when we thought it couldn't get any worse, the privatizers started railing about *us*. They said we were lazy, that we'd spent so many centuries indulging in idle talk that produced nothing but more questions. They singled out poor Confucius in his rags and said he wasn't industrious and didn't deserve a home.

"Those of us who'd practiced enlightenment found we could get paid for certain things, although only a pittance. The population liked books about how to invest your money, and many of our great minds started churning out books with titles like *Make a Celestial Fortune, Eternal Love for Dummies, Unreal Profits from Real Estate.*"

"At least you didn't have to pay for dentists."

"You've obviously never seen Confucius's teeth. While everyone was beautiful in paradise, somehow, in the expensive gardens, you could see flaws you never noticed before. Oddly shaped noses, rolls of body flab, wrinkles and warts. Surgeons did a booming business in changing faces and bodies. Women with bound feet wanted them stretched out, then someone started designing shoes that cost more than the medical procedure."

"You had shoes in heaven?"

"Oh, sure. You even had packaging and branding. We had arrived with nothing, and the money-grubbers declared that that was the beauty of it—a level playing field—so if you didn't have the smarts to launch a business you had only yourself to blame. In fact, they started demanding that you come in with a business plan as the price of admission. I used to watch Jack Kerouac through the hole in my cloud. I was even tempted to enter a mortal body again just so I could get in one of those oil-burning machines and swish along the highways contemplating mortal life."

"My husband liked him—"

"By then I didn't have much time to inspire anyone, since I had to work three jobs just to keep up with my debts, but I did sneak down a time or two and whisper words to Jack while he slept. I was pleased to see that he scribbled them down when he woke up. But when he applied to come up to paradise—actually they called it Paradise Inc. by then—the bouncers at the velvet rope threw him out. Why? Because he didn't have a business plan! They laughed at Jack because he didn't know what a business plan even was.

"You can't breathe freedom until you've walked away from all you know, slept under the stars, and followed the sun as it rises in the east and sets in the west. You're searching for something undefined, and on your way you put it into poetry, you sing it and dance it, and you almost *feel* it for a fleeting moment when you've tasted true love in one person's kiss… then you know what can be. It's art itself that transfigures humanity."

"I won't argue. But you left the woman you loved for *this*?" Ming gesticulated toward the dismal village.

"We staged a demonstration protesting the guardians turning Jack away. We were abandoned, set adrift on an empty cloud until some guys in construction hats came along with a permit to build there. We had a scuffle but they just built right beneath our feet.

"And then Zenia and I got an eviction notice from our slumlord. He wanted us off our cloud so he could build a luxury villa. That was when I decided enough, I'd had it. I vowed I would return to earth to destroy the source of this heavenly covetousness. Some of us had talked about how that was the only way we were ever going to get our paradise back. I didn't know how, but I was going to discover some way to remake the world down here, so that it would be like the heavens used to be, a world where those who have the status are the artists, the benevolent leaders and statesmen, the philosophers; those who can offer reasons to live and love and think, not those who care only about making fortunes and consuming."

Ming, entranced, suddenly wished she could spend eternity there on the Buddha's loin, listening to the mad hermit's operatic voice. "A world where everyone can afford the things they need, and nobody needs to worship money," she said, and sighed. "Would you call it evolution?"

The hermit slid down the Buddha's flank, then took a leap into the distant rice fields. "Where are you going?" Ming called out, and heard her voice echo across the riverbanks. In a flash, though, he returned.

"Do you know what they're doing over there?" he asked, gesturing with his head toward the factory buildings in the distant haze. He had both hands closed, apparently hiding something in each palm. Ming opened her mouth to reply, but he answered himself. "Nothing. The factory isn't worth a rat's nest. The researchers spend their days watching soap operas and soccer games. They hid the TV for your visit, did you know that?"

"How do you know?" But Ming remembered how the pig brains had disappeared so quickly, how the cricket had saved her, and she shook her head with wonder, like a child walking into a fairy tale.

He grinned. "Ah, but I'm Sun Wu Kong, the Monkey King. I can transform myself into seventy-two different forms. I can be a grasshopper or a spider or I can become invisible. I know many, many things, dear Ming. I could be of use to you, if you'd let me." He regarded her intently, then shuffled closer, opening his left hand to reveal a handful of tiny pinkish grains. "Do you know what this is?"

"Soil?"

"And what do they make here?"

"My parents used to make silicon products. Tang Fei pretends they still do, is that what you mean?"

"There's salt in the soil," he pontificated, "and silicon in the salt. That dimwit Tang Fei knows about soccer scores, and he knows how to make up numbers. If I were to take over this factory, I'd have to find something to keep Tang and his buddies occupied, but I've pretty much figured out the rest."

"You, a philosopher, take over the company? Now you want to become one of the capitalists who destroyed your paradise?"

"I don't," he said, and stiffened. "But there are more honorable motivations. Someone who's figured it out might manufacture a biomolecule that looks like a flat grain of rice and processes transactions at the speed of light. The biomolecule is derived from an obscure bacterium that thrives in ponds so salty that the surface is pink and foamy. Cloning the bacteria creates a superorganism that emulates human intelligence. Think of it. This is a biomolecule you can use to create eyes for the blind, or you send man-less combat planes to kill your enemy. And if you are really, truly wise and agile, you can change the very nature of humans themselves. So Ming, tell me, what is it that you really want?"

"I want..." she stopped and looked around as if to make sure no one was laughing at her. But his eyes blazed with nothing but sympathy. "I want to be a writer. I want to wake up every morning and just write. I want to be free, you know, to get in a car and just keep going. I want to love someone who makes me feel transcendent."

"Anybody can make you feel transcendent for half an hour. There must be more. Your true nature lies in the scope of your dreams."

"No, I mean, I want to love someone who knows all about what I did and still thinks of me as his home. And wherever we are, we're at home when we're together."

"Okay. A good start. Believe it or not, there are other investors that would love to be the shark that swallows this factory for a bargain, but if you're going to do that you'd better have what I have. Take a look."

He opened his right hand. Over the layers of dirt on his palm was a miniscule pile of particles that looked like translucent fragments of rice grains.

"An invisible man knows all. I figured it out about a year ago, and I grew this bacteria in the lab during the night. Don't let its small size fool you. This powerful chip is capable of anything. It could be used to manufacture smart bombs. The Chinese government could have weapons of mass destruction like nothing you've ever seen before. Every empire, evil or good, would find a way to get their own. And what will become of mankind then?"

"But you'd use it to change human nature? What do you want from me?"

"Your instincts. My brain. And your brother's private equity." The ragged man grinned, his eyes filled with fiery hope. "The Taoists say heaven and earth are random, but you wandered into my path once,

105

and now again. With one of my seventy-two transformations, I can become tiny and invisible, just a little whisper through your mind, tickling your cerebrum. I could leave behind a nano-sized protein chip in your brain, connected sub-atomically to a central command system."

"A command system that does what exactly?"

"Consider the possibilities. What if a creature the size of a whisper, or a gnat, perhaps, were to plant these biomolecules in the brains of the men of big business, of the powerful and influential? I believe they're mostly men, though there could be some messages for women too. But consider, what does your brother think when he looks at himself in the mirror in the morning? He thinks, 'I'm a guy who's so smart, I'm creating wealth, and if you're half as smart as I am, you can grab a bit of it for yourself.' Well, what if he were to wake up one morning and think something different like, 'What is this all for? Why is the world a jungle dominated by the thirst for power and wealth? Why do I exist? What is the meaning of life?' He'll stand there, shivering like a dying man, but somehow, he'll see marvelous hues—colors he can't even begin to describe in his big important MBA head—he'll hear cymbals clash and a symphony, followed by the sweet birdsong of civilization as it could be."

Ming felt dizzy. "If only. I wish you really were the Monkey King."

"I am a scholarly enlightened gentleman." He held his head high. "I see what money can do if it's finally in the hands of the truly enlightened. Do you know those wacky Taoists used to be obsessed with finding a magic formula for immortality? They made elixirs with mercury and lead and gave them to wealthy patrons willing to risk all for the promise of perpetual life. Of course, everyone who drank it died. The market economy is supposed to be a magic formula, but it operates like a chalice filled with mercury. But it doesn't have to."

The hermit started to move, stretching his limbs and flexing his knuckles until they cracked; then he leapt up and down, and was gone—nothing there but an emerald dragonfly buzzing at Ming's side.

Ming, on a sudden impulse, ran into the cave, pulled the blue-

and-green-striped towel from the little shrine, and ran back out. Out of nowhere, the hermit Monkey King appeared at her side again.

"Do you know what this is for?" She held up the ragged towel. It still gave off a faint whiff of peach-mango.

"Sure. People use these to dry off after they wash in the indoor waterfall. Give it back." His face, Ming couldn't help but notice, was flushed beneath the grime.

"I'll give it back if you'll tell me something. Why did you say, 'Come alone'?"

"I don't have to tell you anything."

You have a crush on my friend. She was certain of it, watching how hungrily his eyes followed the towel as she flapped it around. "I have my hands on the private equity and I can say no to everything if you don't tell me the truth."

He slumped down against the Buddha's foot, looking more wounded than he had that night in the pagoda after Zoe kicked him.

Ming decided to sit down next to him and wait a while. Then she asked, "You must miss your immortal love. Is she waiting up there, or what?"

He buried his head in his shoulders, and when he spoke, it was in a mumble. "She insisted on diving down to earth too. I told her not to. I was the one who'd cultivated conduct, I could come back here and choose my form. She was practicing enlightenment but she had a long way to go. I told her, if you dive down, it's a black hole, and you don't know where you'll end up. Her immortal soul would be unconscious, maybe subconscious at times. I said, 'What if you come back as a rabbit or a deer, and you have to spend your whole short life running from wolves and hunters?'"

"Maybe she thought being prey in the forest was still better than being homeless in the heavens?"

He leaped up again, and for a moment Ming thought he might be on his way. The clouds were beginning to turn a deep violet, a reminder that the day was not eternal.

But he stood still, gazing at the violet sky, then down at the earth, so silent he startled Ming when he spoke again. "She said, 'I'm not as

107

unconscious as you think.' She said, 'whatever fleshly form I assume, I'll try to make it human, and female. And when I see you, I'll have some kind of instinct, I'll beat you with my sideways kick from behind and you'll know it's me.'"

"Whaaatttt?????" For a moment Ming imagined the earth had cracked in half.

The hermit bowed his head again. "For a beginner to kickbox with Sun Wu Kong is like trying to smash a rock with eggs, but she practiced over the centuries. The first time she tackled me with her side kick, I wouldn't speak to her for twenty years. Yeah, it was a big blow to my ego." Then he sank down next to Ming. "Maybe we can get together again in her next lifetime. She saw me like this."

"Poor monkey." Ming ventured a hand upon his filthy shoulder.

A gasp of sun etched itself through the purple clouds, then faded while the two of them pondered silently. Ming let emptiness and thoughts of her own screwed-up life float through her mind, along with a preposterous recollection of a book she'd read in business school called *Transformation*.

"You can transform yourself into a stupid bird or a cricket. So why can't you make yourself a handsome, debonair human?"

He shrugged. "I'd still be a starving hermit in the pagoda."

I have private equity, Ming reminded herself. She wanted, more than anything, to believe everything this squalid creature claimed.

"Maybe," she said, "I can help. You know, my brother isn't going to want to invest in Sunshine Village Silicon Works, but if you come to Beijing looking like a visionary who can resurrect a dead company, maybe we *can* get him to buy it."

He considered that. "When I was a Buddhist believer, we recruited followers by telling them they would get what they wanted if they follow our teachings. Then, when they become believers, they transcended mortal cravings and achieved true bliss."

"See, you're a born marketer."

They talked about Sunshine Village, New York, the New Icarus Capital account that Ming could access, and a great many other things. Ming told him about a special soap he could get in the village.

108

"It'll get rid of the creatures you think are your friends just because they crawl on you. You can get into places without a key, so find a place to wash in the indoor waterfall, every day."

He scratched his head and pulled off a couple of the crawly things. But when he broke into a faint smile the sun beat another faint crack through the clouds. When Ming finally ambled away, a Titian sunset lit the sky. The magical afternoon had her almost dancing along the path, all the way to the courtyard of the guesthouse.

"Good evening, Mrs. Pang," she sang out at the sight of the innkeeper at the front door. Mrs. Pang was scowling, her arms folded like a sergeant in discipline mode.

"You!" Mrs. Pang spat out, her voice shrill. "I don't want trouble in my place. You and your foreign friend get out! Stupid whores!" Her litany continued as she grabbed Ming's arm and pulled her up to the room. "Your American friend is making big trouble. You take her back where she came from. I don't want them coming around here!"

"Them?"

"Stupid foreign devil!" Mrs. Pang unlocked the door to the guest chambers. The interior was as black and airless as the grave. As Ming's eyes adjusted to the dark she made out a trembling form lying on the bed in a heap of torn clothes, with a mass of tangled, copper hair. The pummeled creature lying there was Zoe.

Chapter Eight

The handyman from the guesthouse drove Ming and Zoe to the next village before dawn—in exchange for most of the cash they had left—and dumped them on a sooty thoroughfare, where they sat in a dank restaurant for five hours.

Zoe's muscles screeched with every move. It hurt to even hold the teacup. At intervals, as she told Ming everything, she had to stop and sip tea to wash the gravel from her throat. They spoke in English so that the restaurant proprietor, who sat at the next table watching them, wouldn't understand.

"Thugs in the pay of the police department, no doubt," Ming acknowledged. "That's what's going on; they rule the village. A police officer probably called Mrs. Pang and told her the foreign guest was making trouble and they'd shut her place down if she was going to harbor troublesome guests."

"But what am I going to do about my research?"

Ming shook her head. "You'll have to be patient." Ming was cheerful in a most un-Ming like way, as if some magic formula had cured her stormy sighs. "In *qi gong* you sometimes lose, right? Haven't you ever fallen down and come back up?" Ming had taken a bite of the rock Buddha while Zoe had become like the supergirl from her old commercial, drained of her powers. "We'll go back to Beijing. I'll get Han to take you on as an intern, and you can live in the apartment they put me in. And you can talk to my parents about Sunshine Village and use their stories for your dissertation."

They had just enough cash for bus tickets to Chengdu. From there they boarded a flight—courtesy of New Icarus Capital—to Beijing. On the back roads of Sichuan and in the air, Ming filled Zoe in on her new obsession—the New China.

"Don't you see?" Ming prodded. "That peasant girl Jing Yin's family would own their home simply by virtue of occupying it, and

110

those thugs would go to a jail where they'd have to study new job skills, and read literature and philosophy, like a university with bars!"

It was a fine fantasy to keep Zoe's mind off her defeat. "We could make the rich put a certain amount of their money into investment accounts that go to paying the living expenses of the poor," she offered.

In Han Cheng's office, Zoe followed Ming's lead. "I'm thinking about trying business instead," Zoe told Han. "An MBA, perhaps, combined with Chinese studies."

Han looked at her as if she suddenly mattered. "You can come aboard as a part-time trainee," he said. "We can pay you a little."

And so it was that Zoe slid into a corporate limbo called New Icarus Capital. Three days a week, she followed the hordes along the streets of Beijing's business district, where music synthesizers blared like geomancers coaxing the concrete to keep sprouting new department stores and skyscrapers. New Icarus was in a cinder-gray building on the eighth floor—the prosperity floor, according to feng shui.

In the front office there were two administrative assistants, Tian and Fanny, who'd given herself an English-sounding name for an office where English was required. A corridor diverged, leading to Han's corner office on one side and Tom Wendall's on the other, like the heavyweights of a barbell. The two interns occupied an open space in between. On the other side of the reception area was a conference room that the partners had decorated with sepia photographs of bare-breasted women scrubbing laundry in streams beside bamboo groves, of barefoot peasants carrying baskets of rice balanced on poles over their shoulders, and of a courtesan in gold bracelets playing a lute—Asia before investment capital.

Most afternoons Tom would disappear by three. Ming would step out shortly after, then reappear at five with Tom ten minutes in her wake. Zoe, calculating percentages of profit and loss throughout the day, was developing a fascination with fractions of all kinds.

Tom had come up with the company's name. "You can't fly up to the sun with wax wings, but we've got technology to make anything possible, " he had told Zoe proudly on her first day, at a get-acquainted lunch. Tom's silky strands of light brown hair framed a pliable, pancake face. While Han talked, Tom sat with his hands folded; he wore a wedding ring, Zoe noticed. He avoided looking at Ming when her brother was present.

Like all private equity funds, New Icarus used other people's money to invest in companies. They specialized in taking over companies that remained on the books of provincial and city governments, businesses that had no capital of their own and thrashed about like dogs with distemper. Ming showed Zoe how to write reports adding up building maintenance expenditures, payroll, and raw material costs relative to sales revenue. Zoe's calculations were intended to prove—contrary to company management claims—that debts far surpassed the profits. It was not a difficult job. Sometimes Han and Tom would decide to invest, other times they'd leave the company to die. Zoe assumed the report for Sunshine Village Silicon Works Enterprises would look like all the others, although Ming took on that particular assignment.

When Zoe first checked her email in Beijing, her inbox was overflowing. Three messages from the other side of the world pleaded, URGENT: ARE YOU ALIVE? from her mother. A message a day from Jeff; several from girlfriends with updates on romances that were either too noncommittal or too insistent on commitment; a dozen from classmates who hadn't even known she was in China; and one from Professor Engelhorn. *Hope you arrived safely. I'm eager to hear about your adventures.* Odd word for him to use, adventures. She replied that she was now in Beijing to interview the Chengs and seeking historical documents about the Third Front. There was exactly one message from Danny Hirsch. *Hope you got there safely. Love, Danny.*

Once she answered him, Danny emailed a few more times the following week. Then there was a blank stretch from Monday to Saturday before he wrote, *Sorry been remiss. I've had a friend staying here. We're off to Rio for a little Carnival diversion, so will blow some sea breezes your way.*

Rio. Danny wasn't going to wait. If he had been talking about a male buddy, he would have furnished a name. She foresaw the ritual ahead. She'd seen old girlfriends kiss Danny on the lips at parties. Then they'd kissed Zoe on both cheeks. As an ex, she might run into him at some such party someday, drink too much, remind him of old times, and maybe even have a fling with him. That would be okay, as long as you restricted your bad behavior to no more than once a year. Those were the unspoken rules.

"He's dumping me," Zoe told Ming and felt empty, as if the past three years with him had gone missing.

"It's not your style to be dumped." Ming gestured at the buildings outside their apartment window. "Somewhere there's someone who's really your soul mate, and—who knows?—he might even walk into New Icarus Capital one day. You should get back into your *qi gong*. There's a park down the street and a guy who teaches it at six every morning."

The next morning Zoe kickboxed beneath a grove of poplar trees whose leaves were covered in black soot. Breathing in Beijing car fumes and dust from a neighboring construction site, Zoe exhaled twice for every inhalation. *Enlightenment comes from you, not the air, your brain is a muscle that can master all.* Where had she heard that? She kicked sideways, imagined her feet could lift entirely off the ground.

"Yes," she told Ming when she returned, wiping sweat from her face. "I feel a little less stuck."

While Zoe gathered material for her dissertation in the months that followed, she felt a vague dissatisfaction—as if her time at New Icarus Capital were a perpetual limbo, and the Chengs' accounts of Sunshine Village filtered through too many layers of distant memory. On the two weekdays they had off, and sometimes on weekends, Ming had a habit of disappearing—getting together with old friends from school, she'd claim. Zoe assumed her apartment mate was meeting Tom or perhaps another man. Left alone, Zoe applied for permission to examine Third Front documents in the government archives. Each week she called to see if anyone had reviewed her application, and each time a different person answered the phone

113

and said either they hadn't had a chance to consider it yet or they had no such documents in their possession. She recorded thirty interview hours with the Chengs and several of their employees—all of whom had been happy to leave the village behind. She read six books and took notes for her orals, studying over the clatter of drills and pile drivers outside.

Some nights, Han and Tom would require the young interns to attend New Icarus Capital business dinners, where potential investors would talk about their quarterly performance and look at Zoe and Ming as if they were double-digit investment returns. Zoe changed the subject when they pulled out their phones and asked, "How can I reach you?" She saw Han pretending not to notice Ming making languorous eye contact. He would pimp his sister for a deal.

One morning, Tom told Zoe that the bald investor from the previous evening had asked if she was a lesbian. Tom snickered when he said it. He was all right if you could get past the cheating on his wife.

"Naw, I'm just in training to be a cat lady," Zoe said. The next day Tom brought in a Chinese welcoming cat for her desk.

"Actually," Ming confided on a quiet afternoon in the office, "Tom wants something he can't buy. He just doesn't know what it is. He told me, if he could do anything, he'd fly an airplane. I have to tell you something, because I trust you. But you have to keep it secret. We're seeing each other. Sometimes we meet here in the afternoons and do it on the floor after hours." She grinned at her confession, flashing her Dr. Perlmutter teeth.

"It's the worst-kept secret in the office." Zoe looked down at the shiny parquet floor, imagining puddling sex juices. While Ming was begging her not to tell Han, her own idle hormones shrieked.

One afternoon in late March, Han called Ming and Zoe into his office. "I have to congratulate you," he said. "You're both part of this Sunshine Village deal, so come in early tomorrow and help us see it through. We've got a meeting with a man who is very interested in buying the factory there with us as a partner and transforming it. So we shall see what he has to say."

114

"What's his name?" Zoe asked.

"Be here by eight," was Han's reply. In their own office, Ming explained to Zoe that she had made a grievous *faux pas*. To provide an ambitious intern with the name of a high-value client was simply not done—an intern with real potential would track him down before the meeting and set up her own deal.

"Well…even I don't know his name," Ming segued into a stammer, suddenly flustered. "Tang Fei told me a potential buyer had been looking around…that maybe someone was interested…"

The next morning, Ming was up and dressed by the time Zoe got back from her workout.

"You should wear the black suit," Ming said. The first three weeks of Zoe's intern wages had gone mostly into clothes appropriate for the job.

"Don't you want to wear it?" They also shared clothes.

"No, today it's yours. Like these?" Ming presented a small satin box. Inside was a pair of gold earrings that went nicely with the buttons on the suit that was their joint favorite. "You can borrow them."

Zoe put them on. Ming watched her with the oddest twist of a grin.

When they arrived in the office, Han gave each of them a set of briefing papers. The mysterious potential buyer was due at nine, so with less than an hour before he arrived, Han revealed that his name was William Kingsley Sun. He was an entrepreneur in microchip production.

"Silicon Valley?" Zoe asked.

"All secret stuff," said Tom. "We think he's been working in Russia."

Caterers arrived with coffee and tea and the soggy round things that passed for bagels beyond the borders of New York City. Zoe was trying to get bagel dough off the roof of her mouth when Fanny ushered their visitor into the conference room.

"Hellew," he said, his accent right out of an Edwardian drama, and the symphonic depth of his voice like nature bursting through the walls. Zoe had expected an oligarch jaw and flinty, carnivorous eyes, but William Kingsley Sun had the brooding air of a man who had seen too much and carried the world's burdens wrapped in a shroud of *bon mots*. His eyes were almond-shaped and flecked with gold, his haircut expensively tousled, as if he'd been too busy thinking to look in the mirror. And he was an accomplished seducer—Zoe could tell that by the way he looked into her eyes. He seemed somehow familiar; maybe she'd seen him interviewed on television?

"My son doesn't want to eat breakfast anymore unless it's an Egg McMuffin," Han commenced. That was how he started all meetings—his anecdotal way of conveying that the global economy was at their doorstep.

"When you have a lot, the world seems a better place than it actually is," said William. "Chekhov once wrote that in a letter."

Zoe pushed away the inappropriate thought of getting it on with William Kingsley Sun right there upon the rosewood table; his gaze, intent on her own, implied that he was quite accustomed to sealing deals that way.

A pause, and then it was time for the visitor to make his pitch. "You've seen my business plan," William began, glancing first at Han, then Tom, then Ming and Zoe. "But I haven't told you how I'm going to make this happen. It will be big, I can promise you that. The next Microsoft will happen in the little town of Sunshine Village." Magic words. Han and Tom liked that, someone so cocky he'd do anything to keep from failing.

Han maintained a poker face in meetings, but when he was pleased with a pitch he would lean forward, elbows on the table and hands folded; when bored, he would lean back, toying with a pen or a wadded up piece of paper. He was leaning forward now.

"You've seen Sunshine Village. Now I'm going to show you the chip. Not just any old chip, a nanochip—tinier than the tiniest thing you can imagine." He held up something translucent, less than ant-sized. From his pocket, William retrieved a magnifying glass and handed it to Zoe. His arm grazed within half an inch of hers and the space between them sizzled.

"This nano-sized particle will do many things," William continued. "Manufacturers can use it to make toy dogs talk, or a shirt change from white to purple in the flash of an eye. These chips function according to the particular message they receive. No doubt the military would pay handsomely for such a technology, but I do not plan to sell them to generals and soldiers. I assume you send your employees for regular physical examinations?"

Tom and Han both nodded, although Zoe had never heard anyone in the office mention a required checkup.

"There is a common little medical device called an otoscope. The doctor sticks it in your ear to see if your eardrum looks okay. But a doctor could place this chip on the end of the otoscope, and with one little probe in the ear, the chip is implanted in the outer cortex. Just imagine, ladies and gentlemen, a computer database that sends messages to nano particles that can dance on the head of a doctor's otoscope. To what end? you might ask. Happiness for all."

"Happiness?" Han frowned momentarily over his steepled hands, as if happiness had nothing to do with anything whatsoever.

"What makes you happy, Han?" William Sun asked. "Watching your son grow up? Enjoying a fine dinner? Seeing your business succeed? And how did you arrive at this happy state of affairs? You studied, worked hard, and have earned the right to enjoy the finer things in life. Of course, you incidentally boost the fortunes of others by the simple act of going to buy a new car with a plush leather interior. The salesman is ecstatic."

Zoe could almost smell new-car leather.

"Now suppose you happened to be born into humble circumstances; suppose you live in a dirt shack and work for pennies, or perhaps you are a restless young university graduate who lives in a tenement with three roommates and dreams of becoming a great artist. Being poor, on the other hand, is like being a perpetual child. Your life is always in the hands of someone else—your landlord, your employer, your charitable friends."

Han was listening with something resembling rapture in his eyes. Tom chewed on his lower lip. Ming's lips were curled into a

117

surreptitious smile. It was like landing in a movie where everyone else was brainwashed, Zoe thought.

"Imagine a global economy with no bitterness. With the program we've developed, these little chips can erase all bitterness. I cannot tell you everything. This is classified technology after all. Which brings us to the factory in Sunshine Village. You could buy a stake now, with capital upfront," William said. "They'll go through your money in less than six months—I'd say three, in fact. All the while, they'll repay you in monthly installments at thirty percent interest; that's your terms. When the coffers are empty, we become the new owners. I'm the chief executive, you're the capital partners."

Zoe felt the bagel dough rumbling in her stomach, and was sure she was going to vomit on the table if she didn't flee the room. Yet, in spite of herself, William Sun's next words held her to her chair, as if she were watching a gruesome but suspenseful movie.

"Manufacturing chips is, of course, the primary business," William continued. "But I'm in the refinancing business too. Think for a moment of the majestic cliffs looking over the river at Sunshine Village. I am envisioning luxury condominiums and a golf resort. You build a beautiful village, stores that sell fashionable clothes and fine cars, fine restaurants. You get visitors, but these things are there mostly for the residents, too. How can such things be available to simple village people, you ask?

"That is the beauty of loans. You build, and you offer a beautiful village to your people and you don't even have to spend a lot on salaries. Instead you give them loans. How do you expect these loans to be paid back? Well, you collect from the employee paychecks. This is the beauty of a synergistic town, do you see?" William's eyes gleamed with the fervor of his words. Han's mouth opened slightly, but nothing escaped.

"You can sell the loans on the capital markets, but they won't collapse because the payback keeps coming out of payroll. And you don't have to cut your payroll in lean times, because your employees are paying you interest to employ them. What if people run up more debt than can be garnished from their paychecks? What if an employee quits?

118

Well, that all takes us back to the beauty of these nanochips."

Zoe decided it was time to interrupt him. "Why not just charge people fifty thousand dollars on credit for the privilege of working for you?"

Tom inhaled sharply, Han glared at her, and Ming pursed her lips.

"It's all in the mind," William told her, smiling. "Striving is in the mind. Frustration is in the mind. Even indebtedness is in the mind. We are in the business of making loans, but also in the business of making nanochips with classified software that transmits messages, messages that remind people how much better life is when he or she possesses material things.

"Imagine," he went on, "a world where everyone is industrious. We can make a world where credit is always available, even if cash isn't, so a husband and wife never have to fight about money again. We can make a world where people are focused on making more money, where they're not temperamentally drawn to wasting time in idealistic pursuits that don't pay off. For example, let's say you have a daughter who wants to be a writer instead of obtaining an MBA. You give her two years, see if she makes it; if not, she goes to the doctor for a checkup and the next day she can't wait to start applying to business schools. Now, those with the inclination to be teachers, nurses, police officers, and nannies can pursue that line of work, but importantly, they can still consume. Remember, we're in the business of credit and can make it attractive for schools, hospitals, and government agencies to go private and develop a credit arm, which we can subcontract. You pay wages, you take the credit card payment out of the paychecks at a fair interest rate, and you sell the debt on the securities market. The more people you employ, the more revenue they produce for you as they consume goods and boost the economy. Everyone wins. Everyone's happy." He was still looking at Zoe, and she wondered if his gaze could brainwash.

"Well," said Han, finally. "My old business school classmate, Jonathan Cass, said you could be trusted to have a vision."

"Jonathan..." William Sun chuckled. "Quite a sloop he's been racing."

The conversation drifted to someone's golf score and something about "…married a DuPont, you know." Zoe clung to the table to keep from passing out, picturing a village of people enslaved to a string of company stores. She'd had enough. She pushed herself up and walked unsteadily to the door.

"Got an errand," she muttered, and escaped outside into a chalky noontime.

Zoe was back in the apartment, throwing clothes, shoes, and books into her suitcase, when the doorbell rang. She froze. A scraping sound, then sprightly footsteps retreating down the hall. She tiptoed to the front door and saw that someone had slipped a piece of paper underneath. She unfolded the paper to discover a note, in English, handwritten in elegant sweeps and curves.

Dear Zoe, I had hoped to find you here. I will wait in your lobby. I implore you to allow me a word. It is about a matter of grave concern to your future. I am not at all what I seem. A man with capitalism charging through his soul would have sent you a text message, n'est-ce pas? W.K.S.

"Implore?" Zoe scoffed. She brushed her hair, then picked up her suitcase. If this self-important tech entrepreneur was waiting in the lobby, she would be indisputably on her way out, at least. In the elevator mirror she saw, too late, that she'd forgotten to take off Ming's earrings.

In the lobby, William Kingsley Sun was sitting in a straight-backed chair that offered a view of the elevator doors, reading a print edition of the *International Herald Tribune*. Seeing her, he stood up. "Might we take a walk?" he asked.

"I've got a plane to catch. Anyway, walking around here gives me a giant headache."

"Pile drivers, ground-level ozone, cell phones blasting, trucks with no mufflers—the many delights of Beijing." William sounded almost nice, strangely enough. "I'd be happy to escort you to the airport." He insisted on wheeling her suitcase outside, and helping her scan the street for an empty cab.

"What's this matter of grave concern to my future?" Zoe asked, but her voice was lost in the roar of traffic and pile drivers. Rush

120

hour lasted all day in Beijing. Dozens of taxis limped along in traffic, every one of them occupied.

"What time is your flight?" William asked.

She looked at her watch. It was nearly three o'clock. "Quarter past four."

"What time is the next one?"

"Seven twenty."

"Why don't we sit down somewhere, then you can try for the later flight?"

Other pedestrians shoved and jostled them. The noodle shop down the street was packed. Zoe thought of sitting in the park, but an afternoon drizzle was turning into serious rain. She led William back to her apartment lobby. Two people occupied the only chairs.

There was nowhere to go but her own apartment.

"You forgot to mention during our meeting," Zoe said as she poured tea, "that some enterprising resident of Sunshine Village could put the local jasmine tea into bags, pack them together in a box with a picture of a giant Buddha, and sell it all over the world as 'Sunshine Tea' for ten dollars a box. Then, as it catches on in the best gourmet shops around the world, this enterprising resident could substitute the jasmine tea with chemically scented weeds and charge twenty-five dollars a box."

"Touché."

"So, were you ever even in the village?"

The slick William Sun giggled like a shy schoolboy. With nothing but the cheap blackwood coffee table between them, Zoe tugged at her skirt, her bare knees feeling too naked.

"I'm in something of a hurry," Zoe reminded him.

"Yes, everyone's always in a hurry in this century." He looked nervous himself. He reached for his teacup, but it slipped from his hand and crashed to the floor. "I'm terribly sorry."

Zoe fetched paper towels and sopped up a pool of tea from among the shards of the teacup. "It's just a cheap cup."

"I bet you're good at fixing things." He knelt down and retrieved a large shred of porcelain. "Something you should know," he said,

121

while the two of them were still examining the floor, "I used to be a Buddhist before I saw that the gods were all corruptible." Golden sparks seemed to light up from his eyes, and Zoe had the strangest impression of Buddha surrounded by devotees, stating firmly that it was time to buy real estate instead of stocks.

"You know what the Buddhists say, don't you?" William Sun continued. "Expedient means? Tell people what they want to hear? You might say 'this deal will make you richer,' to the partners at New Icarus, when you really mean 'this deal will make you happier than riches ever will.' I wasn't surprised when you left."

"Well, I'm not really a private equity trainee. I'm an academic doomed to penury. You know, living like a perpetual child."

"Nothing like the word 'deal' to make one's eyes glaze over," William said. Holding up the smallest remain of the broken teacup, he said, "Imagine that this represents the rich." He held up a larger remnant. "The big piece here is the poor. And this is the work of the civilizers." He pieced the two shards together.

"Where did you hear that word 'civilizers'?"

"You might not believe me, but the meeting today was all about expedient means. So this is what I wanted to offer *you*. How would you like to work for a company that plants chips that control thoughts, but it's just the opposite of what I proposed? Han gets a chip. Tom gets a chip. Big shots all over the country get chips—and they wake up one day wondering why are they are devoting their lives to the pursuit of money? Why do their lives seem hollow and meaningless? They start noticing the poverty of those who work for them, of people in the streets who are in desperate need of money. And then they decide to make some changes. It's a revolution that comes from those at the top."

Zoe frowned, pulling her skirt lower over her knees. They were so close she felt a sizzling sensation when he spoke. He's just admitted he's a con artist, she reminded herself.

"There's a job for you, if you'll accept it. Ming is coming to work with me. What do your academic advisors really know about Chinese history?"

She stiffened, nearly knocking the table. "How do you know about that?"

"Oh, I've been talking to your devious but loyal friend Ming. She knows something about expedient means herself. So, I've seen Chinese history professors. They believe a power-hungry eunuch wanted control of the throne so he fooled a young prince; in actuality, the prince was vicious and stupid from inbreeding. Academics believe that women's feet were first bound in the Sung Dynasty, but they have no notion of the fashion designer who made lotus shoes for the dancers and the ladies of the court. What are you reading for your orals? I'd love to see."

Zoe dug out two reference books from her carry-on. No harm in that, surely.

William looked through her books long enough to make Zoe start worrying about getting to the airport. "This is bullshit on page thirty-five," he said.

"I suppose you were there."

"Tell you what," he said. "Why don't you consider this? Go take the orals, just to show these doddering professors what they don't know. Then, when you're finished, come back to Sunshine Village and work with me. I can't pay much at the moment, but I'll give you a signing bonus if you promise to come back."

"Can I think about that? From New York?"

"Well, you're traveling without your survival gear."

William pulled something out from the depths of his beautiful suit. Opening his palm, he revealed a slightly rusted Swiss Army knife, with a blade that wouldn't go in all the way.

Zoe felt the room spin. "William Kingsley Sun.....W.K. Sun Wu Kong?"

He nodded. "If you like this transformation, I'll keep it."

Her knees were way too wobbly to stand up and go anywhere.

"You've taken on quite a fetching mortal form yourself," he said and looked at her, through her, as if he'd known her forever.

"Worst pickup line I've ever heard from a lapsed-Buddhist, self-confessed con man."

William rose to his feet, yanked a hair from his head, and uttered the word "Change!" Suddenly there were two William Suns in the room—both in the same fine suit, with the same dip in their wavy brown hair. Then there were two more. All identical, although Zoe observed that the eyes of the copies were muted somehow, less fiery, progressively tamer, as if they were a photocopy, then a photocopy of the photocopy, and so on. And as suddenly as the lot of them had appeared, they were gone, the room emptied—except for a butterfly with iridescent indigo wings fluttering against her cheek, the way her mother used to do with her eyelashes when Zoe was little and call it a butterfly kiss.

A popping sounded, and William was back in his chair, legs crossed as if he'd been there all along.

"Would you like," he asked, "to know who you are?"

PART II

The Roller Coaster to the Sun

Chapter Nine

Sunshine Village was beautiful in those days. The river was home to plump fish, and a playground for lord and servants alike. The fields and forests were lush and as green as an emerald." William Kingsley Sun seemed to be gazing way past Zoe and the apartment, back a thousand years or so.

He said that Zoe used to plant rice in the same fields where Jing Yin and her mother toiled. "Your name was Zenia. I taught you martial arts, and I used to watch you in the fields. You'd stop to admire the patterns in the vein of a rice stalk, or cock your head to the symphony of swallows and sparrows."

"You're romanticizing the past. I'll bet I hated planting rice."

He told her about the heavens, too, and how they ended up on a cramped slum of a cloud.

"A slum in heaven?"

"It even smelled like moldy cabbage."

"My mom and I were only migraine poor," Zoe acknowledged. "Over-extended credit cards poor. Genteel poor."

The air between them felt electric as they talked and drank wine, way past the departure time of the last flight to Hong Kong. Ming still hadn't come home.

"Ming set all this up with you," Zoe declared as an observation.

The days that followed saw Zoe, Ming, and the un-earthly William Sun begin to make quiet plans to further the spread of enlightenment, with the little corporate apartment as their citadel. As New Icarus Capital interns, Ming and Zoe were compiling the paperwork facilitating the loan that Sunshine Village Silicon Works Enterprises would never be able to pay back. Han and Tom were already making plans to take over the company in a matter of months and install William Sun as the new CEO.

126

In their spare time, the three conspirators designed a software program that harnessed the wisdom gleaned from a thousand years of mankind's blunders. They combed the internet to select potential recipients for their program. William, in the form of a tiny gnat, would visit these individuals and deposit nanochips into their ear canals. They were, as it happened, all men. Men who ran corporations, men who lived to see their stock prices rise and considered it a virtuous exercise to periodically lay off staff so that their shareholders—a tribe that included themselves—could make more money. They were the masters of cold calculations that led to mergers, acquisitions, partnerships, and other deals that combined the manufacture of several products, but mostly earned big bonuses for the men who thought it up. On the list of recipients, too, were government men who believed their power was something close to holy, and men who played investment games that required encroaching upon the squares where pawns dwelt.

"One morning," said William, "they will awaken, and everything will look different. When they ponder the wealth that was so alluring the day before, a nagging thought will wrap itself around their brains like a belt that's too tight. That's the first phase. Then they'll start to see that they have the power to make everyone's lives as bountiful as theirs have been."

Ming danced around the room with excitement. "We should give them—or the program should give them—the idea to set up a national Ministry of Civilization run by a revolving group of writers, sculptors, humanities professors, and all kinds of artists and thinkers. They'll have peer panels that review plans from would-be civilizers, and each year a group of recipients gets enough money to live very well as long as they keep doing creative work."

Zoe mulled that over. "But they shouldn't reward bad art."

"Banality and self-indulgence are disqualifiers," William said, tapping notes into the program. "No funding for blood and gore via special effects, no funding for books that stipulate rules for finding a husband or how to invest like a rich guy. No post-modern gratuitous raunch masquerading as the voice of its generation."

127

Ming sighed. "I'm an awful writer."

"You can work on it," said William.

"Where my mom comes from, in Mississippi, there's a legend of a young blues singer who met Satan at a crossroads," Zoe said. "Satan tuned the man's guitar and made him a master of the blues. Satan, you know, was a god of fertility with horns representing the crescent moon and a pitchfork for tilling the soil before the Christians defeated polytheism and made him the bad guy. We're tilling the soil of the New China. Can't we tune Ming's laptop to make it sing?"

Throughout April they hatched their plans, the three of them in agreement about the messages they'd deliver. William slept on the sofa in Ming and Zoe's apartment or spent wakeful nights tinkering with the software; unbeknownst to his New Icarus benefactors, he had no money for a home of his own. He stashed his clothes in Zoe's closet, and the trousers and soft silk ties filled Zoe with a sense of intimacy. She was holding out, inhaling discipline. She knew it was possible for people to work together and be lovers too; her mother had been happy living and working with Nathan, the theater director. But the thought of her mother, and of home, reminded Zoe that she had a mortal life with obligations of its own.

William had said he wouldn't insist. Actually he'd said, sounding preposterously formal, "I can inhale discipline and exist without carnal pleasure for five hundred years. You tell me when you're ready." The air between them continued to sizzle, and she knew she was denying herself something that would be celestial. But would it swallow her whole?

She grew to know him well anyway, in those close quarters. She knew he liked to shower in the morning and the evening. He would emerge in a black kimono, his hair damp, his skin fragrant with vetiver soap. "Plumbers are deities who have shown us the path for conquering savagery!" he declared to Zoe once. "Standing under a hot shower fills you with love for humanity. Everyone smells like a spring garden in this century."

She watched him discover other delights of urban living in the twenty-first century. He liked to skid in his socks along their hardwood

128

floor and laughed every time they rode an elevator. "Doesn't anyone ever try to take it through the roof and past the clouds?" he asked.

There were also nights when he would come into Zoe's bedroom just to talk. Her double bed had a billowy duvet, inviting as a cloud, and her kimono with the embroidered dragon hung on a peg and seemed to say come hither. They would talk about everything and nothing—of economic equality, of the almond undertones of a Pinot Grigio they'd discovered, and of her impending orals. He read through more of her books and told her what had really happened, and she could tell he thought he was persuading her not to bother with going back. She had to tell him, on a night in late April, that Professor Engelhorn had emailed her with a date and time in mid-May.

She told him, that night, that Professor Engelhorn had provided the money for her to be here in the first place, and that he just might be her father.

"It's just a blip in eternity." William dismissed Professor Engelhorn with a wave of his hand. "Why does it matter who your mortal parents are?"

"It just does. I'm *in* time. I like my mortal life."

William leaned back in his chair; Zoe had insisted they sit in chairs rather than lounging on her bedcover. "Do you know what the human tragedy is?" he asked.

She loved his oratory style, the way he paused just long enough to make you curious. "We have our old savage instincts, but our brains can contemplate infinity. And so we confuse the two. We think we're not safe from the long winter unless we hoard up an infinite supply of salt-cured mastodon meat, or, for modern humans, money. Humans all think they want something specific, but ultimately they want infinity, and seduction is a way of capturing infinity, as is losing oneself in art or poetry or music."

William poured them another glass of wine each, bought with credit cards since wine was expensive in Beijing.

"Did I ever tell you about the argument I had with Adam Smith?" he asked as he handed Zoe a glass, fingers brushing hotly against her own. "He had a habit of watching the rich from our hole in the clouds, claiming that people approved of the rich, that their finery commanded attention, and that the less fortunate sought to emulate the wealthy. I countered that it was the not the rich that people so admired, but their things, their diamonds and gold, and their landscaped gardens. Adam often commented upon how, despite their riches, these individuals were truly unhappy, and none of their worldly goods gave them the serenity they ultimately craved."

"Wouldn't we all be serene if we didn't have money worries weighing us down like a ton of bricks?"

"No," William said thoughtfully. "It's the absence of passion that weighs us down."

Zoe allowed her shirt to slip, baring the curve of her shoulder and upper arm.

"You always made yourself a challenge to anyone who wanted you," William said, his voice husky. "Took me twenty years to win you over. And once we had a fight and it took a hundred years to get you back."

Zoe lay awake that night, not for the first time, aware from the light beneath the door that William was also sleepless, no doubt working on the software. *If the absence of passion weighs you down, would the triple pursuit of romance and paradise and my orals lift me up?* Whatever the consequences, she decided, it would be better than this raging insomnia, which had become a metalcore band of a zillion hormones banging through her limbs.

She opened her door, found him at the laptop, and beckoned, and he followed on cue. In her room she took his face in both hands and claimed his lips in a most carnivorous way. Clothes fluttered to the floor, and he spread her across the bed, painting abstract swirls across her body with his tongue.

So this is what it means to lose your head, Zoe thought.

In the hours that followed, they seemed to float supine above the bed; then with her lover in a headstand; then with her legs wrapped around his neck; finally, she saw only the night sky and celestial blue-white sparks. It felt as if they had opened a secret door to a place far above New York or Beijing or Sunshine Village, and she felt right at home.

After that, he moved into Zoe's bedroom. They giggled and fondled each other while they, together with Ming, imagined aloud, and William wrote code that would make their visions real. Somehow Ming's presence made it seem believable, as if she were the medium between the concrete world and the labyrinth expanse somewhere beyond.

Yet, there were possibilities that one member of their trio might imagine and the others disdain, or possibilities that two might embrace and stack against one. In the second week of May, just two days before Zoe was scheduled to leave for New York, Ming said Tom had told her that he and Han were cooking up a few elements of the Sunshine Village deal themselves. "Han wants to fire all the people who work for the company and make it all high tech."

"So what happens to Tang Fei?" Zoe asked.

"Could be the best thing for him, once he learns enlightenment," William told her.

"You're supposed to be a benevolent leader!"

"Why do we even have to worry about Tang Fei?" was Ming's contribution. "Why do we even have to go back to that damn village? At least Zoe gets to go to New York first! I'll never get to sit on a bench in Prospect Park and write poetry again."

"You can take a vacation before we go underground," William offered.

"Underground?" Zoe asked that with alarm. It wasn't a word he'd used before. .

He nodded. "I'll have to build a place for the computer system where no one can find us. The earth is pliable in Sunshine Village. I'll dig a bunker, and we'll spend most of our time down there, running things in secret. I can, uh, have someone who looks just like me running the company, all very low profile. Just for a few years by your mortal calculations."

"Whaaattt?" Ming apparently hadn't known about it either. "Bad enough that we have to be in the fucking village, but I was thinking that somehow we could turn it into a showplace for enlightenment, not just a hole in the ground. You're going to make me lose my mind!" Ming clapped her hand over her own mouth—much like the way her father was always slapping himself—and burst into tears. When Zoe tried to embrace her, Ming pushed her away and ran out of the apartment, slamming the door behind her.

Zoe and William spent the rest of a steamy afternoon wandering around coffee bars Ming liked, hoping to find her. Outside the sixth café, after three hours of fruitless searching, drizzle poured down upon them. They sought refuge in a gazebo in a park a few blocks away. In the adrenaline-fueled search for Ming, Zoe had said nothing more about her own horror, but in the gazebo, with drizzle turning to sweat-like rain, she said, "Did you think my orals were going to be some kind of vacation, and then we all go into hiding?"

He shrugged in a defeated way. "I somehow thought you'd come back with a thousand-year-old view of things."

A vaporous silence fell upon them. "Ming and I are mortals. We have just one shot at youth, as far as we can tell. We never thought we'd have to be martyrs to save the world."

He shrugged again.

She told him this could be the end of their plans, and they said nothing to each other as they walked back to the apartment under a cheap umbrella that he'd bought from a street vendor. That night William huddled over the computer while Zoe lay awake, wrapped in double quilts against frigid air conditioning.

When daylight came, Zoe rose in a mechanical way, went to the park, and practiced her kickboxing. William didn't look up from his work. She wandered for a while, thinking. When she came back, Ming was in the kitchen, making coffee. Her clothes were rumpled and her hair hung flat. "I was with Tom, but then he had to go home," she told Zoe. "It must be awful to be in a marriage where you feel stuck with each other."

The three of them sat together around the kitchen table.

"I was thinking about something," Zoe said. "I like Ming's idea that we make the village some kind of showplace. Why shouldn't the company we take over be the model for an enlightened company? Why don't we get out and be part of it? We could make it a place where people can come from all over the world and learn to transcend earthly problems with exercises in cultivating conduct. Do you think they could stand the crappy weather?"

Ming shook her head. "I was thinking about that all night too. Can't we set up a place somewhere with decent weather?"

"Maybe," said William, looking sideways at Zoe, "the weather will change. But if you're visible, you'll make enemies."

"We'll have a lot of people who love it," Zoe insisted. "A counterforce."

"Professor Engelhorn would like to know about it," Ming offered. "If we made Sunshine Village a showplace for human rights, he'd want to come and see it."

"This isn't entertainment for the enlightened, or a much-acclaimed new book for Professor Charles Engelhorn," William thundered. "It's a top secret experiment in evolution. If anyone dislikes anything about it and figures out that we're the ones behind it, we're finished."

And so, the next day he watched Zoe close her suitcase and prepare her carry-on, jammed with books to study for her orals during the flight home.

"If I have to do this by myself, you probably won't see me for many years," he told her. "I'm going to be awfully busy."

"Why don't you think about our way then?"

"You've always been bossy." His fiery eyes devoured her. "But if you marry one of your self-important academics or your rape-the-world MBA boyfriends and you have three kids, and if I come out from underground and decide I want companionship and live out this incarnation with someone else, just remember this is a short life in the grand scheme and we're going to be together again."

She had booked an open-ended return ticket because there was always the chance that they'd postpone the date for her orals or that Billie would beg her to stay. Now her plans were open-ended forever.

New York, when she arrived, felt small—cozy and suffocating at the same time. Spring dogwood bloomed on the side streets, and the pansies in window boxes were beginning to wilt in the early heat. Billie looked older than Zoe had expected, her back starting to curve, and new wrinkles evident in the pouches beneath her eyes.

Zoe called Jeff, who answered the phone with a rant about a gallery owner in Chelsea who had told him his work was groundbreaking and strikingly contextual, but hadn't called him back all week. She had dinners and lunches with old friends. Every conversation seemed to hold an undertone of hysteria, as if the world might blow up or her friends might strike gold, and the suspense was eating their hearts away. Her closest friends, including Jeff, found a moment to grow solemn and say "I hope you're okay about Danny." He was engaged to Liesel Morgan. It felt like an out-of-body experience to think of Danny. If Danny had a chip, it occurred to Zoe, he'd throw his finance career aside and write novels. She wished she could say that aloud.

Professor Engelhorn—not quite as tall as she remembered him— asked a million questions about Sunshine Village. Standing before his book-lined walls, he looked like the ruler of a fiefdom of only two hundred square feet. He was full of tales of department gossip. He mentioned a former student by the name of Andrew or Adam, who had run off to Dubai with two chapters written—ABD. All But Dissertation. It sounded like a condition treatable with psychotropic meds. This man who might be her father would be proud of her only if she aced her orals and completed her dissertation; that, Zoe understood with every reflex.

The day finally arrived, and Zoe sat in Professor Engelhorn's expansive office facing a committee of three gray-faced men, including Professor Engelhorn, and one prematurely gray-haired woman. She heard her own voice—like an actor playing at being a graduate student—describing the life of Goujian. She recited a brief introduction, a historical accounting familiar to everyone in the room, of the ancient monarch who was reduced to rags after a rival state conquered his, but all the while he waited until the time was right to resurrect his benevolent reign. Zoe acknowledged, in a voice she scarcely recognized as her own, her own agreement with the theory that Goujian's humiliating defeat and rise back to power were part of the very fabric of Maoist China.

"That theory has received a lot of popular adulation," Professor John Volk replied. "But you make this sound like such a literal interpretation. And how are you so sure it was Mao who believed that and not just some latter-day followers?"

"Mao told the revolutionary troops that they should remind themselves of Goujian sleeping on brushwood and tasting his own gall bladder, and that this was how they should know how much hardship one must endure in order to rise up and win."

"And how is one to determine that?" asked Professor Volk, raising his eyebrows in disbelief.

Zoe inhaled obligatory humiliation, because she couldn't tell them the full truth—that she'd heard the account from someone who'd watched it from a cloud in the heavens.

"Every single Chinese person or movement has been using that story for centuries, to define their particular tale of rising up from defeat and conquering their enemies," another professor chimed in. "It is the eastern tale of the meek inheriting the earth, is it not?"

Zoe reminded herself that she did know some things. "Mao was no exception, despite the fact that he thought he was ridding the world of old beliefs. You can start a revolution and claim everything is going to be different but really, how do you ever make things different unless you put a chip in everyone's brain that reconfigures their worldview?"

Two hours and innumerable questions later, they sent her out to tremble in a chair. After what seemed like eternity, though she saw it was actually just over forty minutes, Professor Engelhorn called her back in, and they told her she had passed.

That evening Zoe had many drinks with her friend Sara.

"You know, Volk and Engelhorn have hated each other for years," Sara told her. "I don't know if I should tell you this, but Volk told people that Engelhorn gave you the money to go to China—implying, of course, that he gave you special treatment for being a pretty female student. For Engelhorn's sake, you have to do a knock-their-socks-off dissertation. We like Englehorn, don't we? A lot more than that asshole Volk. Pity if an Engelhorn protégée doesn't come through. Don't look so scared. You're gonna do it."

Zoe had three years to finish her dissertation.

I'll start first thing in the morning, she resolved. She lay on her bed in the little room that had been her sanctum for so long, in the place that was home as long as they didn't get evicted. Every one of her belongings had its place. The top shelf of the bookcase held a box with faded *qi gong* certificates; the bottom, dusty Mandarin textbooks and yellowed novels about girls who loved their horses. A ladybug crawled across the headboard. "Show your man face or get out," Zoe commanded, but it took no notice.

The next morning, so early the campus was nearly empty, she went down to the fourth level sub-basement of Butler Library, and began reading through a collection of Lin Biao papers. After hours of scrawling notes about plenary sessions on the production of military equipment, her shoulders ached, and she leaned back, closing her eyes and stretching her arms and legs.

"Zoe…." Someone was whispering her name.

She opened her eyes and there was William. She leaped up to embrace him, feverishly pressing her lips to his. He tasted like a plum that wasn't quite ripe.

Then he pushed her an inch away. "You're a beautiful woman. The goddess of academia." His voice was as resonant as a symphony, and his eyes were a flickering fire. Zoe felt warm, imagining she could be desirable even in her old jeans and sneakers, her hair in a careless ponytail. "But I promised I'd be an upstanding gentleman. Let's go for a walk, shall we?"

It was early afternoon and the campus was full of playful sunshine. William stared at two giggly undergrads welcoming spring in skimpy T-shirts and miniskirts. Something struck Zoe.

"You're not William. You're one of his copies."

He giggled in a sheepish and most un-William-like way. "I've been hibernating hundreds of years, but the master called me up because he often needs to be in at least two places at once." His eyes drifted to another co-ed with long legs. "The master knew you would see the difference."

"You call him 'master'?" Zoe tried not to laugh.

"I'm my own man. It's not nice to make fun of me," William-copy protested.

"Well, if you are your own man, you'll need your own name. I'll call you Sun Two."

"Whatever. I have a message for you. The master wants to talk to you but doesn't want to leave messages on that talking machine in case they are intercepted. He says, 'I love you. Please come back. I can't do it without you and Ming. We'll do it your way, and I'll make it work. The company has already burned through their New Icarus loan, and the takeover is coming the first week in July, so we have to make haste.'"

There is, she thought, a great universe beyond these old bricks.

Chapter Ten

In early July of that year, close observers of private equity placements—a rarified breed attuned to fleeting movements in the bush—could spot a short piece of business news on the Chinese internet. New Icarus Capital had bought the controlling interest in a state-owned enterprise in Sichuan province, which they were renaming Sunshine Group, paying an unspecified sum. Insiders knew the word "unspecified" meant a deal no bigger than a sparrow's footprint.

What business insiders didn't know was that an immortal man had pulled a hair from his head, shouted, "Change!" and produced three copies of himself. For five months, three identical men in hardhats spent their nights digging deep underground, eighteen feet below the forest floor. Above this subterranean cavity, they built a spacious house with cedar siding and picture windows facing north, south, east, and west.

A man from some faraway place beyond Beijing—from the distant land known as the global economy, the land where everyone spoke the language of money—came to live in the house. This man closely supervised Tang Fei's day-to-day tasks, and the villagers knew that more would soon come in his wake.

Zoe and Ming arrived in mid-summer, and lived in the guest quarters of the new house. For Zoe it wasn't so much a matter of keeping up appearances as that William Sun was so busy he was rarely at home. The house had a fine library, and among the books was a leather-bound edition of the Mahayana Sutras. Behind the book of sutras was a button that transformed one wall panel into an open door. Through the door, thirty steep steps led to an inclined walkway—also accessible via a secret trapdoor in the woods. The incline terminated at a metal door that had a keypad, and it took a highly classified code of seven numbers to open.

On the other side of the door was a climate-controlled room with a wall of thirty-one computer screens, one for each province and administrative region on mainland China. Brightly colored numbers from 0001 to digits in the hundreds of thousands, scrolled in a continuous loop across the screens. Occasionally a number blinked, which required a vigilant attendant to zap that number with a remote dose of the New China program. The nanochip was programmed to detect brain waves with particular patterns, patterns of thoughts such as, *But wait, I'm the top dog, and my money is more fun if I know the masses envy it.* With a click of the mouse, the New China program could infiltrate the brain with a very different message. The program wasn't active yet, but the three conspirators were almost ready.

To ensure the safety of Sunshine Village, Ming, William, and Zoe had to get rid of the thugs and thwart the industry that had been their livelihood—opium. The forest on the far side of the Tuo River hid acres and acres of poppies and kept the thugs, the police, and even the former directors of the Sunshine Village Silicon Works in working capital. A man of seventy-two transformations could, as a bird, inspect the farms and forest and watch transactions behind old cement walls.

"Opium was initially used as a mild sedative," Zoe said.

"And then it turned people into vegetable brains." William pounded the table with his fist, his eyes molten gold. "Peasants accepted their plight, and emperors ignored everything while they lolled about indulging their appetites. No drugs in the New China."

"I used to like to smoke weed with Jeff in college," Zoe admitted.

"My love, I hope you've given up your childish inclinations. In New China we get high on knowledge, on contemplating the questions and knowing there are no answers. Do you recall the time we spent in the first palace built in the clouds? It reached to infinity itself. We visited, you and I, along with our friend Confucius. The owner offered us white powder from crystal bowls, fragrant little bricks from jade pipes, and the pièce de résistance: A Billion Heavens, a nectar shot from a syringe. We floated in a state of happy delirium from one day to the next. But then the owner informed us that we owed rent for the time we had occupied his house, and it turned out that fifty years had gone by. We started working, with part of our proceeds paying off our debt, forever after. But poor Confucius took to begging to obtain his next fix."

Zoe half-remembered a dream she'd had of a wise old sage, in beard and sackcloth, wandering through a world that seemed to have no floor. "Nonny nonpareil, ai ai ai…" the sage had muttered. He'd squatted down and poked his ass, then rubbed his face with yellow shit. This is what happens to philosophers who can't pay their rent, Zoe had reflected in her dream.

"We need clear minds, and drugs filter everything through a sense of self-absorption," William went on. "You can fixate on a pretty flower garden but not the people who weed and water them. You might hear musical notes you didn't know existed before, but you don't see the lady at the piano pouring her heartbreak into the tune."

⌘

Phase One of the program was scheduled to roll out in November. That month, on a Thursday, as the sun rose above the lead horizon of Beijing, Han Cheng woke up with a hammer pounding his head and a strange sense that his bedroom belonged to someone else. He was wearing the silk pajamas he'd put on the night before and had been sleeping beneath his satin duvet. His thermostat was set to frigid, as always—he liked the elegance of an indoor chill. All seemed to be as it should. But he'd had a bizarre dream. A doctor had stuck an otoscope in his ear, and Han had said, "I have a new parquet floor but below it is sludge."

His wife, Wu Xia, had already fluffed her pillow, and he could smell gunpowder tea brewing. Han stood in the kitchen doorway and watched Wu Xia for a moment. She was dressed, her blouse buttoned to her throat. She used to have long hair, he recalled; she had chopped it off two days after their wedding. She had a fine neck, though, as supple as young bamboo. He started to reach over and kiss her neck.

"It's McDonald's day," Wu Xia said, and glided just out of his grasp.

My wife doesn't like me. The thought blew into Han's mind and lodged itself like a tumor.

Every Tuesday and Thursday Han would take his son to McDonald's on the way to school. That morning Han sat, as usual, in a plastic chair and watched Bo Fu sink his plump little face into breakfast, his world a warm gooey Mount Everest of dough, melted cheese, ham, and eggs. Han tossed a ball of Egg McMuffin wrapping from one hand to another. The hammer beat upon his head again—the lights, that had to be it, fluorescent pinpricks that seemed designed for an inquisition.

"Can we buy my new bike this weekend?" asked the boy, his lips glistening with oil. "I'll have my own money."

The first grade entrepreneurial fair was tomorrow, and Bo Fu was sure he was going to sell the model airplane he'd made.

Han's heart always grew a little larger when he sat in the car and watched his son stride into the schoolyard, his Mickey Mouse backpack swaying side to side. Today, four boys began jumping around him and they ran off in a flock of five. The other children saw his son as a boy worth playing with. And why not—the child arrived at school in his father's shiny new Lexus, the one Han had bought after the Sunshine deal. A gleaming champagne exterior with ivory leather seats. Han reached to turn on the fan and hit the emergency light instead. Where was that button he used every day?

As usual, he arrived in the office before anyone else. The two assistants usually arrived around a quarter to nine, scurrying to their desks in the knowledge that Han was watching. Tom would likely stumble in after nine-thirty looking as if he'd barely had time to rinse the red from his eyes, and he'd say, "Oh, what a beautiful morning!" in English to the assistants and make them laugh. Fanny and Tian liked Tom and were afraid of Han. Han was aware of how they ceased their chatter and sat rigid like soldiers whenever he appeared in the front office.

Fanny was going to be late today. Han knew from experience

that she might not arrive until lunchtime, with a million excuses about taking her child to the clinic again. Her little girl had Down syndrome; the photo on her desk of the defective toddler couldn't possibly be good for the company image, but Han knew everyone would think less of him if he said anything. Fanny kept the photo in a most unprofessional-looking pink-and-white porcelain frame with a heart in the upper left-hand corner. Han had been looking for an excuse to let Fanny go just so that he wouldn't have to look at the awful picture, but she still owed them money from advances on her paycheck, approved by Tom. People who couldn't afford to take care of life's curveballs should think twice before having children, though Han knew better than to say that aloud too.

He knew from Harvard Business School that the market was an elegant machine, the way it could self-correct over-valued companies and goods and labor. And Han had earned his right to elegant things. The old planned economy had nearly starved him to death, but the free market didn't hold people back just because their parents had once been assigned to a forgotten village. The market would forgive Fanny too, if she tried a little; if her labors were worth more than her paycheck, the market would find her and plunk her into a job that paid accordingly.

Fanny's desk and the bothersome photograph were right in Han's line of vision. He thought of getting up and moving the picture a few inches, but his legs wouldn't cooperate. He'd read a magazine article recently about an equation that didn't fit; Nobel prize winning-minds had studied it and found there was no answer, 2 plus 2 to the power of 800 divided by XYZ and something else was plagued by a random N-cubed that canceled out any solution that the mathematical geniuses of the world came up with. Han's life had always added up, but this morning he had a strange sensation that if anyone asked him the simplest question—"where is your car parked?" for instance—a million answers would tumble through his head, and not one would be correct. He knew, though it seemed like a disconnected piece of knowledge, that the car was in the usual place, and the keys were in his jacket pocket—one brass key, one steel, shiny little instruments

142

of torture. Why had he just thought that? Han felt his forehead and figured he must be coming down with the flu.

His computer hit him with yellow lights. In the other hemisphere the Nasdaq had been down at the closing bell, which was less than helpful when he was in the midst of taking several of his companies to their initial public offering. He noticed Fanny arriving, carrying her stockiness like a burden. She sighed with the effort of heaving herself into her chair and rummaged through her cheap canvas handbag. Pulling out a small mirror, Fanny applied lipstick. She wanted to look good for Tom, Han realized, and had a sudden hollow feeling, not unlike what he'd experienced in his childhood when he had little more than a cup of thrice-boiled rice to sustain him from morning to dusk. He watched Fanny put away her lipstick. Then her finger traced her daughter's head in that offending photograph. Good heavens, she wore lipstick for a man who was married and she loved a child who would grow up to be more of an ungainly pet than a daughter.

Han stared at the photos on his office wall and wondered how it felt to look at a fragment of the world and frame it with your eye, capturing the depth, shadows, and texture. *My wife doesn't like me. My sister and my office assistants don't like me.* Han was composing a mental list of others who didn't like him when a rat-tat-tat at his door interrupted his dismal litany. Tom appeared in a rumpled sweater, khaki pants, and moccasins. His face was flushed and sweaty and he hadn't bothered to shave.

"I don't give a flying fuck what time it is," said Tom. "I'm hungover and feeling too good to crunch numbers. I thought about renting a paddleboat, or walking under those dirty willow trees, even though the pollution is yellow today. Then, would you believe, I missed you. You're a competitive son of a bitch but you're my whole world five days a week and sometimes six or seven. And Tian and Fanny. And Fanny's developmentally disabled child that we don't care one hoot about because her mother is for all practical purposes our servant. So, I thought it a fine day to come and tell you all that we shouldn't be sitting at our desks like automatons. Let's take the girls out to a lavish lunch and keep the wine flowing and talk about the meaning of life."

With a feral glint in his eye, Tom called to Fanny, "Make a lunch reservation. For four."

Han found his knees shaking at the thought. "The girls will have more fun with you," he told Tom. "I'm not feeling well."

After everyone else bounded out, Han found himself still unable to concentrate and decided a walk would do him good. The raucous cacophony of pile drivers, drills, and sirens seemed a plot intended to drive him mad. Before, every thud of hammer had sung with the promise of fifty percent growth, a reminder of capital he had invested in companies that would inhabit those buildings.

Han passed the noodle stand his office assistants frequented for lunch. Steam rose from a giant cauldron in the window, and a tired line of people waited inside for their watery bowls. The place smelled like poverty.

Han wondered if Fanny had ever imagined owning her own company or writing a book or doing much of anything besides earning her paycheck. He thought it unlikely—why would she bother? People were like goldfish, growing only as big as the waters they inhabited. A few weeks before he had heard Tian confiding in Fanny; she had had to use her lunch money to cover a cab fare to the hospital to visit her sick mother, and was resigned, therefore, to going hungry that day. Han had slammed his door shut. He had been afraid of her hunger, he realized now.

Han sat on a park bench beside a stagnant pond. By the time he rose to his feet again, an evening mist had begun to fall. He walked to his parked car and somehow found his way to his building and his apartment on the twenty-seventh floor—an extra expense and a highly coveted location, with two and seven signifying "double heaven." Inside, the apartment was dark and airless. He listened for the sound of Bo Fu, giggling and shouting and happy to see him. But there was only silence.

⌘

"Call it Zeitgeist. You know, we ought to have a free-trading World Untranslatable Words Association." William Sun was excited and a bit out of breath, having just sprinted through the door of the

144

underground bunker. He seated himself before the wall of thirty-one computer screens.

"Don't digress," Zoe chided. "What about Han?"

"Han is having an existential crisis. It's an epidemic. Men in suits sitting around on park benches. After Han left for work, Wu Xia called an old school friend and asked if she could come stay awhile, so she could 'find herself.' Bo Fu is with your parents, Ming."

"Maybe it was too much to start," said Ming, frowning.

William gave her an "I'm innocent" look. "Hey, I didn't give the wives chips. I just whispered to them in the night—things like, 'You know you can't stand your husband; if the money didn't matter, would you stay?' The rest is up to them. I'd say Phase One has been a great success. Tomorrow morning, we zap again."

⌘

Three mornings later, Han awoke in the same chair where he'd fallen asleep to television chatter every night since his wife had left him. Wiping sleep from his eyes, Han watched a Cantonese-speaking reporter from Hong Kong satellite television, with Chinese character subtitles for Mandarin speakers. The reporter—declaring he was "on the trail of strange goings-on in China"—was interviewing the CEO of a manufacturing company.

"My company's balance sheet is a pack of lies," the CEO declared. "We get our stock to artificially rise based on how much we think we should be making, and I earn a fortune by laying people off to keep our cash reserves up. I'm laying myself off. I'd like to spend some time fishing if I can find a lake that my company hasn't destroyed with chemical spills."

A shock wave hit Han and he jerked upright. Something was missing and he realized it was his headache. For the first time in four days his head wasn't pounding. He tried to remember what he usually did at this hour. Of course, his office, his work. *I work because in business school I learned to recognize where the soil was conducive to making money grow.* And that was all he knew how to do, Han realized—make money grow.

Something else was pounding through his head. He must, he thought, find a café. The kind of place that barely existed in Beijing, where he could sit for hours and ask other people—the waiters, passersby, anyone—what they thought. Thought about what? Life, presumably. Strangely enough, he found a Parisian-style café two blocks away, with sidewalk tables and a wall of wine bottles. He sat down and noticed a man with an expensive haircut, like his own, sitting idly at the next table. The man turned to him.

"What do you think?" the man asked.

"Everything is finite," Han heard himself saying. "Except knowledge. But what is knowledge?" Something fluttered in his heart, like a caterpillar sprouting wings. "Who am I? Who are you? Is there an 'us' and a 'them'?" The more questions he pondered, the freer he felt.

The other man nodded and moved to seat himself at Han's table. "I trade oil and, in the process, drive up prices so that many people can't afford to heat their homes. What if I put my money into some kind of collective account that poor people can tap into in order to mitigate their heating costs?" The two of them sat in animated conversation until the sun dipped low in a polluted orange sky.

The next day Han decided he might actually enjoy some time in the office. Tian and Fanny told him that Tom had been absent for several days, but he'd left a note. *My wife has left me. She said I bore her. And you know, I really am boring. It's because I'm bored. I'm going to get my commercial pilot's license. Pilots make starvation wages but so be it. New Icarus Capital is all yours, my friend. I'm going to fly to Sunshine Village and visit Ming—don't shoot me! We tried to hide it but we're fond of each other. Don't worry. Tom.*

Han slumped on the edge of Fanny's desk. "Let's go shopping," he said, suddenly. "I saw a silver frame that would look great with your daughter's portrait. My gift."

That evening Han went back to the Parisian café, where he sat with a group of six new friends. Four of them had wives who had walked out. One such wife had left a note. *I married you just for your money. But I can't even stand the smell of you.* Another had told her husband, "You beat me down. Every time I say something, you act like I'm stupid."

The men acknowledged that they hadn't been perfect husbands, looked embarrassed, and began talking of business.

"What if stores charged a sliding rate for their goods?" Han asked his companions. "What if wealthy customers paid more for whatever they needed, and people who made less paid less? Nobody would have to buy cheap crap and nobody would have to go without lunch."

⌘

Throughout the cities of Beijing, Guangzhou, and Shanghai, men congregated—occupying tables for seven—in new cafés that had checkered tablecloths and wine lists priced for a clientele in search of something to show for its money.

"We are seven," observed an economic minister in Beijing. "Seven means lessons learned through loss. You know, the Seven Immortals of the Bamboo Grove used to say that the ruler doesn't take action, but rather just employs ministers who manage the affairs. The ax can cut the tree in the hands of someone skilled. People can live good lives if we just make the capital available."

"I feel like I've gone through my life with a wallet on top of my shoulders, not a head," said the head of a manufacturing conglomerate in Shanghai.

"Your bank account is just a pile of numbers," said the CEO of an investment bank. "Maybe that should be a slogan for something we call the New China."

"Better work on that," said one of the bank CEO's companions. "If we want words to live by, we should look to people who're in the business of writing and thinking."

"People who create words or music or art out of nothing, people who devote themselves to learning. If we don't listen to them, we're nothing but savages."

All over China, men were uttering similar words at that moment.

"Confucius and Socrates left us a master plan for civilization," Han interjected one animated night. "We still have people who can show us the way—I hear songs that lift my mood, and someone

147

wrote those songs, and someone played them. They could do a lot more if their families didn't force them to go to business school. Why do the people who do the *real* thinking make so much less money than I do?"

Chapter Eleven

It was like directing a life-sized theater. "The theater of benevolent madness," Zoe said, perched on the sofa next to William as they watched the premier of China on nationwide television. The premier read a classical Chinese poem about man's inherent wish to be free, then declared that the reigning Politburo had been in power long enough. In two years' time, general elections would be held to choose a prime minister and Parliament.

"Two years," he said, "should give political hopefuls time to prepare their campaigns, and if Politburo members wanted to run for office, they would have to answer henceforth to the populace." The premier stated that the government had recruited a group of psychologists, sociologists, mathematicians, and statisticians to work on calculating the Gross Domestic Happiness Index. He promised tax breaks to any foreign or domestic company that contributed to the happiness of its employees and that of the surrounding community.

The CEO of a major manufacturing company proclaimed that he was going to install a spa, tennis courts, and coffee bar for his sweatshop workers; he would cut their workweek to thirty hours, not so he could pay them less but so they'd have time to go to extension classes at the nearby university and take weekend river rafting trips.

In the days that followed, the leaders of China's banking industry called a news conference of their own and announced that they had devised a new system. The wealth that sat idle in bank accounts of the elite would be turned over to private sector-run offices that would disburse the funds to the poor. The elite would benefit from a return more valuable than money—they would have the privilege of adopting communities.

All over China, bulldozers demolished flimsy buildings and erected in their place glass towers and Beaux-Arts-style brick edifices. The ancient *hutongs* that remained in urban alleyways got new plumbing and fresh coats of plaster and paint; in courtyards, landscape contractors planted willow saplings and hydrangea bushes. Crews of builders and plumbers descended upon the sod huts behind the rice paddies in Sunshine Village and the sorghum fields up north, enlisting the peasants to help rebuild their own houses. The peasants hammered and painted and earned ownership by the sweat of their brows. Over mud floors they laid mosaic tiles or lacquered pine. Exteriors bloomed into pastel stucco, and buried pipes snaked up to immaculate new bathrooms and community spas where a hard day in the fields might end with a soak in a hot tub and a half-hour of acupressure.

Sunshine Village bore a new sign thanking its designated patron, the CEO of an investment bank that specialized in financing pharmaceutical and medical technology companies—a man known as number 2099 to Ming, Zoe, and William.

"Technology is gradually eliminating opportunity for the working class," said one rich banker on television. "While building projects create jobs, when the building is done, what will the workforce do? Stay home and get depressed? Lose their homes and live on the street? I'm putting my money into adult schools so that these workers can learn useful skills beyond building houses and cleaning toilets."

Several months into the renaissance that the world called the New China, a few billionaires thought to invite members of their adopted neighborhoods on weekend sailing trips or holidays at their villas. They hid away their fine art and covered brocade chairs with canvas, expecting a swarm with gamy, accusing eyes and swift hands. But by then the New China had become a temple to the gods of shopping. Lavender-scented boutiques sold fine clothes and cosmetics on every corner; spas and salons kept the citizenry manicured and coiffed and provided consultations on poise and comportment.

Viewers all over the country saw television and internet advertisements designed to help them find their places in the New China. One such video depicted a young, hard-working couple taking a night class in comparative literature, smiling at each other with perfect teeth—thanks to the services of a cosmetic dentistry center that was opening franchises across the country. The central message, across all advertising platforms and products, was that New China had invited you to its dinner party, and in return, you owe it to your neighbors and your patrons to be charming and astute company. Welders, peasants, and penniless writers willingly obliged; they frequented the boutiques and salons, alongside wives of CEOs and soon-to-be ex-wives of CEOs. At the cash register each customer held up their thumb to a scanner. With this biometric identification, any merchant or street vendor would be paid via the customer's bank account commensurate with that person's ability to pay. Every doctor and dentist's office, every school, every of-the-moment nightclub could scan the customer's data from a thumbprint. A pair of shoes might cost fifteen dollars to a shop assistant who earned an annual income of $30,000 while the same pair of shoes would cost five hundred dollars to the wife of a millionaire.

Economic analysts studied the new patterns and found that nearly half a billion people bought something new every day. Fashions changed from month to month. Shopping kept the economy pumped up as if it were running an iron man decathlon and everyone discarded last month's trendy must-haves. But the new phenomenon, which the power brokers called universal gentrification, didn't turn New China into a landfill of plastic and leather and porcelain. Hundreds of aspiring entrepreneurs, benefiting from the stimulus of night classes in every avenue of inquiry, developed innumerable recycling stations. Old porcelain was ground back into soil and re-molded; electronic parts were melted down and reborn as wiring for thumb-scanners; silk dresses were unraveled and woven into vibrant new fashion statements.

Sunshine Village, alive with buzz saws and bricklaying and the smells of fresh paint and lumber, boasted a new square along Market Street. By the end of Year One of the New China, artists and musicians from as far away as South America and the hip Grünerløkka district of Oslo began to hear of an enlightened little town tucked away in the green hills of Sichuan—a place where wondering souls could rise at dawn to contemplate the still river and the quiet sky.

151

Curiously, the weather had also undergone a dramatic change. The dome of clouds just evaporated one day. Rain still arrived in bracing little showers, mostly in the night, and just enough to paint the trees and the rice fields with fragrant chlorophyll. By day, the sun would smile upon the village like a father lavishing gifts upon his only child. It was as if the Monkey King and Zenia had finally arrived at their happily ever after, the villagers told one another, shaking their heads in wonder.

As for Ming—whether it was the devil tuning her strings or something else entirely—she was publishing stories and getting more and more followers every day. "It has to be because I have so many hours free from worry," Ming declared. Zoe agreed. They had empirical evidence, after all. A number of mathematicians in the New China were eager to turn their particular talents to equations that would help shed light on the human condition.

One such scientist had performed an assessment for Ming and found that by not having to worry about money, she had cleared a space in her mind of six hours, forty-seven minutes, and twenty-three and a half seconds a day on average over her actuarially-estimated lifetime. Those newly acquired hours and minutes allowed Ming more time to write—to discard and write something better, but also to read the works of greater intellectual minds. She deleted all the dirty little stories she'd thrown up on her blog just to shock her parents, or because she'd thought it was the route to fame.

Now, dozens of online literary magazines were cropping up in New China and accepting Ming's work. Literary sites devoted to critiquing literary sites began to post reviews of her stories, praising them as "quixotic and rambling, not unlike life itself," and "bursting with random associations that evoke an incurable darkness just below the surface."

Many of Ming's new stories revolved around Sunshine Village, describing a place where characters rose early each day and danced along the riverbank, under the cadence of a blazing sunrise; or spent their evenings drinking fine wine with men and women who guessed at the emotion behind each note in a Beethoven concerto; or sketched miniature masterpieces on cocktail napkins. Ming's stories depicted an ideal, yet they also became a map for visitors to follow.

Even William Kingsley Sun, as CEO of The Sunshine Group, though he still said it would have been better to operate like a Third Front secret site, found himself inadvertently becoming a tourist attraction. A reporter who was writing a story about 2099 and village sponsorship traveled to Sunshine Village and discovered William to be so extraordinarily photogenic and articulate that he featured him in a video podcast.

"If capital were a fresh kill—a wild horse you'd speared and roasted—you could share only so much," William said in the video. "But the world where you buy with currency and credit, it's all just notes that designate a business' worth. We have a division called Sunshine Finance. We provide a loan to a woman who wants to open a boutique on Main Street, which she uses to buy the space, hire carpenters, and stock up on inventory. Customers come and she earns the money back—or if customers don't come and the store fails, either she sells her inventory to be recycled, or she finds new customers over the internet. She uses that money to try another product—perhaps a shoe boutique. If the shoes sell well, she repays Sunshine Finance. We regain our investment eventually, because we allow people to fail; that is, they keep trying until they succeed. Money is like a bamboo shoot—a hardy grass that can grow everywhere if you just let it spread."

Sometimes in the bunker when no numbers blinked, Zoe would catch William replaying his podcast video, and he'd ask her if she thought he should have changed his enunciation here, or looked directly into the camera there. But the video circulated, and soon a group of business leaders came to tour the company's premises, noting the airy laboratory space, the pavilions where the staff met for gourmet lunches and yoga classes, and the weekly meetings at which CEO and janitor alike were encouraged to voice ideas. William found himself on the cover of a glossy magazine with "the newest celebrity CEO" emblazoned underneath.

A private charter flight with seats for eight passengers—a Cessna

Grand Caravan with a yellow nose cone and a logo that looked like the sun—departed from Chengdu every Monday, Wednesday, and Friday at noon. The captain would come out and introduce himself before takeoff. "Good morning, ladies and gentlemen. I'm Tom Wendall, and I'll be flying you into the future of civilization," he'd say. He was a doughy man but he moved lightly, as if he'd shed all that burdened him.

Lulu Pang, the town's director of tourism, often met visitors at the airstrip. "Welcome to Sunshine Village!" she'd say in a voice as rich as an aria. Her bouncy hairdo and even her carriage suggested a former frumpiness that was getting worked away at a gym. She'd lead the guests in a walking tour through grassy pathways, magpies whistling above. A dozen plump-cheeked children with brightly colored clothes would skip up, offering mesh bags full of peaches, bananas, plum blossoms, and lilies. At the village square, Lulu would point out the library, a hexagon of glass panes where visitors could borrow, for two weeks at a time, books and databases, jewels, and fine art. The multimillionaires of China put some of their own treasures on loan, she'd explain, because, after all, if the elite of society found beautiful things soothing to the soul, surely others would too.

The other building, with an imperial roof and a marble entryway flanked by Chinese lions, was the casino. Here, croupiers were stationed behind every table, and visitors could press buttons on a massive board to see a list of stocks on the Chinese exchanges, or click on one and check its share price.

In the village square, fragrant with jasmine blossoms and freshly sawed lumber, visitors and residents gathered each afternoon in the Nirvana Café, enjoying the local jasmine tea and jasmine beer while musicians played flutes and harps. Main Street bustled with renovation, but already it was a temple to enterprise with boutiques springing up like mushrooms, courtesy of Sunshine Finance loans. Antique shops provided wares with dust enough to promise customers the sport of digging through grit to find a treasure; a Chinese apothecary sold one-hundred-and-fifty-year-old curio cabinets, and designer shoes nestled like *objets d'art* on black velvet in the elegant shop across the street. Up the hill, a gourmet market was growing larger by the day, selling artful arrangements of locally made rice pastries and imported dragonfruits, peaches, and lychees.

Some of the visitors stayed, teaching the university extension classes held nightly—with free tuition for all—at the sprawling new high school campus. The new state-of-the-art hospital, with specialty units in dentistry and genetic research, drew doctors from all over the world. Chefs arrived via Tom Wendall's Cessna, too, and worked in the village dining pavilions that made every meal a social occasion, and freed wives from the necessity of having to rush home to cook every night.

Three hours away by car was a New China prison, a complex of buildings that looked like a community college campus, except for the electric perimeter fence. The prisoners—former policemen and the thugs who'd worked for them—were required to spend their morning hours at a recycling plant, and their afternoon hours in classrooms.

Inevitably, the village patron, 2099, announced he was going to come and see the paradise that his money had made possible. Zoe and William met 2099 and his wife at the airstrip.

The village patron was blessed with smooth, glossy skin and hair—as if devoted attendants scrubbed him with rare oils and coiffed his eyebrows daily. Still, there was something unsettled about his eyes and the way he gestured. He was forty-three years old, Zoe knew, and had grown up in Beijing, the son of a high-ranking government official. His wife, who was slender, wore her hair in a globe-sized bun on top of her head. It wasn't an in-fashion hairstyle, but it suited her.

"What are the plans for construction across the river?" 2099 asked, referring to an announcement that a consortium of hotel developers had just released. He was looking pointedly at William.

"It's going to be an eco-resort," Zoe chimed in. She was the one who'd signed off on the plan, after all. "Nestled in the trees with a warm spring that will feed into a natural bathing pool."

As if he hadn't even heard Zoe, 2099 said to William, "There is so much traffic in this town; you will need a bigger airport."

"I don't like our patron," Zoe told William after 2099 was gone. "He's a fucking sexist, for one thing."

"Don't worry about him. The program will bring out his better instincts over time."

The two of them argued that night. "Sunshine Village is like a toy for him, and someday he'll want another toy," Zoe said.

"You, my darling, were born jaded. When you ran the Nirvana Admissions Committee, it was such a select club that, on one occasion, three years went by when no one got in."

"I don't remember that. But I do remember the lessons New York taught me. I had a ring of keys—a big key to the front door of our building, a little key to the mailbox, and two keys for the apartment door. We all knew how to hold the key ring after dark, with the biggest key sticking out between two fingers. Brass knuckles to keep the scoundrels at bay. We had to constantly look around and behind." Even in the now-magical habitat of Sunshine Village, Zoe was still looking behind her. "I know you think this program can instill empathy and compromise, but at the bottom of it all, humans are beasts like any other, and subject to instincts that cannot ultimately be tamed," she told William.

Her lover disagreed; he was insistent that any dissent that might arise within New China was a great opportunity. "A vaccine that makes our systems of reason stronger," he would say.

And soon enough Tang Fei provided them with an opportunity to test their tolerance. Ming, Zoe, and William had agreed that sending Tang to prison for his sideline opium dealing wasn't in keeping with the spirit of New China, so they gave him a chance to earn an honest living as a corporate sales director for the company's nanochips. He traveled around the country with a vial of local soil and a sample chip.

One day in March, in Year Two of the New China, Tang Fei told the three of them he'd met a manufacturer who wanted to build a smart car facility using the nanochip technology in Sunshine Village.

"We're not a manufacturing town," Ming protested. "Sunshine Village is about serenity and enlightenment."

"What about opportunities for the rest of us? We're not all poets or philosophers, you know." Tang Fei glared at her.

William's eyes, though, glowed like sunshine warming the room. "Successful companies thrive on ideas from all quarters," he said. "Bring these manufacturers here for a meeting. We'll have to do a feasibility study and so will they."

Tang Fei left satisfied.

"I don't believe in smart cars," William told Ming and Zoe when the door was safely closed. "People shouldn't be able to go farther than they can drive themselves; but don't worry, these manufacturers will come to Sunshine Village and they'll see that it's just too small."

A few days later, the CEO of the smart car company called and informed William that they had decided to move operations to Guangzhou, where there was already a large base of labor and suppliers.

Tang Fei was livid. "You didn't even try to persuade him!"

"Too much industry would destroy tourism. People are coming here to enjoy all the pleasantries that New China can offer in a small village environment," William said, sounding almost meditative.

"You don't want competition, you mean?" Tang Fei thundered as he stormed out of the office.

"I've decided it's okay to fire him," Zoe said.

"You don't fire people for disagreeing with you," William told her with confident equanimity.

"I want to believe that," said Ming.

⌘

From the old world of New York and academia, Professor Engelhorn emailed Zoe several times a month. His messages grew progressively less curious about how she was coming with her dissertation, and more inquisitive about this miraculous New China and what it was like to be there. He was planning to take a sabbatical the following spring so that he could come to China and write a book about what was going on. It always took Zoe a while to answer his messages. She knew it was a matter of guilt. The reference books that were supposed to be the backbone of her dissertation sat neglected in her apartment. Yes, Zoe now had an apartment of her own—because as it turned out, it seemed important to have her own space. The books got a dusting every week when the household maintenance expert, previously known as a maid, came. The countdown hovered; there was just a little over a year left. Zoe had completed an outline and the first chapter. It was a great misfortune that old Mr. Pang had died while the triumvirate had been plotting things in Beijing; one of her best oral histories gone.

What she really wanted to do was write to Professor Engelhorn and say, "Don't chase false theories. I have all the secrets!" She told Ming, and they laughed together until they both almost cried, knowing they were going to have to bottle in this smug triumph for the rest of their lives.

Otherwise, Zoe's days and nights were filled with bunker duty, and her job as co-director of Sunshine Finance, and, in spite of the New China and its limitless opportunities, people to save. Jing Yin, especially. Her father, Kwan Bai Li, had presented a thoughtful business plan to Sunshine Finance, and now he owned the gourmet market on the hill. An awning with the name Kwan Market in gold characters sheltered a dozen market stalls. The Kwan family operated one stall, selling steamed rice flour buns stuffed with bean paste and egg custard, and turned a profit on renting the remaining spaces.

When international visitors started discovering his market, Kwan Bai Li discarded his Chinese name and renamed himself Bradley Kwan. A gaunt man, he had a face that was elongated like tea stalks drying in the sun. His eyes could penetrate when he looked at you, as if you alone could understand the pain he'd been through.

"You could be on television," Zoe had remarked to him once, though it was his daughter she really wanted to groom. Jing Yin had turned fifteen and was developing a homespun kind of beauty. The problem was that her father was still keeping her out of school, insisting she work in the market stall because her mother, Yu Li, was ashamed to go out, lest people see her cloudy eye.

"You must put aside all this useless philosophy you are learning at school and help the family in the real world," Zoe heard Bradley tell Jing Yin on more than one occasion.

"Mama comes from a noble family," Jing Yin confided to Zoe. The little cousin, who had died in a pile of his own diarrhea before Zoe came back, was the last of the noble stock, she said. "Mama's family never wanted her to marry my father. They said he was a 'wild wolf,' so I must be a half wolf."

"Then be fierce," Zoe counseled.

In the spring of Year Two of the New China, Zoe had a plan for the girl. She visited the Kwan family home, now freshly painted, with a new addition and terrazzo tiles on the former dirt floor. A new sofa with fat red cushions sat across from a flat-screen television that covered the opposite wall and stayed on even when no one was watching. Smoke wafted from a small brass incense burner, and even through the fragrance, Zoe thought she could detect a spectral stink of diarrhea.

"Do you know who Larissa Lee is?" Zoe asked Jing Yin. Subway stations and billboards all over the world featured the shapely movie star in her sequined tunics, leaping into hidden lairs and punching out villains just before they blew up the world. Recently, though, Larissa Lee had been seeking to show the world her serious side. Talk show audiences were familiar with her life story of growing up with a drug-addled mother in Harlem and seeing her father only once before he died in prison. Audiences were also familiar with the star's dual campaigns to feed the hungry and discover enlightenment.

"Larissa Lee is going to come here to make a documentary about New China. I want you to be in it," Zoe said.

Jing Yin hung her head. "My father wouldn't like it."

"But would you like to do it?"

The girl's face lit up enough that the answer was clear. In the next couple of weeks Zoe worked on Bradley Kwan, flattering him with a made-up story that Larissa Lee was going to shoot footage of Kwan Market and Jing Yin would be the spokesmodel for his business. He wasn't happy about it, but the day before the star arrived he said his daughter could go to the welcoming party.

That evening, Zoe—dressed in an ivory sheath silk dress and a necklace of Sichuan opals she'd borrowed from the library—set out to collect Jing Yin at a quarter to five. Bradley and Yu Li said hello to her, then turned their attention to a reality TV show about a tattooed heavy metal singer from the US, dubbed in Mandarin.

Jing Yin emerged in a cloud of strawberry perfume. She was wearing the latest fashion of the peasant teenagers, burlap pants and a sequined t-shirt that revealed the dewy little valley between her fifteen-year-old breasts.

"I went to school today," the girl told Zoe outside the house. "My homeroom teacher is helping me catch up with all the work I missed, but my father says schools are supposed to make some people feel smart and some people feel stupid."

Zoe resolved to talk to Bradley Kwan again, even though approaching him always felt like putting on a suit of mental armor and going into battle.

The bartenders and caterers were setting up tables in the casino when Zoe and Jing Yin arrived. Ming came in with Tom a few minutes later. She cast her eyes upon Zoe's necklace. "Fucking opals," she muttered. "Those prickly little colors look like a thousand ways to die. Anyone want a drink?"

"She's such a tortured poet," said Tom, chuckling as he watched Ming make her way over to the bar and return delicately balancing two vodka and tonics, a fruity punch, and a beer for Tom. "Have you ever noticed how much alcohol is available in New China? Not that I'm complaining."

"It is rather like an artsy bar in Brooklyn," said Ming. Her foot nudged Zoe's and Zoe pressed back, as if to tamp down the wish to say more.

A string quartet began to play, and the first guests filtered in. Just after seven, a man rushed in who, as far as any observer could tell, was William Kingsley Sun. He possessed an air of command. But his eyes, ardent pools of honey-brown, lacked the fiery gold of the original. Sun Two shook hands and air-kissed various people, then, almost as an afterthought, kissed Zoe.

"Sooo…" he murmured after the quick kiss. He had an annoying habit of acting baffled around her.

"Glad you could come," Zoe said, the words hanging dry.

"Now here's a fresh pretty face." Sun Two introduced himself to Jing Yin and did his best to keep his gaze leveled at her pleasing but unspectacular countenance, without a downward glance toward her cleavage. The girl giggled, flustered.

Zoe knew the facsimiles well by then. Sun Three and Sun Four were obedient clones—lithe and simple creatures who could dig tunnels and build a bunker in a matter of days, so shy that they'd disappear at the sight of anyone not their master. But Sun Two, true to his word, was his own man. He had Jing Yin smiling and laughing. But both stopped talking and stared like stunned disciples when the guest of honor glided into the room.

Larissa Lee had skin the color of cappuccino mousse and a little twist in her lips, just imperfect enough to have iconic potential. She was with an entourage of cinematographers, producers, stylists, and itinerant photographers who made it a habit to trail famous faces.

Zoe knew something extra about Larissa; the first professional to recognize her potential had been Billie Austin, at the Harlem workshop. "I absolutely adore Billie! Do give her a big kiss for me," the movie star gushed now.

"Hellew, I'm William Sun," Sun Two bowed in the movie star's direction. "Ms. Lee, I am not only a great fan, but also your humble servant in our little center of enlightenment."

In a casino full of party guests, Sun Two possessed a finely tuned radar for the women most likely to see him as a sexy guru. While William often put him to work zapping blinking numbers in the bunker, Sun the facsimile would rack up "favors owed" which he expected to be repaid with time out on his own cognizance. "Because I know your secrets and I have a great fondness for gossip," he'd say, with a candy-coated giggle that made his threat doubly sinister.

Zoe watched Sun Two separate Larissa Lin from the crowd, the two of them smiling at each other, and she saw Jing Yin slump against the wall.

"I'm going home," the girl mumbled to Zoe, tears welling in her eyes.

Zoe noticed the daggers of pity that Lulu Pang was shooting in her direction—along with the two figures who sat in the shadows of the courtyard. Sun Two was caressing the movie star's supple shoulders, murmuring, "Exhale all the complications of the universe."

Enough. She tore out of her own party and made her way to William's library, then down the stairs and the steep incline to the bunker.

The original William Sun was in the midst of zapping number 98664. The program told him that 98664 was a CEO in Shanghai who used to pay himself a big bonus every time he cut staff, then brag at shareholder meetings about the lean-and-mean operation he was running. Now, like many executives across China, he was hiring civilizers to sit in corporate meetings and offer insights.

"I'd say human incompetence is the cause of ninety percent of the evil in the world," William said, apropos of nothing Zoe could decipher. He kept his thumb on the mouse that was administering zaps. "He's been like this for half an hour. There. I think he's finally got it." The number stopped blinking.

"I think Jing Yin has a crush on your evil twin."

"In another two hundred years we'll have conquered the world and all of this will be as insignificant—"

"How're you coming with *his* face?" Zoe demanded.

William had promised Zoe that he'd work on a new project when he had time. Surely there was room for one more transformation, he'd agreed; it wouldn't be easy, but maybe he could give Sun Two a new face that was not exactly William's own, but that of a flighty cousin, perhaps, and they'd find a superficial role for him that would let him be his own man.

That night she relented and let William remove her shoes.

"The mysteries of the Orient start with the feet," he pronounced, and they both guffawed at the cliché. He ran his fingers down the

162

arch of her foot as if he were plucking delicate harp strings. They found their way to the bed, but afterward Zoe lay awake thinking that Sun Two was an undeniable part of William Kingsley Sun.

"Where'd you go?" Ming asked the next morning. "You've gotta get William to do something about his double. I think he spent the night with Larissa—who, by the way, wants to interview me about my writing."

Ming was happy as long as the world was paying attention to her.

That afternoon Zoe found Jing Yin working in the market, unpacking boxes of cabbage greens, her face pale and expressionless. Bradley was there too. "You know, we could give you some more financing since your market is doing so well," Zoe told him. "You could hire additional staff and Jing Yin could return to school."

"We're not a book smart family," Bradley snapped. "And we're doing just fine."

"Well, I brought you a gift." Zoe held out a book she'd found in one of the boutiques. It was a coffee-table-sized picture book about the heavy metal rocker in the reality TV show the Kwans had been watching.

Bradley swatted the book to the floor with one meaty fist. "You trying to make me look stupid, girl? I don't read so well, but I ain't stupid!"

"Lots of people don't read so well," Zoe replied, shakily. "There are night classes in reading…"

"I went to school till I was fourteen. I can read but they said I was stupid 'cause it took me a long time. Besides, who wants to sit around and talk about fil-os-o-phee?" Bradley howled with laughter—and he seemed to be laughing at Zoe.

Chapter Twelve

Larissa Lee's documentary video, released in July of Year Two of the New China, included footage of Jing Yin stacking rice flour buns into a box for a customer in the market, her expression noncommittal.

"Everyone in Sunshine Village seems to live on a higher plane than you and I," Larissa's voice intoned. The documentary showed cinematic sweeps of tai chi classes at sunrise, of children learning how to prepare gourmet cuisine while their mothers attended classes in yoga or literature, then gathered to talk over bottles of wine. Scenes included life in the orchards and the rice fields, where peasants now worked alongside piped-in strains of Puccini, Mozart, and Chinese classics like "Flute and Drum at Sunset."

Zoe's favorite scene was one of Ming standing atop the restored pagoda, gazing at the pastel peasant bungalows below. An echo of wind chimes bounced off the hills and the sky behind her was a luminous pink.

"An old proverb says that Sunshine Village is just a mile below heaven," Ming told the camera—never mind that it was her own proverb, and only a few months old.

Tom liked it, too. "We are about to land in Sunshine Village. Just a mile below heaven," he'd announce to his passengers as he began the plane's descent. Some of the boutiques printed out business cards with the same tagline.

More tourists came—from Asia, Australia, Scandinavia, Oregon, and British Columbia—with copies of Rainer Maria Rilke in their backpacks. They rented paddleboats and meditated in lotus positions along the cliff top, gazing at the Tuo River. An environmental cleanup company had long since dredged and filtered the river so that it sparkled as it had in Ming's childhood.

The whole town sparkled, but it was still Sunshine Village, the place Ming had hoped to leave behind forever. She set her newest stories all over the world: one in Vladivostok, another in Nairobi, and a third in Mississippi. An astute reviewer had noted, however, that Ming Cheng "was always dropping in on a fantasy world that was somehow reminiscent of New York City."

But anywhere besides Sunshine Village would do. Even Beijing. She saw pictures, from her parents and from Tom, of a city where civilizers were now acquiring the choicest real estate, around Beijing University and much of Beijing Central, through land grants that played into a bold new idea that only artists and thinkers could make a city exhilarating.

Mama and Papa still lived in the Rising Phoenix industrial compound and worked hard, but they sent pictures of the spa and tennis courts they had installed for their staff, and the extension school they themselves were attending after work to take classes in literary criticism, climate science, and the great philosophers. Tom would tell her tales of his travels to the big cities and she'd feel herself emitting deep, wistful sighs. "Don't you ever get a vacation?" he asked more than once.

She couldn't tell him that she and her co-conspirators were way too busy to roam as the summer descended. Summer of Year Two of the New China brought an aura of blue-white heat. Mere wisps of vapor streaked across the sky like brushstrokes, as if the clouds had emptied themselves of tears and were now wrung dry. It was a sweet and raucous summer for the tourists and enlightenment seekers. But Ming heard more fearful rumblings when she visited the peasants' hamlet, where it was her duty to gather intelligence. The ground was too firm, they were saying. It was supposed to be pliant beneath the villager's feet at this time of year, swollen as the grubs came to breed in rain-soaked soil and the moles scurried underground to dine on the grubs. Without rain, the water was running low in the fields in spite of the new irrigation technology, and the rice husks were pale and anemic. The peasants complained that they hardly needed their fashionable new rubber boots adorned with ancient poetry stanzas. The early fruits were small and mealy.

"But the skies tell us the Monkey King is reunited with his true love," said one farmer, guffawing.

"The New China might have changed our houses, but it can't change the laws of nature. Someone is happy, someone else is going without rice," another spat out.

On that particular visit, Ming also bumped into Jing Yin. The peasant girl was Zoe's project, and Ming had avoided getting involved with the whole nasty Kwan family. But when she saw Jing Yin kicking the soil forlornly as a crowd of village teenagers skipped past her, chattering and laughing, presumably on their way to play basketball or watch one of the foreign films at the Cinema Club behind the new stadium, Ming stopped her and told her that she'd looked so pretty in Larissa Lee's documentary.

The girl snickered, then spat. But she didn't move on. Instead she looked Ming in the eye and said, "I wrote a song. Would you like to hear it? I'm not quite finished, but maybe you can tell me what you think of it so far."

"Love be like the earth exploding. You be shreds of fresh-killed prey," Jing Yin began, a rap tune with a raw, searing rhythm. She sang of falling in love; of his eyes that transformed you into a bird with rainbow feathers. "Then he turn away," Jing Yin breathed, kind of heaving her small breasts for emphasis. "You felt the bomb. It tear you apart." When she finished, Ming had a sense of having entered an open wound that would never heal.

"Why use second person if it's about your own feelings?" asked Ming, finally.

"Because I'm just a dumb peasant," she said, her lips quivering, before running off.

In the office that afternoon, Ming told Zoe her protégée was incredibly talented. "Except I thought referring to her character in the second person was a cop-out."

"Did you have to say that? She's vulnerable. She needs someone to encourage her."

"Jing Yin ought to get away from this town and her father," Ming grumbled.

Zoe agreed with that, at least. "And from *him*." It was always clear whom Zoe meant when she uttered the word *him*.

By September, the ground had become cracked clay, with sparse tufts of brownish grass. The drought had hit much of southern China, and provincial coffers paid extra for rice from Vietnam, and wheat and sorghum from the north. The Tuo River shrank to a tenth of its usual size, so that people were able to wade over pink pebbles to the center.

Jing Yin, still manning the market stall, told Zoe it was stupid to bother with school anyway. She was writing a kind of music that was showing up all over China—peasant rap, it was called. "She said I wouldn't like it," Zoe told Ming. "But her father hasn't tried to stop her—it's like he's okay with it if it distracts her from going to school."

Bradley Kwan, in fact, was calling his fellow peasants to meetings in the dining pavilion. Ming watched from the back as one attendee said life was about the land and procreating, always had been.

"Yeah, what do we need with fil-os-o-phee?" Bradley replied, and pounded on the table with such rhythm Ming caught herself tapping her foot.

"Don't worry, it will all wash out in the end," William consoled the co-conspirators later. "Bradley Kwan won't last forever. Jing Yin will grow up and have kids of her own and they'll go to school, and the next generation will have different ideas."

Ming was already tired of waiting, though.

One day in October she saw Tang Fei go into William's office and close the door. Afterward Tang came and told Ming he was leaving. He was moving to Beijing, going to work for an American named Jack Duffy, who was the new head of China operations for the big American pharmaceutical company Plenette-Leuter.

"Do you ever get bored with this place?" Tang Fei asked her. "I used to think, 'I was born here, I'll die here.' But this isn't my home anymore. So when Jack Duffy called me one day to ask about the price of nanochips, I wasn't shy about letting him know I was looking for a new job. They've got big things going on. One of the company's scientists in Beijing had suggested using nanochips in the brain to rewire a depressed person's brain to be happy. But Duffy decided they should work on a drug in the end. He said you can rewire the brain, but it won't change body chemistry. So now he has some kind of information that suggests things are going to come crashing down, and that when people realize all this equality isn't working, there's going to be a big market for anti-depressants in China."

"I like equality," Ming said, her voice rising into the soprano little-girl tone that felt too much like weakness.

"You wanna know something I know, that you can't get from books? People aren't all equal in their heads. Some of us work hard, and then we just want to go home, have a beer, turn on the TV, and watch a bunch of good guys shoot up a bunch of bad guys, or my team grab the ball and beat the hell outta your team."

"I looked up Jack Duffy," Zoe reported later, when the three of them convened in the bunker. "He was in Jordan for five years, and now he's in China. Could be CIA, you know. Undercover. He doesn't have a chip, does he?"

William checked the database. "No. He's new in town."

"Well, go get him."

"We've got our test subjects going, and their influence should be sufficient for the foreign regional managers who find themselves in China," William insisted. "Next phase, we go to the power brokers in America."

"Soon, I hope," said Zoe. Ming watched the two of them graze each other's knees, still silly in love when they weren't fighting.

Above ground, December provided the longest sequence of dry days on record. At the dining pavilion, Ming mingled with the peasants at yet another meeting. They smelled like spa soap now, but they seemed almost rapturous in their righteous indignation.

"They won't send us rain!" one woman lamented. While none identified who "they" were, the peasants all nodded agreement.

"It's just nature," Ming ventured.

"The government gave us this fancy New China, they can just as easily take it away. They've got some kind of machines to control the weather, too—that's what I heard."

168

"Yeah, big government will kill all of us in the end."

Ming briefed William and Zoe on the new conspiracy theory, but William wouldn't waver. In January, the official beginning of Year Three of the New China, the whole village grew abuzz with talk of the first elections. In November, everyone in the country would be able to vote—for town mayors, city councils, provincial governors, all the way up to members of Parliament and the prime minister.

Bradley Kwan himself was running for town council. He'd even started his own political party, which he called the Raindance Party. Ming went to watch the candidates speak at the village amphitheater one evening in February. She'd hoped a developer would demolish the old amphitheater and rid the village of its raging spirits, but there it remained, atop the fourth hill, moss and weeds cracking through the cement.

The worst of the spirits, she saw, were alive in Bradley Kwan. "How can you trust a government that made our country a hellhole, and then a paradise? Because, you have to ask yourselves, what are they going to do next? We're plainspoken folk and we matter!" he thundered, spittle cracking against the metal of his microphone. "We're the world's engines—spending our lives stooping down to plant rice shoots, picking the harvest, and building offices. We feed the world with our rice, and some people in this New China would have us think that we should be looking for the soul of those rice plants. How's that meaning of life thing going for you?"

Laughter from the bleachers crackled like an old soundtrack, and Ming saw black heads bobbing in formation, as if no one dared sway left while others swayed right.

"You might ask me—if I win, what am I gonna do about the weather? All we need is rain, my friends, and they don't want us to have it." The menacing way Bradley Kwan uttered "they" made Ming's toes shiver. "We ask for rain in the summer so we can make honest tea, and what do they give us? Poetry. University extension classes. Music. Fil-os-o-phee. Health care that they say is free. But I want to know, what is all this costing?"

The crowd roared like ravenous bears.

"What do you want? Questions or answers? I'll tell you the answer, and it ain't more questions. What good are fil-os-o-phers, and these folks who call themselves 'civilizers,' when your crop has blight? You wanna study useless things at night school?"

"Healthy dissent," William insisted, later that night in the bunker. "He's spouting idiocy, and people have to figure that out for themselves."

"We need to get a better assessment of the landscape," Zoe said. "See if people are discontent in the big cities. Ming, you should go. I know you'd like to get away for a bit." She rubbed Ming's shoulder. "And when Ming gets back, I'm going to take a nice vacation myself. With Sun Two, if you won't go with me, William."

"I could take a road trip!" Ming cried out. "I could get away from this damn town. I'll take a slow train to Beijing."

Zoe was plotting something, Ming could tell by how magnanimous she was being. "You have to let Professor Engelhorn know you're there. He's writing a book about the New China and he's looking for people who know how it happened. Tell him you heard he's looking for help. You could tell him what he should know and find out what else he's heard."

Ming could barely answer; her hands were trembling, imagining the illicit love affair that might have been, and now Zoe, with a look of innocence that Ming didn't believe for a moment, was sending her to his door. "So why don't you go?" Ming asked when the words came.

Zoe looked her squarely in the eye. "He'll want to know why I'm not immersed in my dissertation."

A few days before Ming left, Zoe let her know, as if in passing, that Professor Engelhorn and his wife had split up, and he didn't quite know what to do with himself these days.

Ming stared in the mirror that night and defined herself aloud. "Writer, yes. Feeder of false information. Counter-spy, maybe? On the road, at last. I'll be a love vagabond." *Love on the road. I'm going to be a vagabond.* She repeated the refrain in her mind, and felt almost happy.

Chapter Thirteen

Ming left on a Friday in March, Year Three. The immortal lovers spent that weekend underground, indulging in acrobatic love and smoky music. Only once in a while did an occasional alarm interrupt them, and they'd have to stop and zap a number.

William had allowed Sun Two a bonus weekend of roaming free. "He'll get laid, sure, but I told him to stay away from Jing Yin or I'll never give him time off again," William assured Zoe. She chose to trust that her lover's copy would have that much sense, and lost herself in a cloud of incense and sweat, the electric mix of Nina Simone and saxophone jazz and samba. They drank champagne in bed, and she pondered her own madness aloud.

"I sent Ming off to have an affair with the man who could be my father. Don't you wonder why?"

For William it was a blip in the cosmos. What he said was, "It was rather sensible, I thought, to send her off to gather intelligence."

In truth, the dissertation and the professors who would judge it seemed a million lifetimes away. "Well, I kind of felt like this could be a test of human nature. Is Ming loyal to me or her own quests for whatever? I told her to tell him she heard he's looking for help, but what he actually told me is he's looking for a research assistant, and he's going to think she's applying for the job. She's going to be pissed, or maybe she'll play along."

"And you're the director from afar? Darling, we're not gods, and gods are flawed themselves."

"It would be good to be a benevolent god who was really in charge," she admitted. He said isn't it enough to be a sex goddess, and proceeded to levitate a few inches above Zoe, pulling her up so that they lost themselves again, making love in mid-air.

But Monday morning came, with inevitable news from the world outside. William summoned Sun Two to the bunker, and the lovers went above ground. A story in the *New York Times* quoted an international bond-rating agency analyst who claimed the New China had a staggering amount of debt, and that it was time to downgrade the A-grade rating on their sovereign bonds—bonds which the outside world had bought to help finance the grand social experiment.

"This is how Wall Street can stop the progress of New China," Zoe cried. "Danny told me about it. When a country swings too far to the left, some right-winger on Wall Street is sure to counter with a statement that that country doesn't deserve a high credit rating. So then China has to repay its debt at higher interest rates, so the debt mounts, and the whole bullshit analysis becomes a self-fulfilling prophecy, and wealthy investors stop buying Chinese bonds. We need to use the chips on Wall Street powerbrokers!"

"Not before we're ready," William insisted, and lost himself in one of his distant looks. "Do you remember when Janis Joplin came to Nirvana? She went on stage and poured her very soul into her singing, never knowing if the audience was going to swoon and sigh and smother her with adoration or stomp all over her. We hung out with her after that. She told us, 'I'd rather be the audience than me. They're seeking pleasure. I'm begging for love.'" Zoe must have rolled her eyes, because he glanced at her just then and said, "Don't look so impatient, I'm making a point. We suffer. We shape our creation, which in our case is the New China, and we fine-tune it. We let critics stomp on us, but we persevere."

"Speaking of, I wonder what jagged shards *he* left behind him in the village."

William agreed they should go on a village crawl that evening. They had dinner in the Nirvana café while a violinist played. After dinner they strolled along Market Street. The night air carried the fragrance of wine and spices. Lovers laughed, a classical quartet played, and a group of teens in canvas jackets and hemp pants were gearing up to play drums. Then a singer stepped up to the mic. Zoe did a double take.

"It's Jing Yin!"

The girl held the microphone and raised her arms as if in some kind of worship. She wore a tank top with a pitchfork in rhinestones; emblazoned below were the words "Unschooled and Proud." A roll of young fat hung over her pants.

"They wanna reform this town," Jing Yin began, her voice husky, her palms slapping out the rhythm of her rap on her hips. "With their mental masturbation. Yo, Will Shakie-speare, what you hear? Was you queer? Bet you fuckers got no hoe. What you say now we got dough…." The youthful group gathered about Jing Yin began to stomp their feet and whistle their appreciation.

"What is that?" asked William, shaking his head.

Jing Yin, surveying her audience with an almost diva-like appreciation, caught sight of William and Zoe. With a guttural noise, she hurled a thick wad of yellow phlegm from her mouth, landing with an unsavory dribble on William's shirt. "What the hell?" he muttered.

"Promises, promises." Jing Yin resumed her rap-song. "Don't never believe a man. Lyin' eyes say it's me. Lyin' cock say she and she and she—"

"Let's go," Zoe hissed, seizing William by his arm and pulling him away. "It's gotta be your copy." They fled from the village square, the fierce laughter of the young rebels echoing behind them. "I had a strange dream last night," Zoe told William on the way home, "that we broke up because you were fucking around with Lady Godiva."

William offered a melancholy smile. "That was eight hundred years ago. I thought I was entitled to everything and everyone. But you did break up with me, and I was miserable, wandering around without you. I started talking to you as if you were a ghost that was haunting me. I could hear you laughing except you weren't there."

"But you had a subconsciously wandering eye, didn't you? It never went away."

They stood on the road to his house, silent and indecisive, until Zoe began to walk away in the direction of her own apartment.

William caught up, though. "You want me to hurry up with more chips. You want me to change his face. You're in such a big hurry for everything. Is this what you learned from your New York mother and your New York schools, find true love, then nag him to death?"

"You think I'm a *nag*...?"

"You always nagged me, actually." He grinned.

"Where I come from Sun Two could go to jail if he slept with Jing Yin. She's a minor."

"I don't think he slept with her."

"You don't know that for sure. You can't control him."

"You say he's part of me, then you say he has his own mind."

And so they fought again, with no resolution.

"The peasant girl has begun to live," he insisted. "She's had her first crush, and turned it into street poetry. There *is* something rather grand in that."

"Her name is Jing Yin. Why do you and Ming persist in calling her 'the peasant girl'?"

"Yes, we're a class conscious folk here in China, haven't you noticed? We even had a little revolution where the intellectuals were supposed to learn about life from the peasants, but the peasants were still peasants. I'll bet if I were to whisk you off to your beloved New York, sooner or later I'd hear you condescend—you'd look down on someone who prefers a beer and a ballgame to spending their nights studying Mandarin. But what's wrong with a little class-based tribalism? Your Jing Yin could become a guru of peasant hip."

Zoe spent the night in her apartment. She had been happy, and now she wasn't.

As the co-head of Sunshine Finance, though, she practiced discipline, pushing away the urge to touch William and rage at him all at the same time. The two of them had a meeting with a contractor the very next morning to look over the construction of the eco-resort across the river. The contractor had assured everyone that the main building, atrium, conference rooms, and twenty guest rooms would be ready by June, as long as the weather stayed dry. Walking together and fighting the magnetic force between them, the CEO of The Sunshine Group and the co-head of Sunshine Finance walked around the foundations and examined the blocks of Ferrock—

composed of recycled steel dust and ground-up glass—that would make up the floor. They toured the patch of land that would be planted with moss and host the guests' morning yoga and *qi gong* sessions, and the frame for a natural rock bathing pool. Zoe drew in a few particles of contentment, imagining splashing amongst the rocks someday.

"Look there," said the builder, pointing to a lush valley just below where the jasmine tea flowers grew. Then he snickered. "They say you can get another kind of flowers from those fields way out there, beneath the forest camouflage." He gestured toward the west.

William looked agitated; she could sense it by the way his forehead crackled. When they bid goodbye to the contractor and headed toward the dock where paddleboats ferried visitors back to the other side of the river, he stopped. "We need to see what's going on with the *papaver somniferum* flowers."

"How?" The impenetrable bamboo forest was visible to the west.

"I guess you don't remember the time you flew? Just a little liftoff, but you'd be surprised at the miracles you can make happen if you try, Ms. Zoe Austin from New York. Close your eyes, inhale wisdom. Arms high; slice through the air. Imagine you're an eagle, and if anyone sees us, we'll look like eagles to them."

She inhaled all the wisdom she could imagine and lifted her arms high. Nothing happened. William hovered and told her to try again. The fourth time, she took a deep breath that seemed to send heavenly breezes fluttering down to her toes, then felt herself gliding over the crests of trees, following a form that felt like William, aglow and familiar and sinewy, as he swooped below the treetops, following a floor of pine needles and weeds and grasses.

A dazzling field of poppies—vibrant red with black seeds, hot pink, and fireball orange—materialized below, so bright that they seemed to beckon.

Zoe dipped closer. Then a death rattle thundered right in her direction. She saw the earth shake beneath the flowers and felt an arm grab her waist and swoop her into the forest.

They were in a thicket of trees, standing in tall grasses. Zoe blinked. William held her by the shoulders. "Don't go so close. They shot at you!"

She found herself shaking all over.

He led her through the trees to a rock along the cliff. There they perched side by side and contemplated the sky and the river and the eastern bank. They were miles downriver from the Buddha and the factory and the village proper, though they could see the airstrip and the pagoda-shaped roof of the terminal on the opposite bank. A small plane was taking off, carrying passengers to the east.

"I don't know what to do," William admitted. "Who are these people who insist on holding the world hostage at gunpoint so they can make money from fools who've become prisoners to their false cloud of bliss?"

"Make another program. Give them chips."

He shook his head. "They're not the leaders. It's those who lead who are the wind that bends the grasses."

Zoe knew he was paraphrasing Confucius not from her memories of Nirvana, but from books. Poor Confucius. She was still shaking from her mortal brush with death, too much to challenge William on whether the world was always going to be too power-mad for purists.

Yet with a lot of effort she could fly. As the dry spring grew balmy, Zoe practiced flying in the woods beyond William's house. She managed to take off alone and leap into an arc before landing.

In her regular rounds walking about the town, Zoe found the Kwan Market growing. Jing Yin was still there, selling homemade jams, a condiment of hot peppers and peaches, and an assortment of steamed buns with poppy seeds on top. Next to the edibles she'd stacked a dozen paper-wrapped CDs, with a picture of herself and the title "Do You Dare?"

"I always knew you had talent," Zoe told the sullen girl as she purchased a CD. Jing Yin lit up, seemingly in spite of herself. Then they talked for a while, woman to woman.

"You're a business partner to him. You're a nice person, but I'm young and fresh." That was what the girl confessed. She tossed her head as Larissa Lee might, then giggled with a heavy dose of fake modesty. "I bet he tells you we haven't...you know...*done* anything. Well, I won't give him what he wants 'til he's mine."

Shrewd girl. When Zoe told William about the conversation he begged her to rise above it. There would be time to get back to work on the face in a few years, maybe, after they launched Phase Two. She pushed him away.

Lulu Pang, with her bluntness reminiscent of older, crueler times, told Zoe she'd been smart to get that philandering man out of her life. "I always wondered how you could let him do that to you. Sure, sometimes he looks sad, like somebody's broken his heart, but it's probably for show. That type never changes."

On the riverbank she would see young lovers on benches and old lovers strolling, hands clasped. An occasional interesting man passed through town, but Zoe felt like the keeper of so many secrets it was hard to imagine an intimate conversation with someone new. If only Ming were here, she could talk to someone about body doubles and flying. Sometimes in the dappled light of a spring evening she'd think of old friends from home, though. If Jeff were here, he'd at least make her laugh. One night in April, not quite eight a.m. in New York, Zoe pulled out her cell phone and hit his number.

Three rings and he picked up. "Zoe? At the bottom of the hole I've been digging to China? I nearly broke my neck on a pile of shit, getting to the phone, but at least it's worth it. I'm supposed to be exhibiting at a gallery show, but they didn't pay the rent and they got evicted yesterday. Can you fucking believe it?"

How forlorn and strange his problems sounded. And so easy to fix.

"I miss you. Why don't you come to China? I mean fly to Chengdu and then to Sunshine Village. Ming isn't here..."

"Shit, I can tell by the tone of your voice—trouble with Mr. Sun and Moon and Stars? Tell Uncle Jeffrey all about it. But I don't have any money to come to China. My estranged wife left me with a big credit card bill, remember?"

"I think she's been meaning to pay you back. But I'll take care of it. And your ticket."

177

"I'm touched. But how could I let you—"

"Everything is different here. You'll find the strangest words you can hear are 'I can't afford it.'"

"I miss you too," Jeff said.

Five days later—on a day that Tom Wendall's alternate was flying the Cessna—Zoe met Jeff at the airstrip. He was wearing a torn T-shirt. He'd made friends with the other passengers on the flight—a backpacking couple from Sweden, two businessmen from Seoul, three earnest-looking women from Toronto.

"Hello, welcome to Sunshine Village." Lulu shook hands with the passengers as they disembarked.

"You look like a movie star!" Jeff gawped when he saw Zoe. "Hell, I thought I was gonna land in rice paddies. Holy shit, we got to what's that first place I landed in China—Gwang Joe?"

"Guangzhou."

"They've got a casino in the airport, can you believe it? Where's your boyfriend? Mr. Fun in the Sun."

"You are photographer?" Lulu asked in stilted English. "My great uncle was a civilizer too, a well-known playwright." Self-aggrandizing had become common practice in New China.

"A syllablizer?" Jeff asked, perplexed. "I saw your mom, Zoe. She almost lost her funding for her Harlem classes, but that gorgeous actress with the preternatural tits—the one who made the documentary about Sunshine Village, what's her name?—heard about it and put her own funding in. What luck!"

"I know."

"So when did you turn into a fashion maven? Is the Dragon Lady gone? Promise me she's gone. It's a big country but, I swear, if I bump into her, I'm on the next flight out of here. I must be jet lagged—kind of feels like an invader from planet Klingon has scooped out my brain with a spoon. What do they have to eat in this town? Is there a bar where we can get some irony on the rocks? Where's Mr. Sun anyway? Didn't I come here to see if he gets my seal of approval?"

"We sort of broke up."

"You don't sort of break up."

At the Nirvana Café, Jeff nursed a jasmine beer. "Not a macho brew," he pronounced. "Produces only a nice Jewish boy kind of belch." He poked chopsticks into green curried chicken. With a morsel still in mid-air he paused to notice three young Chinese women at the next table and two German-speaking blondes at the bar.

"That girl's got an intriguing take-me-as-I-am look. Her friend's got a sweet face; dare I say nice tits?—yeah, slap my face. How come they all look like they're dressed for a fashion spread?"

Zoe looked up to see that Sun Two had come into the café. He was peering sideways at the five women. Then he saw Zoe and strolled over. He kissed the air in proximity to her cheek. "This is the famous William Kingsley Sun," she felt obligated to say. He shook Jeff's hand and took it upon himself to sit at their table. He ordered tea and braised tofu with black bean sauce. His dinner break from the bunker; he'd be in no hurry to return to relieve his master.

"Are you a Yankees fan?" Sun Two asked Jeff.

"Is Buddha a Buddhist?"

"Yes, I can see your true nature," Sun Two laughed his un-William-like chortle. "I met your mayor several years ago when I was in New York—"

"You and your master both have attention deficit disorder in common," Zoe muttered to Sun Two in Mandarin.

"For a thousand years she's had a cruel streak," Sun Two said in English.

"I don't do past life regressions," said Jeff. "That's not required in this town, is it?"

After Sun Two finally departed, Jeff leaned back in his chair and looked Zoe in the eye. "I've gotta ask you something. Dead serious. How is this guy your type? Sure, nice if you like 'em lean and handsome, but you never went for guys who look like a male model with the depth of a fruit fly."

"He…has a bit of a split personality." Her voice came out weak. "Seriously, he takes medication for it."

179

On Jeff's second night in town she took him to one of the pavilions for cocktails and dinner. He appeared with a tidy haircut and new loafers as shiny as mirrors. Before an hour had passed, the real William arrived.

"Jeff," William said, extending a hand, his fiery eyes gleaming and sparks electrifying the air. "May I steal Zoe away, for just a moment?"

Steering her by the elbow, William drew her to a quiet table. "I just wanted you to know I almost got his face. He was mute, though. Then 2099 went on a blinking rampage. I've got Number Two down there and I think he has it under control so you can stay out and entertain your friend. But some others blinked today. We've got to spread the program. I can hurry up with Phase Two or work on Sun Two's face."

"Are you asking me to choose?"

William ran his fingertips along her back; each spot he touched seemed to burst into a freeform dance. "I know what your answer will be. You look scrumptious, by the way."

I would have said save the world, wouldn't I? She told herself that if he'd wanted to test her, she would have passed.

"Your boyfriend you sort of broke up with was in rare form," Jeff conceded the next day. "By the way, if you have work to do, don't worry. Some people I met invited me to a concert tonight."

By his fifth day, Jeff had a new laptop with hundreds of photographs. He had magpies pecking at plums and children kicking balls, arms and legs in motion. He'd captured a pensive series of a young peasant man in galoshes taking a tea break on one of the wrought-iron benches that dotted the rice fields as he browsed Plato's *Republic*. Jeff's camera had caught open-mouthed tourists in the casino, stockbrokers in their striped shirts, children bathing at the river, and bevies of pretty young women.

"This is the one you should do something with though," he told Zoe, clicking on a picture of the giant Buddha just after sunrise, with the ruff of clouds around its neck—clouds were appearing over the village again. "It'd better sell after you dragged me out of my cozy bed to take the damned thing."

Jeff's visit drifted into weeks. He enrolled in a Mandarin class and learned how to say, "You're very pretty," and "Would you like a drink?" On many evenings, Zoe would see him strolling in the village square with Lulu Pang. Zoe showed the Buddha photo to an entrepreneur planning to export the local jasmine tea and beer. With a loan from Sunshine Finance, the entrepreneur purchased the rights to use Jeff's photo of the Buddha on the tea boxes and beer labels. Jeff had little interest in traveling beyond Sunshine Village, however. "I know it's a fucking big country," he said, "but what if I bump into the Dragon Lady?"

Zoe threw herself into her work, meeting with people seeking capital, discussing the company and the state of New China with the man who drew her like a magnet.

"I can fly on my own," she told William. "But Jeff feels sorry for me because he thinks he saw my ex-boyfriend making out with some 'cutie tourist' as he put it. At least Jing Yin is out of town, I hear."

William inhaled self-denial and sat rigid. "Do you know where Jing Yin has gone? I get out *sometimes* and I hear what's going on. She's in Chengdu with her father. Some kind of Raindance Party conference. And all we can do is keep showing everyone how much better New China is than they say."

But he looked worried.

Chapter Fourteen

On the train to Beijing, Ming was an escapee once again. *Born to be an outlaw. A love vagabond. What if I just don't go back?* Zoe and William might even understand, she told herself. She sent them innocuous texts about heading north on trains that smelled like newborn technology and the towns where she disembarked.

"I feel like I'm playing inside a computer," Ming told the man seated next to her. They laughed together. Ming got off the train with him in Xian and let their conversation draw out. She stayed two nights, a love vagabond gorging on time. Ming filled her laptop with fanciful descriptions of the man from Xian and the people she encountered on the train, embellishing lives with tragedies and meanderings.

When Ming decided to move on, she told the Xian man, "I'd like to spend a year writing on a train," and he understood. All over New China, people were starting to appreciate such dreams. Ming traveled to Linfen, Shijiazhuang, and Baoding. Other passengers also tapped away on laptops, and a violinist tried out a new composition two rows to her rear. Trains were, Ming found, a delightful way in which to travel—the seats tilted back into loungers, and the dining car, with its peach-colored tablecloths, served mid-morning lattes and late-afternoon cocktails. At night, passengers scrambled for seats in the dome cars, where they gazed at constellations.

"I'm on a road trip under the stars," Ming texted Zoe. Then suddenly, alone beneath the dome, alone in the world's most populous country, Ming felt adrift with no one to rein in her euphoria or shadowbox this dark mood and stop it from devouring her.

She disembarked in cities where the tiny buds of spring were beginning to appear, where teenagers raced bicycles down willow-shaded paths, and children's laughter tumbled out of pools and playgrounds. She lingered at cafés, drinking cool glasses of lemonade and jasmine beer, and listened to poets in outdoor literary performances.

Everywhere, she tried to lose herself in observations. People seemed to have seized one end of the spectrum or the other; they were either ravenous for this new way of living or staunchly opposed to it. *Richly Civilized Dad, Poorly Civilized Dad*—a book that expounded on the value of learning—was a bestseller, beckoning from many a bookstore window.

In Baoding, posters plastered on market walls advertised help for those still struggling to find their way—*Let Dr. Wu confiscate your emotional baggage*, and *Tonight: If Life is Perfect Why am I Still Searching? A trip to Nirvana with Guru Xi.* And with China's first-ever nationwide elections approaching, political propaganda posters sought to galvanize the discontented—*Stop the conspiracy, Equality is for wimps*, and *Education and health care won't solve your problems—Tien for Governor will.*

"I don't think the crazies will get elected," Ming wrote to William and Zoe. "I have faith in reason."

As the silvery sprawl of Beijing came into view, however, Ming felt an iron band start to tighten across her chest. Han and her parents would have their usual onslaught of questions. "Are you going to divorce Jeff and marry Tom? When are you going to have children?"

In the greeting area of the Beijing station, amid a sea of people sporting high-fashion spring coats of candy-apple red and deep periwinkle, Ming spotted her parents, still wearing their oft-washed taupe-ish parkas. Papa drove home to Badaling, the road fringed by tall willow trees. Beyond the hills, Ming could see clusters of new villas with brightly painted pagoda roofs, outdoor cafés, bicycle lanes, and a hiking trail.

"Grown-ups playing," said Papa, and slapped his cheek.

"Are you still married?" Mama asked.

Her parents had made a few improvements in the Rising Phoenix compound. The glass shards that used to line the walls were gone, as was the rusted iron gate. Now, the entrance consisted of an ivy-covered wall with a welcoming archway and paths that directed workers to the tennis court and swimming pool.

Inside Mama and Papa's apartment, though, a garden hose still functioned as the shower, and the same frayed towels hung on racks, grayer than ever.

Han and Bo Fu were there, waiting. At dinner, Papa announced that Ming was going to be staying with her brother, since he lived closer to the city, in the Shunyi district. Ming would have preferred to stay northwest of the city, where civilizers inhabited luxury skyscrapers between Beijing University and the Summer Palace.

"I can afford my own place," she protested.

"You'd get lonely," Han said. "Anyway, the shared solar-battery-powered taxis will take you anywhere you want to go."

"Please stay with us, Aunt Ming," pleaded Bo Fu. The boy was nine now, and had shot up into a handsome, slender child. He still liked McDonald's, but its new vegetable buffet was apparently proving to be just as popular as the Egg McMuffins had once been.

Han's home, Ming was gratified to see, was in a new compound known as a balance tower, a community of graceful residential and office buildings clustered around courtyards. He'd moved his office to an adjoining building.

His routine, he told Ming, was to work until noon, then go to the indoor solarium, which housed a pool where he swam laps before lunch. While he was swimming the next day, Ming strolled through the garden. Children's laughter from a jungle gym and swing set filled the air.

"Ming?" a voice called. She turned and saw Fanny, flushed and smiling, pushing a heavy girl in a swing. "This is my daughter," Fanny enthused. "She's in a nursery here, and I can take breaks to play with her."

"You look happy."

"Oh, Ming, I am. So very happy to have my daughter nearby. Tian went back to school, did you know? She's studying to be a nutritionist."

"What about you?" Ming asked. "You're still working for Han?"

"Oh, I don't care about fil-os-o-phee," Fanny shrugged, and took her daughter's hand. The three of them entered the solarium.

Han was just finishing his swim. Toweling his wet hair and dangling goggles, he nodded at Fanny.

"You can go shopping," he said. Fanny and her daughter went off, and Han gestured to Ming to sit down at one of the café tables.

"When business gets slow we send our staff shopping to ensure that money keeps circulating," he explained to her. "Nowadays, we figure it scarcely matters so long as the money keeps getting made somewhere and moving around. When I look at a company now, I want to know how my investment can help them fuel the economy—"

Yes, I know all about it, she forced herself not to say aloud.

Han's phone interrupted his lecture on the fundamentals of New China. He picked it up and spoke for a few minutes. "I'm just about to close a deal," he told Ming. A waiter brought them lunch, *zhajiangmian* noodles with soybean paste.

Ming nodded. All around them, men wrapped in towels were talking about "percentage" and "structure" with each other or on their phones.

"Why be stuck in a stuffy office?" Han toyed with his chopsticks as if he were about to use them to write instructions on a whiteboard. "Swimming laps makes us more alert, more aware. I've found that when you contemplate the human element in a transaction, rather than just the spreadsheet, it's better for all parties. A matter of paying attention to the ambiguities. If you're spending in ways that help other businesses grow, prosperity spreads like a thriving bamboo weed. And what is it you occupy yourself with these days, little sister?"

"I make time to write."

"Why does everyone think they have to write something? Bo Fu's mother says *she's* going to write a book."

"I should visit her."

"She's living with a group of women who have left their husbands to find themselves. I told her, 'Keep Bo and get your mind off yourself, like I do.' You think my life is so perfect? I work, I swim, I visit my parents, I look after my son. I make money. I had a girlfriend, but she decided some musician guy was more her type."

185

Han isn't happy, Ming realized.

"The air's gotten cleaner, and my money helped do that," he continued. "I suppose you think there's supposed to be something more? Do you ever see Tom? Are you still fond of each other?"

"Sure. He's the only person I know who doesn't pass judgment. But I like writing, he likes flying, I don't think he's the man I'm going to marry…"

"You *are* married. Aren't you?"

"Oh…I dunno, what happens when you live apart for so long?"

"You still have to make your separation official." Han shook his head. "You're an executive at Sunshine Finance and you don't know how the laws work? What brings you to Beijing, anyway?"

"Research," Ming said, the first word that came to mind.

That afternoon, in Han's guestroom, Ming began a new story. She brought back the character Mimi and had her living in Beijing—the old Beijing of toxic skies and limousines splashing beggars with black gutter water. Mimi earned her living as a high class escort until one night, in a hotel suite with a captain of industry, she discovered she had a superpower. Mimi could sing a bluesy tune, lulling the man into slumber, and whisper things as he slept that would alter his conscious mind. This influential man woke up dazed, full of existential questions about the purpose of his wealth.

"Aunt Ming," Bo Fu called, rapping on her door. She let him in, and he said, "Come with us! We're going to the pavilion for dinner."

"I have some work to do," Ming told him, depositing a kiss on his cheek. "I'm writing. Sometimes when you write it feeds your mind and that's all you want."

"My mama's writing too, but I like to eat," Bo Fu giggled.

She wrote into the night—not just the Mimi story, but also an email to Charles Engelhorn: *We met last year. I have a book of Du Fu's poetry for you. Do you remember? Zoe Austin said you're writing about New China. I just arrived in Beijing. Maybe I can be helpful?*

Charles Engelhorn's reply came within the hour: *I do remember.* He suggested meeting at a café near Beijing University the following day.

In the morning, en route to the café, she bought a fine leather-bound copy of Du Fu—since the copy she'd claimed to possess had been abandoned to Jeff's clutter long ago—and explored a city born anew. Urban planners, architects, and engineers, their minds ignited, had constructed a frenzy of subterranean pedestrian passageways and Wi-Fi enabled stations where sleek hybrid vans departed to every part of the city at fifteen-minute intervals. Private vehicles were banned. "A city for the new millennium," the planners had boasted.

Ming jostled pedestrians, walking elbow to elbow beneath the welcome shade of the willow trees, circling around the occasional street comedian or ballet dancer.

"It's like a city of boulevardiers, flaneurs—the kind that are engaged in the study of humanity and how to live well in a post-capitalist world," she said to Charles Engelhorn as they found seats in an expansive café with white walls and carved rosewood tables. A flute player provided soothing sound, and a fusion scent of wine, coffee, and mossy tea filled the air.

"It's nothing short of amazing," he agreed. "Amazing that government and business leaders have not only dreamed up everything a city should be, but actually built it!"

Glad you like my ingenuity. Just once before I die, can I stand on a big stage and say I did all this? His appreciation hit a chord in her heart, though; there was something so eager about him, the gangly youth peering out beneath his crinkly middle-aged skin even though he'd aged, with grayer hair and an anguish in the way he moved. She stared for a moment at the blue veins in his hands and the conspicuous absence of his wedding ring.

Ming ordered bean-paste buns for them both, while Charles idly stirred his green tea.

"So," he said, "have you worked on books before?"

Odd question, she thought. "I write short stories, but someday—"

He wasn't really listening. "I want to discover the seeds, the roots of this transformation. I always assumed that if there were any entity that could implement mind control, it would be the Chinese government, but whoever imagined they'd do it this way? Makes you wonder... is this brainwashing or freedom? Is this an experiment

187

that will abruptly end, leaving a repressive reactionary regime in its wake? Might the roots be found in Confucian thought—?"

"Confucius was a purist," Ming couldn't resist interjecting.

"Perhaps it speaks to an ingrained guilt complex in Chinese corporate leaders. I want to talk to business and political leaders, to civilizers, and to ordinary folks. Would you be willing to help with interviews? Zoe recommended you so I know you can do the job, if you want it."

"The—?" She stopped herself. Zoe had said *tell him you heard he's looking for help*. And Ming had taken the bait. He wanted an academic handmaiden.

"I'd want to obtain a variety of views, though I don't usually do oral histories," he was going on. "You were here when it all started, weren't you? I am sure your life changed dramatically."

"Yes, I'm a writer, after all."

"Well, if you'd like the job, we can keep the hours flexible. The only thing that concerns me is that you haven't been living in Beijing."

Zoe did this to me, sent me off to play this role. But I'll be a double agent. That bit of adventure appealed to her, though she wondered how long she'd be able to play the innocent researcher.

"I went to high school and university here." The co-head of Sunshine Finance and author of minor acclaim was suddenly pleading for the job. "I can introduce you to plenty of people. You might even want to meet my family—we've got the old guard and a financier and me, a civilizer." *Besides, you're a convenient cover for me to stay here a while and inspect the world I've designed.*

"You know, you have quite the mysterious smile," Charles murmured, almost without thinking.

Just call me Mysteries-of-the-Orient Ming. Would you like me to seduce you?

Before she started the minimum wage undercover job two days later, she finished the Mimi story, carving a trail of powerful men who tell their underlings, "I don't need to hoard my earnings because money is a bamboo weed, here's a cutting for you and for you and for you."

Poor Charles. She was going to have to lead him down a path of theories with no conclusion. The thought made her feel protective of him all over again, somehow.

She led him first to visit Wu Xia, Han's ex-wife, in a neighborhood of villas dedicated to cooperative feminist living. Wu Xia, her hair now long and her face serene, took them on a tour of the compound, showing them the common kitchen and nursery, and a starkly bare room with mirrored walls and floor. "When we have our women's sessions, we take our clothes off in here," Wu Xia confided with a giggle. Charles flushed.

"Our group has read some of your erotic stories, Ming, in our effort to rid ourselves of inhibition. We examine ourselves, our minds, and our bodies. I care about Han, but I can't be married to a man who holds everything inside. One morning, I suddenly realized that being a good wife and mother, agreeing with everything Han says, just isn't enough. He didn't really love me, you know. You can tell him I said that. When I find myself, I'll be ready to find my true soulmate."

I know too much, and if I find true love I'll always harbor secrets, it occurred to Ming.

In the weeks that followed, she accompanied Charles to meetings with professors and minor government officials. "The consensus is that the seeds grew from a century of being open to whatever revolutionary thought works best," Charles pondered late one afternoon. "Can you type up the notes under that theme?"

Ming had a sudden urge to throw her arms around him and tell him everything, but she stopped herself. They were in his Beijing University visiting faculty apartment, a place that had become familiar to her by then. Someday, she was sure, they were going to find their way to the bedroom.

It happened in May. Han and Bo Fu were away with the boy's class for a father-son weekend of rock climbing, fishing, and paintball at the Baihe River. Charles had an invitation that Friday night to a party celebrating Ma Fu Gang, the recipient of a prestigious literary prize for his stylistic novel about life among the Americans and their "primitive addiction to paychecks." Ming had known Ma Fu Gang

189

in New York. He had been one of her roommates in the basement apartment. He used to read his political poetry aloud late at night and distract her from studying. Once, he'd thrown one of Ming's MBA textbooks across the room, then told her that only a bourgeoisie fool would study business when she could be learning anarchy right here in this hovel they all called home.

Charles and Ming stopped at a bookstore before the party to buy a copy of Ma's new book; Ming was sure the great literary prizewinner would have humiliating words for any guest who couldn't quote a line or two.

"You haven't read it yet?" the bookstore clerk asked, casting Ming a look that made her feel like a bumpkin from Sichuan. "It's being called the definitive work on the dystopic horror that China could have been. But frankly, I find him a tad predictable on the plight of the starving artist."

"Why does everyone in New China think they're a literary critic?" Charles asked. "We've got to look into that."

Fu Gang lived in the Summer Palace, the most magnificent building in Beijing, the former playground of emperors set on the placid Kunming Lake. Charles and Ming arrived early—Fu Gang had promised that his assistant would provide a pre-party tour of the quarters that now housed the country's most famous civilizers.

They met Fu Gang's assistant beneath an archway that had no number but, like the entrances to each of a dozen courtyards, was delineated by the shapes carved out in the stone; this one had a circle, a bottle shape, a crescent, and a dragon tongue. The assistant was a willowy young woman who strode on silver stilettos. She ushered them through a courtyard with lilacs in bloom, to an expansive room with a polished granite floor. They could hear the strains of a cellist and pianist rehearsing somewhere within.

"As a writer, Ma likes it quiet," the assistant murmured, invoking his name as if he were a god. "His chambers are back there." She pointed a silver-tipped finger. "Those are all closed-off residences, you understand. But I can show you a model apartment. So you're a professor? Are you looking for accommodation here?"

"In my dreams," said Charles.

The assistant pressed her thumb against a brass circle on a door and it swung open. They stepped over a traditional Chinese threshold, raised to trip evil spirits if they tried to glide through, into a hushed room with blackwood floors, perfect lacquer furniture, fine art, and white silk upholstery. The apartment smelled of spring blossoms. An empty side room featured a vast glass door that slid open to a patch of manicured woodland, with a view of rolling hills beyond.

"That, of course," said the assistant, "is the creation room. Every apartment has one."

"I want to live here," Ming declared.

"These apartments used to be reserved for the very wealthy, but money isn't what makes the world a better place. Art holds that honor, and artists now live here so they can better focus on the colors, sounds, and words that describe what humanity most needs to know about itself," the assistant recited.

A familiar soliloquy; Ming had written those words, more or less.

"You'd have to be a very accomplished artist to qualify," the assistant continued. "And it's always conditional—if you stop being productive you have to move."

"That clerk in the bookstore thinks Ma's work is predictable," Ming muttered to Charles as they made their way to the grand hall where the party was just beginning.

"Well, maybe someday you *will* live here," said Charles.

"Why not? I invented New China, after all."

He laughed.

They walked through carved doors into a vast room with mosaic floors and gilt molding. A string quartet played, and a number of guests were dancing. A long way from the nights Ma Fu Gang had read his poetry from a perch on his cot, with springs that rattled any time he moved, Ming thought.

Lean men in silk T-shirts and well-toned women in sequined cocktail dresses chattered in both Chinese and English, with a thousand different upper-class accents. Everyone seemed to be holding poses, like sculptures on exhibition.

"What earth-shaking advances did you create today, darling?" a green-eyed man asked Ming, his gaze drawn to her cleavage. A wave of chatter and head-turning announced the arrival of Fu Gang, who entered amidst his entourage. "Oh, there's the artist of the moment. But his book will be passé when mine comes out, and, as his friend, I'm going to have to tell him so," the man remarked.

Ming strode over to Fu Gang and threw her arms around him.

"Hello," the artist of the moment said, startled. He had more flesh on his frame now, with love handles that stretched the seams on his shirt to the point of unraveling; or perhaps the shirt was intentionally frayed, along with the pre-cut hole that showed off a bat tattoo on his left tricep. Fu Gang's hair hung about his ears in spikes, and he dangled an herbal cigarette stump between his thumb and forefinger.

"I'm Ming Cheng—remember the bad old days in the basement dorm at NYU?"

"Oh, of course, Ming. My ex-girlfriend used to read your blog. Not my thing, of course, that porno chick lit genre."

"Must have been a long-ago girlfriend. You had a great description in your book of the highway in Jersey City."

"Great? Now there's an all-encompassing chick lit word. As in 'great cock,' I suppose."

A reed-thin woman in a copper dress blew Fu Gang an air kiss in the general vicinity of his cheek.

"Hello, darling," he responded. "This is..."

"Hello, I'm Xiao Ming Cheng."

"Ming does a racy blog."

"Yes," the woman said. "I've heard of you. The writer from the small town—what was it called, Sunny Town?—nobody visits anymore because it's become a tourist cliché."

"Bad girl, you've hurt her feelings," Fu Gang fake-berated. "I was at your gallery yesterday, darling, and I wondered what possessed you to start carrying Wong Qi Yan? He's a banal would-be wit, really, that sunflower with Van Gogh's ear embedded in the crevices? Simple-minded."

Ming let her own eyes drift. Across the room, Charles was standing

192

beside a skeletally thin woman with a bored expression, despite the fact that she was the one talking. Charles raised his eyebrows in relief when Ming appeared beside him.

"You should come and see my performance piece next week," the woman was saying. "The Anomaly. I invite everyone under thirty-five in the audience to splatter themselves with paint because, these days, we know the artist is the message." She beckoned toward two handsome European men with wind-burned faces and sun-kissed blond locks. "This is Lars and Johann. They are the real estate developers who renovated this palace, and *they* don't qualify to live here."

"We applied," said Lars. "We're a gay couple—wouldn't you think that might count for something? We read up on art and philosophy for our meeting with the board, but they got us with trick questions. They said we didn't have reserves of a sufficiently rich inner life, that our views were too derivative."

"Somewhere there's a loophole," Johann contributed.

"Turn, darling, and show us your steely buns," the woman purred. "I'm going to be thirty in three months, and it's time I got to pronounce a living work of art."

Ming felt a hand groping her arm and turned to see Fu Gang at her side. He drew her away slightly to whisper in her ear. "You are with the venerated professor, I see? The thought of you fucking the bearded old man makes me want to get to know you better. I won't suggest coffee every morning for the rest of my life, but novelty is man's nature, you know, and I hope in your case woman's too." His breath reeked of herb tobacco.

I can make you wake up one morning and wonder why you're such a disgusting prick. The words came to her but didn't come out. He laughed at her when she shoved his hand away; anything she uttered would be the words of a lesser civilizer in his mind. How had she strayed so far, getting stuck down below her godforsaken village while writers like Fu Gang consumed their newfound fame as if it were their due?

She found Charles and told him she was ready to get out of there. He said he was fine with leaving, too. In the taxi outside his building

Charles asked if she'd like a nightcap. She didn't feel like being alone.

"These civilizers are rather drunk with power," he observed as they sat sipping mint tea in his living room. "Living like emperors. The next thing you know there'll be a revolution against *them*."

"You think?"

"You look like I've hit you with a shock wave, my mysterious Ming." Charles was caressing the top of her hand in a strictly friendly fashion.

She pulled her hand away. "You made me think of business school. In the one class I liked, we examined strategic scenarios. The professor was always saying, 'But now let's consider what the unintended consequences might be.'"

"Well, China's most esteemed civilizers might find that the country's most royal real estate has a price tag. Especially if ordinary people start a backlash. It's a lot easier to be a successful capitalist than a successful civilizer." Charles leaned toward her then, and tentatively kissed her. She let him.

In the bedroom he kept his shirt on, tails flying out like a reminder of some important business that would eventually need tending to. Ming had steeled herself for gray hairs and the musty smell of old books, but even when his old-man whiskers scraped her thighs she found herself feeling safe, as if they were somehow protecting each other.

As dawn began to glimmer, she jolted out of sleep and screamed. On the pillow beside hers was a face in a black mask.

"Oh…." The man in the mask was upright now. "I have sleep apnea. It's an asthmatic condition."

"Isn't asthma hereditary?"

Under the sheet she felt a five-alarm lurch.

After that, she had to straighten things out. Her older-man lover, presumably, was imagining that she might want to have a baby with him. She made a point of snickering at children in the street and calling them annoying nits. *This mission is all for New China and for you, Zoe,* she thought. While she never thought of the relationship with Charles as exactly a romance, they made love again, many times, and she began confiding stories from her adolescence so that he'd do the same. He told her about his boyhood in Cambridge, Massachusetts, with his Harvard professor father. He told her of his ex-wife's accusations that he played cerebral, macho games to torment her, the same kind of games he, his brother, and his father had inflicted on his mother. His benighted faculty wife of a mother now had dementia, and even his brilliant brother, a physician who had found a way to restore the memory of a brain-damaged accident victim, couldn't do anything for her.

He even talked about his two sons, and said he would have enjoyed having a daughter.

"Didn't you do the whole party scene as a teenager?" Ming asked. "You know, when you smoked pot and jumped into bed with everyone?"

"Oh no, I was what they called a nerd." He shook his head and looked the part.

Ming took to coming home late, tiptoeing into the dark guestroom so that she wouldn't wake her brother and her nephew. Nothing escaped Han's notice, but he just said, more than once, "You're chronologically a grown-up, so I hope you're being sensible." She wasn't always with Charles; she made some friends of her own and attended other artists' parties in handsome high-rise buildings between the Bei Da campus and the Summer Palace.

Some nights, though, Ming huddled in the guestroom and wrote. Having an affair—that was the term she used in her mind—gave her further inspiration, and she began a novella about Mimi. She had Mimi deciding to run for president of China, against a dozen men. One of the opponents was a pompous real estate executive, the son of a party leader, who kept saying he'd change everything but didn't say how. Ming attempted several scenarios, including one in which Mimi won the election and then evicted the Summer Palace artists in order to accommodate poor people who needed to learn about beauty to rehabilitate their souls.

William called from Sunshine Village and suggested a very special research project. "Our village patron lives in Beijing. You should visit

195

him. Up there on the two-thousand ninety-ninth floor somewhere; what do I know about skyscrapers here in our little village?" It was a coded message; 2099 must be blinking.

"I've set up a meeting with the Sunshine Village patron," Ming announced to her employer/lover Charles a few days later.

They met 2099 on the thirty-eighth floor of a building in the financial district. He was the CEO of a "boutique investment bank"—as if a bank might sell trendy clothes, and, in fact, his firm engaged in mergers and acquisitions that fit the prevailing fashion. The offices were full of art—everything was full of art in Beijing now—and there was even a larger-than-life Buddha sculpture in the waiting room.

Number 2099 looked Ming, then Charles, up and down, as if they might be in possession of something he was searching for. Zoe didn't like him, Ming recalled. He was friendly, though, pumping their hands with what seemed to be genuine enthusiasm.

Ming had told him that Professor Engelhorn was writing a book about the transformations life had taken in New China.

"My life hasn't changed much," 2099 proclaimed, gesturing for them to sit on the other side of his massive mahogany desk. "I still try to put companies together in a way that makes sense. Perhaps in a way that makes even more sense now, but you know, we money men have always been the backbone of China, and now, in New China, we are truly servants of humanity."

"I see you've worked with pharmaceutical clients," Ming said, eyeing a bronze statue of doctor with a syringe under his arm that adorned 2099's desk. She knew—because she had invented the idea—that less famous civilizers were frequently hired as corporate artists, playing live music during the workday, writing entertaining narratives about the corporation, or creating art objects that reflected themes of the company.

"Yes," 2099 replied. "This sculpture came from a pharmaceutical company that's working on a drug to rid the world of depression and lethargy. Despite the fact that we are living in happy times"—his eyes searched Ming and Charles' faces, as if to ensure they hadn't brought any tainted particles of unhappiness into the room—"people aren't always content. We are currently assessing potential partners for distribution in China and exporting overseas."

It wasn't difficult, here in 2099's office, to think of people who could use a good antidepressant. Han, in particular. It was easy, too, to say, "I know of someone who might be a good partner." She dropped the name of Jack Duffy and Plenette-Leuter.

"I've heard about Duffy," 2099 replied, with a regal nod of his head. "I'd like to talk to him."

Charles was unusually pensive when they left, looking down at the sidewalk. "I had a feeling he was leaving a lot of things out of the conversation," he said, finally.

That same evening, Ming went home and found Han sitting in front of the television, as he so often did after work.

"Have you thought about taking anti-depressants? This existential angst wasn't supposed to last—"

"Angst? There's a word for writers." Han threw a wadded-up paper ball across the room. "How do you know what's supposed to last?" Then he scrolled with the remote, to Tiger News, a new cable TV station that had Bradley Kwan, of all people, as its chief commentator, Monday through Friday at six o'clock. Ruben Spurlock, an American media mogul, had attended the Raindance Party congress a few months before and been impressed with a speech that Bradley had made.

"Now China is free, and the people deserve balance," Spurlock had stated in a news release, above the Tiger News logo—the words *Balance* and *Harmony* intertwined.

"Remember when you were struggling to get rich?" Bradley Kwan thundered now, on the TV screen. "What's gonna happen when New China goes broke taking care of people who can't be bothered to work hard?"

Bradley Kwan from Sunshine Village was becoming a new celebrity. At a recent party, Ming had overheard rumors that Ruben Spurlock paid Kwan via an offshore account so that he wasn't obliged to share his money. "Smart man," the woman at the party had pronounced.

197

"You never know what's going to happen."

Ming talked to William and Zoe about it on the phone, and William insisted, as he had so many times, that toleration of dissent was critical. Ming was growing dubious. One evening, Bradley Kwan delivered his commentary in front of a large green screen with billion-yuan figures rolling down. The numbers, he claimed, proved that China had diminishing reserves compared to five years ago. Government figures demonstrated a surplus, but Bradley cupped his hands around his mouth in a way that had become his signature, and yelled, "Don't trust the government, they're all liars! At this rate we're going broke. Ask for answers, not fil-os-o-phee."

In late June, Ming received a text from Zoe that simply said, *The summer rains have returned*. Was that because Zoe had broken up with William? The two of them had been businesslike in their calls. On the phone, Ming sympathized cryptically. "I guess it's good for the peasants and bad for you." She said nothing about Charles; Zoe knew only that Ming had the job as his research assistant.

But Zoe was chatty on that particular call, telling Ming all about the Kwan family. Jing Yin was finally back in school—but it turned out that the boarding school in the southern town of Liangshan she'd gone off to was a Bible studies institute. Jing Yin had emailed Zoe apologizing for her lusts of the flesh. Worse though, Bradley Kwan had built a massive villa on the edge of town, and rumor had it he was holding Yu Li there like a prisoner, bringing in other women now that he was a star, and telling his paramours that the stooped woman with the blind eye was the gardener and the maid.

Ming didn't tell Zoe that Charles was becoming frustrated with his book.

He told Ming that this New China was too of-this-world to have a basis in Buddhism, and too non-hierarchical to spring from the deep roots of Confucianism.

"It makes me think of the way the European powers and the U.S. carved up China after World War I. Chinese intellectuals sought to specifically understand what had brought the culture of this once-great Middle Kingdom so low," Charles droned on one afternoon in

July. "But capitalists asking what's wrong with themselves? Someone might as well have brainwashed them—an extreme version of Mao's reeducation camps."

"I brainwashed them."

Charles looked annoyed, not amused. It made Ming truly sad, watching him push papers off his desk because he knew they were meaningless. He wasn't eating or sleeping much, and his face showed tracks of defeat. And now, that night, she was dragging him to Badaling to have dinner with her parents. He had become a frequent guest at the Chengs' apartment, and he seemed to enjoy escaping into talk of the past with Mama and Papa, but she knew he'd rather be dining with some hotshot official who'd been privy to the conversations that Charles was sure must have taken place among a select secret group of leaders.

That night, Han and Bo Fu came too, and instead of dwelling on the past, they watched Bradley Kwan's show. A senator from Washington was his guest. The senator proclaimed that the United States had better eliminate its social programs and rid itself of the federal deficit, or it would end up becoming a colony of New China.

"Not so long ago, we had to work ourselves to the bone just for a bowl of rice," Bradley bellowed. "We knew the meaning of money, and we respected those who worked hard. Senator, tell me, what do you think is going to happen to a country that pays people to sit on their bottoms and contemplate fil-os-o-phee?"

"He was out of work," said Ming.

"He was a peasant," said Han, sneering.

"We respect peasants," Ming reprimanded her brother.

"China has always been a class-conscious society just below the surface," Charles pronounced. He knew when he should play referee. "And even in this New China, I can't imagine that changing overnight."

"I hear this 'peasant,' Bradley Kwan, has built a fifteen-room mansion just outside of Sunshine Village," Papa contributed. "He's still in the running for town council, but some suggest that's only a ploy, and he intends some bigger scheme. Maybe New China

199

represents the next phase of evolution, but it's going to take thousands of years to evolve that wiring for facing adversity out of our brains. You know what our staff do on weekends? They go wild boar hunting. It is not as if they really need to hunt. Barbecued boar is pretty tasty, though."

Thousands of years? Ming shuddered. "Bradley Kwan's dissent is conditioning us all for the insanity you can get with free speech," she said aloud. "It ought to help people learn how to rebut stupidity in the voting booth. We just have to provide them with the tools to come to sensible conclusions for themselves."

"Ming invented New China single-handedly, don't you know?" Charles said. The three men at the table laughed as if they were watching a five-year-old turning somersaults. Papa chuckled so hard he began to turn purple, and Mama had to hand him a glass of water.

Ming passed the platter of spareribs to her brother, determined to change the subject. "Han, how is the deal business going?"

Han clicked his chopsticks together like dancing puppets. "Things move slowly, but I'm in no hurry."

"Han wrote a great business expansion plan for us," said Papa, his face beaming.

"I'm writing a new novella," Ming announced, and saying that to her family still felt like an act of defiance. Several editors at publishing houses had asked to see her manuscript when it was completed, but nobody around here was going to applaud her for that.

"I have to write a story for school," her nephew piped up, "but I don't like writing."

"I'll help you," Ming promised.

"You see, not everyone even wants to be a writer," Han persisted.

"Yes, Charles thinks it's easier to be a capitalist," Ming replied.

"You know all about easy capitalism, little sister. Everyone knows why you came back to China. We know you worked for that scumbag Li Nan and you're a wanted criminal in New York. Tell me, Ming, do they have wanted posters with your face plastered everywhere?"

Mama frowned but remained silent.

"I might not have artistic talent, but at least I'm not a criminal on the run—"

Ming closed her eyes and gripped the edge of the table; the world was blood red behind her eyes and venomous retorts swarmed through her head. She ran her tongue along her Dr. Perlmutter teeth and remembered the reign of fear in Li Nan's boiler room—and how Han could have transferred some money to avoid it all. She'd siphoned thousands out of the New Icarus account to rehabilitate William Sun, and Han hadn't even noticed. A teapot, still steaming, sat on the table. Her hand reached out with a life of its own, and flung the contents in Han's direction.

"Aaahhhh…" Han shrieked as porcelain smashed on the table and hot tea splashed all over his face and torso. "You're crazy!"

"We are leaving," Ming said stiffly, taking Charles by the arm. "And, yes, I'll be staying with him. And we're having great sex, by the way!"

Papa choked, turning violet as Ming stalked out the door. She heard Charles saying, "I'm so sorry," then following her and grabbing her arm as if to restrain her.

In Charles's apartment, he poured two glasses of whisky. Ming sank into the couch. "My brother loved making money while other people starved."

"Our brains are wired for the jungle, mostly. We love it when people envy our success," Charles acknowledged. He sat in a chair, opposite her.

"I hate my brother."

"Did you really commit a crime?"

"I needed to make money and an old friend hired me," she muttered, avoiding his gaze. "Why don't you cheer me up and tell me about life in the '70s? Did you ever take a road trip? I had plans for one once, a long time ago now."

"A buddy and I took off together on motorcycles our senior year in college; we only got as far as the East Village, though. We slept on the floor in somebody's place—there must have been twenty other kids, some of whom were in a rock band. The whole building shook

201

when they rehearsed," Charles said, smiling in recollection. "My buddy got me stoned every day, except I could only take about two hits before I started coughing. I even had a girlfriend, for a while."

"Who was your girlfriend?"

"Oh, some ambitious girl just passing through."

Ming rocked forward, almost cheerful with excitement. "What was her name?"

"Alicia. She was from Connecticut. She was shy like me, which made us gravitate together in that crazy stew. I saw her wedding announcement in the *New York Times* a few years later. Why are you looking at me that way?"

Might as well go for broke. "Did you ever know a girl named Billie Austin?"

Charles froze, his face flushing a deep red. "Yes, I…"

"Zoe Austin. Did you ever connect the two?"

Charles's lips drew tight together and he rose abruptly to his feet. "I think it's time for bed," he said. By his tone, Ming could tell, he didn't mean anything but sleep.

The next morning, Charles was already dressed when Ming stirred.

"Listen, I've got meetings." He was clearly not inviting her along. "Then I'm going to meet with some historians at a retreat outside of Shanghai so we can plan a conference on New China."

Charles Engelhorn had a fine grasp of Chinese etiquette, Ming thought. A polite escape, to a retreat she hadn't heard a thing about. He even promised to transfer some money into her bank account. A very polite way of firing your casual labor.

Chapter Fifteen

I'm on my way back," Ming told Zoe. "I'm on a train now. It's all been so awful. Is Jeff still in Sunshine Village?"

Zoe didn't want to talk to Ming about Jeff, who had sent his estranged wife an email several weeks before with a photo of himself with his arms around four pretty women, and the message, *Greetings from a mile below heaven.*

"And the weather's awful here," Zoe told her. "I've got a terrible cold. William's sequestering himself, the roads are flooded, people are staying home, and the stores aren't getting their deliveries. You might have trouble getting in."

"I'm meeting Tom in Chengdu. I guess we'll just have to wait it out."

Tom? Zoe didn't tell Ming that on recent flights, Tom had brought along a curvaceous woman from Beijing whom he'd introduced as his fiancée. Zoe had dined with the betrothed couple one night, and Tom's fiancée had talked all through dinner about her "self-actualization journey." She had been an interior designer, and a wealthy man had set her up with her own business, but she'd woken up one morning feeling like she couldn't breathe and told him she was giving it all up. Tom had looked fat with contentment.

"I'm sure the rain is all your fault," said Ming on the phone.

"No doubt." Zoe stifled a sneeze.

"You sound terrible. Get some rest."

⌘

There were so many songs about rain: love songs, protest songs, life in the rain. But songwriters didn't write about the slimy roadblock in your nostrils, or the heat of fever making your bones feel as if they were breaking. Just four days ago, Zoe had inhaled wisdom, lifted off through the downpour, and saved a battered wife.

But then, of course, Zoe—Zenia—knew how to stop the rain.

She'd worked hard the last few months, side by side with William but resisting the electricity. Zoe's grandfather, Grandpa Stork Austin, died in May, but Zoe didn't even go back to Mississippi for the funeral. Though the musty smell of academia still wafted through the back of her mind, she had trouble remembering what it was like to examine little pebbles of history.

Jing Yin had been emailing regularly since her departure, saying in every message that she wanted to atone for her sinful ways. She'd sent a recording she'd made in the very targeted musical genre of Christian peasant rap. The lyrics referred to "the land" and to the "wayward soul that saw the light," concluding with, "I am alone no mo'. I got Jesus as my bestie."

"Jesus? That hippie self-promoter," William had scoffed. "He got himself a great piece of real estate in the heavens, and he told me he's never coming back. But, of course, people are free to join cults and free to love Bradley Kwan."

William didn't sleep anymore, as far as Zoe knew. His hair fell every which way, like sentries too fatigued to stand. He didn't tell her exactly what he was doing.

June had brought a torrid spray each afternoon, and, by the second week of July, the rain was so fierce that it woke her in the night, tearing trees from their roots and leaving rocks and tangled branches at Zoe's front door. The river rose to the cliff's edge and puddled at the feet of the big stone Buddha.

The weather was not the only thing that raged that month. Five nights ago, Jing Yin had called, sobbing into the phone. "Zuo Yi? It's my papa—he's been stepped on like an ant all his life, and now that he has a little power, he is crazy. My mama tried to get away—he's got her locked up in that house—and he said he'd kill her if she tries again. We're all going to hell anyway, but can anyone help her?"

There's no need for hell, Zoe wanted to say, though she had her own vivid pictures of Satan and fire and brimstone from Mississippi Sunday school.

A women's shelter, just beyond Market Street, accommodated women from the village and villages beyond who'd fled their husbands. At the shelter, they could take classes in house wiring, plumbing, business initiatives, and the marketing of handicrafts and homemade sauces.

"They'd take care of your mother there," Zoe told Jing Yin.

"So she can learn how to market her own homemade pepper sauce?" the girl spat out. "Or fix the toilet?"

"So she can be independent," Zoe said in defense.

"She's gotten, uh, slow. She won't try leaving again unless someone drags her out when he's away, and he'll find her and kill her if he knows where she is."

Do good deeds, Grandpa Austin's voice whispered in Zoe's head.

She put on her galoshes and slogged through the muddy path to William's house. She found him, as usual, in the bunker. He was immersed in a computer program and looked up only to say, "Everyone's behaving, don't worry."

"I need your help. We've got to rescue Jing Yin's mother."

William turned from his console at last. He had a rainbow of circles around his eyes and stubble darkened his chin. It was not a small matter that she was proposing, Zoe knew. Bradley Kwan had the power to ruin people now. When a provincial police chief had dared to announce a crackdown on opium sales, a few days later on Tiger News, Bradley condemned his "corrupt practices," and the police chief was now under investigation.

"Since the roads are flooded and the guards would hear a car, I was thinking we could fly there, and between us carry her out," Zoe told him.

He agreed to meet her at four, when Bradley would be off at the studio. And so, in the forests behind William's house, Zoe attempted to fly again.

She inhaled wisdom, though breathing felt like drowning. After five false starts, she felt her body rising into the pelting rain. The wind swirled, yet it seemed to carry her along.

At last, Bradley Kwan's villa came into view, shrouded in sheets of gray, the grounds sodden. Through a window in the guard station, they saw two men in uniforms playing cards. The front of the house was quiet, the walkway lined with bushes sculpted into the faces of hideous devils. Two painted statues of naked warriors stood on either side of the door.

"I thought we'd banished bad taste for good," William whispered. He grabbed her waist and soared to a sturdy tree branch overlooking the house. "Stay here," he instructed. Zoe wrapped her arms and legs around the branch, shivering in the dampness. Suddenly a blue butterfly hovered beside her, then flew toward the house.

The butterfly found a window left ajar, and fluttered through McMansion-sized rooms that were mostly empty. It was a house without possessions, no books or sentimental treasures: life with nothing to show except the price of the real estate. In a vast room with a dining table, three triple-tier crystal chandeliers hung from the ceiling, and at the end of the hall, the butterfly saw what made the crystals sparkle so. Yu Li stood at the top of a ladder, dipping a cloth into a cup of vinegar solution and polishing each crystal so vigorously that he could imagine a layer of skin being scraped away. A bruise bloomed beside her cloudy eye and a vacancy had settled in her clear eye. Yu Li sang as she worked—an off-key and incoherent song of dying in the Sichuan soil. Spying the butterfly, she made a hissing sound, spittle hurling through her teeth.

"Bug!" she slurred, in her rough peasant dialect, cocking her head slightly. Her peasant clothes had a waft of black magic, William thought.

To subdue a wife, you didn't need leg irons, only an opium pipe.

"If you want to be free, follow me," the butterfly whispered in her ear.

"Whaa??" Yu Li lurched back on her ladder, which teetered beneath her feet. William rapidly transformed himself into an invisible flying creature and swept the woman into his arms, out the window, and into the forest.

A dazed Yu Li found herself standing beside a path, swirling with the rush of rain, on the outskirts of the village. The tiny peasant woman gaped at Zoe, who arrived breathless as if she'd just come out of the woods.

Rubbing her good eye, Yu Li peered down at the muddy water that rose up to her shins and up again at the horizon, as if searching for visions more strange than those immediately before her. Uncomprehending and almost as small as a child, she let Zoe guide her through mud and water, squishing through back roads that might as well be canals, to a modest stucco house, where a bevy of women seemed to know just what to do, pressing her with hot tea and warm towels.

Zoe returned to the bunker mortal style, sloshing through the pathways, and by the time she arrived down below, she was shivering all over.

Sun Three, with his tidy hair and pale, puzzled eyes was at the console. He jumped when she entered, a copy who'd become capable enough to watch the computers when things were calm, but so shy he could barely even speak to her.

"Where is William?" Zoe demanded.

"He's…he's on a b-b-business trip."

"Just like that?"

The next morning Zoe dragged herself into the Sunshine Finance office. William was not there. A pile of business plans awaited her, but the words and numbers danced across the page. She tried to rise from her chair but her limbs were like iron, her head a ball of fire. Her eyes began to weep with a life of their own.

"Are you all right?" The Sunshine Finance executive assistant had poked her head in the doorway. "You've got quite a cold."

Zoe recalled that her mother would get dreadful colds, mostly when a callback hadn't come. Billie would stay in bed for days with rheumy eyes and a crimson nose, the apartment stinking of eucalyptus vapors.

Zoe was still sneezing when William sauntered into the office the following day, sporting a ruddy glow and a new haircut.

"Did you have a nice vacation?" Zoe asked in a bleary voice.

"Very funny. Go home and take care of yourself. I'm working on something I want to share with you, but don't come to me until you get the message."

Zoe took his advice, leaving with business plans under her arm. She could work as well from bed. A day passed without a word or a sign from a butterfly. She even wrote a few pages of chapter two in her dissertation, though the words themselves felt musty. On the second day, the phone rang and interrupted her progress.

"Zuo Yi, I'm back!" Jing Yin said the rain had started to dissipate to the south in Liangshan, and the school principal had allowed the bus driver to take her home. "The road into Sunshine Village is like a river!" Jing Yin exclaimed. "We prayed, Zuo Yi, and a miracle blew my mama through the woods. The rain is getting tired of falling. I'm a peasant, I can tell these things. Come to the shelter? Mama's safe, but she's sick."

When Zoe arrived, Yu Li was in bed, her face pale and chapped, her brown eye almost as vacant as the blind one. Jing Yin, looking older than her sixteen years, perched on the edge of her mother's bed, a gilt-edged Holy Bible in Chinese in her lap.

"I keep telling her Jesus will guide her through," Jing Yin said. "They want her to go to rehab. My father asked if I knew where she was, but I told him no."

Zoe comforted both mother and daughter as best she could, though a fever rattled her brain. They all agreed Yu Li should stay in the shelter, where night duty nurses and police guards stood watch.

The rain in Sunshine Village was showing no signs of relenting when Zoe left the shelter that evening. *We must write a program for Bradley Kwan*, she thought. *Injured creatures could become a deadly force.*

"Zoe!" a voice called from the Nirvana Café.

She turned and saw Jeff sitting at a rowdy table by the big window, Lulu by his side with a possessive arm around him. He introduced those at the table with him as Zoe apologized, between sneezes, for dripping on everyone. Jeff's other companions were a group of performance artists.

They told her they were preparing a Sun Dance, a show that would present an antidote to the Raindance Party rhetoric. "Here's a chair," one of the performers said.

"Thanks, but I'm headed home." Zoe felt simultaneously hot and cold and the thought of a cool jasmine beer made her head ache. "I'm not feeling well."

"I'll check on you later, okay?" Jeff called, as Zoe left, hunched beneath her coat against the rain.

She was half asleep in a hot bath when the doorbell rang. She slipped into her kimono. Jeff stood there. "You look awful," he conceded as he shrugged himself out of his dripping poncho. "Do you want some chicken soup? The Dragon Lady emailed me, by the way. She hopes we can be friends. Can you imagine—after she fucked me over? I've decided to leave Sunshine Village, go traveling. I'll have to tell Lulu she doesn't own me, never thought I'd be the one to break someone's heart. Why don't you come with me?"

"Oh, I can't. I'd love to, but I can't." Zoe sneezed again.

"Get into bed. I'll take care of you. Of course, I'm soaked through, too. Does this fucking rain ever let up?"

Zoe put on sweats and gave Jeff her winter bathrobe. They curled up on her bed to watch a Hollywood comedy—just like the old days in Jeff's New York dorm room. Thunder shook the walls, and rain pounded ceaselessly on the roof.

"You're still hot. Even when you're sick," Jeff said. "Come see the rest of China with me."

"I have a job here—I can't abandon it. Don't you want Ming to see that you're a successful civilizer with a girlfriend? Don't you want to rub that in her face, even just a little?" The thought of Jeff leaving made Zoe feel abandoned. She muted the television, and as if to keep him there, began relating feverish tales about how Jing Yin's mother had mysteriously escaped from the evil Bradley Kwan, despite her opium-induced haze, and was now suffering withdrawals in the women's shelter, while her husband was issuing death threats and her daughter was trying to summon Jesus.

"Shit," Jeff said. "What a fucked-up family. Maybe you should adopt Jing Yin. "

Zoe, wracked by a coughing fit, was unable to reply. Jeff massaged her back and shoulders, his fingers probing tightly wound muscles and tortured knots. Jeff's body, leaning against her own, felt alien, scrawny; she longed for dexterous sinews, smelling of earth and fire. He rubbed a stiff spot on her spine and fever shook through her all over again, pouring out in tears that felt scalding.

"You're not still crying over William Moony, are you? You can do so much better," Jeff murmured. The softness of his words made her cry even more. "Intervention time," he went on. "I think you're gonna have to quit this job. As long as you see him every day, how are you ever going to move on?"

"I can't."

"Sure you can. What kind of weird spell does he have over you? Tell me. Otherwise, I'm going to have to start spying on him and see if he's got some kind of secret nanochip he's planted in your brain giving commands. Or some thousand-year-old aphrodisiac snake powder he slips in the water."

She turned her tear-streaked face toward Jeff and kissed him lightly on the mouth, just to distract him. *I'm as bad as Ming, leading him on like this.* But Jeff forgot about snake powders and nanochips in an instant, and began to tug at her sweatshirt.

"Let me just make you happy," she coughed out, pulling away from his hands. Ducking under the bathrobe, she tickled his hard-on with her tongue.

"Oooohhhh, baby!" Jeff moaned. "I could let you do that all night…"

Twenty minutes later, Jeff let out a long moan, squirted in her face, then, mumbling "best ever," drifted off to sleep.

Thunder crashed like a thousand baseball bats against the roof. *I'll never get to sleep, I don't deserve to sleep,* Zoe thought. But sometime in the night, a noise shook her awake. She tiptoed to a window, and, through a musky sky, a full moon grinned. A golden moon. In Manhattan the full moon sometimes hung bigger than life, as if it were preening for some Broadway director, but in Sunshine Village the craters looked deeper and darker, the man in the moon staring down with Svengali eyes. The peasants still warned against looking the full moon in the eye because it might hypnotize you.

She heard a howling, followed by high-pitched yips. The peasants also claimed wolf-dogs came out when the full moon shone, lone beasts from the litter of a dog who had bred with a wolf. The shaggy animals mated with their close relations when the moon was full, then stalked off on their own to give birth to deranged loner pups. Two howls sounded, then six, from hilltops and caverns. They sounded like they were preparing for a feast.

Her limbs called out for rest, finally, and she turned away from the window and crawled into bed. A cloudy sunrise was pouring through the room when the phone rang.

"Zuo Yi, help me!" Jing Yin cried.

"Where are you?"

"Papa did it! The police station… Oh, I pray to God! Please hurry!"

Zoe heard voices in the background, Jing Yin screaming, "No!" and the sound of hanging up. She shook Jeff awake and scrambled into her boots and poncho.

Together they sloshed through the rain to the neighborhood car park. Starting the ignition with just her thumb print, Zoe sped to the police station.

On most days, the Sunshine Village Police Station hummed with the pallorous sounds of files being shuffled, computer keyboards clicking, and bureaucrat staffers conversing about movies and sports. Now, though, an unruly spectacle greeted Zoe and Jeff. Police officers, their jackets askew, and teenagers with pierced noses and lips swarmed about. Zoe spotted the Kwans' former neighbors and several members of the Sunshine Group staff. Jing Yin, in bloodstained clothes, twisted about in a big wooden chair, her face streaming with tears.

At the sight of Zoe, the girl began to shriek, "He did it! I didn't kill her. My papa did…I swear I didn't kill her."

A policewoman directed Zoe and Jeff to the evidence room, where she showed them photographs of the crime scene. Yu Li's body sprawled on the bamboo floor in a thick pool of blood, one clouded eye open, her throat a ragged wound as if a wolf-dog had tried to gnaw her voice out.

"We know a man broke into the shelter, sprayed the police guard and the woman on duty with chloroform, and threatened the women with his knife until he found Yu Li's room," the policewoman said. "We've got a posse of police out looking for him."

"Bradley Kwan?"

The policewoman nodded.

"So why are you holding Jing Yin?"

"We just want to ask her some questions. We're trying to understand how Yu Li escaped from the family's house. It seems likely she had help, and we need to know who that was."

"Can I use your phone?" Zoe asked, trying to suppress a shiver.

She left a voice message on William's house phone.

By the time the policewoman let them back out into the front office, a television news crew had arrived. And so had William. Zoe plunked herself into a chair beside him.

"What's going to happen to Jing Yin now?" a peasant woman in the crowd wondered aloud. A reporter within earshot caught up the refrain.

"Jing Yin, where are you going to live now?" the reporter shouted, holding the microphone out to catch the girl's response.

"She can stay with me, if she likes," Zoe spoke up, without thinking.

"Zoe's apartment is small," William announced, rising to his feet. "Jing Yin is welcome at my house until she works things out."

Once the police were willing to release Jing Yin, William and Zoe bundled her into a car. In William's house, Zoe gave the exhausted girl sleeping tea from the local chamomile flowers. Jing Yin obediently took a bath, put on a pair of William's too-big-for-her pajamas, and knelt at the side of the bed to pray.

"Now I lay me down to sleep…" she intoned in Mandarin. "Do you know it?"

"I pray the lord my soul to keep…" Zoe said, almost in a whisper.

212

"Are you a Christian?" Jing Yin's eyebrows shot up.

"Not a good one."

"Jesus will save you if you let him."

Once the girl had fallen asleep, Zoe found William in the library. He shook his head with disapproval when she came in. "The peasant girl is beyond your help. She needs a psychiatrist and meds."

"She's my business. You can ask her to leave any time you want."

He shook his head again, then rose. "Before you make any decisions, I have something important to show you. Down below." They went down the steep flight and the incline. At the door to the bunker, William put his hands over her eyes. "No peeking," he whispered. She felt the hot brush of his breath against her ear and the leap of sparks between them.

When they entered the bunker, William removed his hands. A man stood in front of the computer screens.

The man's demeanor was familiar somehow. While he bore a vague resemblance to William, he was taller and carried more weight on his frame. His face was round and serene, like the face the giant Buddha might have had if the sculptor had finished it. He had ohm-chanting eyes, clear as spring water, that surveyed her body as if lust were an involuntary reflex; eyes that looked as if he had subsisted all his life on spirit-searching and sex. Neither cosmetic surgery nor magic could change a person's eyes.

"This," said William, "is a man I call my cousin. I've named him Simon Sun. He attended Oxford but was expelled for partying, as well as a little sex scandal we don't talk about in the family. What do you think?"

"She's speechless," the not-quite identical copy, Simon Sun, cheered. "You see, Master? She still loves you. The master decided to make me before he saves the world, Zoe. He did it for you—I'm a gift. I can even undertake a few limited transformations of my own." In an instant, Simon Sun's complexion became ruddy, his features European, and then darker, so that he resembled a man of Indian descent.

"And just so you know, I would never chase young girls. I'm

213

chronologically about thirty-three in this life, wouldn't you say, and to tell the truth I think mature women, older than I am, are really, really hot."

Simon Sun spent the afternoon lounging at the Nirvana Café, spinning tales about enlightenment to three young British women who'd arrived just before the storm. They were happy to have him distract them from the gruesome murder everyone in town was talking about.

Below ground, the two re-ignited lovers let themselves forget both the madman and his sleeping daughter for a little while. William presented Zoe with a small silk box. Inside, she found a chiseled stone that cast a million rainbow prisms against the walls. Sichuan mines produced opals both ordinary and extraordinary; this one, affixed to a ring, was absolutely celestial.

"Will you marry me?" William asked, dropping to one knee.

He slid the ring on to her finger. The stone was heavy on her hand, massive enough to skim the borders of vulgarity. "Yes…but it's…so big!"

"Just think of the new consumer society we live in. If everything is so affordable, maybe we can re-think being blingy." When he expounded that way, she knew he wasn't telling her everything. "All right," he admitted. "It's not just an engagement ring. Don't take it off. Ever. Think of yourself as the guardian of our future, just in case the opposition wins."

"Does it contain a camera? A recording device?"

"Nothing like that."

Before they could leap back into bed, however, someone knocked at the door. Simon Sun entered the bunker. "News flash. Bradley Kwan has been found floating face down in the river," he said.

"Stay down here," William instructed the man he called his cousin. "And keep an eye on the screens." Number 2099 had been blinking again. "We should make some rounds," he said to Zoe.

They found Jing Yin in a trance-like sleep under the quilt, then went to the police station. The captain was closing the file on Yu Li's death, calling it murder and confirming the murderer's death. The villagers had seen Bradley Kwan swimming through the rapids, until he reached the thousand-foot drop-off known as Suicide Falls. The captain said his body was probably shredded to pieces by the rocks.

When they emerged from the police station, the rain had stopped.

The newly engaged couple spent many hours in a café where champagne flowed and patrons toasted to the fitting end to a crime and the future for the engaged couple. Only later, as they strolled home, did William tell his fiancée that something was on his mind. "Maybe Bradley Kwan knows how to survive the rapids. People have forgotten how the skies over this town grow dark when a villager dies. There's no darkness."

⌘

Around that same time, Jing Yin awoke, yet still heard voices from the land of dreams. She rose up and walked out the door, wading barefoot in rolled-up pajamas through the storm-soaked grasses that led to the cliffs, following a bloated moon on its first night of waning. From the forest she heard the long, baying cry of a wolf-dog. She looked at the moon and it seemed to drip with the same blood she'd seen on her mother's savaged throat. A voice told her where to go, and she made her way to the yawning mouth of the cave on the riverbank, venturing behind the stalagmites that resembled magic mushrooms. There, seated on the cool ground, Jing Yin began to inhale until she heard the voice of God himself, a voice that bellowed in a strange and foreign tongue. She would listen and listen until she understood, she resolved. *Inhale the heavenly,* the mushrooms told her, *forget the language you left behind, make room for the new...*

Chapter Sixteen

Rains were still bombarding the city of Chengdu, northeast of Sunshine Village, where Ming spent four days in a hotel room, mostly in bed with Tom. Dear Tom. Ming dared to imagine he was the man who would bring comfort. They spent many hours watching the news. The politically progressive channel—one that Ming had labeled anti-Tiger News—depicted cities and villages shimmying under water. Agitated news commentators described houses washed away by floods and scores of people drowned.

Breaking news interrupted the weather reports. "Anti-New China talk show host, Bradley Kwan, fled his home in Sunshine Village this morning after an incident that left his wife dead," the anchorwoman spelled out. "Mr. Kwan, whose body was last seen in the Tuo River rapids, is presumed dead."

Ming burst out of bed.

"Bradley fucking Kwan?" Tom exclaimed. "I saw him on TV and kept thinking, 'Why does he want to send us all back to our lives of greed?'"

"When my mother was a girl, before the revolution, they used to say that if the summer rains didn't arrive on time you had to split a stone with an axe, which would bring the rains. The peasants still believe that if one bad thing happens, it's a portent of something else looming. It is a sign, you see, that whoever's in charge has lost the mandate of heaven."

"Huh? Who's in charge of what?"

"I'm in charge of New China." She said it with gravity in her voice.

Tom wrinkled his face and looked lost, as if she'd just said something vicious in a language he didn't speak. So much for permanent comfort. Tom was no Professor, just a nicely padded lug.

She paced, watched the ceaseless lightning outside. *Would they never get out of here?* Tom was not the answer, she realized. She was getting tired of the earnest way he stared at the TV, as if the news from New China were a lecture on something as indecipherable as how to plant rice on planet Jupiter. And the room had grown stagnant with the smell of flesh and beer.

They made love again, just to have something to do.

"I'm going to lose my mind," Ming said afterward.

He nodded in agreement.

But on the fourth day, she watched Tom stride across the room, naked with his flabby stomach, and open the window at last. The scent of freshly washed air poured in.

"A blue sky," Tom said, smiling. "I'll phone the airport."

He arranged for his plane to be ready in a few hours, which gave them time to order breakfast. She watched Tom overload his rice porridge with peanuts, scallions, pork, bamboo shoots, sliced wheat gluten, and a fried egg on top. He ate, then put his hands on the table.

"There's something I have to tell you," he announced. "I'm moving to Beijing. I've been offered a route starting in September, flying to Hong Kong. I should have told you before, but you know... didn't seem like the right time."

"Have you met someone else?"

"You'll always be special to me." He put his arm around her as if he expected her to cry.

Ming had a window seat on Tom's Cessna. The plane was full; tourists had been waiting for the flights to start up again. Two passengers behind her were talking about their plans to experience the poetry of laboring in the fields alongside the peasants of Sunshine Village. Just after one o'clock, the plane began to descend over the forest, and Ming could see the banks of the Tuo River through a familiar scrim of clouds. This was the time of year when the yellow rapeseed would be rearing up and the path through the orchards would be lined with squishy black plums. Soon, the hard green apples would appear and old peasant men would play mournful tunes on their lutes. Civilizations would come and go, but the ghost-clouds and rapeseed would be steadfast.

217

When they landed, Ming bid Tom a hurried goodbye and ran off, so that she wouldn't beg him to stay with her and make a fool of herself. *You'd be bored with him anyway,* a voice chided, but she'd never felt so alone before.

Her old apartment was hushed and cool inside. A parade of tourists had rented it out in her absence, yet her big jade plant still thrived, sprouting a woody trunk and six new branches. The tourists had read the instructions she'd left and watered it; a couple had even left notes saying so.

When she went out, though, the air was full of voices, and from the hill she could already see a crowd swarming the village square at Market Street.

"This village is decadent!" a man standing on an overturned box thundered. "There are homosexuals who call themselves married, despoiling the sacred union…"

Ming, blending in, found villagers shouting all around her.

"Bradley Kwan was a good man. Demons made him kill his wife!"

"Or those foreign spies who watch us from the pagoda!"

"Or the devil himself!"

"Mrs. Kirschenbaum, I presume?" She turned to find none other than Jeff standing behind her. A transformed Jeff, in fine Italian shoes, a crisp linen shirt, and trendy rectangular glasses, his face sporting the glow of a man who hiked the hills and breakfasted on brown rice.

"Jeff, I'm so glad you're still here!" She threw her arms about him and had a sudden urge to laugh with him again.

He disentangled himself and gestured toward the mob. "I saw this town change overnight and not for the better. But I stay because, unlike some people, I can't abandon my friends. Zoe is sick as a dog. Didn't you bring your sugar daddy professor with you?"

"I have a lot to explain. Can we have a drink tonight?"

"Not tonight. I'm kind of spoken for." Then he said something about being on his way somewhere, and left her alone in the crowd.

But, of course, Ming had places of her own to go. At the offices of Sunshine Finance, a new assistant occupied the front desk.

"I'm Ming Cheng. I work here—in that office. Is Zoe here?"

"In a meeting."

"Can you buzz her, please? Tell her Ming is here."

The assistant led her to the conference room as if she were sure Ming didn't know her way around. William, rumpled and unshaven, sat at a round table with the two young women who used to sit in the front office, each with a stack of proposals. Zoe was halfway to the door as Ming entered.

"You made it!" Zoe gave her a fierce hug, and in that proximity Ming saw crusty redness around her nose.

"We'll finish this later," Zoe directed the assistants and gestured for Ming to sit down in their place. That was when Ming noticed Zoe's hand. *Horrors, a giant Sichuan opal.*

"We're engaged!" William announced.

"We found Jing Yin, did you hear?" Zoe asked, her voice stuffy and almost baritone. "She's hiding in the cave. A psychiatrist keeps going and trying to talk to her but she just screams gibberish."

"Everything's crazy here," William said, and even the fire in his eyes looked overworked. "We've got people begging me to run for mayor and others who insist I've been diverting money into offshore bank accounts."

Later, Zoe agreed to go home and rest, and William took Ming down to the bunker. "The thing we have to keep secret," he confided, "is that Zoe and I, with the help of a little magic, got Mrs. Kwan out of the house. That family has been her curse. I understand that Zoe's mother and unknown mortal father are a part of the family I'm marrying into, but I draw the line at the mad girl in the cave."

He seemed to have something else on his mind. "I don't think Bradley Kwan is dead."

"I saw his picture on television and I thought something was missing. I didn't feel any darkness," she agreed.

"They never found the body, you know. If we accept Jing Yin into our family, Bradley Kwan will come gunning for us someday. Zoe doesn't believe me, but you and I, we have a sense of what death in Sunshine Village feels like. Welcome home, Ming."

Chapter Seventeen

There are reasons to go back to where you came from, Ming decided. Ideally, you sit on a sun-warmed rock and speak to the ghosts of your childhood. But with a business to run, and a country to save, she had little time for communing with phantoms.

What Ming found readily visible were amoebic life forms flailing about in stagnant puddles as the rains dwindled. She toyed with an end to the Mimi novella in which Mimi was elected president, but overnight a resistance faction sprang up, a faction of men who'd heard a rumor that she planned to take away their jobs and replace them with women.

In the office, she watched Zoe zip about like a fevered hummingbird. "The feng shui man says the last Saturday in August is the most opportune time for a wedding," Zoe told her, and sneezed into a tissue before she continued. A doctor had diagnosed her with a sinus infection and prescribed antibiotics, but she refused to rest.

"We should have the ceremony when the sun is at its height, and facing water to ward off dangers. He said no guests who've just crossed the ocean, and expect disaster if the rain starts to fall or if anyone uninvited shows up. Not that I really believe this stuff, and of course I offered to send my mom a ticket. So can you believe it—I think you can, actually—Billie the diva said, 'Honey, I miss you like crazy. Just have another wedding for your old mom and your grandma and your friends when you get back here, okay? 'Cause you can imagine what a plane ride like that would do to my back. You'd be pushing around your crippled old ma,'" Zoe said, in near-perfect mimicry. "What mother doesn't come to her daughter's wedding? Of course, if she did come, the wedding would be all about her."

Zoe was silent a moment, and Ming was sure she was thinking of the would-be father, who wouldn't have to cross the ocean. Coincidentally enough, that night Charles sent her a to-the-point email. *I heard about the mad Bradley Kwan. Have you heard from the folks in Sunshine Village?*

Time to let him know his "researcher" has some authority, Ming decided. *In fact, I'm back in Sunshine Village, back at my job as the co-head of Sunshine Finance.* And time to give Zoe the gift of truth. He'd need to be there for that to happen, so she wrote, *Zoe is getting married to the CEO, William Sun. She's been pretty busy, so I'm supposed to invite you. It would mean a lot to her to have you come.*

She'd tried to find refuge in Tom, then lost herself in work, but when she saw the name "Charles" on the screen, a sword pierced her heart. This was, presumably, her punishment for deceiving Charles and Zoe. It was four weeks until the wedding—twenty-eight days, to be exact. She gave herself exactly that length of time to get over him.

His email address taunted her again the next day. *I should see Sunshine Village. Very interesting. I've read about William Sun. I'll see if I can make it. Thank you for passing this along.*

This message, like the one the day before, was unsigned. Was he trying to leave her uncertain as to whether she should call him Professor Engelhorn or Charles, or maybe she was supposed to forget she knew his name altogether? Maybe when he referred to "the folks in Sunshine Village," it was strictly a fatherly concern about Zoe?

But to worry over love and paternity was an indulgence. William asked Ming and Zoe to come down to the bunker, and he showed them Number 2099 on the screen. The number had been steady and unblinking for the past week, but William's immortal eyes had detected a slight fading in the pixels. Ming didn't see any difference. Neither did Zoe.

"Stop staring at the screens and get out more," Zoe rasped.

Three weeks before the wedding, Charles sent another non-signed message saying he was going to come to Sunshine Village soon, and he hoped to be there for the wedding. Perhaps the message foreordained that Ming would prepare a pot of jasmine tea for her ailing friend and censored wisdom would come pouring out. Zoe was telling Ming about a business plan, but she stopped to sneeze and threw a wadded-up tissue into the garden of Kleenex carnations that had piled up in her wastebasket.

"You ought to be in bed. Did you ever suffer from childhood asthma, by chance?"

Zoe shook her head. "I've never been sick, ever."

"I just wondered because Professor Engelhorn had it—" Ming stopped herself too late. They stared at each other.

"Jeff has a very big mouth." Zoe bounded out of her chair, paced about, then stood over Ming with her arms folded, like an interrogator. "And how many other intimate details do you know about Professor Engelhorn?"

"He left me." Ming hung her head. Then she confessed everything, a guilty party hoping for mercy—including how she'd uttered Billie Austin's name and Charles had turned as red as a stoplight. The only lie Ming uttered was the biggest one of all—

"I'm over him," she swore. "He might come to your wedding."

"He doesn't go to ABD weddings," the cross-examiner declared. "Or is he thinking of coming to see *you*?"

Ming hung her head again. *Twenty-one days,* she reminded herself.

"I have some important things to do," Zoe snapped. Ming saw how her shoulders were trembling as she stomped out of the office.

She observed, also, the tissues in Zoe's wastebasket. Ming had in mind a good deed she could perform; as long as Zoe was mad at her anyway, might as well seize this opportunity to come forward with the tough-love gift. She seized the clean corner of a wadded up tissue. Ming happened to have struck up a friendship of sorts with a lab technician at the Sunshine Village hospital named Ning Bao, who had applied for funding to start a business testing biomarkers. It was time for a little quid pro quo.

Two weeks before the wedding—thirteen days before Ming's self-imposed deadline to banish Charles Engelhorn from her heart—he appeared in the doorway of the corporate headquarters of Sunshine Finance. He'd had a New China makeover—his beard trimmed neatly, a crisp new summer tweed blazer.

"Hello," Ming said, willing her voice to stay low and formal.

Charles sported a wide grin, and she noticed, for the first time, the slight gap between his front teeth.

She saw Zoe do a double take, then recover and step forward. Even her face had a sudden healthy bloom. She'd gotten into character, Ming saw—Zoe might as well be on stage, playing a character who wasn't sick and was capable of uttering the words, "Professor Engelhorn, how wonderful to see you. You must come to dinner with us tonight. You too, Ming."

"I'd be delighted," Charles replied. Ming detected a trace of anxiety in his voice. He'd like to play a role of his own, it occurred to her: the role of Zoe's father.

That evening at Zoe and William's house, the three conspirators drank vodka martinis and said nothing of Ming's guilt, and when Charles arrived Zoe mixed more martinis.

"The emphasis on fine wine and elegant cocktails in the New China is really intriguing," the professor intoned about halfway through his cocktail. "There is plenty of bonhomie, without much evidence of alcoholism. As if the entire enterprise were the brainchild of New Yorkers who wanted all the world to be a party."

"Yes, it was my idea—mine and Zoe's," said Ming.

"New China is merely a front, actually," said William. "What we really do is drop drugs in the water supply."

Charles laughed, and the party went on.

The four of them dined on sautéed monkfish, spicy noodles, baby eggplants in a garlic sauce, black mushrooms, and chicken with oyster sauce, with a white Cotes du Rhone.

"I'm getting spoiled rotten," said their clueless guest. "All this food prepared by professionals, and costing only so much as you can afford. But I look around and I see that even though Beijing and Shanghai had a utopian appeal, the people didn't seem to know how to be content. Americans ask me what I think is going to happen in China, and I tell them I'm an historian, not a soothsayer. Still, if New China retains a semblance of democracy, well and good, but whatever the political system, inequality will inexorably rear its head again."

"Have you found the roots of this noble experiment?" Ming had to ask, and didn't dare look her co-conspirators in the eye.

He shook his head and looked bewildered all over again. "I can only surmise that it had something to do with this being a civilization that has always been on a search for perfection." His gaze rested on Ming for about a nanosecond, then he looked at William. "I would respectfully submit that China has been the only society that keeps trying to examine the nature of perfection and strive to achieve it. In the West, we ushered in the age of enlightenment and democracy and called it a day."

William told Charles he might be on to something—and he sounded totally sincere. "We have a tendency to get a big idea and spread it overnight," William said. The men expounded with each other, like two sages grafting theory onto theory. Ming poured more wine for herself and Zoe, while William and Charles kept on, reaching back into loftier and loftier texts that shed light on the character of China; when William cited a few philosophers so esoteric Charles admitted he hadn't known their writings existed, he didn't grill his host on how he'd found such obscure texts. *Alpha men respect other alpha men; how very primitive,* Ming reflected.

"Evolution is stalled, right here," she whispered to Zoe. "I'm going to get some sleep. You should too."

Zoe nodded, and they bid the men goodnight. As Ming was closing the door behind her, she saw Charles and William, brandy snifters in hand, settle into comfortable armchairs in the library. It was if they were plotting the country's next strategic move.

In the morning, Ming had a piece of unfinished business to attend to, and she'd thought of someone in town who could help her. Her heart beat in nervous staccato as she hit Jeff's number.

He picked up and said, "To what do I owe this summons from my strangely estranged one?"

"I need you to do something special for Zoe. Tell Charles…"

"Ah, you *are* on a first-name basis."

"Shut up. Anyway it's over; I'm completely over him, and he's avoiding me like he thinks I still care and I really, really don't."

"Aw, he broke your heart like you broke mine."

"Promise me you'll help? It's something you've been wanting to do for Zoe for years. Tell Charles that Sunshine Group has appointed you to make the rounds of all visitors. Tell him that the summer rains left us with a few cases of malaria and that everyone needs to be tested at the lab. They just need a dab of saliva. Ning Bao is on duty this afternoon. She will swab his inner cheek, and it's all done. But be sure you see Ning Bao."

"Malaria? You *are* an evil genius." As she'd suspected, it was a game of intrigue he couldn't resist; he even said so.

Just before six that evening, Ming received a text from Jeff: *Your X-lover & I are bonding at Nirvana. Spit accompli. Please come, need your help, damn it.*

Ming had a couple of hours before she'd promised to do bunker duty, so she scrambled into a jade silk dress with a wide sash and spritzed herself with ylang ylang perfume. At the Nirvana Café, she found her estranged husband and ex-lover drinking jasmine beers and looking engrossed in a discussion that seemed to involve a claim that the sky over Sunshine Village had been a moldy green in the rainy season. She stood beside Jeff's chair and said, "Hello," to get their attention.

"Well, well, if it isn't my dear wife," Jeff murmured, pretending surprise. "Pull up a chair, Mrs. Kirschenbaum." When she sat down he reached over and stroked her hair as if she were a cat preening for his attention. Charles flashed a crooked grin at her and kind of slouched over his beer.

"Oh my god. Vegetable brain drugs!" Ming thundered at Jeff.

"Just one, dear wife." He kissed her ear and whispered, "for the cause."

There were places in the peasant villages, Ming knew, where tourists would go and buy herbal cigarettes laced with opium. It might have been a harmless quest except that rumor had it the cash from the opium trade was funding the campaigns of Raindance Party politicians.

"To think," Jeff continued, his eyes looking half-mast, "I wasted four years of undergrad at Columbia and never took Professor Engelhorn's Chinese history class. Oh, and you will be pleased to know, Ming, that we both had our malaria tests this afternoon, but I'm pretty sure we're both negative."

"Malaria," Charles muttered. He raised an eyebrow at Ming. "I have a suspicion. More than a suspicion. There's no malaria really, is there?"

Ming dug her elbow into Jeff's side.

"Oh, I told Charles all about it." Jeff leaned back and reached his arm behind Ming's chair. "That I married a damsel in distress who worked for a crime ring to pay for her pretty teeth, and then became a fugitive. Did I leave anything out, Ming? Opiates are the true confessional of the masses."

Ming pinched Jeff's thigh under the table; he pinched hers back, then traced a long line up her thigh, followed by a short one—as if he were casting an I Ching message.

"I have another confession," Jeff went on. "The malaria test was, in fact, a paternity test. A dear friend of ours grew up without a father, and now that she's about to get married, we think it's time she finds out who he is. Apparently, a little over thirty years ago you might have known her mother very well?"

Charles's mouth dropped, then his face lit up like a kid in a spelling bee who had given the wrong answer but inexplicably won the prize.

"Our friend's mom ran away with a Christian rock group in the 70s. Then she defected to New York and got into sex, drugs, and rock 'n' roll. And God delivered her a pregnancy."

Charles turned as red as he always seemed to do at the thought. "Billie...." He spoke her name as if it came from an immortal ballad.

"'I live upstream and you downstream, from night to night of you I dream,'" Ming quoted softly in Mandarin, a troubadour's love song by Li Zhiyi from the Song dynasty. The troubadours of medieval China and Europe, she reflected, worshipped love and lust for their own sakes. The pain arrived when your passion had an object. She had a sudden urge to ask Jeff what he thought about that.

"Billie Austin sang at a club in the East Village," Charles said, his voice reverent. "It was the end of the summer, and I was staying at an apartment with my aunt and uncle. One night, when my aunt and uncle were away, I...I invited some of the East Village students over for a party. Billie came with some guy, a college dropout who played the guitar. She pointed to me and said—and I'll never forget this—'He's smart, he's going to be somebody.' The absurd thing was, at that moment, I wanted nothing more than to be a guitar-playing dropout. Anyway, they fought, Billie and the guitar player; he was quite a jerk. He walked out, and I persuaded her to stay and talk. I had some good dope and told her I'd teach her some words in Mandarin." He shook his head over his own youthful machination.

And so he mastered the art of chatting women up, thought Ming.

"She was the most beautiful girl I'd ever seen," he confessed. "Idiot kid that I was, I thought we might have something going after that, but two days later I rang her doorbell, practically panting like a lovesick puppy. I heard a guitar playing before she even opened the door. Later, somebody told me the boyfriend had skipped out and left her pregnant. She was still in New York, and I—I had this crazy dream that I was the father and that we would marry and live in one of those apartments with cardboard walls and shag carpets, pinching pennies and feasting on love. She'd work as a secretary while I finished my PhD. Stupid, I know. I decided to propose to her anyway, planned it for weeks. There was a miserable snowstorm the night I went to her apartment, but I didn't care. I slogged through it, all the way out to the East Village."

He took a long swig of his jasmine beer.

"Turned out she wasn't alone," he continued, "and she wasn't moping like I'd imagined. They were having a party. Billie was dressed up like the Virgin Mary, wearing a paper halo, in a white gown and bare feet, even though the floor was cold. I told her that I wanted to marry her and take care of the baby. She laughed so hard she began to cry. Someone actually opened the door, like I was a dog that should go home."

"What was the guitar player's name?" Jeff asked.

"Something that suggested he should be playing bagpipes...

Baldwin? No, Malcolm." Then, as if remembering who he was now, Charles rose to his feet, saying he had calls to make and was sober enough to get back to work.

"Well, well," Jeff pondered. "Sorry he didn't ask you to come nurse his old wounds. We do make a good interrogation team."

"Actually, I have to get to work too." She longed to stay there, safe with Jeff in spite of the inebriated way he slurred his words, but of course she didn't have a choice.

"You're going to leave me after these surreal revelations?" He looked as if she'd socked him. "I thought we were friends again."

"Oh god. What about Zoe?"

"He'd like to be her father, Old Engelhorn. He's not a bad guy, even if he did fuck my wife. Don't say anything to Zoe until we get the test results tomorrow. But stay. We have a lot to talk about."

"I know, but I can't, really."

"Well, then, darling, I wish you goodnight." Jeff's lips grazed across her cheek, and then he was off, sauntering toward a group of tourists at the bar. Ming let herself out the back door of Nirvana. A moon beamed through a light drizzle. It was a night in which you could tell the difference between visitors—with their slickers and neon umbrellas—and the villagers, who strolled through the mist as though it were sunshine.

At the end of the pine grove, she felt a tap on her shoulder. Jeff had run and caught up with her. He was panting. "I followed you. A crazy stalker, I know. I just want to talk. Can we?"

Ming hesitated, biting her lip. "I'm hoping Engelhorn is her father. Maybe just because I'm hoping that Malcolm asshole isn't." The mist enveloped them. "But I have to go. Really, I have a company to run, you know." She turned and began to walk away.

"I had a tryst with Zoe," Jeff blurted out. He did know how to stop her in her tracks. She glanced back, then made herself move on. "One of these days you and I are going to have to meet in divorce court," Jeff called after her.

"What if we don't?" Ming asked, finally, over one shoulder.

"You know, if you had told me you were in trouble, I'd have

figured out a way to help." He was behind her again, and puffing. "How about a peace pipe before you go? Yeah, I know it's gauche, but I did it for the cause. Then I promise I'll quit." Jeff pulled out a homemade cigarette and a match. "Relax. This some pretty fi-ine stuff, mellower than pot. I can see how people get addicted."

She took a hit, then another, then said, "I really do have to go." It seemed funny, somehow, that she would be standing there at the edge of the pine grove and there was Jeff, like an apparition. As a parting gesture she took his face in her hands and kissed him. She waited for him to leave. Dear Jeff, he knew they should be spending the next few hours laughing together.

A wicked idea swirled through her head. There must have been a reason she'd worn this dress; she removed the sash, wrapped it around his eyes, and tied it in a figure-eight knot. "I'll take you with me," she announced. "But you can't see anything."

"Is this going to be kinky?" he guffawed. "Hey, how about you and I get middle-aged together, and then old together?"

Something giddy danced through her veins as she led him through the trapdoor and down the steps into the tunnel below.

"You *are* a spy," he prattled on. "Or you're planning to kill me. Is this where William Sun Moon has his orgies?"

"I show you, white man, the true mysteries of the Orient. Don't take off your blindfold or you'll be back in Brooklyn without a penny in your pocket."

"You are so cute when you talk like a sorceress whore."

Ming walked him past the computer console, where 2099 was blinking in steady beats about half a minute apart. She pressed the button, then drew Jeff onto the bed. "Wait here," she told him, her voice a husky whisper.

She made a strong chamomile brew with a generous dose of whiskey. Another number was blinking but at longer intervals. She zapped the number for a full minute, until it held steady. Then, with the screens looking stable, she peeled Jeff's clothes off, massaging him all over with sesame-jasmine oil. She fed him sips of whisky, then pulled a thread from her dress and tickled his bare orifices.

"Tiny butterfly tongues," Ming whispered in his ear, as he shivered beneath the warmth of her breath, the fall of her hair upon his skin. "They are blue and white; they like the taste of you, but if white man looks they all shrivel into little shit pebbles." It felt like coming home, in a way, to play this ridiculous sex game with Jeff, and his New China coiffed hair smelled downright scrumptious. She mounted him face-to-face; then, with his feet on the floor while she sat on him; then, she made him stand while she wrapped her legs around his torso. Finally, he collapsed in a poppy haze. Ming collapsed beside him.

She had a dream about being on train, and when she opened her eyes, she didn't remember where she was supposed to be. Jeff was making contented snoring sounds. Good heavens—she had lost her mind, bringing him down there. She shook him out of his slumber and helped him—blindfolded still—put his pants and shoes on and got him outside into the dewy forest.

"What the fuck…and what's the deal with all those computer screens and numbers?" he mumbled as she led him away from the trees and all the way to the river ledge, trying to make sure he wouldn't find his way back.

The blindfold must have slipped sometime in the night. "My head is killing me. Did you try to kill me? I had this dream that you and Zoe were taking over the world with computer screens. Don't worry, though. All I want to do is take my pictures and have my life. Don't tell me things I don't want to know. I loved your hundred little butterfly kisses. You're the best lover in the world when you want to be."

"Maybe it was another woman," Ming said, finding her voice at last.

"No, I know just the way you feel and smell."

"I must go, and you must go home or I'll have to kill you."

She threw down his shirt, socks, and underwear, and took off at a run. She could hear him stumbling after her, but when she turned, she saw that he'd kind of collapsed below a grove of plum trees. Jeff would be safe; he'd wake up drenched in dew, he'd stagger home and doubtless hate her all over again. The thought made her shrivel inside, but she had her duties.

Back at the bunker, Ming sat before the screens, the numbers quiet as the grave. She peered closely at 2099 and thought it did seem ever so faintly less green. The software measured conscious thought. Ming wondered how deeply it could penetrate the subconscious.

⌘

A month before Ming and Jeff's bunker tryst, Number 2099 was already growing restless. The air of Beijing was leaden with the summer heat, not as it had been in previous years when chemical compounds burned through your nose, but still, the heat of the devil. 2099 should have been in a mood to celebrate—he was about to close a deal he'd finagled with Jack Duffy. Plenette-Leuter China was in the home stretch of acquiring a controlling stake in 2099's pharmaceutical client, which was itself on the verge of launching the perfect anti-depressant. Hardly anyone knew of the Chinese company—it operated a hundred miles west of Beijing and wasn't listed on the stock exchange—and they were keeping the deal quiet for now, but the new formula had all the makings of a blockbuster drug. It was an intravenous solution instead of pills, and it contained a secret ingredient that would induce such a euphoria that people would line up to get it.

It was a perfect deal except that Duff, as all of his associates called him, wouldn't stop nagging 2099 about the labor costs. All that blather on Tiger News about the country going broke didn't help. He had reassured Duffy that the workers made very little actual money, and that capital in circulation was good for everyone.

Still, every deal demanded his negotiation skills in one form or another. Without some highs and lows, wouldn't business be *mon-o-tone-ous.*

Number 2099 was pleased when the right word came to mind. He didn't know what else to do with the word, or how he might describe his life, or why he might bother. Yet an alien voice had been badgering him, insisting something was missing, and he knew it had to do with the spoils of power. Every time he thought he came close to figuring it out, a live volt shot through his head. He traced the confusion three years back, to one morning when he had woken with the strangest thoughts swimming through his head and the vague recollection of a bug scratching his ear. After that, 2099 had begun to understand that he had important responsibilities in New China; he started to read voraciously and began to socialize with a witty group of artists, filmmakers, and writers—all of whom had biting comments about popular culture, world affairs, politics, and economic theory.

Number 2099 had always felt inadequate among the people who had witty, biting comments to make. He *was* good at golf, which he played periodically with a group of high-powered businessmen. Even his golf buddies, though, weren't immune to the trends that seemed to be sweeping throughout New China.

"I'm writing a novel," one had confided. "I'll bring copies next week so you can read it." 2099 nodded, though he recalled a witty writer declaring that it was the mark of a true amateur to share his novel-in-progress to all, an amateur who sought nothing but assurance that he had a bestseller in his leaden prose and inane revelations. Something 2099 had come to realize in New China was that he adored novels. They made him believe that there was a story to tell in any life, including his own. The voice came after him again, whispering a persistent message in a language he could not yet understand.

Number 2099 didn't know quite where to begin but decided he might start with his own childhood. He could write a book about being young and horny. If others could do it, why couldn't he, a powerful man who knew how to make millions? He had, after all, made both his mistress and his secretary scream in bed and rewarded them with jewelry afterwards, and even set his mistress up in a little business of her own. Both later deserted him—his former assistant was now studying gender politics, while his former mistress was off in some flight school.

After two weeks of writing about a man a bit like himself, who was horny in youth as well as in maturity, 2099 thought he had a moving story. He gave the story to his wife to read. He'd developed a new appreciation for her noble gaze and the way she listened when he pondered questions he couldn't answer. He left the room, but his heart drummed with expectation as she stared at the computer screen.

She was still engrossed when he came back. He waited while she stretched, and turned and said, "The boys want one of these." She tipped up her screen to show him an ecommerce site.

"What did you think of my novel?"

"Oh, kind of sweet," she'd said with a smile and a shrug of her shoulders. She didn't even take him seriously enough to say it wasn't good.

He lay awake that night, watching his wife sleep. Her skin sagged in spots, and the way she lay—with her left arm outstretched in his direction—seemed like a demand that she find him there. He remembered other women he'd known, and imagined other women he might someday meet, yet his emptiness seemed like a black hole in space.

On a whim, 2099 tracked down his former mistress. She said he couldn't come to her apartment. He told himself she was fighting temptation, and persuaded her to meet him in a café. At the table he'd caressed her hand, with her long red fingernails, and observed she was wearing a big Sichuan opal—way too commonplace a stone for a woman of her talents, he told her. She sipped from a teacup without touching her lips to the rim, and said she was engaged to a man named Tom who flew a shuttle to Sunshine Village. "He's good friends with William Kingsley Sun," she'd said with excitement. Just the week before she'd been down there and William—she called him by his first name—had told her all about the principle of a business investing its money back into society at large. Number 2099 had wondered—aloud—if she was in love with her fiancé or with that William Sun.

Now, on a morning that happened to be just around the time William detected the slightly faded pixels, 2099 found himself in a sour mood, missing the simplicity of deal-making in the old days, when it was all about making money for your client and yourself.

When he had these thoughts, he could feel his head vibrating and a bullet rattling around inside. The bullet kept rattling, all through dinner with Jack Duffy and his team that night.

"This New China economy is doomed!" Duff thundered. "Who ever heard of a world where people are *not* driven by the prospect of making more money? How is it possible that the Chinese economy is doing better than ever when people are obsessing about their quality of life instead of their bank accounts?"

Number 2099 paid attention. Yet, as if he were viewing a split screen, he had a sudden recollection of construction workers employed at a site next to his office a few years back; they had all stopped working to stare at him when he exited his office in his glossy shoes and pressed suit. He'd seen the envy and hate in their eyes, and felt powerful. After all, he knew more about economics than these struggling workers. He was a walking incentive; they would work themselves to death to attempt to acquire what he had. It was a strange recollection, and as he sat with Duff, he felt the bullet rattle like sonar waves trying to map out every millimeter of his brain. If you laid the complexities of life end to end, 2099 considered, you'd have an array as infinite as the universe. *Respect those complexities and don't ever presume to solve them,* ancient philosophers said. Perhaps he was a bit of a Taoist sage himself.

Growth, growth, growth, Duff was expostulating. "I think we could get our share price up to $145 by next year. And $180 by the year after that. Yeah, I like the sound of $180."

After dinner they went to a tasteful nightclub, where a woman with a rich voice belted out big band songs in English and French, and a man in a tuxedo played the piano. 2099 ordered a bottle of champagne for the table, and when Duff and the other Americans finished it, another appeared. In old days the bottle would have been Cognac, which had always left 2099 feeling stuck together inside.

Their waitress was young, and she told them she was going to be leaving the job to act in a play soon. She wore a slinky evening gown. Number 2099 wondered about the smoothness of her thighs beneath the fabric, hoping she'd say come see me on opening night.

234

She didn't. She had no need for him to pay her rent or set her up with a business; she'd probably think a little electric Alfa Romeo was just a showoff toy. There was nothing he could offer her.

"You know…" Duff continued, putting his arm across the back of 2099's chair. Americans did that, he knew—it made you feel like they loved you, like you were so important to them that they were about to ask you for a very large favor. "We just laid off about a thousand people at our plant in Ohio. We solved the problem with the rest. We just told them they've gotta take a pay cut and pay for their own health insurance. Our share prices went up the next day. You know what one of the Chinese guys here said? He said we should have told the insurance company we're gonna give them a pay cut! Can you beat that?" Duff laughed so hard his pudgy cheeks shook. "The insurance company takes a pay cut! Sometimes, I swear, you Chinese sound like a buncha' communists."

"I tell you," Duff went on. "There's a hedge fund on our ass back in the U.S. They're asking me what's with all this equal distribution shit in China? We've gotta get our share price up to $180 or the predators on Wall Street will eat us. Isn't there anything someone can do?"

The sonar bullet exploded in 2099's head—as if it had accomplished its mission and was now done with him. He muttered, "excuse me," and beat a path to the men's room. Bending over a urinal, 2099 felt the nausea rise in his throat and expected to throw up.

"Get my friend a whiskey straight up, no more faggot champagne," Duff shouted to the waitress when 2099 returned to the table.

"No, I'm fine," 2099 insisted. He held his head up and tried to look like the kind of man that would appeal to a young actress, but the waitress brought him a whiskey and didn't even glance his way as she set it down.

"Maybe you could eliminate half the jobs in the company so that you're producing half as much but showing twice the profit," 2099 suggested. Another bullet exploded in his head, and he heard himself uttering a whimper, like a wounded dog. Duffy's eyebrows knitted into concerned question marks. But as 2099 drained his whiskey, he

235

felt his mind begin to grow calmer. He observed pinpricks of light. He thought how infinitely complex the universe was and how much better it would be to master one little zillionth of infinity. Maybe he was kind of a sage after all, a sage at producing profits.

Miles away, in Sunshine Village, the number 2099 flickered into a soothing liquid crystal display, one pixel paler than it had been before. This was the flaw in William Sun's technology—the system couldn't detect the brainwaves of a man who'd reverted to old beliefs and found true virtue there.

"You know," 2099 told Duff, "a few years ago we heard about a great new business model that was taking China by storm. It started with an obscure silicon company. The brainchild of William Kingsley Sun—you've heard of him, I assume?"

Duff had indeed heard of William Kingsley Sun. It was a small matter to take Sun's former sales manager, Tang Fei, on a golf outing and find out more. Somewhere near the sixteenth hole Duff slapped his underling's thigh and exclaimed, "So, the Sunshine company makes loans! Do they have a banking license?"

Now, Jack Duffy was a much subtler man than almost anyone realized. He spoke Chinese better than he generally let on, and he had committed to memory all of the Chinese laws that weren't actually on the books, but which a business executive with good connections could have invoked if someone happened to get in the way of his company making money. And it was getting to be time for Duff to have one of his intelligence briefings with the Ministry of Industry.

Soon after, Duff attended a garden party at the US Embassy. Someone introduced him to that professor who used to write op-eds about human rights in China, Charles Engelhorn.

"You must be out of business these days," Duff joked.

"It's a good feeling to have won the war and be in the country with the peace-keeping forces."

Smug, what else would you expect from these Ivy League intellectuals? Duff thought to himself.

"And what about crime in New China?" Duff asked as he scooped up a spring roll from a roving waiter. "Like that village in Sichuan where the talk show host killed his wife?"

"Sunshine Village." Engelhorn nodded. "Yes, a student of mine is there, and she's getting married to William Sun—" He stopped as if he thought he might have said too much. "And you, Jack, I hear Plenette-Leuter has done very well under your watch." Duff detected suspicion beneath the Professor's flattery.

Before he could say more, a woman from the embassy exulted, "Jack, here you are!" and swept him away. Out of the corner of his eye, he spotted the professor talking to the guy from the *New York Times*, both of them looking in his direction. It was impossible to hide from the gossip that went around these Beijing ex-patriate circles; the expressions on their faces said "CIA" as if it were a bad thing.

Chapter Eighteen

In one part of Sunshine Village, Jeff was waking up beneath the plum grove. That same morning, Zoe was in the office, wondering where her co-conspirators were. William had woken at dawn, said to Zoe, "I had a dream something was going on in the bunker," and hurried down there. No one knew where Ming was.

Zoe filled in for William at a meeting with two entrepreneurs from Australia who had an idea to use nanochips for a process that would wring salt out of seawater inexpensively. *Play the role, the executive of Sunshine Finance,* she told herself. She enjoyed the role, in fact. It was like directing real life. When she sniffed the seawater sample they'd brought, it seemed to soothe away the fever that remained in her sinuses.

The meeting ended, and still no sign of anyone. Time to go down.

She made a detour to visit the cave, as was her habit now. A crowd clustered outside. Some had brought food, pillows, and quilts, while another faction hovered there to make their views known.

"You see? Here is all that is wrong with New China!" a member of the Raindance Party hollered. "Too much knowledge turns the human clock backward!"

Jing Yin had become live entertainment.

Zoe had thrust note after note into the cave, hoping to coax the girl away. "They're waiting for you to show your face," she'd written. "Don't be their freak show. Just come out, and go back about your business." She'd added, because Mississippi Sunday School teachers used to say such things, "I think God would want that." But Jing Yin stayed inside the black mouth, poking her head out just often enough to titillate the spectators. That day Zoe heard her howl three times. The howls sounded rehearsed. She's trying, it occurred to Zoe, to talk to God.

It was time for Zoe to disappear from view, though. Down the stairs and the incline. When she opened the door, she saw William pacing, his feet hitting the floor like a martial drumbeat. Ming was there too, seated, head bowed. Their mouths dropped when they saw Zoe. As if she were an intruder.

"I was going to call you," William said.

"I did a terrible thing," Ming said in that little girl soprano voice.

"You might as well sit down." William gestured to a chair. "Ming brought Jeff to the bunker."

Ming began to let tears fall. "Jeff and I got a whole confession out of Charles Engelhorn. He used to be in love with your mom. She had a boyfriend named Malcolm, but they had a fight and she slept with Charles. She got pregnant along the way. Either the good one or the bad one could be your father. Malcolm walked out on Billie. Charles asked her to marry him, but she laughed in his face. Jeff was stoned and...I brought him here. I was lonely, and we'd just found the key to the mystery of your life together. But...I'm not that stupid. I blindfolded him and made him think he was hallucinating..."

William shook his head, then pointed out that an invisible man could steal opium from a dealer in the peasant village, and then a bug could fly into Jeff's room at night and slip a dosage into his veins. He would wake up to beautiful colors.

Ming stopped crying and shrieked, "If we let Jeff go free, we might be spoiling everything for a billion people who are finally starting to get their opportunity to evolve to some higher rung of humanity. If we destroy his mind, we're the cruel ones. And then how can we be arbiters of this higher rung of humanity?"

"Ming's ruined everything, but even so she's right," Zoe said. "We've crowned ourselves arbiters." She stared at William. "This is a test, right? And we've passed it."

William looked truly incomprehensive.

"I mean, you weren't really going to drive poor Jeff to insanity!"

He still didn't answer, and that told her everything.

Was she going to marry a ruthless man who would destroy Jeff to protect their paradise? Zoe stormed out the door. Back in the office, she looked out her window and watched a mist overtake the

239

afternoon sun. She thought about returning to America, perhaps finding a Danny Hirsch replica. She shuddered, imagining a place where she could never fly again, where she might live with a husband and kids whose imaginations might reach only as far as what they had in the bank. And she recalled that strange thing Ming had said. *The mystery of your life.*

Might as well get on with business for now, so Zoe checked her email. There was a message from Professor Engelhorn, addressed to her and to William. The subject line said *Emergency Trip.* The message was terse. *I have to go to Beijing on some emergency business. Not sure I'll be able to make it back for your wedding, so best wishes to you both. Best, Charles Engelhorn.*

When was there ever emergency business in academia? Zoe felt a sickly blob begin to regenerate in her sinuses.

"Zoe, are you here?" The voice from the hallway was Ming's. So she showed Ming the message.

"Oh my god." Ming turned pale and twisted her shoulders in a way that looked apologetic. "What time is it? I'll be back in just a little while."

Ming was back within the hour, and she presented Zoe with a crisp white envelope. Inside was a single sheet of paper covered with boxes and codes, a lifetime lost in two dozen rows of numbers. A footnote below declared, *The tested man cannot be included as the biological father of the child.*

"The mystery of *my* life." Zoe glared at Ming, not sure if she wanted to deliver a kickpunch or fall into her arms for comfort.

"I'm sorry," Ming said, then took it upon herself to squeeze Zoe's hand. "I was, well, I was hoping he'd be your father and we'd all fall into place." She looked eager to please in a way that reminded Zoe of Professor Engelhorn himself. It occurred to Zoe that Billie would have eaten such an eager-to-please young pup alive.

"Maybe..." Ming hesitated. "Maybe you'd like to call your mom?"

Good idea, though it was just before six a.m. in New York and she knew Billie wouldn't pick up.

Zoe listened to her mother's voice belt out "Hello, you have reached

240

212…" like an acapella choir resounding through a Mississippi heat wave. They had never left their names on their outgoing voicemail because it might be the landlord calling.

Zoe could just see her mother—in her darkened room with a white noise machine, ear plugs, and a sleep mask; the landline in the bedroom would be shut off, but Billie would still hear it from the living room, and for the rest of the day, she'd complain that she had bags under her eyes because the phone woke her at some ungodly hour.

"This is your daughter, Zoe. Call me as soon as you can. This is very important." She slammed the phone down. "Aren't parents supposed to answer calls from their kids at any time of day?" she pondered aloud, then realized that Ming had left the room and it was William standing there watching her.

"Darling," he said. "I know I failed *your* test, somehow."

"Just leave poor Jeff alone."

William shifted about like an unwelcome guest. "I have enemies," he said, finally. "You should know that before you marry me. I can't promise you we'll be able to live happily ever after."

Instead of breaking up, the two of them spent the evening walking along the cliff, saying little, just watching the river lap the shore while a lutist played beside the big Buddha and other lovers sat on rocks, drinking wine and laughing. At this hour the spectators had abandoned the cave girl, though there were plates of fresh food outside.

Around twilight, they settled on a bed of moss, and Zoe called home again. This time Billie's live voice croaked, "Hullo?"

"Mom…."

"Zoe? That you, darlin'? Whatever bee you've got in your bonnet….I'm sleeping. Was that you who woke me up this morning?"

"Don't hang up."

"You're drunk. Is William…?"

"I'm not drunk."

"Then I'm going to strangle your pretty little neck."

"Just tell me—how well did you know Charles Engelhorn?"

"Who? Oh, your professor. You have such a good memory, darling, makes me feel like I've got early dementia."

"I know he isn't my father. Who was my father?"

"C'mon baby, I have an audition this afternoon and I'm going to have ten-ton sacks of lead under my eyes. You always were special. I had dreams that you were going to save the world."

"I have reason to believe my father was someone named Malcolm."

"Who told you about...?" Billie's voice cut like lightning. "We were better off without him, honey. I should've married the very smart Charles Engelhorn. Are you happy with William? If you have a man who's got a lot on the ball and wants to accomplish big things *and* he's devoted to you, for god's sakes marry him."

"Your mortal genealogy is just a blip in the heavens," William said afterward.

Zoe examined her own mortal hands and feet. "I'd like to have children and earthly descendants into the next thousand years, and they should know who they are. But I'm not going to sit down and write about history; I'm never going to finish the dissertation. You missed a meeting today with people who might use our chips to make sure the world has enough drinkable water. We've done something. I like directing this theater of life."

She didn't call off the wedding. The infamous fog rolled over Sunshine Village, though it didn't rain. Zoe appointed herself emissary to Jeff, who hadn't left town after all, and wanted to ramble about nothing else but the night of true confessions.

"Do people even get malaria in these parts? I think he kind of wanted to be your father all along. Wish you'd been there to save me, though. Evil Ming, I'm sure she slipped something in my drink. Someday we'll find your asshole father, Malcolm."

Two days before the wedding, Jeff told Zoe he'd been to the cave, imagining he might crawl in there with the Cave Girl. "She let me take her picture," he said, and held up his camera like a trophy. "I'm going back today. Do you want to come?"

They went together. The crowd had fashioned its own line of demarcation—on one side Raindancers, on the other civilizers

242

wearing T-shirts that said in English and Chinese, "Knowledge is for everyone."

"It's all alive," Jeff said. Zoe noticed a slur in his words. Jing Yin sat cross-legged and chanting.

Zoe called out her name. "The moon will come out twice, then when the sun is up again I'm getting married. Come to our wedding."

She saw Jing Yin look up.

"Both sides want the Cave Girl as their mascot," Jeff observed. "I think she might come to your wedding, though. Should I drag her out?"

The shrine adjoining the resort across the river was close enough to completion, and Zoe had thought it would make a perfect spot for the wedding. The shrine was a solarium, with cedar-frames around walls of glass, with a view of the woods and the Buddha across the river, but also the sky, so that any god could peer down through the stubborn fog. Zoe and William had written and rehearsed the ceremony; they had stage-blocked Ming as maid of honor and Simon Sun as best man—Number 3 could work the bunker for a little while. They had ordered lavish altars of oranges and grapes and flowers, the fragrances mingling with incense and fresh cedar. And as the guests assembled, Zoe saw the sun wink through the glass walls.

Zoe wore a red gown, Buddhist style, and carried a bouquet of lacquer-red roses and mandarin-orange orchids. A Buddhist priest shifted his feet at the makeshift altar; the bridegroom was late.

"Sometimes you wait and sometimes you rush. You see, that's how you recycle minutes," Zoe whispered to Jeff, who had agreed to give her away.

"I'm getting older with each minute," he grumbled.

William appeared, finally, aglow in his tuxedo. "Sorry," he whispered in his bride's ear. "Numbers. You look ravishing, Mrs. Kingsley Sun. By the way, look who followed me."

Jing Yin stood in the doorway, so frail that her limbs seemed pieced together like pottery shards. Her clothes hung in threads about her scrawny frame, and her dirty feet were bare.

"I see we have some more late arrivals. If everyone will find their seats," said the priest in a voice that sounded like a tranquil stream, "we will begin."

Zoe glanced toward the back of the room. Good heavens—Jing Yin wasn't the only one who'd come through the door. Standing in the back was none other than Charles Engelhorn. And beside him, Tom Wendall, still in his pilot uniform. She nudged Ming and whispered, "Do they know each other?"

A choir of villagers in saffron robes began the ceremony with a chant: *Namo Tassa Bhagavato Arahato Samma Sambuddhassa*—Homage to Him, the Exalted One, the Supremely Awakened One.

"We are uniting two people bound by a commitment greater than religion..."

A violet cloud sailed across the sun, and Zoe, glancing up, saw raindrops gathering in rivulets across the glass. William's face had taken on a grayish hue—was he ill? His hand crept beneath her bouquet and tapped her ring. He smiled at her faintly.

"Friends, we are together today in the presence of this congregation, and in the sight of the Buddhas and Bodhisattvas, to witness the vows of William and Zoe. I earnestly ask anyone who knows of any impediment to this marriage to make it known now, or else remain silent." And after the obligatory pause—"Now you may exchange rings."

The bride and groom each placed a plain gold ring on the finger of the other.

"May its circle remind you both of those things that are eternal," the priest continued. Wrapping a string of beads around their wrists, he urged, "Be compassionate to all, and set your feet on the Path which leads from illusion and sorrow to Enlightenment and Peace. I pronounce—"

A shriek, followed by a stampede of boots drowned out the priest's soft words. Zoe heard crystal shatter and guests run amok like wildebeest before a tiger, just as a horde of Chinese police charged into the solarium and swooped down upon her groom. She saw his wrists in handcuffs and screamed.

"Run—" William whispered to her. Why didn't he transform

himself into a microscopic creature? Zoe tried to say something, but Professor Engelhorn was seizing her arm and dragging her from the solarium. She kicked and kept screaming, but Tom Wendall scooped her up and deposited her in the back of a crowded van. "This is for your own good, Zoe," he insisted, and held her down with his meaty paws.

She tried to move and get out the door in the back of the van, but someone else grabbed her and she felt a sharp prick in her arm. Then the faces around her started to fade. She heard Ming's voice, as if it were coming from a faraway room, saying, "Sorry, no room for Jing Yin!"

When Zoe awoke she was lying on a narrow bed in a room. Tatami mats covered the floor, and she could hear the muffled noise of traffic outside.

"I didn't think you'd get hysterical, but they all insisted. Men," Ming shook her head in disgust. She pulled a pair of jeans and several T-shirts out of a shopping bag.

"There's a bug in the room," Zoe rasped. A dull pounding echoed through her head.

"I won't kill anything," Ming promised.

"Where are we?"

"Tokyo. We're leaving for New York this afternoon. Put these on." Ming held up the clothes, and Zoe saw her hands trembling.

On the plane to New York, Zoe found herself wedged between Ming in the window seat and Lulu Pang in the aisle seat. "Leaping continents," Zoe mumbled. Ming, staring out at the clouds, ignored her. Zoe saw that she was trembling again.

"Can we trade seats for a while?" Zoe looked up and saw Charles Engelhorn speaking to Lulu. When he took Lulu's seat, it turned out he wanted to talk to her, not Ming. "I'm so sorry about the way your wedding turned out. The authorities claim that the Sunshine Finance Company was operating without a banking license, and they claim the money for loans came from the sale of opium. It's all ridiculous, clearly, but that's Chinese justice for you. They want to stop someone and they find a way to do it, and unfortunately some people saw your husband as a danger to the old capitalist order."

"We didn't finish getting married."

"You came close enough," the professor offered, and patted her hand. "There are preposterous rumors circulating about William brainwashing the populace, about deliberately contaminating the water supply. I'm so sorry, Zoe."

"Have you heard that?" She was asking Ming, but their companion in the window seat just kept staring at the clouds, in a world of her own.

"My mom remembers you. She said she was stupid. Did you two really talk about getting married?"

"*I* did." Heat rose to his cheeks. Then they sat in an awkward silence until the plane landed with a bump of the wheels at JFK.

"Zoe has the only mom in the world who'll say, 'Sure, you all come and camp on my floor!'" Jeff told Lulu as they disembarked. "Assuming she hasn't been evicted. Have you called your mother, Zoe?"

"No, and I don't even have a key."

Charles, the only one among them who had foreseen the trip, had his cell phone, and handed it to Zoe. *Hello. This is 212…*

"Mom, are you there? I'm coming home. With friends."

There were five of them, and they had to separate at the immigration line. After the three Americans passed through, they scanned the crowds for Ming and Lulu. At last, they spotted Lulu, chewing on her long hair like a frightened child. "The customs officials pulled Ming into a room," she told them.

"Oh motherfucking shit…I'd practically forgotten!" said Jeff.

"She was scared," Zoe whispered to him.

The bedraggled party lined up against the wall and waited.

"I'm going to go talk to the airport police," Professor Engelhorn said. "And I'll stop at an ATM. You might have all forgotten—in America you need legal tender. Why don't you wait at the bar? Order something and I'll pay when I get back."

Maybe he's going to desert us, it occurred to Zoe. But no, he handed

246

Zoe his leather satchel and cell phone to look after. He would be back.

"Let's get a car and drive across America looking for your father," Jeff whispered, as they hauled their meager baggage to the nearby bar. "I'll take photos of spool museums and sharecroppers and pay our way." His face shone with sweat, and his complexion had a greenish cast to it. *How much opium did he smoke in Sunshine Village?* Zoe wondered.

Charles's phone rang. "Zoe?" It was Ming, and she was weeping. "I am having some trouble. Can I talk to Jeff, please?"

Zoe passed the phone to Jeff. He listened without speaking, his mouth falling open. "Holy shit. What the fuck am I supposed to do?" Jeff was ashen when he hung up. "They *did* arrest Ming. I'm not feeling so good, either…"

Chapter Nineteen

Four travelers adrift on the Long Island Expressway, in bumper-to-bumper traffic. "You could save the world from money to finance terrorism if you got a hybrid car," Jeff told the Pakistani taxi driver, who ignored him and inched the car forward.

"Didn't she know she'd get caught?" Zoe asked.

"Zoe, my love," Jeff began, while Lulu frowned and Zoe sensed Jeff had meant to insult the woman who considered herself his girlfriend, "that's only the beginning. Ming knew she might get arrested in America, but it was a better alternative to her possible fate in China. An American bedbug-infested cot surrounded by girl-thug rapists has nothing on a Chinese *lao gai*. Oh, sorry, that's insensitive of me."

Certainly, William had escaped his mortal body, and was even now leaping across the Atlantic? Zoe tried to assure herself.

Professor Engelhorn—even after all they had been through, she still couldn't imagine calling him anything else—sat in the front passenger seat. "Well," he offered, "you can all come to my apartment. I have room if you need to stay over."

They plowed through Harlem, where shirtless black men stood on street corners, dragging on cigarettes. The taxi stopped in front of a row of brick buildings adorned with griffin gargoyles. A cliff across the street wound down to Morningside Park, where birds tweeted and chirped instead of the exotic whistles of magpies and shrieks of starlings. Rap music blared from a car nearby. It felt like home.

Professor Engelhorn's apartment was cavernous, dark, and cool, as if it knew nothing of summer. Once, Zoe had imagined living in a place like this, with Chinese rugs and book-lined walls that proclaimed a home for existentialist theories and languages not our own. Yet this apartment had a despondent feeling and many layers of dust. Zoe left another message for her mother, then the four of them went to a nearby restaurant that served hamburgers, soy burgers, and salads. A rowdy group of teenagers with rings in their noses and gelled hair drank coffee and shared French fries at an adjacent table.

"I thought people in New York would wear more evening gowns," said Lulu.

"Now is when she dumps me for a rich guy," said Jeff.

With no word from Billie, they went back to the dusty apartment. Charles directed Zoe into his sons' room, and she scrunched herself into a twin bed beneath a Yankees pennant. In a just world, she'd have played with her two little half-brothers in this room. In a just world, she would wake up twenty years younger, sit down to a bowl of granola and soymilk, and say, "Good morning, Daddy"—after which her father would walk her over to a playdate with another faculty kid, practicing the Mandarin words for tree, bird, and car on the way.

"I can't sleep." In the dark she heard Jeff's voice. He sidled up next to her in the small bed, and Zoe could feel the clamminess of his skin. "I just can't get over how weird this is," he whispered against her neck. "The Dragon Lady and your William Sun Mung Moon both get arrested? I knew they were up to something diabolical. He even lured you into marriage too. Tell me, is he after your nonexistent fortune?"

A mosquito buzzed around Jeff's shoulder and he instinctively raised a hand to slap it away.

"Don't kill it!"

"What are you, a bugs' rights activist now? You know, I had the weirdest hallucination that night I got stoned with Engelhorn for you. Ming took me into some strange room with computers and numbers, where somebody was trying to control the world. I woke up later, outside, half-dressed. I hope she rots in jail."

"You're sweating. And you don't eat." Zoe spoke with deliberation. "How much opium did you do there?"

"Can I stay here with you and never come out?"

The mosquito buzzed near Zoe's feet.

"I'm going to make a movie about a handsome, evil genius who hardwires brain chips and sends out technological whispers that say, 'Share your money, make life fair!' Oh, shit, we're home and we're fucking homeless. Can we start a revolution here? Penthouses for all the starving artists? Gotta work on that fucking slogan, millions for the masses, champagne for the civilizers."

"Calm down. Stop saying fuck." Zoe stroked his damp hair. For the rest of the night, Jeff tossed and turned, threw out his arms, and kicked his feet, and he didn't seem to sleep at all. Eventually, Zoe felt her eyelids growing heavy.

The next morning, the light warmed her face through a dusty Venetian blind. Jeff lay on his side, clutching his chest, his eyes fluttering in a half-asleep stupor. Her mouth felt bitter. She padded out, headed for the kitchen for water, but on the way she spotted Lulu in the living room, her face blotched and unhappy. She turned at the sound of Zoe's footsteps, and got chatty.

"That Charles, he's nice. Doesn't he have a wife and children? I saw pictures of big new skyscrapers in New York. Where are they? That's where I want to live. Maybe I can get a job here, do you think? I'm sorry, Zoe, you must be so sad. Charles is looking for news from China online."

A little later, Professor Engelhorn shuffled into the living room, dressed but barefoot. "The Chinese authorities are blocking all news from Sunshine Village," he announced. "The provincial governors are gathering there for a summit to discuss measures to stay competitive in the global economy while practicing sound environmental policies. How about some bagels?"

Charles, Jeff, Lulu, and Zoe sat at a picnic table in the park and said little while they drank coffee from paper cups and ate warm buttered bagels wrapped in greasy white paper.

"Butter—*phew!*" Lulu spat out her first bite.

"Someone should start a business selling the delis cheap Chinese porcelain, instead of these landfill-destroying paper cups," Jeff said. "There's something you can do here, Lulu. Cheer up, you're gonna be rich in America someday."

Zoe watched a pigeon alight at her feet, glancing at her with beady, indifferent eyes as it swooped down on a piece of bagel. Professor Engelhorn read a section of the *New York Times*, while Zoe scanned the headlines about a congressman under investigation for ethics violations.

The paper rustling ceased when the professor arrived at page five. "Oh god, Zoe. Look here. 'The Chinese authorities said they had reason to believe that William Kingsley Sun, recently arrested entrepreneur who created a model village in Sichuan, had been supplying silicon dioxide to certain pariah countries in the Middle East. Code-named *Sand* by the U.S. military, the silicon dioxide substance can cause military hardware and other machinery to jam, engines to seize, and air filters to malfunction. An official from the Beijing government said they believed it was something enemy countries could use against the United States.' It's all fiction, clearly. But it looks like the notion of sharing corporate wealth has officially gone out of favor. I'm afraid William may be locked up for a while."

Professor Engelhorn's cell phone rang just then. "Hello…are you all right?… yes, right here…." He handed the phone to Jeff.

"Yeah, it's me." Jeff's eyes narrowed, sweat beading on his forehead. "Uh huh… That's a shitload of money. Got a sugar daddy you want me to call?" He hung up, rubbed his eyes and the stubble on his chin. "Ming, of course. She gets to talk on a pay phone for ten minutes every two hours. Get this, for the crime of telemarketing something bogus from some boiler room in Chinatown, they've set bail at $10,000 plus a $100,000 bond, because they figure she could so easily flee the country."

A few fat raindrops splattered into the paper cups, and Professor Engelhorn gave them sections of the newspaper to hold over their heads as they raced back to his apartment. Inside, Zoe pretended to read the paper, while Lulu flipped through year-old magazines, and Jeff stared out the window.

"I have to do some work," Professor Engelhorn muttered, and disappeared into his office. After what seemed like days, though, he rushed out with his cell phone live in his hand, playing its jazz piano ringtone. Billie used to tell Zoe that in the days when telephones were mystery boxes without caller ID, she nevertheless always knew when a call came from an agent, or a man worth talking to. "The ring is the same, but there's something you *feel* when it's important—something that pounds at your heart and says this is about to be a day to remember." Now Zoe knew it was Billie calling mostly by the bewildered look on Professor Engelhorn's face. He handed the phone to her; he had come into the room to do that. *Coward.*

"Baby!" Zoe could feel her heart lift at the sound of her mother's voice. "I heard something awful happened in China? I met a guy this weekend and we were stuck in traffic for five hours—five hours can you imagine?—and there you were, just arriving back in town, trying to find your momma. Come home, baby, and bring your friends."

Charles the Chickenhearted walked with them as far as the street, where they all huddled beneath one big black umbrella, watching taxis stream by until finally one slowed down, the light on top illuminated in the dark.

"Why don't you come over for a while?" Zoe asked him.

"Thanks, I'd really like to, but I've got work to do."

In the building that Zoe knew as home, the elevator sometimes worked. This wasn't one of those times, and they had to climb five flights of stairs. It had been a grand building in the nineteenth century, with a wide staircase, but now Zoe—as she had always done after visiting friends whose homes had managed to stay grand—found herself counting every paint flake on the floor.

"This is not as nice as the professor's building," Lulu observed.

So now it's okay to let me know I'm a financial failure, Zoe thought but didn't say. She'd heard people make pronouncements on the value of homes and possessions fairly often in pre-New China times.

When they finally made it to the sixth floor, they found Billie waiting in the doorway. She wore an orange and white sundress and white sandals, her face pink and her hair meticulously windswept. "My baby, look at you! I'm a mess, sorry—I've gotten so fat, my hair's a disaster. Hello, I'm Billie, do you speak English? Jeff, my favorite boy—"

Billie was not alone. In the living room, a man rose to his feet.

"This is Rafael. Darling, this is Zoe, and Jeff and—what's your name, dear?"

That was when Zoe saw his face, the face that could have been the rock Buddha's if the sculptor had finished it. Rafael was lean, his hairline slightly receding, and his demeanor one of European solipsism.

"Have I met you before?" Zoe asked the revised work of art.

"Rafael produces music videos," Billie chimed in, wrapping her arms around the creature. "We met at a party in Greenport."

Jeff nudged Zoe and said, "He looks like a Eurotrash version of fucking Simon Sun."

Why, Zoe raged inside, couldn't William have left Sun Two stewing in prison while he became a little creature with wings? *But I sent him to check up on you,* she imagined the real William replying. Someday they would have a big fight about it. She might be old by then. It might be in their next incarnation.

Zoe sank into a chair. Billie commanded center stage, as usual, while her audience chattered, ate, and drank in a semicircle around her. Somehow, her mother had produced a pitcher of margaritas and a platter of tortilla chips. Zoe could hear the rain outside slow to the kind of patter that brightened the plum blossoms in Sunshine Village.

"Oh god, Zoe, your ring—it's massive!" she heard Billie exclaim.

"Two more seconds and Zoe would have been a married woman," Jeff said. "We were living the American dream in China—the real one where you can be a respected artist *and* make a living. And then somebody decided they didn't like it."

"Sunshine Village is..." Rafael began.

"Yes... do tell," Zoe moved closer to the imposter. "Where is William?" she hissed in his ear, in Mandarin. Rafael, startled, splashed his margarita over the couch.

"Don't worry; it's had a million drinks spilled on it." Billie was already there with a sponge.

"My eight-year-old son," Rafael said when he recovered, "is learning Mandarin. His class did a play about the Chinese Monkey

King. His teacher said the Monkey King personifies the reckless instability of genius."

"Are you reckless and unstable?" Billie asked, batting her eyelashes. Good god, all it took was the presence of a man and Billie reverted to all the Southern belle ways she claimed she'd spurned.

Zoe had had enough. She said goodnight, and, before anyone could stop her, turned down the hall into her room, with the walls she'd painted chrysanthemum years ago. She inhaled emptiness, meditating on a patch of peeling paint. The walls were cracking, but everything was just as she'd left it. She must have dozed, because sometime in the night a cry broke through a dream about floating on clouds—"Ooohhh…yes, oh yes!"

"Does a listener, like an observer, equally affect the action according to the law of quantum physics?" Zoe asked aloud, hoping there might be a gnat in the room to hear her. She heard sighs in the next room, followed by silence except for the usual roar of engines and horns from the street outside. "People don't change," she said to the non-existent gnat, then sank into a sleep that felt like a black hole.

Chapter Twenty

Down near the bottom-most tip of Manhattan, about six miles from Zoe's chrysanthemum bedroom, was a granite labyrinth named the Manhattan Detention Complex, though New Yorkers called it the Tombs. Everyone knew of it, though no one in Zoe's orbit had ever set foot inside, until now.

The walls, the ceilings, the doors, the tables, even the shower stalls were painted gray. The prison scrub suits were navy blue, some so laundered and bleached that they had also turned gray. Ming would observe the cracks in the gray walls and imagine monkeys leaping and a sun with rays around it.

"They got some beastly ghosts in this room. Better make friends with them, China Doll," her cellmate Delia said, languidly flipping her prematurely gray locks over one shoulder. Delia's fingernails were three inches long and painted crimson. Vanity was all they had in the Tombs. In her second week, Ming let Delia paint her nails with purple and white stripes. Inmates earned twelve cents an hour to do the laundry, peel potatoes, or stack library books; they used their pennies to buy beads and nail polish in the commissary. In her third week, Ming dyed her hair auburn like Billie Austin's, just for something to do.

Delia was almost fifty and came from out West. She liked to talk and Ming was a good listener. Delia had left her first husband, not because of his cocaine habit, but because she'd caught him getting a blowjob from the drag queen at his Las Vegas club. She'd moved on to Arizona, where she used to coax brightly colored peonies, vibrant cactus flowers, and even healthy rosebushes out of the scrawniest seedlings. Delia's flowers had bloomed so lush that they had hidden her cash crop for years.

Three years ago, Delia's luck ran out and the police busted her for her horticultural enterprise.

255

"I should have known better. My customer said he had an aging mother with glaucoma, and he wanted five pounds. I should have known it was too much, but he knew all my regulars. The narcos get to know you real, real well."

Delia had been transferred from federal prison to federal prison for the past year—from Arizona to Florida, and now New York—and she'd just received a sentence of ten years, with the possibility of parole for good behavior.

"My beautiful ranch and one hundred acres—it's all going on the auction block if some dirty-finger cop don't squat there himself," Delia moaned.

At first, Ming had thought she'd be better friends with Jennie, the butch with roan-colored skin and a trim Afro cut. Jennie had been the administrative manager of a medical clinic and was in for insurance fraud. People couldn't afford the doctor if the insurance didn't pay for their visit, she told Ming.

"We're all political prisoners," Ming declared, earning a dirty look from Rosa, like what do you know, Ms.-Attended-NYU-Business-School.

Rosa, the fourth cellmate, had a father who'd beaten her often, for partying all night, getting bad grades, and dropping out of community college. "My daddy was, like, a busboy forever. I saw how people pushed him around, and I said, 'I ain't gonna be no servant.'" Rosa was twenty-one and had three children. She had been arrested for helping her boyfriend sell stolen car parts at his shop in the South Bronx.

"What if you could live in a place where you could afford everything you needed?" Ming asked. Jennie threw three dead roaches at Ming's bed to teach her not to indulge in fantasies.

"I always liked the bad boys," Rosa said. "I bet you went out on dates with good little business school boys with itty-bitty-eeny-meeny cocks. China Doll, you wanna bury them bugs and light a candle?"

They all knew Ming screamed in protest if they tried to throw their regulation tennis shoes at scuttling vermin. She told them it was a religious thing.

The inmates were allowed only one visitor a month—in addition to their court-appointed lawyer—excluding bugs, mice, or invisible men, though what, Ming wondered, could an immortal do for her now? During her first week in prison, Ming had waited for Zoe to come, hopefully with some magical access to the bail and bond that would get her out. But her former Sunshine Finance co-head was having her own crisis over money.

"The landlord found out my mom isn't Brennan Leichtling," Zoe had wailed on the phone. "We got an eviction notice. I feel like Sunshine Village, all of it, was some bizarre dream. All except for the opal ring. Which is in a safe deposit box. I can't walk around here flashing that thing."

Instead of Zoe, her visitor for the month was Jeff. He had stopped shaving and his hair stood out in greasy tufts. "How did I manage to marry a fucking rapscallion?" he asked from the other side of the glass. "I've always wanted to use that word but preferably while floating down a raft with Huckleberry Finn."

"I'm innocent." You had to say that if anyone asked.

"Yeah, the illumination of your halo is absolutely blinding. I know you'd rather have a rich husband to bail you out, but I brought you this." He opened a bag and produced three spiral notebooks, one yellow, one red, one blue, and a box with a silver pen inside. "From Zoe and me. Great works have been written in longhand, you know." He slid them into the metal drawer that a guard inspected before Ming could retrieve them.

"Thank you," she said. "Tell me how you are. Tell me really."

"Oh, fine, a bit dopey. Zoe dragged me to a clinic in Harlem. She's convinced I turned into a drug addict in Sunshine Village. I'm taking a mild dose of clonidine."

"I wish I could help you." She meant it.

"She wants to *help* me now! Ha!"

That night Ming drew lines and arrows in the blue notebook. She fashioned them as pathways, tracing the stories Jeff had told her about his movements since he'd arrived back in New York and taken Lulu to stay with his sister, Tracey, in Short Hills, New Jersey. Ming drew Jeff's path in a continuous pencil line, with Lulu's running parallel in short dashes, like two opposing I Ching modalities.

In Chinese characters she composed the scene that Jeff had described—a family dinner with the toddler eating organic macaroni, and the adults dining on some gourmet dish. Tracey's husband had talked through the whole main course about his technology business that was on the brink of going public, then made fun of a Democratic politician—knowing Jeff would fume, but happy to test the endurance of his houseguests. Jeff had taken the bait and called his brother-in-law a fucking dumbass.

Lulu pushed her food around with a fork while Tracey apologized for not having chopsticks. Eventually, the brother-in-law turned to Lulu and asked loudly, "Good? You like the chicken? I'm sorry, I don't know Chinese. You want more? *Uno mas?*"

And Lulu, seizing upon her limited English vocabulary, replied, "I have rich friend in New York. He comes long way, like me. From Sunshine Village."

That night, according to Jeff, Lulu crept into the study where Jeff slept on a fold-out couch. "Not in my sister's house," he protested when she tried to caress him. "I'm sorry," he told Lulu. "It's too much. You need a man who can take care of you."

Lulu had sat up and sobbed, but said in a rigid, defensive voice, "I know one. He imports Sichuan opals and jasmine tea."

The next morning a man in a BMW came for Lulu, and no one had seen her since. Jeff had left his sister's McMansion and now occupied a corner of a friend's row house in Astoria. He spent his days taking photos of the neighborhood and its inhabitants and surfing the internet.

"What's this?" Rosa asked, flipping through Ming's notebook. "I speak'a ze Chinese, you know. 'And there was his giant cock, and I couldn't help myself. He was wanted in every state but I loved him…'"

"Aw, go on, leave her alone," Delia said, glowering at Rosa. Shortly thereafter, Delia positioned herself on Ming's bed. "They're auctioning it. Shit. My ranch near Sedona—I did tell you about my ranch, didn't I? The rocks there are the deepest red you ever saw. Full of heavenly energy, and as remote as remote can be. Wish you could go there, sweet Ming. I'm going somewhere new when I get out."

Ming developed a habit of writing late at night, an hour after lights out. She would wait until Delia's feet hung limp over the top bunk—she was too tall to curl up like a fetus without her knees hanging off the center—and that was when she'd start writing, a faint hallway light guiding her along the page. One night in late September, she scrawled a few lines, then a shadow distracted her. Beside her bed was a scrawny little mouse. The creature waved its tail up from the left, then down to the right, as if it were trying to form the character *ren*—person. Its eyes had a golden glow.

Ming scrambled to the edge of her bunk. "Say something!" she whispered in Mandarin. It poked at its mouse-groin with a forepaw. "God damn it...!" At Ming's exclamation, it bared its rodent teeth and scampered off into the dark.

"China Doll was speaking Chinese in her sleep last night," Delia remarked the next day.

The next night a furry tickle roused Ming from sleep.

"Someone's gonna throw a shoe at you," she warned.

The mouse fixed its golden eyes upon her, scampering close to her ear. Squeaky words rasped from its mouse-sized larynx. "Buy ranch...."

"Ranch?"

"Se...don...ahhh."

Sedona, yes!

Chapter Twenty-One

Zoe pushed button number seven. "A *mouse* was in the cell," Ming said on the phone, with a particular emphasis on the word "mouse." She didn't give Zoe time to ask if the mouse had said anything. Or explain why he didn't come to see his almost-wife.

The apartment was already starting to feel cavernous, though Billie had only begun to take things to the thrift shop. She had checked listings and called realtors in Brooklyn, Queens, Inwood, and as far as the beginning-to-gentrify Yonkers. Everything cost more than she could afford. The real Brennan Leichtling invited her to stay at their sprawling estate in the Hamptons for a while, and Billie figured she'd go, abandoning the kids in Harlem.

"What else can I do?" she asked Zoe, as if pleading for forgiveness. "I'll walk on the beach and think about suicide and I'll jump in, maybe. Maybe someone will give me thousands of dollars to start a theater up there."

Zoe accompanied her mother to Fairway, and it felt like a pilgrimage, going to the market that they had considered theirs for so long. Walking along upper Broadway, they scanned faces that seemed full of anticipation. They eyed the restaurants and hardware stores, the Starbucks and the banks, the shoe stores and the Barnes & Noble—as if they were taking notes on a civilization about to perish. Teenage girls emerged from Sephora holding their faces to the sun to show off sparkle makeup. Young mothers in yoga pants pushed strollers, loaded down with organic groceries. Old couples carried Zabar's bags and argued over where to go next.

"These people are us and we are them," Zoe mourned. "Except they all have apartments they can afford, somehow."

A middle-aged man walking with a little boy cast a long look at Billie. Before the eviction notice, Billie would have fluttered her lashes. She'd had one date since she'd thrown Rafael over that

Thursday after Labor Day. Zoe had watched the battle from a corner. It had started with the man of many transformations alluding to his ex-wife.

"Funny, at the party you said your wife was dead."

"Awww. She's dead to me."

"Who the fuck are you? What am I doing with you? I like to think I'm ageless, but you know what? I'm way too old for a guy who can't decide if he's divorced or killed his wife or whatever your problem is. In a movie this would be the part where the woman says I've been faking all my orgasms. Absolutely no one says that in real life, but you know? It's like there's no 'there, there' in your head. No coherent thoughts, no depth. It's like you're some kind of incomplete sketch, and maybe the master copy is hanging on a wall a million miles away."

But that was all before the registered letter.

The landlord offered a temporary reprieve; Billie could stay until the end of the year. But she was purging things as if preparing for her death. The good furniture went into a Manhattan Mini Storage space; her one thread of hope was that someday she'd reclaim it.

"Might as well kill myself," she muttered through a haze of cigarette smoke. "You know, I always wanted to be a bulwark, to give kids in Harlem something to aim for. The doors of my glamorous paid-for theater penthouse would be open, and 'inside everything's beautiful.'"

"Cabaret."

"Can't you say it like you're actually talking about a cabaret, rather than a coffin?"

"I'm supposed to be married," Zoe moaned. "I've never finished anything."

"Zoe darling," Billie replied, stamping out her cigarette. "You're supposed to be the sane one. When was the last time you got up at sunrise and did your kung fu?"

"*Qi gong.*"

"You don't have to be miserable, and you don't have to be broke. You speak another language. You ran a company."

"What does an ABD do for a living in America?"

"Does that stand for 'Awfully Boring Despairing Damsel'? I didn't raise you to wait for a man who isn't there."

Riverside Park, three blocks away, was a place where Zoe used to jog along the Hudson and feel thrilled to be alive. When her mother pushed her, Zoe strolled down the old riverfront walk, past the dock where it segued into a newer walkway. An elderly couple threw breadcrumbs to pigeons. Joggers passed her in a heave of sweat and panting breath. Even in the park no one looked idle; they were New Yorkers bracing themselves with the giggly morning breeze for a day of auditions, or nursery school, or a deal, or a date.

In spite of herself, she stopped in a grassy place beside a rock formation, stretched into the warrior pose and did battle with the breeze. School bells had rung and commuters had poured into the subways by the time she turned into the apartment walkway. She rode the elevator—working at the moment—with two women she'd never seen before. They pressed the button for the seventh floor. One was heavily made up, and her younger companion, about Zoe's age, was bursting with a radiant pregnancy, flaunting a diamond even bigger than Zoe's Sichuan opal.

"My husband's a lawyer, and he works so late we thought why not live near the office instead of in Greenwich," the radiant mother-to-be was boasting.

"You'll love this neighborhood," the older woman gushed. "It's a nice walk to Lincoln Center. And you have such interesting neighbors in this building. There's a Broadway actress, there's a Columbia PhD who spends a lot of time in China…"

I'm a poor academic, can you lend me $100,000 to get a friend out of jail? Zoe squeezed her lips together to stop herself from uttering the words, all the way to the sixth floor. In the kitchen that would soon not be hers, she held down the button on the coffee grinder, blasting the beans as if she were digging up the sidewalk. Billie sat watching, still in her white nightgown. *You could have played a realtor in real life and made enough money to stay here,* it occurred to Zoe. When she spoke, though, the words that tumbled out were, "Who is my father? Is his name Malcolm?"

262

The flames in Billie's hair seemed to flicker on the spot. "What the hell, I'm about to be homeless and my one and only daughter hates me. I saw a vision once."

"No doubt you were stoned out of your gourd."

"Do you want to hear this or not?" Billie glared, and Zoe raised her palms in mock surrender. "I told you about the guitar-playing half-wit? Well, that was…him. Yes, the name you said. You have his complexion and his profile, but my brain. Anyway, I had a vision of a creature who told me that my child was going to save the world."

"I've lived my whole life under a delusion. What was Malcolm's last name?"

"I saved you from him! He would have been an awful father. You're giving me a migraine!" Billie stormed back into her own room.

That evening Zoe huddled in her chrysanthemum room idly watching a movie on her old computer, one of the many releases she'd missed while she'd been occupied with trying to save the world, when her mother made a grand entrance.

"Zoe," Billie's voice sounded like the cry of a wounded sparrow. Her hair was tousled, her eyes bleary. "I have something I want to show you."

Billie handed Zoe a dusty envelope with paper inside and a separate letter on lilac stationery, folded in thirds and cracked with age. The faded handwriting on the envelope was lean and angular. It was addressed to Billie Austin at an apartment on East 3rd Street. The postmark indicated that it came from Grass Valley, California, in January 1976. In the upper left-hand corner was the name *M. Samuelson.*

The one-page letter inside began with: *Dear Billie (aka Red, My Virgin Mary).*

Guess you never thought you'd be hearing from me, and can't blame you if you burn this. But don't think I didn't think a lot about how I could fix things. But let's be real. How long were we going to live on this vision that came to you in the night? I'm not good for much when it comes to growing up and being a husband and a father. But I guess that's proof to both of us, I'm not Mr. Fix It after all. I'll never forget you. Malcolm.

The other letter was written in a hand Zoe knew well. It was dated two days after the date on the envelope.

Malcolm: Since you didn't even provide me with an address to write to you, I'm just pretending I know where you live, so I can stick this in the mailbox with a bomb inside. I hope someday you will understand how stupid I feel now, to think that I—who gets standing ovations in New York—could have ever been in love with a guy who tried to kick my baby. You are evil, Malcolm Samuelson, and you tempted me like the Devil that night, with your damn electric blue eyes and your hint of exoticism. Truthfully, it was like we were dancing on the moon, looking down at the lights of Manhattan and the universe was banging cymbals and blowing trumpets in a Wagnerian score just for us. I thought at the time if I die tomorrow I'll at least have known the rapture.

Billie's letter went on for eight pages, and it didn't have a finite ending, just a paragraph that said: *This baby really kicks—maybe she's trying to get back at you. I ask myself every day what I'll do if the baby looks like you or has traces of your Persian mother and all I can think is I'll just consider you a gorgeous spirit that never lived, and this an immaculate conception.*

"Malcolm Samuelson." Zoe uttered the name and felt the walls of their soon-to-be-lost home tremble.

⌘

Somewhere across the Pacific Ocean and three thousand miles off the coast of China, Zoe's fiancé—or one-minute-short-of-being-husband—had recently inhabited a dungeon where rats and spiders were his masters, and the rice gruel tasted like a broth of human shit. The Chinese government had re-opened its most secretive corners and filled them with prisoners whose heinous crimes included questioning a governor's motives, carrying a protest sign, writing an essay citing evidence that someone had bribed a mayor to obtain a contract, and running a business that didn't offer fifty percent of its equity to the provincial minister of industry. One of the most prominent among these prisoners, William Kingsley Sun, was, like others, incarcerated on vague, trumped-up charges, uncertain of his crime.

264

"Congratulations on your new career as martyr," he whispered to himself.

The healthier among his dungeon-mates also conversed with themselves, a sign that mental gears were still grinding.

"Thank you, but what went wrong with the middle ground? We weren't decadent. We weren't cynical," he muttered back.

"You think the whole world wants to drink fine wine and talk about ideas?"

William closed his eyes and imagined the smooth sweetness of icy champagne and his would-be wife. "We were presumptuous, maybe. Everyone wants to be on top whether they understand ideas or not."

"Some people will even be martyrs to be on top."

"If my mortal body dies here, perhaps a few might remember me as a hero, but I won't do anyone any more good."

"Quite so. That is the height of arrogance, of course, to see yourself as so important."

"Arrogant, you say? If that's my only flaw—"

The voice in his head was persuasive, and William had decided that, in fact, he had bigger things to do than be a martyr. He calculated he'd been in the *lao gai* for about three weeks at that point, long enough to describe the inhumanity to the world beyond. Now it was time for someone to take his place as prisoner William Kingsley Sun. The guards counted inmates every morning and every night, and a missing body would mean protracted torture for all those left behind. He could fake William Kingsley Sun's death, but that would prove problematic when he wanted to appear in the outside world.

William searched his head for hairs—fewer of them now—but in the dark of night he pulled one out, chanted, and a figure that looked just like him appeared. "You can have your Simon face back someday when we get out. It'll be an untroubled, handsome visage. I'll make all this up to you," he promised his copy.

"Yeah, you're going to have to make me king of something for a century. Oh yes, I'll sleep in the bowels of hell for you, my master and creator. I will swallow my own gallbladder to taste bitterness. But at a price—you'll owe me a solid gold Rolls Royce, champagne, and lobster tails every day for fifty years, ten beautiful women every night, even if they're fucking cunts like the ones in New York." Then Sun Two bent his head and wept. "I'm going to be the part of you that never goes away," he said. "You can hide me but I'll come out and turn your happy home with a wife and kids upside down, just because I can."

William abandoned his copy to the cell in spite of the threats, because he had no choice.

The inmates, who lived without expectation, were not the least bit surprised that a business leader known in the outside world for his charisma—a man who might have riled the other prisoners to storm down the walls—would slink silently through his workday. The prisoner named William Sun began to look like a faded facsimile of himself, with eyes like doorways to a vacant building. To inquiries he might mutter, "I'm just a copy of William Kingsley Sun, don't bother me." He wasn't the first natural-born leader to lose his will in a *lao gai*.

The immortal himself, after weeks of nothing to eat but shit-infested gruel, his legs stiff from the chains, kicked up his heels like a fawn and leapt over the land mass. He had many destinations to traverse, starting with Beijing. There, as an invisible presence in the room, he observed a meeting of powerbrokers who looked simultaneously smug and scared as they exchanged views about how China needed a bold new vision. He followed twelve dignitaries and their bodyguards to a meeting on the executive floor of Plenette-Leuter China, where twelve government officials and twenty top executives, some from the US, talked about the importance of inoculating the population with a vaccine that had been developed to treat depression, but would be just as effective at warding off all fears of a deadly strain of bird flu that had made headlines in recent weeks.

Two days later, the invisible man sat in at a television studio as the premier of China broadcast a live address. The premier told his people that the government was ready to protect them from a bird flu epidemic. The camera cut to footage of wasted, deathly ill people hooked to tubes and ventilators. The premier assured his people that a certain heroic pharmaceutical company was working with the government and starting the very next day would provide free inoculations for all across the entire country.

The unseen immortal flew to hospitals in Beijing, Shanghai, and many cities north and south. Not one had patients dying of bird flu; the wasted bodies in the television footage were digitized images. The same images were now appearing in posters, internet ads, and television announcements urging the public to get their shots. He observed, also, that the share price of Plenette-Leuter tripled in a week.

While the immortal was in Beijing, he also found Mr. and Mrs. Cheng, looking stooped and troubled, moving into an apartment near Han. In his invisible presence, he witnessed a series of discussions between son and parents; Han had sold their company because it was time for them to retire, time for a filial son to look after them, time for him to take them to a nearby clinic for their bird flu shots. Mama and Papa Cheng didn't so much protest as look disappointed, as if they knew their son was saying all the right things but the words were counterfeit.

The invisible William somersaulted through the sky to Sunshine Village. He tumbled through a cloudbank and landed in the peasant hamlet, where weeds grew outside the pastel stucco houses and wound their way around foreclosure signs. A bulldozer detonated the earth in an empty lot; an adjacent sign announced the new development of luxury condos. The rice paddies were similarly lifeless, the seedlings strangled by wild dandelion, the once-neat rows now neglected. His own house, too, was gone, luxury condos under construction on the site. Good thing he'd thought ahead and had Sun Four cover up the secret passageway just before his wedding. Along the cliff, he found a crane and a shopping mall coming up, polished pavement covering the ground even where the giant Buddha had been, and a sound-and-light show taking place in the cave.

He searched for Jing Yin's whereabouts and found no sign of her at the old Kwan villa, which had a real estate sign out front announcing "Sold!" It was an easy feat, of course, for an invisible being to hack into the computers at the real estate office, and there he found the name of the seller—Bradley Kwan. The dead man had a new address in Chengdu.

He found Bradley very much alive in a spacious apartment there. Oblivious to an unseen presence in her new home, Jing Yin sat slumped on the couch, her eyes obediently glassy, a Band-Aid on her upper arm. Everyone got a Band-Aid after the vaccine.

In a rote voice, she asked her father, "Do you have money?"

"Some," said the man who was no longer dead.

"Can I have a new iPhone then? And I couldn't possibly go to school without a Louis Vuitton bag..."

That same night the man of seventy-two transformations returned to Sunshine Village, where he sat on the condo construction site and shed tears for all the work that was now undone. But he had a mission, and he must not give up on human nature's ability to evolve. From the secret entry in the forest he crept down to the bunker, where he found his thirty-one computers intact. He extracted the data to an external backup drive, then smashed all thirty-one computer screens and buried the remains. Perhaps in another millennium an archeological crew might puzzle over the significance of this shrine.

Then it was time to leap across the Pacific and go to his co-conspirators. Sun Two had told him of their whereabouts. Whether Zoe still loved him or not, she was walking around with the key to civilization. But he decided it would accrue good karma to check in on Ming first. And as it happened, karma seemed to visit him instantly; as a scrawny mouse within the Tombs, he eavesdropped on Ming's cellmate when she met with her lawyer, he viewed the specs on her foreclosed ranch in Sedona, Arizona, and he listened to Delia try to ply Ming with the fantasy of buying her ranch at the upcoming auction. It was a property with much to offer, he decided.

Though he wished he could clean up first, he was going to have to enlist Zoe now that he had a plan. As an invisible human form, he reached the Upper West Side in one swift leap. A neighborhood that seemed designed for lives filled with words and music, he observed.

268

A luminous October sun lit up the nineteenth-century edifices with their scrubbed bricks and lacquered doors.

At the address he'd committed to memory, William rang the bell for the apartment labeled "Leichtling." When there was no answer, he sidled in behind another resident and flew up six flights of stairs.

If Zoe was home and in the throes of passion with someone else, he decided, she would know only that a gnat had whizzed by. In that particular life form he slipped through the keyhole into her apartment. He found a home that was eerily empty; boxes were strewn about the living room; there were no dishes in the drainer; the teakettle was stone cold. He did, though, catch a whiff of peach mango in the bedroom with chrysanthemum colored walls. He would stay invisible and wait until she came back, he decided. He would write a note, and when she came home she'd find it and know he was about. A legal notepad sat right there on her desk. It was turned to a page with the words *Suzanne Hirsch* and *Benefit* with a phone number, all in a handwriting that made his heart turn a somersault of its own. Other notes on the same page seemed to refer to job applications; she'd written *Translator* and underlined it, beside the name of a person and a company.

Beside the legal pad, he noticed a cracked and yellowed envelope addressed to Billie Austin.

A hero doesn't snoop, he told himself. But he was looking for clues to his darling's whereabouts, wasn't he? He began to read.

Chapter Twenty-Two

Zoe was seated in a hospital room. Around her were a dozen actors and actresses, playwrights, singers, make-up artists, and yoga instructors. They occupied chairs, leaned against the windowsill, or sat cross-legged on the floor. All gazed upon the woman who lay in the bed, unaware of anything—Billie, her hair spread across a pillow, her eyelids translucent and closed. A tube fed oxygen through her nose, and a needle filled her veins with nutrient components.

Grandma Austin, who had arrived from Mississippi the day before, held one of Billie's hands tightly within her own, her chestnut eyes alive with sorrow. Jeff shifted about in a corner, and the real Brennan Leichtling busied herself arranging flowers. Others provided explanations to new arrivals: "A frigging SUV. The driver kept going but somebody actually saw the whole thing and gave the police the license number."

"Did they catch him?"

"They charged him with felony hit and run."

Zoe hadn't told anyone about the letters Billie had shown her. Or how she'd come out the next morning wearing a diaphanous white dress and no makeup.

"I think I'll take a walk to the river," Billie had said, with an English tilt to the word *walk*. Zoe had had a sudden image of Virginia Woolf walking into the River Ouse, but Billie wasn't wearing an overcoat and had no pockets to fill with stones.

She just needs air, Zoe had told herself. Billie had taken along a shoulder bag, with her wallet and identification, even a card that said *In case of emergency notify*——.

"Your mother's SAG insurance will cover two weeks of hospital care, but I'm afraid there's a pretty big deductible, and the doctor thinks she needs at least a six-week stay in a rehabilitation facility. After that she can go into a nursing home. You'll just have to spend down all her savings, then she can get on Medicaid," the head nurse told her.

"That's our health non-care system, for you," Jeff contributed. Then he turned to someone who'd just come in. Zoe heard him delivering the account she'd heard a million times now. "The driver was depressed after his wife left him and he'd been downing sleeping pills with vodka. You know what the motherfucker told the police? He was late for his men's sensitivity group and he didn't realize the light had changed."

Later that day a massive bouquet of yellow roses appeared in the doorway. Zoe saw gangly legs and polished loafers below the flowers, and as he entered the room she saw that Charles Engelhorn was the bearer. While someone found a space amongst a dozen bouquets and someone else proffered a chair, Professor Engelhorn sat down and leaned against the bed railing as if he aimed to stay for a long time.

He was still there when evening descended and someone suggested Zoe and Grandma go home and get some rest. "I knew her a long time ago. I'd like to stay a while," the professor told them. And before they left he said, "My brother in Boston is a neurologist who specializes in brain damage. I think I should talk to him."

In the apartment, Zoe and Grandma set out old family porcelain and decanted Chinese takeout food into the flower-pattern bowls.

"Tell me about that nice man, Charles, with the doctor brother," Grandma said.

"I have it on good word that he wanted to marry Mom and be my father once upon a time. But now I know who my real father was. Mom was madly in love with some guitar-playing—" Zoe felt her throat thicken and her eyes prickle with tears. "He tried to kill me before I was born."

"Oh, honey." Grandma patted her hand.

"Charles was in love with her, but she laughed in his face."

Grandma nodded. "Billie always did have a bit of a cruel streak. She asked me once, 'Mother, why doesn't God just get rid of people who are ugly or boring?' When she grew up and had you, she called

271

us and said, 'The baby cries. I can't stand these smelly diah-pers.' So we took you in."

"She told me you didn't approve of her life."

"Yes, I'm sure she remembers it her way. When you turned five she came and begged us to give you back and your grandpa gave in. You seemed like you knew you had to be an interesting little person to your mama. Oh, sweetie. Do you want to come stay with me?"

"No," something whispered. Zoc was sure a voice had said that.

"Goodness, I didn't think we ate that much." Grandma surveyed three bowls with nothing left but rivulets of sauce and slivers of onion.

"I'll clean up," Zoe said, and Grandma went into Billie's bedroom, moving as if a thick cloak of sorrow were weighing her down.

Zoe poured the remaining wine into her glass and left it on the table while she carried the dishes into the kitchen. When she returned, the wineglass was empty.

"A truly enlightened man would help with the dishes," she said aloud.

She waited. The room was still. "I'm going to take a shower," she announced. Her words kind of echoed, mocking her certainty that she wasn't alone. She took her time in the shower, then wrapped herself in her old blue kimono from Chinatown and floated on a waft of peach-mango soap into her bedroom. She hadn't been in there yet, all night. The room felt alive. That was when she saw that there was a note on her desk, in Chinese characters—*Darling, I'm here waiting for you.*

"Show your face," she called out.

The visible transformation appeared in the chair beside her desk, sitting with one leg crossed casually over the other. "Needless to say, I eavesdropped on your dinner. I'm very sorry about your mortal mother," he said. He was the very picture of a man who'd escaped from hell, with raccoon circles around his eyes and unruly hair thinned on top. He was dressed in clean but faded scrubs, a blue shirt and drawstring pants; he must have stolen them from the penitentiary after he visited Ming.

272

Zoe flew to him, and they somersaulted onto her bed, body heat as florid as a summer garden, glorious infinity melting all thoughts of hospital and prison walls. Except that, after they made love, William held her left hand to his face and stopped.

"Where's your ring?" he asked.

"In a bank, in a safe deposit box. For safety. "

"I suppose the bank is closed at night."

"Of course. We can go there first thing in the morning."

He shook his head. "Way too late. It's Wednesday. Lots to do. I'll tell you as it unfolds." He sank into her pillow, battling the urge to sleep. Zoe, on the other hand, eyed her computer.

"I have something important to show you," she announced.

"Letters? I came and looked for you…" William confessed. "And I saw them."

"Look at this." Her computer was still on, just in idle. "Malcolm Samuelson is a common man with a common name, but I found something on Google."

What she showed him was a web page with a banner advertising *Malcolm's Auto Repair.* Beneath were the words, *Need a tune-up? Overhaul? Emergency? 24/7 emergency towing. Malcolm will fix it all 4 U.* In the center of the page was a photo of a cinderblock establishment, and in the left-hand corner were directions to an address in Edgewood, New Mexico. *Half a mile past the First Baptist Church, 300 feet from Taco Bell.*

In the lower right-hand corner was the photo of a man with a gray ponytail and wiry build. He wore a black cowboy shirt with embroidered swirls that, upon close inspection, turned out to be tiny guitars. Malcolm had electric-blue eyes and laugh lines deep as canyons. The cleft in his chin matched the proportions of Zoe's own.

"I found the site, and that was precisely when the phone rang. It's like he hit my mom with a bolt of fate."

"Edgewood, New Mexico," William read aloud, caressing her shoulder.

"Edge of nowhere. I could have come from a village full of the ghosts of cowboys and Indians, like a parallel life to Ming's."

273

"New Mexico is on the way to where we're going. Did Ming tell you about Arizona?"

"Arizona?"

"There's a property auction going on Friday. There's a ranch with a starting price at half the market value. Good soil for digging underground and the nearest neighbor is two miles away. Zoe darling, the key to the deposit box please? I'll go get your ring, then we can fly before dawn…"

Zoe retrieved the key, and he was off, a butterfly zooming out her window. She couldn't sleep, so she trolled through pictures of mystical red sandstone formations and thick pine forests around Sedona, Arizona. She checked her email. Suzanne Hirsch had sent a message about the gala dinner to raise money to address the plight of William Kingsley Sun, Chinese political prisoner. "Everyone wants to support human rights in China again," Suzanne's message gushed. "I'm so happy to be able to make this happen." And then, a new message, composed at an insomniac hour, from Charles Engelhorn. *My brother would like to conduct tests at his hospital in Boston, and we can arrange to transfer Billie there, but the hospital wants to know about your insurance.*

He signed it *Charles.*

How would she ever pay for special care? She was pondering hospital expenses when a force pounded against her window. Zoe opened it to an invisible gust which then materialized into a man in sweaty prison scrubs. He opened his right palm to reveal the opal ring, casting prisms against both of them.

"You'll need to wear it," William insisted, slipping it on her finger. "And you'll need some nice clothes. And your passport. We're going to Bermuda."

"How am I going to fly that far?"

"Inhale conduct. You can do it."

She dressed up in a silk blouse, trousers, and pumps. Then they stood together on the balcony, amidst the potted asters. The sky was just beginning to grow a lighter shade of nighttime black.

As she inhaled, a shift occurred below her feet, the ground

transforming from a solid surface to something invisible and infinite. Nothing but clouds above and an inky ocean below, and a hand boosting her that seemed less like flesh than an endless current. When she stood upright again, she was breathless. William stood beside her, barefoot and sweaty for a moment before his corporeal form disappeared.

"I'll be with you," he whispered, invisible now, "but best that no one see me. You look fine, just a little windblown. Rich people with offshore bank accounts get to be windblown and eccentric."

Zoe entered the marble lobby of an offshore bank, where two guards asked for her security code. An invisible hand guided hers, punching twelve numbers into a keyboard. A third guard, a woman, took her down a series of steps to a subterranean vault, to a safe deposit box not much bigger than the one where she'd stored the ring. With the invisible hand guiding her, she pressed a miniscule lever on the side of her opal ring that lifted the stone. Beneath the opal was a tiny plastic card, which the hand helped her hold up to the scanner beneath the deposit box handle. Gears whirred, and the door opened.

Zoe gasped involuntarily. A creature grinned at her from the darkness—a stuffed monkey, all of six inches high, with a Sichuan opal around its neck. Next to the monkey was a manila envelope.

"Thank you. I'll take it with me," she said to the guard.

The two of them flew back, William grasping the monkey toy and the envelope, over the tempestuous waves of the Atlantic, through fiercely whipping winds—a flight that lasted forever and yet no more than a second. They landed on her balcony with a thud that shook the rail and sent flowerpots crashing to the floor.

"Work on slowing down before you land," William murmured in her ear, disheveled but triumphant. It was just after ten a.m. Grandma had left a note on the kitchen table. *I see you've gone out. Glad you're getting back to your morning exercises. Take your time. I'll be at the hospital when you get there.*

"I need a sharp object," William said. "And just in case Grandma decides to come back, let's go behind closed doors."

The monkey grinned at them. With a knife from the kitchen,

William sliced its head off, then disemboweled its torso with one stroke. Buried in stuffing was a small plastic bag. William emptied the contents on to the desk—a cluster of miniscule translucent grains. Zoe counted ninety-seven of them.

"We'll have to save these for the most influential people in the world," he said. "No more manufacturing facilities—all we have is this ranch, and that's only if I can get out there before someone else buys it."

Zoe kept staring at the chips.

"Open the envelope," he said.

Inside the envelope was a stack of papers and a plastic card, which he held up as if it were the spoils of war. The card was from the bank in Bermuda, and the name on it was Zoe Austin. The papers were full of numbers—numbers that bounced off the page and boogied about her room, critical inspectors of her life. Nine million, nine hundred ninety-nine thousand, nine hundred ninety-nine dollars.

"All nines for long lasting fortune and a life of harmony, " said William. "Of course it has earned interest. I only hope we have enough. Come, we have to go. We have to buy the place in your name, since both of your partners are technically in prison. We should go right now."

She kept staring at the numbers, and the mocking grin from the monkey's severed head. "Where did it come from?"

"A smart business leader puts something away for an emergency. I haven't even told you what I saw in China." He described to her, all the while glancing at her clock, the bird flu vaccine campaign and Jing Yin's telltale bandage and how alive Bradley Kwan had been.

Zoe suddenly felt damp and deflated. "About ten million dollars plus interest and ninety-seven chips are nothing against what China has."

"We have to try. We keep honing the program 'til we get it right. We thought everyone would want to be a civilizer, but turns out that what everyone wants is to be the star of their own movie, at least in their own microcosm. I say we go after ninety-seven top dogs and

276

drill their brains with empathy and benevolence. Including the top dogs at Plenette-Leuter Pharmaceuticals, of course."

Zoe stared at the plastic bag and the subversive little miracles inside, then shook her head. "No more secret operations. It's dangerous to play god. I guess Jeff did kind of have a drug problem, but I convinced him it was worse than it really was just because I wanted him to think he couldn't trust his own eye. I thought my mom should face the truth, and it sent her into such a trance she didn't see the car coming at her."

The room spun around her, and something that had no name tugged at her. She saw her own hand reach to the plastic bag, and she heard a voice asking, *What would he do if there were no chips?* She felt her feet rustling through the living room and out of the French doors. She held the bag precariously over an unbroken pot of purple asters and heard herself saying, "I bet these little miracles would make the flowers grow."

He was behind her. He shook his head and grabbed the bag of chips. Of course, she knew he was going to do that, didn't she? "I can buy the place as your representative and I won't use more than my third. I'll be fair. If you change your mind you know where I'll be. I presume there are lots of ways to transport yourself to Arizona."

With that, he took a deep breath and disappeared, a gust of wind somersaulting across the balcony and into the sky.

Chapter Twenty-Three

She had tried to save people and instead destroyed them. Zoe thought of dying there on the balcony, waiting for winter. She thought of the man who'd given her this mortal form, the man who made his living off the pickings of the highway. Perhaps he thought she was already dead.

She didn't know how long she'd been out there when she felt someone shake her, but late afternoon sun illuminated the face of Jeff. Unshaven, a whiff of subways coming up from his shoes. Of course, he had a key from his time staying here.

"Everybody was wondering where you were." He pulled her up by the armpits. She tried to kick but felt too weak. "Your grandma's going to be home soon. You want her to see you like this?"

"I have the money to get Ming out," she mumbled.

"Then you better do it."

Jeff told her to take a shower, and knowing he was outside the door waiting gave her the strength to wash. When she finished, he followed her into her bedroom.

"Whew," he said, taking in the rumpled bed sheets, the room intoxicant with sweat and sex. "I won't ask questions. Not married man Danny, I hope. Someone new? What the fuck is this?" He picked up the stuffed monkey's severed head.

"An old toy I found. I was in a bad mood and I felt like cutting someone's head off." The monkey head seemed to flash her a sinister grin. Then she showed Jeff the old letters. She even showed him the bank statement, saying it had arrived by mail. When Grandma came home, Jeff was sitting on the chair, Zoe on the bed, wearing her kimono.

"Are you kids okay?" asked Grandma. She brought them sandwiches, as if they were indeed children.

"I'm going to stay here," Jeff told Zoe while they were eating.

"On the sofa bed, of course. Who ever thought you'd be the crazy one?"

Two days later, Jeff and a lawyer accompanied Zoe to the gray place. Morning ticked past noon. Finally, a prison guard brought Ming out. She kept her gaze on the floor, as if she'd lost the right to look anyone in the eye. Her hair hung with indecision, wiry ringlets sticking out amongst sullen strings. She wore an electronic ankle bracelet.

That night Ming slept on the sofa bed, with Jeff. And the night after. Jeff began to mark his territory. By the end of the week there were two laptops, three cameras, and a cluster of found bottles and toy cars on the living room floor. They had three months yet before they had to vacate the premises.

"You are quite the accumulator," Grandma told Jeff, with a tight smile. Not being Southern, Jeff didn't seem to understand that the laugh in her voice was a hint that he ought to straighten things up.

"I even accumulated a wife." He flashed Ming an uncharacteristically indulgent smile. But Grandma liked Jeff, in spite of his trove. Zoe could tell.

Grandma didn't ask where Ming had been, though Zoe could surmise by the faintly patronizing undertone when Grandma addressed their new guest that she considered this a worthwhile charity, putting up a wayward girl.

The wayward girl asked Zoe to stay behind one morning when Grandma departed for the hospital and Jeff for a day of wandering. "You have to see this," Ming said. She clicked on a Chinese website and pulled up a reality TV show entitled *The Kwans*.

A camera panned to a man's face: Bradley Kwan. The man spoke. "My name is Bradley. I had an argument with my wife one night. I killed her. I escaped from a vengeful mob. I did wrong. But everyone deserves a second chance."

The camera cut to a classroom, and zoomed in on Jing Yin. "She looks drugged," Zoe observed. Another girl in the classroom whispered something to the girl across from her and they both giggled. When Jing Yin glared at them, the first girl said, "Ha ha.

Your father is a murderer." Jing swung a large designer handbag at her.

In the next scene, the teacher was reprimanding the girl who'd begun the taunting. "Jing Yin is a little older because she dropped out of school, but her father makes a lot of money and someday *you* might work for them. No matter what he's done in the past, if he's making a lot of money, we should look up to him."

Ming clicked on another episode, in which Bradley and Jing Yin were having breakfast on a terrace high above Chengdu. "Isn't it fun being rich?" Bradley declared. "If this show gets canceled, you know it's the *lao gai* for me and planting rice for you." He chuckled at his own joke, before the show cut to a commercial—for the Plenette-Leuter pharmaceutical company. Footage showed town after town where doctors and nurses were giving people free bird flu vaccines.

"You see," said Ming, "my country needs you."

"Someone is always going to undo what we've done."

"My lawyer thinks that when I have my trial they might not put me in prison, even if they find me guilty, since I've already done five weeks. So Jeff and I are going out west if it all works out."

"What's that, gratitude?"

Ming looked pensive. "As long as I'm with him, he won't start blabbing about what he saw. So that's my punishment—a life with Jeff. There are worse things. Sometimes I think I do love him. Don't you want to go to Arizona? I, uh, told Jeff you bought the ranch and you need to get it ready, as a place for William to recover and write a memoir once he gets out. Actually, I'll write his memoir while he saves the world. And Jeff and I might go on to California before he pokes around and finds out too much."

Ming and Jeff even told Grandma they were dreaming of going out West. "We'll get a car and take the old Route 66," Jeff said. "I'm going to make a road movie. We'll stay in crumbling motels with flamingoes on the marquee and hope we don't cross paths with some Billy Bob cowboy with a machine gun. Hey, Zoe, you're the director, see, you have to come."

Zoe envied their ability to imagine a future. But even Grandma told her she should think about taking a trip with them. The doctors said it would be all right to send Billie up to Boston by air ambulance, and Grandma was planning to go with her. The insurance would cover part of the transportation, but Zoe began mentally putting aside funds.

The day before they left for Boston, Professor Engelhorn was sitting at Billie's bedside again, grading papers.

"Are you thinking about your dissertation?" he asked Zoe that afternoon.

"Everything changed."

"Yes, it changed and then it went back to being the same, or worse. Did you know Bradley Kwan isn't dead?"

"I heard."

"If I believed in crackpot conspiracy theories, I'd swear the leaders decided we'll give the country a taste of freedom and equality and show them how human nature itself is what gets in the way of equality. But think about it. Maybe you just need a break, but you can re-apply and start over when you're ready." He looked at Zoe, then at Billie in her coma as if she had some kind of answer.

"Or maybe you'd like to write a book with your husband when he gets out," Charles went on. "Who better than William to raise awareness of all the ways this stepped-up hyper-capitalism is destroying human rights? It could even be the subject of your dissertation, and if you did that, I'm sure you could get a good teaching job."

He talked as if he thought Zoe were still whole. She looked away for fear he might read her thoughts. She stared at the vegetative patient who had once been Billie Austin. An aide had cut her hair, and the tendrils on the pillow were mostly the color of ashes. Her Technicolor life had turned a grainy black and white.

"I know, you have to get through Suzanne Hirsch's benefit," Charles said, smiling as if they were allies in the ordeal. "But if she helps get the word out, and gets you the funds for a high-powered international lawyer…."

Suzanne Hirsch's William Kingsley Sun Defense Fund gala took

281

place a few nights after Grandma left with Billie, two weeks before Thanksgiving, at the Metropolitan Club on the East Side. "Danny will probably be there," Jeff reminded her, "with or without Liesel, did you know she's about to pop their first heir?"

"We need dresses," Ming said. "You know, we could go to Bergdorf."

"Loehmann's," Zoe heard herself insisting. "Don't think Suzanne's friends won't know it if we're wearing Bergdorf dresses and whisper among themselves about how could we afford them." How long had it been since she'd made an authoritative pronouncement? In the store, she convinced Ming to get a black dress instead of the blue one with the sexy cutout back. The backless blue dress was tarty, like a fashion statement Ming might have acquired from her cellmates. Zoe, the daughter of Malcolm Samuelson, with no fiefdom left to her name except Empress of Going to Loehmann's, at least ruled her square inch of turf with good taste.

On the night of the benefit, as they primped and zipped themselves into their designer-discount finery, Zoe stared herself down in the mirror. Her dress was deep purple satin, approximately the same color as the circles around her eyes. "I look awful," she observed.

"Don't worry, you're supposed to look bereaved." Ming winced when Zoe put on the garish ring, though.

Charles Engelhorn was also a featured speaker. He introduced Zoe, in fact. As the guests were finishing dinner, he stood at a podium and talked about *lao gais* he had seen ten years before and the underground reports that told him the dungeons were even worse now, with chain gangs forced to break boulders, often dragging companions who'd dropped dead of starvation.

Behind Charles, projected on a screen, was a photo of William Kingsley Sun. His gaze seemed invincible, his eyes fiery. Zoe had taken the picture. She could feel the sinewy body that had held her just a few weeks ago.

While Professor Engelhorn was saying, "It's a great honor to introduce William Sun's fiancée and one of my favorite students," she observed Danny Hirsch strolling in late, without Liesel.

Zoe made herself stand up to the microphone and step into character. "I feel William's presence here," she said. Except she didn't, not in a literal way. She delivered the lines Ming had said would work, about how the man of the moment had been arrested just before the priest pronounced them married. "And that was the last time I saw him." She spoke about the New China and how quickly the government had buried all traces.

"We have it on good word, there's no bird flu." She heard gasps of astonishment or maybe skepticism. That at least she could do. "Those vaccines, I can tell you, are to brainwash the little people." There might be executives from the Plenette-Leuter company in the audience, it occurred to her. Maybe they'd have her shot.

"When influential people mention the name William Kingsley Sun to Chinese government authorities, the powerbrokers will know that William has powerful allies. I leave you with this thought: those who serve an authoritarian regime live in fear." That was the note of hope; Ming had told her she had to end with optimism.

"That was so moving," someone said afterward, as Zoe floated through the crowd. Of course, they would say that.

"Suzanne Hirsch is such a one-woman tour de force," someone else effervesced.

The mob blurred, except for someone just beginning to fill out into his grown-up self, his jaw a tad fleshier than she remembered, his hairline receding in slow motion.

Danny kissed her on the mouth, then said, "So, you married a hero."

"We didn't finish getting married."

"You look beautiful. A little too wise for your age, maybe. Have a drink with me?"

Zoe looked around, wondering if someone was going to try to stop her. Even Ming and Jeff were lost somewhere in the traffic. At the bar it was hard to move without hitting someone's elbow. She saw Danny whispering something to a bartender. Then he put his lips against her ear and said, "Come with me." His breath tickled.

He steered her into a smaller ballroom where gilt-edged chairs lay slanted against barren tables. A waiter, whistling and patting down his pocket, brought in a bottle of Van Gogh Blue vodka and a bucket of ice. Danny pulled out chairs.

"I kind of suspected," he said over the clink of glasses, "that you were going to do something bigger than a dissertation if you went off to the wilds of Sichuan."

She let Danny put his arm across the back of her chair. The tart taste of alcohol made her feel pretty again. She told him a tale or two from her life in the New China.

"Civilizers." He rolled the word around. "Did I tell you I'm quitting the hedge fund world? I'm going to write a novel."

"How does Liesel feel about that?"

"Aw, lemme tell you something about my lovely expecting wife. I haven't told her yet. I just decided it when I saw you." Danny was leaning close to her now. "Actually, it's not my decision to quit. We had a bad year at the old fund. A bad two years, in fact. All our big investors have been taking their money out. Last year I put my own money in to keep the assets up. When you do that and you have another bad year you're fucked. So I'm going to have to close down the fund. So I'll have plenty of time to write a novel."

"I'm so sorry. But you can start over."

"I put in *all* my money. Liesel's not into cutting back."

Zoe took a greedy sip of vodka.

"You're different, somehow. Did I say that? Not that I didn't like you before, but I like the way you seem different."

Maybe she looked like someone in a position to lend him a million dollars?

She could feel Danny's eyes surveying her hair, then her shoulders and cleavage. No, he didn't want her money. He was sizing up the body parts of Malcolm Samuelson's daughter.

"It's getting kind of late," she said.

"Oh, I'm not worried. My wife isn't worried. You know what's really funny?" Danny drained his glass and poured more vodka for both of them. "I have an idea for a novel about China."

Then he kissed her with purpose.

Was it possible to die of carnal starvation? Yes, but I can inhale discipline and fly. The daughter of Malcolm Samuelson reached for her immortal mantra just as Danny was kissing her shoulders and making his way to her breasts.

She pushed him off with a gentle forward thrust.

"Oh…" he said. "Presumptuous of me."

She held out two icy glasses, which they both sipped for a moment like cold showers.

"Life is crazy, isn't it?" he said. "You know what could have saved my fund, except I didn't do it? I didn't buy stock in Plenette-Leuter. Just two weeks ago, someone told me Plenette-Leuter had proprietary medical evidence that a global bird flu epidemic was on the way, so they were stepping up production of the vaccine. All I knew at the time was this could be a piece of inside information so I resisted buying. I obeyed the law and so I missed out. Their share price has quadrupled since I got the tip."

Zoe shivered. The empty ballroom was frigid.

"A global epidemic?"

"Yeah. And then when you said that tonight, about there being no bird flu, well, I thought maybe I'll write a novel about a pharmaceutical conspiracy to brainwash little people all over the world, except it isn't fiction and I don't think it has a happy ending unless someone has a *really* powerful antidote. " He touched her chin and held it up as if she were a kitten. "Would you consider being my muse?"

The only possible hope.

What she said was, "Didn't you know? I'm going out West."

Chapter Twenty-Four

Do you think she jumped off the roof?" Jeff asked Ming. They'd lost sight of Zoe.

When they finally found her, she was wandering out of an empty ballroom. And who should be right behind her but Danny Hirsch. Danny hovered about Zoe and wouldn't let go. The four of them got into a cab and went back to Zoe's apartment. In the living room, Danny told them all that he'd decided to start writing a novel that might not be fiction at all.

"Whatever came over China, when all those business and financial leaders decided to be generous, that then gave them a reason to think of themselves as archangels who could do no wrong," Danny pontificated. "We're on a precipice now. I mean, what would you say if you were writing a novel about what happened? Are you writing a novel about China, Ming?"

"I'm writing a story that has to end with someone left to start things over," Ming said. "If you have, say, a mad captain who rams his ship right into the great white whale, someone has to be a survivor who tells the story." In the prison library she'd read all kinds of stories told by survivors.

"I beg to differ; it has to end with the power elite saying, 'Okay now it's time to crack down,'" Danny persisted. "That's what those who believed in the New China experiment overlooked."

"Maybe we're in a war between good and evil and there's no end, just one battle after another," Ming countered.

"Whoooo, a pissing contest," said Jeff.

Danny leaned close to Ming. "Tell you what. In fifty years let's meet on the Upper West Side—or appoint our heirs to meet if we're not around—and draw up a point-by-point review of where I was right and where you were right. I'm betting my list will be twice as long as yours, but what the hell, we'll let posterity be the judge."

"Ouch, Ming doesn't like to think about judges," her husband muttered.

"Who'd have ever thought Danny would be the despairing one and me the one who believes you can improve humankind?" Ming whispered to Zoe later, after Danny finally left.

"I thought I'd given up, but I can't afford to give up," Zoe said. "There's going to be a global epidemic if we don't stop it."

Jeff was still awake when Ming tiptoed back to the sofa bed. She didn't feel like sleeping either. They had developed a kind of circadian rhythm together. They sat with their heads against the back of the sofa, his feet nuzzling hers.

"If I get locked up, you can go to Arizona with Zoe." The offer made her feel a little bit heroic.

"Fuck. Why did you have to do it?"

In the lamplight she saw how his face hung, though he was weightless compared to the things she knew. A wild beast yowled in her head. "You know all my dumb erotic stories that you laughed at? I didn't make that stuff up."

"Of course you did." He looked frightened, more than anything.

"You know how I was making money before?" He tried to drown her out but she kept talking. She told him about the man who wanted a golden bath. And the mere $150 she got for each trip to some hotel at the shabby edge of midtown. "Some of them said I could get more for this if I got my teeth fixed."

"Noooo…" He stood up. She watched him open the door to the balcony and go out there. He was wearing nothing but boxer shorts and a T-shirt.

She fished his jacket and her own coat from the closet, then followed him out.

He didn't put on the jacket. *That's hostile,* she thought.

"This just gets better and better. Mom, Dad, this is my wife of sorts. She's a professional whore."

"You don't have to tell them anything. I'll be out of your life."

"Did you have to tell me?"

She considered going out and wandering New York. Instead

287

she crept into the bathroom and filled the tub. Wasn't a hot bath supposed to be a form of rebirth?

At some point Jeff came through the door. The steam fogged his glasses. He sat on the rim of the tub. It was an old-fashioned claw-foot tub, in need of new enamel. In a couple of months, some new tenant paying five thousand dollars a month or more would be lounging in this tub, or maybe in a renovated bathroom.

"I wish I could have helped you. Paid for your teeth, I mean."

There was no resolution.

In the morning, Ming woke to an empty space in the sofa bed. *If he's gone, that's that.* She closed her eyes again because she didn't want to look and see if his clutter was still there. Her senses adjusted and she smelled something. Coffee. In the kitchen, she found Zoe and Jeff watching a news video on a laptop.

"Ming—you've got to see this!" Zoe was practically bouncing off her chair.

The president of the United States—a Republican who had been adamantly against legislation that he claimed would "force" Americans to have health insurance—was speaking. "I was wrong when I said freedom is all about choosing your health insurer," he said. "Nobody chooses to get hit by a car and be rushed to the hospital. Some things aren't meant to be profit-making. Patients should spend their energies combating their illness and injuries, not fighting with the insurance company or worrying about whether they can afford treatment. I am committing myself to legislation that makes insurance available for everyone, where doctor visits and hospitalization costs will be funded by the federal government. I am going to push this bill through, or I'll pay these costs for the uninsured myself. What the hell, I'm a very rich man...."

Zoe pulled Ming aside. "It's a gift," she whispered in Mandarin.

"Ha, must be mind control," Jeff quipped. "What do you think, wife? Pretty funny, me having a wife. Pretty funny word even. Life. Strife. Knife. Rife." He gave Ming a sly smile that felt a bit like moving on.

They got a call that morning from Grandma. "Dr. Robert

288

Engelhorn says the tests show Billie still has some potential brain function," Grandma told them, her voice teary and exuberant at the same time. "We don't know…but we'll stay here a while and he says he'll see what he can do. By the way, did you hear the good news about health insurance?"

The president's about-face gave Ming's high-priced attorney some brand new ammunition, too. A week later, he argued to a jury, "Ming Cheng got mixed up with a bad element because of a barbaric practice familiar to all in our country, a practice where the cost of essential medical care—like the replacement of rotten teeth and the associated dangers of gum disease—are out of reach."

Ming watched the court reporter typing as if her hands were made of lightning, and the jurors begin to shuffle out.

"Expect the worst, hope for the best," said Jeff. The two of them, and Zoe, waited for more than three hours in a small room off the judge's chambers. A court assistant brought them sandwiches and water.

A knock on the door. The jurors were back. Same serious faces, all checking her out.

The clerk, a thin young guy, picked up a piece of paper. "Count one," he said.

The room spun around her.

He said, "Guilty."

It wasn't over. The judge said she could go home but she had to come back for sentencing next week. Ming's world became narrow again. She walked across Manhattan, and almost the length of it. She even saw Charles Engelhorn, who came by one evening to visit Zoe and tell her he was going to Boston that weekend and would see Billie.

"It might seem preposterous, but I'm entertaining the idea that maybe the corporate leaders themselves started the New China, as a way of selling products, then raising the prices. It's dumping consumer products to get people addicted to them," she heard him telling Zoe.

"At least you're not imprisoned in a coma," Jeff said to Ming. He brought her little gifts, things she could stash away. A bangle bracelet, the complete collection of Elizabeth Bishop's poems.

It was worse the second time, waiting and waiting and waiting in the judge's chambers. Someone brought sandwiches again. Ming studied the sliced ham, the orange cheese, the three pickles in a triangle, like two wide eyes and pair of pursed lips. She tasted a pickle and the brine burned her throat.

"Oh my god!" Zoe read aloud from the news app on her cell phone. "'Dr. Blake Gower in Ohio has reported a patient who recently traveled to China testing positive for bird flu. Dr. Gower has treated the patient with the bird flu vaccine that stopped the epidemic in China....'"

The knock came.

Ming's lawyer was smiling.

A fog descended over her, but Ming thought she heard the words "suspended sentence."

"The judge said you've already served a reasonable time," Jeff explained, as if he were translating. "You're on probation for the next year, but you can go anywhere in the continental U.S., without an ankle bracelet *if* you check in with your probation officer and your very law-abiding husband keeps an eye on you."

From Ming's Notebook

You'll see. All our friends in New York will get jabbed with bird flu vaccine while they're walking through a crowd. We've gotta stay out of big cities," my husband said just now.

It's a little past two in the afternoon. A while back we passed a Welcome to Pennsylvania sign. Zoe is driving, with Jeff in the front seat.

"This," Jeff is saying, "is a car that can easily break down just outside a mechanic's shop in New Mexico." Zoe insisted we shouldn't blow our money on a new car, so we got a ten-year-old Volkswagen Passat.

Zoe says she'll think about it. She's playing "Rhapsody in Blue" for the sixth time, so I know she's already missing New York.

We're fighting battle by battle. The Republican senators who suddenly agreed with the president on universal health care and passed an emergency bill have, by my count, brought us down to fewer than ninety spare nanochips against an infinite supply of the vaccine. Still, I'm writing a story that ends with the chips winning. It's my tale against Danny's.

"We'll see tumbleweed," says Jeff. I'm not sure what tumbleweed is.

There's an eagle soaring over the highway. It swirls about, then flies off over a rolling green field. I tell Jeff and Zoe there's an old Chinese proverb that goes, *If you're facing the right direction all you have to do is keep on walking.* The afternoon sun has begun to ignite us through the windshield, and we're headed straight into the blaze.

Acknowledgements

I wish to thank my publisher, Jaynie Royal, and editors, Teresa Blackton, Katelynn Watkins and Ruth Feiertag. And special thanks to many friends and colleagues who helped point the way: Geoff Fox, Peter de Lissovoy, and Dirk van Nouhuys of the Thoth Books Editorial Collective; Beth Neff of Sparklit; Sarah Stone; Janice Horowitz, who tirelessly read and critiqued my early drafts; Richard Bulliet; Sara Klatchko; Samantha Marshall; Raquel Scherr, the participants in Karen Braziller's writing workshop; and the "Cheng" family. Also to my cousins Bill, Carlisle, Jane, John, and Ilya, who have always encouraged me to tell stories.